MW00368238

Praise for The Sicilian Inheritance

"*The Sicilian Inheritance* is an addictive family saga with a rich abundance of strong women, quick wit, immersive history, and page-turning suspense. What else could one want from a novel? With her wise prose, Piazza grabs us by the hand as we journey through the picturesque Italian countryside while our heart thumps in anticipation of what Sara will find next. Mined from Piazza's own family history, this novel is a lyrical elegy to the past and its influence. . . . Narrated by two powerful women who refuse to let others define them—Sara, a butcher, and Serafina, an Italian woman healer—will steal your heart and threaten to never give it back. Piazza is a master storyteller with a voice of deep wisdom, and *The Sicilian Inheritance* is don't-miss historical fiction with a dash of Mario Puzo and a hint of Nora Ephron."

—Patti Callahan Henry, *New York Times* bestselling
author of *The Secret Book of Flora Lea*

"I loved this epic tale of one woman's quest to learn the truth about what happened to her great-grandmother a century ago. A gripping story of motherhood, ambition, misogyny, and female power, now and then, it is also a great mystery that kept me guessing until the final pages."

—J. Courtney Sullivan, *New York Times* bestselling
author of *Friends and Strangers*

"Strong women, rich history, and page-turning suspense make for a rich and satisfying read . . . In *The Sicilian Inheritance*, Jo Piazza turns her formidable talents to the dual present/past timeline of a woman who goes to Italy because of a bequest but discovers much deeper—and more dangerous—family secrets."

—Pam Jenoff, *New York Times* bestselling
author of *Code Name Sapphire*

"*The Sicilian Inheritance* is a thrilling adventure throughout a beautiful landscape that tells the stories of two women who persevered despite the many factors working against them. It's enjoyable, satisfying, but also motivating. It might just inspire more underestimated women to make bold moves, defy the odds, and redefine success on their own terms."

—*Forbes*, "One of 2024's Most Anticipated Novels Is
Actually a MasterClass in Leadership"

"A sweep-you-away story about three generations of women who rebel against the expected in search of their own sense of self—it feels as much a feminist adventure as a redemptive family mystery, with as much wit and humor as heart and soul. Jo Piazza gives us complex, original heroines, a rich Italian setting, and a puzzle-piece journey that keeps the pages turning. There's nothing not to love here—I was gripped and entertained from start to finish."

—Ashley Audrain, *New York Times* bestselling
author of *The Push* and *The Whispers*

"All of *The Sicilian Inheritance* shimmers and stuns: the gorgeous writing, the complex and fascinating history of Sicily, the immersive Italian setting, and the propulsive family mystery that had my jaw hanging open. But what leaves a mark most of all are Piazza's heroines, the unforgettable and inspiring cast of women who defy the patriarchy and the odds stacked against them and learn to live life on their own terms."

—Carola Lovering, bestselling author of
Tell Me Lies and *Bye, Baby*

"*The Sicilian Inheritance* is the perfect travel novel! A fiercely original family saga that you need to pick up for your next flight."

—Jane Green, *New York Times* bestselling author of
Sister Stardust and *Jemima J*

"Equal parts rich historical fiction, gripping murder mystery, and a moving exploration of identity, grief, and the long shadow of the past. With lush prose and airtight plotting, Piazza's novel made me laugh, cry—and start planning a trip to Sicily."

—Andrea Bartz, *New York Times* bestselling
author of *We Were Never Here*

ALSO BY JO PIAZZA

FICTION

The Knockoff (with Lucy Sykes)
Fitness Junkie (with Lucy Sykes)
Charlotte Walsh Likes to Win
We Are Not Like Them (with Christine Pride)
You Were Always Mine (with Christine Pride)

NONFICTION

How to Be Married
If Nuns Ruled the World
Celebrity Inc.

The Sicilian Inheritance

A NOVEL

Jo Piazza

DUTTON

DUTTON

An imprint of Penguin Random House LLC
penguinrandomhouse.com

LIBRARY OF CONGRESS CATALOGING-IN-PUBLICATION DATA
Names: Piazza, Jo, author.
Title: The Sicilian inheritance: a novel / Jo Piazza.
Description: New York : Dutton, 2024.
Identifiers: LCCN 2023035750 (print) | LCCN 2023035751 (ebook) |
ISBN 9780593474167 (hardcover) | ISBN 9780593474174 (ebook)
Subjects: LCSH: Women—Fiction. | Inheritance and succession—Fiction. |
Family secrets—Fiction. | Sicily (Italy)—Fiction. | Thrillers (Fiction) lcgft | LCGFT: Novels.
Classification: LCC PS3616.I214 S53 2024 (print) |
LCC PS3616.I214 (ebook) | DDC 813/.6—dc23/eng/20230828
LC record available at https://lccn.loc.gov/2023035750
LC ebook record available at https://lccn.loc.gov/2023035751

Printed in the United States of America
3rd Printing

For my dad, John Piazza,
who started all of this with his curiosity
about our family history . . .

And my daughters, Beatrix and Eliza,
who inspired me to finish it.

All of Sicily is a dimension of the imagination.
—Leonardo Sciascia

In Sicily, women are more dangerous than shotguns.
—Mario Puzo and Francis Ford Coppola

The
Sicilian
Inheritance

PROLOGUE

––––––––––

2016

The room was freezing. No windows, one rickety table, two metal chairs.

"L'ha ucciso?" the detective asked with an uncompromising glare.

I was lost in a fog as I blinked up at the kind-eyed older woman they'd assigned to help translate for me even though I didn't need her. I understood exactly what he'd asked: Did you kill him?

My whole body ached. At least one, maybe more, of my ribs was broken, and the pain in my abdomen throbbed hot and sharp. Fat, salty tears rolled down my cheeks. Not for him, the man up on the mountain, the one whose blood was dried on my skin and my clothes. I couldn't cry for him at all. These tears were for me. For what I was about to lose.

Would I ever see my family again? My daughter? Why had I thought coming here would solve any of my problems?

The questions were merely my brain trying to escape reality because I knew exactly what happened up there.

And so, I nodded.

ONE

SARA

Two weeks earlier . . .

I often tried to pinpoint the exact moment when the life I'd worked so hard for began to fall apart. Because there's always a beginning, a place where you've screwed up so badly there's no putting it back together.

It's what happens when you slice through the wrong tendon in a flank of meat. I ran a restaurant for years, but I started as a butcher, so I still think in terms of joints and muscles, the connective tissue of life. Cut the right one and you end up with a perfect steak. Cut the wrong one and the whole system breaks down. The meat falls apart in the places where you want it to stay close to the bone. Once you make that single wrong cut it's nearly impossible to keep everything else intact.

When did I make the wrong cut?

I thought about it, obsessed over it really, as I closed up my restaurant, probably for the very last time. I was so deep inside my memories that I didn't hear the knock on the door. The sound didn't register until it became an unrelenting pounding.

"Mommy, let me in. I need to come in there right now!"

Few things are more persistent than a four-year-old faced with a physical obstacle. Sophie's dad brought her over early. Jack was always early these days, probably because he was trying to catch me doing something he disapproved of.

My body lurched toward my little girl's voice. I flung open the door and the two of us hurled ourselves at one another with a feverish intensity, colliding in a smush of skin and lips and complete and total adoration. I never realized how much I would miss this little creature until I could no longer see her whenever I wanted, until my custody of her hung in the balance.

"Who's my best girl?" I asked her.

"Meeeee. Who's my best mamma?"

"Me?"

"You!" The part that both killed me and kept me getting out of bed every morning was that she meant it. This gorgeous, brilliant child of mine truly thought I was the best despite all recent evidence to the contrary.

Jack, my almost ex-husband, was certain I was no longer the best at anything. I could feel his bitterness as he stood behind Sophie and took in the nearly empty restaurant. The tables, chairs, and furniture I had painstakingly selected only five years earlier had been sold to a new place opening down on Passyunk Avenue. Various kitchen equipment was pushed against the walls, ready to be hauled off to the highest bidder. All that remained was our mascot, a massive plaster pink pig flying from the ceiling, its lips curled in a cheeky smile and the restaurant's name emblazoned on its flank, La Macellaia—the butcher woman.

The plaster pig was a joke at first, before he became the symbol of the place. Jack had him made for me by a local artist. Because for all the years I'd dreamed of having my own restaurant, I'd never

4

believed it was possible. When other people told me it would happen one day I'd laugh like I didn't care if it did or didn't and say, "Sure, when pigs fly." Jack surprised me with the statue on opening night. I wondered when I went from being someone he'd design a custom pig statue for to a person he could barely look in the eye. It happened bit by bit, and then all at once.

I looked up at him, hoping to see some of the old soft devotion, but Jack just seemed annoyed and sad. It was impossible to tell what he resented more, me or the restaurant that stole so much time from him and our marriage.

"Let's go outside," I suggested, not wanting to see my failure through his eyes. A small part of me still hoped La Macellaia would reopen in a new location at some point in the future, but I couldn't see how, not with the mountain of debt we'd taken on, the skyrocketing rent, or the nasty rumors that continued to dog me. I knew I'd made so many mistakes with my restaurant. I'd poured my heart and soul into it, but also my hubris. I'd pushed us to expand and grow too fast to make my investors happy, to make them money. I took on more than I could handle, and in the process, I lost almost everything. Another part of me also hoped, on some days, that with the restaurant gone Jack and I might find a way to work things out. But that seemed more unlikely with each passing day. Our marriage had become merely a bundle of services that neither of us could fulfill well enough for the other.

Once we made it to the sidewalk Jack thrust a handful of mail at me.

"This all came to the house for you," he said. Since we separated Jack had been living with Sophie in our sweet little brick row home, the one we bought together the year we got married. It made sense at first, since I worked most nights and could sleep in the studio over the restaurant. But once La Macellaia closed I'd have nowhere to live.

Mixed in with the overdue bills and junk was the letter I'd been waiting for, a brown envelope scrawled in my aunt Rosie's perfect penmanship, gorgeous cursive that only ancient nuns could beat into you.

I didn't want to open it because the second I did, my aunt Rosie's death would be as real as the end of my business and my career. I knew that the letter contained the last words she never got to tell me in person because I was too busy working to go see her one last time. Yet another regret.

Jack cleared his throat the way he did when he was about to say something I wouldn't like. "I hate the idea of Sophie going to your aunt's funeral. She's too little to learn about death."

"Sorry it bothers you. But please be reasonable, Jack. Sophie adored Aunt Rosie as much as I did." I swallowed my irritation and managed a contrite smile. "And all her cousins will be there. It won't be creepy and morbid. Rosie wanted more of a party than a formal church funeral. It'll be fun for Soph."

"A fun funeral? Who throws a party when they die? Your whole family is nuts. Rosie was nuts." His annoyance had nothing to do with the funeral. He was pissed because he was supposed to leave for vacation with his parents and I was making him wait until Sunday night, after the funeral.

"We've gotta get going, sweetie." I said this to Sophie, but really I was saying it to Jack to let him know our conversation was over. "We've got a two-hour drive up to Scranton and Carla is on her way to get us."

"To visit Aunt Rosie?" Sophie jumped up and down and clapped her hands.

"In a way, my love."

"See, she's too young for this, dammit," Jack said.

"Let me handle it," I said with all the conviction I could muster.

He sighed and shoved his hands in his pockets. "You know I loved her too. Rosie."

"Even though she was nuts?" I asked.

He shot me a regretful smile.

"Especially because of that," he mumbled.

It used to be one of the reasons he loved me too.

———

It was true that my aunt Rosie didn't want a funeral, but man, that woman could throw a party, even from beyond the grave. She'd made it very clear that she wanted all of her "people," all three of the boys she raised and their families, all the staff at the school where she was the principal for half her life, and pretty much any-one else in town who wasn't "gonna be a crybaby" about her death, to get drunk at her favorite pub to celebrate her.

I wore a bright red jumpsuit that had been sitting in the back of my closet for the better part of a decade with the tags still on. I couldn't afford anything new. I'd applied for and been approved for seven credit cards over the past three years. Six of those cards were currently maxed out. The jumpsuit was too tight and too low-cut, but I knew Aunt Rosie would have loved it.

The bar was loud and rowdy. I hadn't seen my cousins and the rest of my extended family in a couple of years, but folding myself into their comforting melee felt like sinking into a warm bath. There were hours of toasts and storytelling. Aunt Pat baked a mas-sive cake with a picture on it of Rosie at her seventieth birthday wearing a T-shirt that read SEXY AT SEVENTY. There was Aunt Rosie trivia and eventually Dolly Parton karaoke.

My sister, Carla, and I eased our way around Aunt Arlene, who was in the midst of a stunning rendition of "Islands in the Stream" on the karaoke machine with my mom and Arlene's daughter, Little Arlene.

Mom was really belting it out. She shimmied with Sophie on her shoulders. I wanted to grab my daughter, spin around with her, and hold tight to her spindly little body. I knew the next month of vacation with her other grandparents would do my daughter some good. I also knew Jack's mother would use the time to determine if I'd somehow caused Sophie irreparable damage with my recent personal miseries. Sophie has always been more resilient than me, but I still worried about her. Since I had to file for bankruptcy I could hardly drag myself out of bed except to handle the logistics of shutting La Macellaia down. There was a hell of a lot of grief involved in losing something you built from scratch, in losing the future you expected to have. I often drank too much at night to fall asleep and mainlined coffee all day to stay awake. Even when I was with my daughter, I wasn't always really there.

I tugged on Sophie's naked big toe and kissed her foot. She'd thrown her shoes somewhere in the corner during an earlier dancing session.

"Who's paying for this?" I asked Carla as we walked across the room, balancing two trays of shots to bring to our dad and uncles.

"I think Rose stashed some cash away," Carla replied. "She knew this day was coming."

At ninety-one it was always coming. Rosie had been fading for a year at least. The last time I'd seen her, a few months ago, she'd hardly gotten out of bed except to make the two of us a pair of strong old-fashioneds and to light the living room fire with a single match.

"A real woman makes a good drink and lights her own fires, Sara," she always reminded me. She told me lots of brilliant things over the years. I wish I'd written them all down. As Rosie and I had sipped our drinks, she said, "This is how I want you to remember me. A sexy, well-seasoned dame drinking her whiskey and getting ready to tell you a filthy joke."

"That's how I want to remember you too," I agreed, and begged for the joke. Toward the end she wanted me to come one more time. It was urgent, she told me. There was something we had to discuss. But I was never able to make the trip.

Carla squinted out at the scene in front of us. "I think Dad and the boys must be paying for some of it." I'd actually assumed my sister had thrown some cash in the kitty. Of all the cousins she was the big success story, at least in terms of how much money she made. She was the youngest partner in a fancy Philly law firm, the mother of gorgeous twin boys with a beautiful, brilliant wife, and they owned a fancy town house off Rittenhouse Square. Carla had earned her success, but it was also due to Rosie paying part of her college and law school tuitions.

Rosie was my great-aunt, my dad's aunt, but she raised him and his two brothers when his parents, Santo and Lorenza, died in a car crash when Dad was a kid. So many boys, all of them little assholes, she used to say with complete and utter devotion. She'd never married, though she had a string of loyal and usually much younger boyfriends. I'd always assumed she was sick of living with men after raising three of them.

"The bar is probably covering some of it," Carla added. "They all loved her."

"Everyone did," I agreed, and swallowed one of the shots. The fiery liquid tickled my throat and warmed my insides.

Uncle Mario raised a half-empty glass and shouted an old Sicilian saying Rosie taught all of us.

Cu picca parrau mai si pintiu.

Those who speak little never have regrets. Ironic since Rosie rarely shut up.

Even though she came to the United States as the baby of four siblings, it was Aunt Rosie who kept the family legends alive. She told and retold the coming-to-America story of our great-grandfather Giovanni, Gio to his friends. The first American of the family, the one who worked himself to the bone in Sicily's sulfur mines and then bravely came to the new country to labor in a toilet factory in Queens. He slept in the attic of a funeral home in Astoria owned by other Sicilians for more than ten years.

"Slept up there in a coffin like a goddamn vampire, Sara. Now he was a man," Rosie had told me more than once.

Eventually, Giovanni saved enough money from the factory to bring his children to America and they moved from New York City to the Pocono Mountains, where they'd been told there was a fortune to be made in the coal mines. Someone promised him Scranton was exactly like Sicily, but with snow and coal instead of sun and sulfur. That someone had clearly lied, or perhaps they hadn't been to either Scranton or Sicily. Then the story turned tragic. Giovanni's wife, Serafina, never made the trip. The kids apparently traveled across the ocean first while Serafina stayed behind to sell the family land, but she was killed by the flu before she could join them. In the memories of the family she left behind Serafina grew more pious and devoted with each year that passed. She essentially became the Madonna. Saintly, pure, a loving mother and a martyr who had selflessly raised the children in Sicily while Giovanni built a future for them in America. Once they made it to Scranton, Gio and his sons toiled in the coal mines and then saved enough to open a small auto body shop that flourished until my uncle Mario lost it in a high-stakes poker game in the early nineties.

My father named me after his grandmother Serafina, a name that sounds like an angel or old movie star. But for all of my life no one has ever called me anything but Sara, and my mom, whose parents were a mix of Polish, Irish, and German, distinctly not Italian American, insisted on spelling my nickname in the more American way, probably to get back at my dad for his various marital shortcomings.

The drinks disappeared the second I dropped them on the table. My dad and his brothers didn't even take a break from telling their favorite Aunt Rosie stories to down the shots.

Remember the time she dyed the pond behind the school green for Saint Paddy's Day.

The time she stole a tractor to drive in the Founder's Day parade.

When she went skinny-dipping with the mayor and got caught by his wife.

I tousled Dad's hair and kissed him on his bald spot. He smelled like booze and the Ivory soap he had been using as shampoo, conditioner, and body wash for the better part of six decades.

He was properly sloshed. Rosie's death was hitting him hard. He was the youngest of the trio of brothers when his parents died. He had a heart tattoo on his left biceps, the kind that usually read MOM, except his read ROSIE.

"Don't stay up too late," I whispered to Dad before slipping away to finally read Rosie's letter to me. I'd put it off long enough.

I nodded to the bartender Jimmy and pointed to my uncles, making a little slashing motion across my throat in the hopes Jimmy would cut them off, and then snuck out the back door, searching for the gap in the chain-link fence that would lead me to Rosie's backyard.

A rustle ran through the bushes behind me and I paused, my skin tingling, feeling eyes on my back, but there was only silence. The sensation remained as I let myself into my aunt's dark house and banged my hip on her dining room table. Rosie left her epitaph there, the one she'd been writing and rewriting herself for the past twenty years.

The Body of Rosie M.
Lies Right Beneath This Stem
A Tough Old Broad
Those Who Knew Her Were Awed
She Really Was Quite a Gem

My great-aunt loved a fucking limerick. I could see her scratching out the final version on this rickety old table, maybe right after she penned me that letter.

The house murmured as I lit a fire in the old woodburning stove with a single match just like she taught me. The place was haunted for sure. Rosie's father, Giovanni, died in the bedroom upstairs at age ninety-three. Rosie's brother Vin too. Rosie was with them now, but I hoped her spirit could escape this house and travel around the world. She'd always wanted to see the pyramids, the Eiffel Tower, the Great Wall of China, but after coming to America she'd never left the States. Even after she got each of her nephews out of her house, she kept inheriting their kids for long stints at a time. Someone was always handing off a wayward teenager who needed an Aunt Rosie–style kick in the ass or whose parents needed a break. My sister and I had lived with her for six whole summers and I moved in for my entire freshman year of high school. Plus, her work at the school never really ended. She was the vice principal, then the principal for four decades. The school never had a guidance counselor, so the kids went to Rosie with all their drama. She exuded a vibe that let you know *Oh yeah, I see you and I'm here for all your crap.* Even after she retired, she substituted just because she loved it. She also loved the slots and blackjack and frankly her gambling often got the best of her. All of that meant there was never any time or extra cash for Rosie's international adventures until all the nieces and nephews were grown and it was impossible for her to make it to the casino on her own.

That was when she started planning a big trip to Sicily for just the two of us. But then I was busy opening the restaurant and then I had Sophie and then the restaurant started doing really well so how could I leave? I promised over and over again that we would go. By the time she got sick my restaurant was bleeding money, and the trip never happened. Remembering all the times I put her off hit me like a punch in the gut.

I fixed myself a sobering cup of tea in one of the hundred mugs littering my aunt's kitchen cabinets. Whenever any of us went on a trip she insisted we bring her back a mug. I once asked her what the hell we would do with all of them when she died, half joking, and she'd replied with all seriousness, "You take your favorites and then leave the rest of them on strangers' stoops as a surprise gift. Who wouldn't want to wake up to a THE POCONOS IS FOR LOVERS mug on their porch? Talk about making someone's day."

I sipped from the NOBODY DOES IT LIKE NIAGARA cup that Uncle Mario picked up a few summers ago and opened the letter.

Rosie wrote that she already missed me, that I was the daughter she never thought she wanted, that her only regret was not seeing

13

everything I would one day accomplish. I was blubbering by the time I got to the tough love. She told me I needed to get my shit together. I never should have let my dream die, I could have asked her for help. (*With what money, Rosie?*) Irritation and love seeped into every sentence she wrote.

She waited until the end for the surprise. *Surprises are the best thing in life and there are too few of them*, Rosie used to insist.

I've got a plan for you, gioia mia. You trusted me your whole life. I need you to trust me now.

I'm sending you to Sicily. You and I should have made the trip there together a long time ago. Now don't go feeling sorry and blaming yourself. I'm not mad at you. Life got in the way . . . but we're not gonna let death hold us back.

You're going to take my ashes to Caltabellessa. I want you to know the town where I was born. You're lost, my love, and you need to get back to your roots. But I also need you to do something for me. If I had tried to explain it, you would have thought I was nuts, but I'm sorry I didn't try, so here it goes . . .

I'm enclosing a deed in this letter, a deed for what I believe is a small plot of land that belonged to our family in Sicily before they came to America. The owner is listed as my mother, Serafina Forte. It's been mine for a long, long time and I always told myself that when I retired, when I had the money to fly off to Sicily, I'd go back to our land. I'd hoped I would be able to do that trip with you, but time ran out. And to be honest, I was a little scared of digging up the past. But I've gotten sentimental in my old age, and I think we need to know our family history. That's what people do when they're close to death. They try to learn more about the people they're gonna meet on the other side.

So here we are, my love. This is my last wish from the great beyond. Spooky, eh? I need you to go back to Caltabellessa. It's all taken care of. The hotel is booked for a week, the plane ticket is bought and it's nonrefundable. No more excuses. I want you to investigate whether this paper is worth anything and if it is, I want you to take all of the money you can make from it and rebuild your life. Reopen your restaurant and take care of your girl. I'm sending you on an adventure, my love. Don't you dare waste it.

TWO

SERAFINA

1908

The girl is cursed. My mother whispered this to my father late at night, even though she knew I could hear her through the wall. Mamma sensed I'd been wicked, that I'd brought shame on our family, but all she muttered was *the girl is cursed* like what was happening to me was all the result of the devil's magic.

Before the sun rose the next morning Cettina and I visited *la strega*, the witch, to try to undo the terrible thing I had done.

The old woman lived beyond the end of the road. As we walked higher and higher around the steep curve of the hillside the stone path turned to gravel and then to dirt. My skin tingled with the uncomfortable feeling I'd been tricked, like maybe Liuni and Gio would jump out from behind a tree and laugh at us for believing in fairy tales.

Sheep bells chimed in the distance calling us back home. Cettina, my oldest friend, the closest thing I had to a sister, led the way, gripping my hand so hard my bones ached.

Visiting the witch, asking her for help, had been Cettina's idea. *La strega* was a distant relative of hers, one her family never acknowledged. No one with half a mind would admit to being the witch's kin even though every woman in town depended on her healing powers for something or other. Men never visited the witch. She only ever tended to the women and then only in secrecy. I didn't know if she chose to keep away from the whispers and stares from our villagers or whether she was asked to live just beyond the town's border to keep her magic separate from the sacred sphere of the church. Most likely a combination of both. But Cettina cared for the old woman. My friend had a beautiful heart—bigger, perhaps, than was good for her—so she'd sneak away once a week to the woman's cottage on the edge of the cliff, bringing things the witch needed from town—flour, lye soap, sugar, copies of the *Giornale di Sicilia*.

"She can read?" I'd asked.

"I think she learned in Palermo," Cettina said.

The capital might as well have been on a distant star for how far away it seemed. That the witch had once lived in the big city and chose to return to our dusty rural village of peasants only added to her mythology.

Cettina added, "I have seen her reading long books and articles."

None of the old women in town could read. Even many of the girls our age didn't know how to decipher more than simple sentences. Some of them, including Cettina, had quit school long ago to help their mammas raise little ones. The state required children to attend school for just four years. At fifteen, I was the only girl left in our class, a fact that my own mamma often complained about because she wanted more help at home. My love of learning made no sense to her. It was impractical at best and dangerous at worst. I hadn't told my mother that I was at the top of all the students in my class, one of two who would be sent down to the upper school in the city of Sciacca to receive more education. A girl from our town had never done it before. My teacher was going to ask for special permission to send me. One day I could maybe even get my teaching certificate, become a *maestrina*. I'd asked Papa months ago, and he'd been skeptical, but my desperate enthusiasm won him over and he promised to try to convince Mamma.

It was the only thing I had ever truly desired. It was the only thing that could offer an escape from our tiny village. Generations of women before me had lived their entire lives circling the tip of the small mountain doing nothing but caring for babies and husbands. For me that life seemed the worst kind of prison. But leaving would be impossible if the witch couldn't help me.

Cettina knew what the witch could do because she had the ears of a wild boar and had listened as her mamma's friends discussed the work of *la strega*, her spells, her healing. We had not had a midwife in town for many years, not since old Nunzia followed her sons to *la Mérica*. The physician, Peppe Spica, lived far away in Sciacca and did little to treat women's troubles. It was said that *la strega* could deliver a baby without pain to the mother, an insult to God since the Bible insisted women deserved pain in childbearing in penance for the sins of the first woman. Cettina had also heard that the witch had medicine that could solve my particular problem.

"What if it does not work?" I asked as we neared the witch's home.

"It will," my friend promised. "I will be here to help. I will take care of you." Cettina's voice was brave with conviction.

We swallowed our breath and held it tight in our chests as we passed the cave where the dragon had lived hundreds of years before, the terrible reptile who ate the bad children, or so our parents and grandparents had told us. Everyone knew you had to hold your breath or you'd bring bad luck on your entire family.

"Do you want to stop at the dragon's ear?" Cettina asked.

When Saint Pellegrino eventually slayed the dragon many hundreds of years ago, the beast had turned to dust, all of him crumbling except for his giant ear. The ear turned into rock, becoming one of the outer walls of the cave on the mountaintop. The villagers believed you could tell the dragon's ear your darkest secrets, the things you could never confess to the priest.

I nodded and walked to the crumbling side of the cliff to mumble into the sun-warmed stone, quiet enough that even Cettina couldn't hear me. "This is all my fault. I am a terrible, sinful girl and I deserve all my ill fortune."

Cettina pulled me back to the trail. Our village grew smaller and smaller behind us. If we turned to the right and walked a few paces from the path we'd tumble off the edge into the valley below, a deep crevice filled with thorns and gnarled olive trees too tough and old to bear food.

I thought to turn back when the witch's house came into view, as if my doubts willed it to appear. The structure was built directly into the mountain, not unlike the dragon's ear, but with a crooked door and two small windows on either side. A century ago, this building used to be a stall for the militia to look out for invaders coming in from the sea. The windows were just big enough for arrows to fly out. Most of these places were abandoned now, but the witch had moved here because she had no family that wanted to claim her, no husband, and nowhere else to be.

Or so the stories went.

Cettina paused outside the door. Perched on her tiptoes, she grasped the sides of my face in her palms, her fingers cupping my cheekbones. Cetti's large eyes grew even rounder as she pressed her lips softly onto my forehead, a drop of sweat falling from her upper lip. "I love you."

"Come in." A strong voice bounced off the old stone walls inside the house. She sounded younger than I expected, but when the woman stepped into the doorway I saw that her soft baggy face was impossibly old, the skin mottled like an old log. Her narrow marzipan eyes held on to the two of us. A tattered blanket fell over her shoulders like a cape tied at the hollow of her neck. It flapped a little in the wind as she led us inside.

The witch's home smelled like an animal right before slaughter: wild, anxious, clinging to hope. Blood mixed with something sweet: ripe lemons and rosemary. Six dark wood chairs with high backs sat around a table that gleamed like it had been rubbed over and over with oil. A quilt sewn from rag scraps was tucked around a straw mattress in the corner of the room. Meat, maybe rabbit, roasted in a fireplace as high as the ceiling. The stones of the hearth were lined with uneven shelves: on one side were rows and rows of glass canisters of all shapes and sizes; on the other, stacks of books and periodicals. There were more words in that tiny room than I had seen in my entire life. I ran my fingers along the spines of the volumes.

"Fina is a very clever girl," I heard Cetti brag about me to the old woman. "She is at the top of the class. They have invited her to be the first girl to go to Sciacca to study."

When I turned away from the books the woman motioned for the two of us to sit at her table. I pulled my hand away from Cetti's grip and tucked it into my lap, squeezing my palms together between my sweaty thighs. My friend's free hand moved to caress my back, running her index finger up the knots of my spine.

The witch nodded to a plate of bread smothered in honey and fresh fruit, sliced apricots and ripe plums with their maroon skin scored to allow the ruby pulp to ooze onto the plate. I hadn't realized I was ravenous until that moment. I'd hardly kept food down in weeks, but I'd tried to hide the sickness from Mamma, making sure to leave our house early in the mornings to empty my stomach into the alley.

We filled our mouths before speaking.

"Tell her," Cettina finally urged me.

"Tell her what?" I replied, as if we'd just walked all the way to this strange place for nothing more than a meal.

"Everything. You can start from the beginning."

Something about the warm hovel and the woman's calming silence made me feel like it would be fine to repeat the things I'd previously only told Cettina. This witch on the edge of the world possessed a kindness I hadn't expected. Sunlight snuck through the slanted window, sending a sliver of light over my face, the warmth a false comfort.

I went back four months ago, to the start of summer. Papa had come home after spending two months in Palermo, where he'd been digging out ditches for the new grand road that would circle the city. He had a little extra money and he wanted to take me and my little brothers down the mountain to the beaches at Eraclea Minoa. He could get us there in half the time it usually took because he'd gotten the mayor's son a job with the company that was building the grand road and the mayor returned the favor by letting him borrow his modern carriage and his fastest horses. Three of us children crowded onto the front bench of the cart. There was never a question about whether my mother would accompany us. She had to stay home with the littlest ones.

I'd never seen anything so spectacularly perfect as the sapphire sea emerging from the edge of the soft pine forest. Pristine white sand stretched for miles. A small patch was speckled by striped umbrellas and blue and yellow chairs. Papa parked the mayor's carriage right up at the edge of the beach, and everyone stared at our scraggly family as we tumbled down.

Papa handed some coins to a boy at the entrance, and he gave us an umbrella with three chairs. I had no proper swimsuit, since Mamma told me it would be sinful for me to wear one. I stretched out on a chair like a wild cat in a warm patch of sun and listened to the waves lap against the shore. I knew it was exactly what heaven would feel like. When I opened my eyes my brothers and father had gone to the edge of the sea in their short underpants. I watched Flavio, always the most daring and headstrong of the boys, dive under the waves and held my breath until he resurfaced.

A woman and a man curled up together on the chair in front of me. The woman's hair tumbled in tight dark curls down her bronzed back and she wound her fingers around the man's neck. She couldn't have been much younger than my own mother, but she was an entirely different creature than the stooped and wrinkled figure stuck at home with a baby suckling at each of her breasts. I couldn't take my eyes off the lovers, at the way the woman pulled back from him and teased him, at the way he gazed at her as if she were the most perfect thing he'd ever seen. My stomach tightened and tumbled as I imagined what it would be like to have that kind of power over a man.

When the woman walked to the toilets, I followed.

By the time I reached the small cabanas with a hole dug out of the ground that served as a latrine, the glamorous woman was applying a deep red color to her lips.

"Would you like some?" she asked innocently. I nodded. She steadied my face and painted the bottom lip, then the top.

"You are beautiful as golden grain," she announced when she was finished. My face went hot when I looked in the small, cracked piece of glass that hung on the canvas wall of the tent. It was such a small thing, to have fiery lips, and yet also so wonderfully different.

"Are you from here?" I asked her.

"No, no, my pet. I'm on vacation from Naples. Just a holiday to your gorgeous island."

I'd never thought of my home as gorgeous, or as anything special at all. I would have given almost anything to travel to where this woman was from, a place where ladies wore bright red lipstick and kissed men out in the sunshine, where they went on holidays to foreign beaches. My eyes crawled over the woman's body. Her stomach was flat in a way that announced she had never carried children. The curves of her breasts pushed up over the scalloped edge of the top of her red bathing uniform. She smelled like salt water, sunburnt skin, and men's cologne.

"What do you do there? In Naples?"

"Many things. I'm an adventuress." Her silky voice made me want to wrap myself up in her words. "I'm teasing. I work in a shop sometimes. Sometimes a restaurant. That is where I met my love." She did not call him her husband.

It was sinful to brag, but I wanted to tell her everything about me, how I had only recently learned about my high scores in school, how I had been recommended for the special classes in Sciacca, how one day I too might make it to Naples, but I merely thanked her for painting my lips.

By the time we'd trudged back through the trees to the sand I had already swiped away the red makeup with the back of my arm, knowing my father wouldn't approve.

An hour later my family piled back into the carriage to make it home before Mamma became cross, all of our skin pink, sand between our toes.

The next night the village celebrated the Feast of Saint Antonio with dancing, masquerading, and feasting. Boys dressed as old men and played practical jokes on us all. Liuni put on the costume of a circus bear and begged for sweets. The wine flowed freely for everyone and the usual lines of decorum blurred. Rich mingled with poor, young with old, boys with girls. Feast nights were the only times when fathers lost track of their daughters.

The four of us danced away from the crowd. Me, Cettina, Liuni, and Gio. I was already too tall for most of the boys in town, but not for Gio, who grew like a weed and was already a head taller than me. Gio, or rather Giovanni, even though no one called him that, was the only boy who met my eyes when I talked to him, who didn't have to look up at me. We wandered out to the fields to look at the moon and the stars. Liuni had swiped two bottles of wine and we passed them between us. Eventually Cettina and Liuni wandered off over to the other side of the hill. I kept drinking the sweet liquid while Gio lay on his back and invented constellations in the sky—the angry dragon, the lazy sheep, the tipsy priest, the horny old man. He traced their outlines on my palm with the tip of his finger. I could still feel the woman from the beach's hot breath on my cheeks and the traces of red paint in the grooves of my lips. When I closed my eyes, I saw the woman grip the back of the man's head and pull his face into her own, bending him to her will. That scene played over in my mind as I rolled toward Gio and gripped his dark curls. I lost time after that.

Gio was a kindhearted and gentle boy. He never would have done anything without my permission, and I knew I had given it to him that night. He showed up at my house in the following weeks and we held hands when no one was looking. He was quiet and listened when I talked, laughed even when I wasn't very funny. He never did more than kiss me again with both of our mouths closed and he always asked before he did it. *I would like to kiss you now, may I?*

A month or so later my breasts began to swell and my blood didn't come. I didn't bleed the next month either, or the month after that. Cettina was the only one I told.

"We'll have a double wedding. Liuni and I will get married earlier than I planned."

"But I don't want to marry Gio."

"Who else will you marry?"

"I don't know. Maybe no one. I want to at least go away to school before I think about marriage."

Cettina only laughed because all the girls we knew, even the ugly ones, got married at sixteen or seventeen. I knew Gio wouldn't be a terrible husband for me. He was kind and gentle. Cettina was already engaged to his best friend. We could continue through life as a foursome. But a baby with Gio would tether me to this village on top of the mountain forever. Like my mother and her mother before her, I would probably never leave it.

La strega hardly blinked through my story, her expression remained unchanged, as if she'd already heard it and I was merely confirming the details. Her hands fluttered in her lap, and her eyes rolled back in her head, which made her look like she was dying. My limbs stiffened and I reached for Cettina. The woman looked down and moved her lips slightly, twitching each of her fingers as

25

if she was counting on them. Then she placed a hand on the lower half of my abdomen, cupping the tiny curve, just nearly visible beneath my dress. Her warm palm pressed against me as the sunlight shifted to cast her in a jaundiced glow. We sat like that for a minute and then a minute more.

When she spoke her voice was sad but resigned.

"My medicine will not work. It is too late for you."

THREE

___

SARA

Viewed from above, the shapely boot of Italy appears to be kicking the island of Sicily into the tumultuous crease between the Mediterranean and Tyrrhenian Seas. The color of the water beneath us shifted and swirled from light blue to navy to an emerald green. Our plane nearly grazed the severe cliffs lining the shore as we swooped above the burnt-orange rooftops of Palermo.

It was gorgeous and otherworldly and still I thought, for maybe the hundredth time since I took off from Philadelphia, *What the hell am I doing?*

"It's an adventure, baby girl." I heard Rosie so clearly that my eyes watered. The fact that I didn't make this trip with her when she was alive weighed me down and yet it still felt like she was right there with me.

A painfully young and striking Italian flight attendant made me put the box with Rosie's ashes in it in the overhead compartment before we landed. Until then I'd had it in my lap. I imagined it warming my thighs even though that was impossible. It was just a box.

Rosie's last voice memo to me on the day before she died played on repeat in my mind.

Buck up. Get your ass out of bed and seize the goddamn day.

I hoped that she had managed to seize her last goddamn day.

"Do you think she was losing it?" Carla asked when I told her about what Aunt Rosie wanted me to do here in Sicily, about the all-expenses-paid trip, about the deed for land that might or might not be worth anything. "Did she have dementia at the end that we didn't know about?"

"She was sharp as a knife."

"You sure? Everyone sort of loses it when they're that old," Carla said.

"I'm totally sure she hadn't lost it."

"I wish I was going with you. I mean it's not like she bought me a plane ticket or anything, but I wish I could have gotten out of work to come, even if I had to pay my own way."

"I know," I said. "And Rosie probably knew you had a big case going on, plus the kids." I lied to assuage my sister's quiet jealousy. We both knew I was Rosie's favorite and most of the time it never bothered Carla because she had been everyone else's favorite for our entire lives. She was bouncy, sparkly, and liquid magic. In addition to everything that made Carla so outwardly lovely, she also made you feel like the most captivating person in the room and that made *her* the truly captivating one. Things just worked for her while I struggled for everything. I never resented her though; her charm worked on me most of all. Rosie had understood from the very start that I needed one person to love me a little bit more than they loved my sister.

But Carla still felt the need to add, "Also she knew you needed cash. And that getting away would be good for you. This was like her final way of taking care of you. You've hardly changed your clothes for the past two weeks."

"That's not true." It was true.

"So do what the letter says. Go to Sicily. Figure out if this deed is real or not. It's probably not, but whatever," Carla said. "Have sex with some hunky Italian men who don't speak a word of English. Eat good food and drink all the wine, eat and pray and love and all that shit, and then come home and put your life back together."

In that moment we both pretended like food and sex could be the answer to what had broken me instead of therapy, pharmaceuticals, and a time machine. I promised her I would try my best.

The pilot announced something so fast it was impossible for me to understand despite the fact that I've managed to retain a decent proficiency from the Italian classes Rosie enrolled me in as a child. She paid for them for all her great-nieces and great-nephews starting in elementary school. It was so important to her that we embrace our heritage. Rosie's father, Giovanni, spoke only Italian at home and she remained fluent until the day she died. All my cousins dropped out after a year. I was the only one who kept it up, spending Saturday mornings in the smoke-filled basement of Saint Rita's down by the baseball stadium for more than a decade. Even though Rosie's Italian was speckled with her father's Sicilian dialect and mine was more basic, the two of us used it as our secret language to talk shit about everybody else at family gatherings.

On the way to get my bag, I tried to call Jack to say good morning to Sophie, completely forgetting the time difference and getting his voicemail. I recorded a quick video message for my daughter instead, making funny faces and pantomiming eating a lot of pizza, her favorite food.

I'd never been truly away from my daughter for a long period of time. Since I'd moved out of our house six months ago, I'd been busting my ass to keep the restaurant alive. We began offering delivery service for the first time. Came up with a scheme to curate customized meat boxes every month. We stayed open for more hours. None of it was enough to make payroll and rent and health insurance. But I still made it over to the house every morning to take Soph to day care. Then I picked her up most days and brought her to the restaurant while I prepped the dinner service. I tried to give everything to both my babies, Sophie and La Macellaia, but I was running on empty all the time and it wasn't enough for either of them.

I had thought Jack and I were still figuring the arrangements out, figuring *us* out. I didn't expect him to hire a lawyer to officially file for divorce and full-time custody of our daughter, but he did, a month ago. I'd been trying to hire my own legal team to fight back ever since, no easy task when you have no cash or credit for the hefty deposit they all required.

My bag was the last one on the carousel. The second I made it into the arrivals area I ran into a meatball-shaped man hoisting a sign with my name above his head like I was someone who mattered.

"Sara Marsala. *Buongiorno. Come stai? Spero tutto bene.*" I translated in my head. Good morning. How are you? I hope all is well.

The meatball kissed both of my cheeks like we were old friends and switched to a heavily accented English.

"I am so sorry for the loss of Rosie. Such a woman! A good friend. A compadre."

His intimacy surprised me. "You knew Rosie?"

"Of course I knew Rosie. We spoke many times on the computer and the WhatsApp. Many times. She was looking for a driver for you, but she got a friend in me." He pounded on his chest like a proud ape.

I wanted to interrogate him, to know everything they talked about, what saucy jokes she served up, whether she flirted with him the way she did with gas station attendants, bank tellers, and supermarket cashiers, whether she told him all the things she never got to tell me.

"Rosie is the best." He said it like an indisputable fact.

"She is." I managed. "She was."

"Let me feed you. She would want me to feed you." Before I knew it, he'd led me by the elbow to a small outdoor café just past the taxi line. He introduced himself properly while we walked. "I am Pippo." It was pronounced Peep-*poh*. He drilled down hard on the last syllable like it was a surprise, a puppet jumping out of a jack-in-the-box. Pippo abandoned me at an unsteady table for two and quickly returned with a tiny paper cup of espresso and a soft sugary doughnut the size of a baby's head.

"Ciambella!" He announced the name of the pastry like he was presenting me with an Oscar.

I could almost see my reflection in the pastry's thick sheen of butter before I devoured it in seconds. For the past couple of months nothing had tasted good. In fact, almost everything I put in my mouth since I learned I'd have to close the restaurant tasted like cardboard. Eating, once my greatest joy, turned into the most mundane activity of my day. The *ciambella* was the first time in a long time that I actually derived pleasure from something.

"Your aunt was very proud of you. She sent me this."

He reached into his bag and I knew what he was gonna pull out before he showed me.

"You are famous in America. The queen of meat!"

31

The *Philadelphia* magazine cover with my face on it was a print-out from last year's July issue when La Macellaia won an award for the best new steak house in Philly. The photographer for the piece, a hawk-nosed twentysomething in thick glasses and a polka-dot dress that smelled like an old lady's closet, asked me to grab the biggest knife I could find. On the cover I'm brandishing a massive meat cleaver over a pearly pink pig belly ready to coax a coppa steak out of an obstinate pork shoulder. Given the state of world affairs, a lot of people saw a picture like that and created a story about empowerment and agency and how the future really was female. Others hated it, particularly the establishment chefs who thought I got recognized only *because* I was a woman.

I once thought I looked strong and powerful in that cover photo. I loved everything about being a butcher and a chef and owning my own business. I loved the little ecosystem of local farmers that I could pay a fair wage for their meat. Success for me was never about being on a magazine cover, though I did get off a little seeing my picture on newsstands. Success for me had always been about feeding the people in my neighborhood really good food, sometimes things they had no idea they'd love until I convinced them to try them. I relished the art of carving a perfect steak, of knowing exactly how to slice any cut of meat to find the most tender and juicy morsel. My restaurant gave me a purpose, made me feel useful, needed, and loved.

Yet, when I saw the picture of myself in Pippo's hands, I cringed. *Look at that ridiculous woman holding a knife as a prop, someone in costume. That's not me*, I wanted to say. *Not anymore.* The picture had come to represent what can happen when, for once in your life, you thought you actually deserved all the nice things that were happening to you. In the end I had wanted too much. I wanted success and love, a career and a child, a marriage and freedom.

I'd wanted it all and I'd ended up with nothing.

The article didn't mention that my restaurant was leveraged to the hilt, that I'd maxed out all my credit cards to keep it going, to keep expanding the space, building out the back deck and a bigger kitchen. It didn't say that no banks wanted to give me another loan, that our landlord, a skeezy slumlord who owned half of South Philly, tripled the rent after I won Best in Philly and then charged me extra for all the renovations I'd done, claiming he hadn't approved them. The magazine never printed the rumors started by my competitors, the ones that said I sourced my meat from disgusting factories instead of the local farms printed on our menus. I had no idea winning that award would shatter the eggshell egos of the mostly male chefs in the meat industry who had previously treated me like a precocious little sister. Those kinds of whispers in such a close-knit business quickly turn to murmurs and then shouts and then accepted truths. Most of my competitors found a certain amount of glee in declaring me a fraud, and maybe they were right because I had screwed it up. I'd been sloppy with the renovations, taken shortcuts, ignored codes, in order to get everything done in time, to expand, to make more money, so I could finally take a break and enjoy the life I had built. But the truth about the restaurant business is that you never get to slow down. So when someone called the inspectors on me I didn't stand a chance. They fined me for violating three archaic codes. It was the final straw for my investors, who had already stopped putting up any more cash because we didn't see fast enough returns. The restaurant failed because of me and in spite of me. Both things can be true.

But that was too much to explain to a stranger in an airport parking lot and my heart surged a little remembering how proud Aunt Rosie had been when I was on the cover of that magazine. I managed a humble smile for Pippo and shrugged like it wasn't that big of a deal before attempting a change of subject.

"You must have much better restaurants here in Sicily. And you probably know the best ones with your job, with showing people around. You're a taxi driver?" I asked.

"I drive here in Palermo, but mostly longer trips. Foreigners, especially Americans, do not like driving here in Sicily. None of you can drive a manual and we do not have many automatic rentals for you. How do you live your lives without knowing how to drive a real car?" When he grinned, I noticed he was missing his left incisor, which would have made him look menacing if his smile weren't so wide and honest.

I didn't tell him I *could* drive stick; Rosie had taught me in her pristine Mustang convertible. We began lessons when I was ten because Rosie said you never knew when you'd need to "get the hell out of Dodge." We were the same height by then, so reaching the pedals wasn't a problem for me.

Pippo nodded to the box I placed on the seat next to me. "You brought Rosie with you?"

He said it as though she sat in the seat next to me on the plane, sipping a chilled martini.

"I did. She told me she wanted her ashes to be scattered in the town where her relatives were from. Is it close to here?"

"The village of Caltabellessa. It is ninety kilometers south," he explained.

Less than sixty miles. "A quick drive."

"The roads here are different than in America. Not so good. And the traffic will be bad. We will be there in two hours, maybe three. But the views are spectacular, the most beautiful you will ever see."

I lapped up the last drips of espresso. Two to three hours before I could lie down and get some real sleep. I could smell myself. I needed a bath and a real meal of something besides butter and sugar.

"We'd better get going, then."

"Would you like to see anything in Palermo before we go? I can take you on a walking tour of the historic district, through the beautiful Quattro Canti, a masterpiece of baroque architecture. We have the very best cathedral, the most spectacular palace. Our Capuchin Catacombs are much more interesting than the ones in Rome, not so big, but much better. And there is the Teatro Massimo, the third-largest theater in Europe, and the fish market. Oh, you must see the fish market."

I cut him off more abruptly than I meant to.

"I'd love to get to the town while it's still daylight," I said with all the conviction I could muster even though I knew Rosie would have wanted me to linger. Maybe it was lack of sleep. Maybe it was the intense familiarity this man seemed to have with my dead aunt, but I was on edge and ready to know exactly how this story would unspool. I hated surprises as much as Rosie loved them.

Pippo mumbled something in Italian under his breath but stood quickly, slinging my battered old duffel over his shoulder and gesturing to a shiny yellow Fiat parked practically on the curb.

Traffic around Palermo was a special breed of chaos. There might have been lines on the freeway but they were clearly a suggestion since no one acknowledged them. Cars and motor scooters wove in and out of them without using turn signals. With its rugged cliffs leading to faded golden hills tripping down to the sea, the landscape reminded me of Northern California where Jack and I once went to the wedding of one of his colleagues. We'd snuck out after dessert and had sex in the crumbling old wine cave, passing out naked and surprising the vintner with a view of our bright white butts in the air first thing in the morning. The memory brought me a twinge of joy before I could catch myself.

I let my hand float out of Pippo's car window and bobbed my head up and down to an Italian pop song with the English refrain "Baby, you ate my heart."

The same vines and olive trees they had in Sonoma terraced the Sicilian mountains, except instead of neat rows of grapevines, these plants trailed up the hills in chaotic clusters, interspersed with fat palm trees and prickly pear cacti.

When Pippo pulled over for gas and a pee, I called Carla, and despite the early hour in Philly, she answered right away.

"How's your road trip with Aunt Rose?"

"Great. We're just arguing over who gets to be Louise and who has to be Thelma."

Carla flicked a lighter. Both of us had recently started smoking again and we were trying to hide it from everyone else. I did it because of the stress. Carla did it in silent protest against her wife's ultra marathon training. I could picture my gorgeous older sister inhaling on her back patio, her two boys about to wake up for school. She probably had a black leather jacket wrapped around her slight frame, her curly red hair loose and messy. Carla began dressing like Mick Jagger when she was fifteen: spandex pants, tight T-shirts, and tiny leather jackets. At thirty-nine not much had changed even though she was a fancy-ass lawyer now.

"You're so Thelma. You would never have done this unless Rosie made you. I feel like a good old-fashioned road trip is exactly what she had in mind. An adventure for the two of you."

"Rose even hired a driver."

"I bet Rosie made a bunch of secret money in the end at the slots. She loved the slots."

"Maybe."

"Is the driver hot?"

"He's, like, Dad's age."

"Which means he would definitely hit on you."

Our parents' forty-year marriage and the fact that they're still together confounded the both of us. Mom probably got Stockholm syndrome from being with Dad for so long. She'd been an honor student at Archbishop Ryan, only a junior, when they met. He was at least ten years older, a jack-of-all-trades—a bartender, a welder, a drummer in a wedding band, and an extra in *Rocky IV.* Dad spent the better part of the past forty years living up to his high school superlative, "most likely to hit on your mom." He'd allegedly curtailed his extracurricular activities ten years ago though, right after his first heart attack. Mom had convinced Father O'Brien to inform my father, in no uncertain terms, that God was punishing him for all the other women.

"Stop tomcatting and whoring, John Marsala, or the Lord is going to nail you to your cross," Father O'Brien told him. Powerful words from an eighty-year-old Irish priest who'd survived Bloody Sunday and probably had a crush on my mom.

I peered through the window of the gas station, where Pippo appeared to be telling the attendant an elaborate story, judging by the fluttering of his hands in the cashier's face. "The driver's not my type," I told my sister.

"Not a self-important mamma's boy with intense delusions of grandeur about his place in the world?"

"That's an OK description of Jack."

"Thanks. I've been waiting to use it."

Carla was never a fan of Jack's, not even in the beginning, when all of us were still on our best behavior. He once made some comment about how it must be nice to sell out to Big Law, and Carla retorted that it must be nice to have rich parents footing the bill for your Ivy League college, top-ten law school, and civil service job. I spent a lot of time trying to make them love one another as much as I loved each of them.

It was actually Jack's mom who gave me his number when she met me at the farmers' market out in the suburbs. I had been running my own little butcher shop and food truck out of a refurbished Airstream I bought on Craigslist. "The roving meat monger," they called me.

"I like the way you trim a roast," Jack's mom, Zelda Grossberg, informed me the second time she bought a steak from me. I told her it would be my last day at the market since I needed a new special permit to stay there. "My son's a lawyer. You call him," she'd said. "I'm not losing this brisket."

Zelda was just looking to do me a favor, not hook me up with her son. I did call Jack because I wanted that permit and he called a friend in the local municipal office to get it for me. I offered to cook for him at my place to thank him. When I saw how cute he was I decided I would try to sleep with him too.

As I prepped a porterhouse back at my tiny studio apartment he asked about how I became a butcher.

"You don't see that many women in the meat business."

I rolled my eyes like it was such a sexist thing to say even though he was right. "I probably shouldn't admit this to a lawyer, but I was a middle school juvenile delinquent," I told him as I mixed finely chopped garlic and balsamic vinegar for the marinade. "I kept getting into fights, mostly with boys who were picking on my sister because she wasn't into them. I got suspended a bunch and the school said they'd expel me if my parents didn't figure something out. So Mom and Dad shipped me up to the Poconos to my aunt Rosie's house for ninth grade and Rosie decided I needed to get my own ass kicked a little. She had a pal who ran a farm that employed former convicts right after they got out of prison to help them transition back to life in the real world. Rosie sent me there every day at dawn before school. It was just me and a bunch of ex-cons mucking shit out of stalls, hauling bags of feed, castrating the bulls, all of it. I loved those guys. I loved those early-morning hours." I didn't talk about how the stench of manure clung to me while I slept through my first year of high school or how I smoked rolled cigarettes and sometimes the odd joint with the guys every morning.

I did say that they were the hardest-working dudes I'd ever met in my entire life. Them and the farmers. The farm did all their own butchering. After a couple of months, I convinced the bull master, Frank, to let me watch the slaughter and quartering of a cow. I threw up when the cow collapsed on the ground in front of me. Frank said I should become a vegetarian if I couldn't stomach where the meat came from. I cleaned up after myself and helped him butcher the whole animal and then we did the pigs and then packaged it up for restaurants all over the East Coast. I learned the difference between happy meat and industrial meat. I could taste it even then. I also loved preparing dinners for the men on the farm and for Aunt Rosie. I kept up the cooking when I got home and eventually saved up enough money for culinary school because I thought it might give me more job options, even though all I wanted to do was get back to the basics of butchering. I'd explained all of that to Jack while I cooked. By then the steak was out of the cast-iron skillet and resting on my counter. I sprinkled it with salt and pepper and served it on my two chipped plates that I'd taken from my mom and dad's house.

"This steak tastes like Christmas morning," Jack gushed.

"You eat steak on Christmas morning?"

His cheeks flushed pink, which was terribly sexy. "No. I mean it tastes like pure joy. My Waspy friends had Christmas trees and got all these presents, and all my parents ever gave me for Hanukkah was socks and boxer shorts and acne cream. For me Christmas morning was this magical perfect moment of wish fulfillment. That's what this steak is like, the perfect gift."

I couldn't think of a better thing to be than someone's perfect morning.

He ate the rest of it in five swift bites, pushed his chair away from the table, and kissed me. That kiss was like Christmas morning and later that night I had my first orgasm with another human. All the men before had made me finish the job myself. I had filthy dreams about him for weeks until our next date and we were inseparable after that. Poor Zelda Grossberg didn't know the price of that brisket.

With his tiny cherubic face Jack looked like a little angel even though he carried himself like a very serious man, always walking faster than anyone else on the sidewalk. I was two inches taller than him, more if I wore heels, which he encouraged me to do. By then I'd outgrown my teenage awkwardness and embraced my height and strength. I loved being strong enough to throw a two-hundred-pound beef quarter over my shoulder with nary a grunt. Jack had no interest in lifting anything heavy. He didn't even know how to change a tire when we met, bless his well-mannered Main Line soul. The two of us fit together in unexpected ways—Jack was organized to a fault where I was messy. I taught him how to have fun, drove us through the night to Montreal just to try a specific poutine, painted our bedroom electric blue, enrolled us in a kickball league. Jack encouraged me to stay in, to rest, regroup, and snuggle.

We were both young and ambitious. I started doing small catering gigs and then this fancy restaurant asked me if I wanted to do a pop-up with them. I was featured on a TV show on the Travel Channel about food trucks. My reputation swelled along with my bank account though neither really had anywhere to go but up. Some investors offered to put up a little cash for my very own restaurant. My. Very. Own. Restaurant. I was an accidental success and it always felt like it could be snatched away.

Once Sophie came along, I brought her with me some nights. I nursed her in the pantry while eking out a menu with one hand and squeezing my boob into her mouth with the other. But mostly I left her with my mom, which Jack hated. What choice did I have? The first couple of years are all that matter in the food industry. I guess you could say the same about the first years of having a kid. Still, I wanted my little girl to see me succeed. That's what I told myself every time I left her, that I was modeling what a strong, successful woman looked like and wasn't that as important as any of the other parts of parenting? That's when Jack started pressing me to have another baby, when he told me maybe I should slow down at work. That's when we started resenting each other, when our marriage began to fray around the edges, and I was too busy to see it. And then came my betrayal, the one he wasn't able to forgive. I hated thinking about it, hated remembering how we'd once loved one another so much we couldn't breathe without the other one and then how we'd lost track of why we'd chosen each other in the first place.

41

Carla thankfully changed the subject. "Where are you now?"

"A gas station in between Palermo and the town where our relatives are from."

"The legendary Caltabellessa." We'd grown up hearing Rosie mythologize the village like it was Atlantis.

"Dad is so jealous," Carla said. "You know that, right? He has been dreaming of a find-your-roots trip forever."

"Yeah, yeah," I said to my sister. "But Dad doesn't have a passport, or any cash, and Mom only leaves Philly to go down the shore."

"Well, bring him back a flag or an apron that has the flag on it," Carla said.

"I'll get him something nice. I'll call you when I get there. I'm hoping to figure all this out as fast as I can and get back."

"You're so crazy. Why don't you stay for the week and enjoy yourself? That's what Rose wanted. It's all paid for and who knows, maybe that deed is real."

"We both know it isn't. And I've got a ton to do back in Philly." The last of the bankruptcy paperwork, making sure my workers would get unemployment, finding a divorce attorney who would work for pork chops.

"Sara, chill out. Everything will still be there when you get back. All the paperwork, all the problems."

Pippo walked out of the gas station, his hands filled with caffeine and more pastries.

"I gotta go. Love you." I ended the call with my sister and rushed over to help him.

"You like cannoli?"

"Do I look like a savage? Who doesn't? But, cannoli from the gas station?"

"The gas stations have the best cannoli. You trust me."

"'Leave the gun, take the cannoli,'" I joked. He smiled, but he'd definitely heard this line from every one of his American clients.

"How much longer until we get there?"

He gestured down the road. "Fifteen minutes and then we go up the mountain and then maybe another thirty more. When we arrive, I will take you to the hotel and you can sleep."

Once we were back on the road Pippo asked me, "How much do you know about Caltabellessa?"

"Only what I heard from my aunt Rosie over the years," I admitted, slightly ashamed that I hadn't done more research before coming. "Her father left because there were no jobs and he wanted to make a better life for his family, but he never stopped loving his village. He told Rosie it was the most beautiful place he had ever laid eyes on, that food tasted better there, that the air always smelled of delicious things to eat and to drink. That the streets were always filled with laughter and musicians and the most beautiful women you had ever laid eyes on."

"What did you think of that?" Pippo asked me.

"I thought it sounded like a fantasy. Like the grass is always greener somewhere you will never be again."

He rolled his eyes at my cynicism.

"You will have to see for yourself. It is an ancient village, your Caltabellessa, settled by the first people of the island, the Sicani, in one thousand BC."

"You're a historian?" I teased.

"I did my research for you. For Rosie. Shall I continue?"

"Please do," I encouraged him warmly, worried I'd hurt his feelings again.

"It was a special place for the Sicani, a holy place, many say. There

43

are two caves on top of the mountain where ancient rituals were practiced. It was eventually invaded by the Greek peoples. They say it is where the brilliant inventor Daedalus, the one who built the labyrinth, fled after escaping the Minotaur and King Minos. The legend says Daedalus built Caltabellessa like the maze of the labyrinth to be impenetrable to enemies. Because the city was so high on the mountain it felt separate from the rest of the world. But the Romans eventually sacked it and then so did the Byzantines and the Arabs and eventually the Normans came. There is a very large and beautiful castle on the top from when the Normans invaded in the eleventh century. That is the main reason the tourists come."

"Are there many tourists?"

When he shook his head his jowls jiggled. "We would like to have many more, but we do not get so many on this side of the island. We get the more adventurous ones, also those looking for their ancestors, but most of the tourists visit Taormina on the eastern shore. The cruise ships stop there and give the visitors eight hours of Sicily before heading off to Greece or Amalfi. Though some developers have been buying land and making spas and golf courses for the rich Russians and the Chinese. But I like Americans. I wish more of you would come to the island. You must tell all of your friends."

"I promise I will."

"And you will give me a five-star rating on the Tripadvisor?"

"Absolutely. This has been a five-star journey so far."

I was ready to close my eyes for the last part of the drive, but Pippo started rustling around in his bag and handed me a brown envelope, the same kind that came in the mail two weeks earlier, the same handwriting, except this one was addressed to me, care of Pippo Turturici. I slid my finger beneath the seal and a laminated photograph fell onto my lap. It used to hang in Rosie's hallway with all of our school pictures. It was the only photograph she had of her mother, one taken in 1925 right before Serafina died. The boys in the picture, Cosimo, Vincenzo, and my grandfather Santo, looked like teenagers, almost as tall as their father. Serafina stared directly into the lens. I'd never thought much about this picture before. Despite knowing she was younger than me when she died, I still always thought of Serafina as old, matronly. But looking at this photo in a new light, I noticed her sharp cheekbones, her smooth skin, almost childlike, though there was nothing innocent about her eyes. Her stare was hard and timeworn. Her lips were full, not unlike my own. They formed a slash across her face. Not a scowl exactly, but more a look of displeased resignation.

I took one final look at the photo, Serafina's eyes boring into my own, before I read Rosie's script.

> *My darling girl. There's another reason I wanted you to come all the way here. I didn't want to tell you at first because I know you hate surprises and you're in no mood for a real adventure. This trip is first and foremost for you. I want you to figure out if you can get any money from this tiny plot of land and use it however you need to solve your problems. More than anything I hope this time away will bring you back to your true self and get you back on your feet. But I'm also a selfish old broad and I have one favor to ask now that you are here.*
>
> *There's something that has never sat right with me about how my mother did not join us here in the States. I was always told she got sick, that she died of a flu. But as a girl I heard things I was never supposed to hear. I didn't dare ask any questions. Children didn't ask them back then. I know there is more to my mother's*

story. I did some research while I've been stuck in my damn bed but no one in Sicily will really talk to me while I am still in the US. You gotta be there to get people to open up. I was hoping this would be something we could do together, but if I can't figure it out for myself I need you to do it for me. I don't know why it gives me peace now to ask you to do this, but like I said, I'm a selfish old broad.

I want you to find out what really happened to my mother.

FOUR

SERAFINA

1908–1910

Gio kept calling me "Mamma." He'd never lived with another woman besides his own mother, and he simply didn't know any other way to be. As the youngest son he'd grown up firmly attached to his mamma's skirts and he was not ready to tear himself away.

We moved in together, into the small building across the back alley from my parents, the week of our wedding. The dirty, stinking space used to house chickens and the goat and it was so small you could clean it with one sweep of the broom. Its gypsum rock walls were covered in the thinnest of plasters, easily penetrated by rains in the winter.

My own mamma had insisted I was old enough to get married. Papa didn't agree, but this was the one and only time his opinion didn't matter to anyone but him.

"*Chista è a zita,*" Mamma said, her voice directed to the floor she was on her knees scrubbing even though it would never look clean. She would scrub that floor until her fingernails fell out. "I was thirteen when I married you. She is almost sixteen. She is a woman."

Papa shook his head at that, like he didn't believe I was even a teenager but still five years old, a little girl in lacy dresses baptizing my dolls in the town fountain with Cetti.

"We can send her away," he begged. "To my aunt in Catania. She will be discreet. By the Holy Virgin I swear she will work with the sisters to find a family for the baby."

"There is no other option, Santo. She is ruined now so she will marry Gio." One of her babies wailed and Mamma dropped her rag so she could pick him up from the cradle in the corner. She rocked back and forth as she nursed and picked up the rag to wipe crumbs off the table. Papa didn't lift a finger to help. I saw my future reflected back at me. School in Sciacca was already a distant memory.

"Do not make this worse than it already is," my mother said. "There will be a wedding and then there will be a baby. That is the way things are supposed to be. Do not behave as if this is the end of the world. Your soft spot for the girl is shameful. Many fathers would have killed a daughter for this kind of sin."

I said nothing. A well-brought-up daughter, a modest girl who would make a good marriage, was a reflection of the family's honor. Gio's family was even less well off than my own. Given my circumstances and the role their son had played in them they wouldn't require a dowry from my family. This, my mother made sure to tell me, was no small amount of grace.

"A good marriage for you would have bankrupted us. We do not have an extra bay mule or gold coin to our name and times are only getting worse."

A girl's dowry payments ruined families like ours, the ones who made only enough to get by. How many times had I heard the old sayings: "Blessed is the door out of which goes a dead daughter, and the older and uglier she is the greater the comfort" or "I have five children. One boy and four burdens."

I bit my tongue to stop from replying that my having no marriage at all, that a life far away working as a teacher in a city would have cost them nothing.

The wedding had to be small. Everyone in town had already remarked on how fat I was. Mamma saw no point in showing it off some more. People would stop talking after there was a ceremony. I wore the church dress Mamma had worn to mass when she was with child and added a lace ribbon and my mother's wedding veil. The ceremony and mass were just me, Gio, our parents, and the priest. Father Caputo's breath was sweet with the smell of wine. Gio traced a shape in my palm with the tip of his finger. I smiled at the memory of the made-up constellation, the tipsy priest.

We had only a month living together as husband and wife before Gio took a job at the sulfur mine in Sciacca and stayed down in the bowels of hell scraping the minerals from the earth for two weeks at a time. When he came home I fed him and listened to his raspy breath on the nights when I couldn't sleep because my body was too large to be comfortable in any position. No matter which way I rolled, it felt like I was crushing the baby or the baby was crushing me.

Sometimes my tossing and turning would wake Gio and he'd tell me stories about the men who worked in the mines with him.

"These men have become my *cumpari*, my greatest friends. I am closer to them than even Liuni," he admitted.

He talked about a small one-eyed man named Cloru, who had seven fingers on his left hand, which meant he could play the harmonica better than anyone Gio had ever heard. Sometimes Cloru would drink too much, put on a skirt, and play the miners lullabies while he stroked their heads like he was their mother. Cloru caught a rat underground that was as large as a tiny dog and he kept it on a leash tied to his belt. He was training the rodent to dance along with his harmonica. I laughed at these stories, imagining a small man in women's clothes doing a jig alongside a monstrous rat.

Sometimes when I laughed I got a cramp in my belly so bad I'd have shooting pains down my torso for the rest of the night. Gio would rub small circles into my lower back and aching hips.

None of my friends had yet been pregnant and Mamma would not speak to me about my aches and pains. I had no one to ask what was normal and what was strange to happen to a body about to have a child.

"We can go to see the old woman again," Cettina said when a yellowish paste started leaking from my nipples.

"I can't walk that far," I said. I hardly left the house. A woman in my condition became an object of fascination and I hated it, hated the eyes on my body. By the end of it I felt obscene being out in public at all.

"I could ask her to come here," Cettina said with uncertainty because we both knew the old woman came only when the baby was ready to be born.

The labor pains arrived early one morning while I was using the toilet, soon becoming a white-hot sharp thing that felt like someone lit fire to all of my insides. I barely made it across the alley to Mamma's house, where I collapsed in front of her door.

I awoke on the straw mattress I had slept on as a child, stripped naked and writhing in pain and terror. My body had been trying to do the work as I slept, but something was very wrong. Mamma was in the room along with my grandmother and two aunts, the ones Mamma liked the best. Cettina stood in the corner with a red face and puffy eyes. Mamma's fingers worked a black rosary that Papa had brought her back from the Feast of Saint Lucia in Palermo. My body felt as though it were being sliced in two and all I wanted to do was close my eyes again. My heart pounded like it wanted out of my chest. I no longer cared if I was dying; I let myself fall into the blackness. When I opened my eyes again the witch was there and all I could see was the map of wrinkles on the old woman's face. The lines formed grooves and canyons around her eyes and her mouth, which had been touching my mouth only a second before. I realized the woman was trying to give me breath, trying to keep me alive.

Maybe my baby will die. I did not wish it, but I let myself think it. If the baby died, my life could go back to the way it was. Maybe the school would take me back. Maybe I could leave here.

"He is backward," the old woman whispered when she saw my eyes open. "I am going to turn him around." She poured a foul-smelling liquid down my throat and maneuvered a stick in between my teeth and instructed me to bite down. Cettina released a blood-curdling scream from the other side of the room as the woman reached her hand into my body, the arm going inside me up to her elbow. I felt the witch's hand turn, could feel every muscle and tendon in her forearm scraping my insides. Then one last sharp pain, like a knife being twisted into an open wound, and I felt nothing more. Mamma cried, helpless beside me, gripping my limp hand, whispering prayers. The witch slid her hand out and the baby soon followed, a writhing purple thing. He didn't make a noise. Someone slapped him on the back and he released a low whimper. The old woman poured another drink that tasted like dirt and blood into my mouth and began washing thick white paste from the baby. I fell asleep again and by the time I was awake the witch was gone, no trace of her left behind and no mention of her ever being there at all.

When I asked Cettina why she had left she looked at me like I was stupid, which I was when it came to the ways of the world. "She slips in and she slips out. She stays invisible to the men so that the

51

women can go to her for what the doctor will not or cannot give them."

As Cosimo, Cosi for short, grew I knew he was happy. I knew it because he smiled earlier than other babies and he never cried. He was so silent my mother found him unnerving and strange.

"Something is wrong with him," she insisted. "Babies need to cry. It helps them release the demons."

The blood boiled in my veins.

"He is thinking," I snapped while Cettina held him. My friend came to the house every day to hold the baby and talk about her own wedding, which would take place during summer. I felt a fierce need to defend Cosi to my mother, a baby I'd never even wanted to exist, a baby I'd hoped would somehow be knocked loose all those months he lived in my body. But once he arrived and it was just the two of us living in our one-room apartment while Gio worked far away I began to enjoy the child's silent friendship.

After the birth I sent a letter down the mountain for Gio. He sent back congratulations with extra money but stayed away for the next three months. It was for the best. Everyone knew a man was useless around a tiny baby. The winter grew frigid and sometimes we didn't leave the house for days. I swaddled the baby tightly to make sure his legs would grow straight and then burrowed into a nest of quilts with him, rising only to grab a hunk of bread and cheese, enough to keep my milk flowing.

Taking care of the baby was second nature after helping to raise my younger siblings. But it was different with Cosi. He was a piece of me. I talked to him like I'd never spoken to anyone else, told him stories about our family and the town, told him how, initially, I didn't want him or his father, how I'd wanted something more, even though I didn't know exactly what *more* meant.

I told him how I wished I could have gone to school longer. I taught Cosi all the numbers I knew, counting everything in the room and his fingers and his toes over and over for hours on end. Somehow neither of us ever got bored of it.

When spring came, I tied the baby to my body with a tight muslin and walked him through the village. Cosi made everyone smile and they gave him presents, a crusty slice of bread to cut his teeth on, fresh whey skimmed off the milk. The cheesemonger asked both of us to open our mouths and close our eyes before placing velvety ricotta directly onto our tongues.

My husband had been a boy of fifteen when I married him. After a year of working in the mines with men twice his age and living apart from his mamma he started to grow into a man. The muscles in his arms and chest hardened. And even though he always smelled of smoke and brimstone, some nights in our bed together I began to feel a warm stirring between my legs for him, but he was always too tired to reach for me.

The stories he told were no longer sweet and funny. "It's too hot for clothes in the mines anymore. Even a thin shirt feels like flames on your skin. We work naked most days since the air is on fire," he whispered. His once smooth olive skin was burnt and warped on the backs of his thighs, the bottoms of his feet.

Each mine employed a group of boys as young as six years old who could fit through the tunnels and carry messages between the groups of miners. These boys came from the poorest families on the island and were usually sold to the mining companies when their parents could no longer afford to feed them. Gio had taken a liking to one of the boys assigned to his group. *Donnola,* they called him, the weasel, because he could contort his body into the shape of even the narrowest spaces. Gio shortened it to Donni out of affection.

"Maybe I can make enough money for the boy to come to live with us one day," Gio said.

I didn't bother to point out to my husband that he was barely making enough money to feed the three of us.

The next time he came home Gio didn't mention Donni or Cloru. He stopped laughing and smiling too. He stayed home for two weeks and then another. He was there when Cosi celebrated his first birthday.

"Mamma will be so happy you are here for the celebration," I lied to my husband. "She made Cosi a little white suit encrusted with tiny pearls she'd pulled from the hem of her own wedding dress. He looks like a shiny doll when he wears it." I told Gio this hoping he would get excited, but nothing could make him smile. We went to the one restaurant in town and ordered a feast, seating Cosi at the head of the table like the man of the family, propped up with pillows so he was nearly looking down on us. Mamma beamed at her grandson and even at her son-in-law, who she usually tried to ignore. It was a momentous day for Mamma, her first grandson turning a year old. Many of her friends' daughters had babies who hadn't made it through the first year—pneumonia, influenza, burns, one child who simply never learned how to swallow at his mother's breast and starved by the time he was two weeks old. The mothers blamed themselves and the grandmothers blamed their daughters and themselves. Despite everything I had ever done wrong in Mamma's eyes, I'd managed to keep Cosi alive for the first year and it might have been the first time my mother was truly proud of me. My papa had changed too, but his feelings for me were different from Mamma's. Before the baby came, he had been proud of who I might turn out to be. Now he looked through me, not unlike the way he looked through my mother and her sisters. I was no longer special to him.

"Gio, when will you return to Sciacca?" Papa asked as the food began to arrive, platters piled high with olives and artichokes, sun-dried tomatoes swimming in oil, bombettes, pork necks stuffed with herbs, crushed almonds and cheese roasted over a bed of hot coals in the garden, and slabs of swordfish so fresh you could still smell the blood on the fingers of the man who brought the plate. "The mine can do without you for so long?"

"I am not returning to the mine," Gio whispered. It was the first time I had heard him talk of the mine since he returned.

"You will stay here?" Gio shook his head and lifted a glass of wine to his thin lips. Cosi inherited my lips, full and red like the meat inside a tomato. Gio's lips were narrow, a thin line across his otherwise unremarkable face.

A shudder of panic ran through my body as I considered what it would be like to have my husband living with me and my son every day, not the sweet, clumsy, gentle boy I'd married but this new miserable husk of a man. What would it be like to have the three of us in that one room every day and every night?

It must have been the first time Gio's own mamma had heard of this too because she turned to him with a look of surprise. "The mine is a good job."

"There was a fire," he murmured. "Six of the tunnels fell down and they do not need many of us anymore. I was told not to come back."

His mother crossed herself and pulled her son's head to her breast, offering up a prayer to Saint Rosalia that he had made it home safe, murmuring about the many accidents in the mines.

"It was not an accident," Gio spat. "The mine owners did not secure it properly. The tunnels never should have collapsed." I could feel his anger like a pain seeping into my own skin. I knew without asking him why he no longer mentioned Donni.

I looked to Papa for help. He must be able to get Gio a job in Palermo working on the grand new roads. But Gio spoke first.

"There is a job for me in Calabria."

Il continente. The mainland. "How long will you be gone?" I plucked Cosi from his throne of pillows and clutched his squirmy frame to me. He reached his fingers out to grab a fistful of peaches smothered in honey and shoved them into his mouth.

"Most of the year." Gio's words sent a surge of relief through my body. "There is work for me on the docks."

"It sounds like a good job," Gio's mamma said.

"Auguri!" Gio's poor wretch of a father raised his glass of wine in congratulations and the rest of the table did the same. *"Auguri e figghi masculi!"* I congratulate you and wish you more male children. Everyone looked at me and laughed with their mouths wide open because now that Cosimo was one year old they expected me to be pregnant again. I raised my own glass and placed a hand on my belly because that is what they wanted to see me do. The tips of my fingers curled inward, my nails digging into my skin until it was painful.

I passed Cosi to my mother, who did not notice my agitation. Only Cettina stared at me with any kind of concern and gripped my knee beneath the table. "Don't make that face," she whispered. "You have to pretend to be happy. You have a beautiful child, and your husband will soon have a good job on *il continente.* What more do you wish for? Do not be greedy."

Cettina was now officially betrothed to Liuni, but he didn't make it to the party. He was in Palermo taking political classes at the university. "Liuni will be an important man one day," my father said. "He'll help us get those bastards out of Palermo."

There were so many bastards in Palermo, so many bastards in

charge of our island, that I was never certain which bastards my father was referring to. I had learned about politics in school from a teacher who was sympathetic to the causes of workers and peasants. Maestro Falleti had explained that ever since the Risorgimento, when Sicily was forced to become a part of the Kingdom of Italy in 1861, the rich leaders in the northern cities on the mainland had been bleeding our island dry. "Sucking the life from our blood and our soil," he told us. "They take our sulfur, our good grain and our grapes, our fish and our meat, and they give us the lowest possible prices for it because we are all one kingdom now. But what do we get from them in return? Nothing. Sicily may have no choice but to be a part of Italy. But our people will never be of Italy. We are not Italians. We are *Siciliani*." And the leaders in Palermo, according to Maestro Falleti, were not much better. They did everything they could to make sure people like us, poor peasants, did not have any control over the direction of our lives. We were helpless as the rich ruling class made life easy for their wealthy friends and taxed the poor into debt.

"*Surfaru sugnu*. I am just sulfur. They want us to have no control over what happens to us, no sense of self-determination," Falleti said.

It was the first time, but not the last, that I would understand how the new unified Italian state and the rich ruling class in Palermo were making sure we rural Sicilians would always remain poor. Liuni was sympathetic to Maestro Falleti's views. He'd been his most eager student, working secretly with the *fasci del lavoratori*, a group of men trying to unite the farmers, the industrial workers, the tradespeople, and the guild members in a single *fasci*, or bundle, to fight for less taxes, more rights, and better conditions for the common people. All this knowledge was still in my brain, now dusty and useless. The women in town did not talk of such things and the men did not talk to women about politics.

Liuni's older brother, Marco, escorted Cettina to dinner in place of her fiancé on the night of Cosi's birthday. He had been many classes ahead of me in school, but we knew one another because there was only one classroom for all the children in town. He had been smart but also kind. He used to help Falleti by giving the younger children our lessons when the *maestro* became over-whelmed or got too drunk during the day. I always tried to impress Marco with how well I could read and write. He was the first boy I ever thought of as handsome, and as a married woman I could only allow myself to take the adult Marco in with small glances. He'd been sitting next to Cettina for most of dinner but now he leaned against the doorframe, his bearing calm and curious, his jet-black hair longer than any of the other men's in the room, nearly brushing the collar of his freshly ironed shirt. He was newly mar-ried too, to the daughter of the richest man in town. Before he left that night he came to our table and handed me a small envelope. "For the little one," he said. It was the only time I allowed myself to meet Marco's clear green eyes. The envelope contained ten lire.

Later that night I put Cosi in between me and Gio. I stroked my son's silky hair until he fell asleep. He'd eaten everything we put in front of him at dinner, the artichokes, the pork bellies, the squid, and even the grilled cow tongue, proving over and over again that he was a healthy specimen of a little man.

When I woke at daybreak my husband had moved our child off the bed. Cosi was grunting and snoring in the blankets in the cor-ner of the room and Gio was turned away from me facing the wall. His body shook with sobs he tried to keep silent. The contours of his neck and shuddering shoulders were visible in the dark. Gio always slept with no clothes. No matter how cold it was in our room he sweated through any sheet I tried to put on top of him. I flinched at first, unsure what to do. I'd never seen or heard a man cry before. My own father would never shed a tear, much less allow Mamma to witness it. Slowly I reached over to stroke Gio's back, the way he'd done for me when I was aching and pregnant. I rubbed figure eights and then traced over the trails of my finger with light kisses. My lips fluttered up and down his spine and I felt his body relax into me. I pushed him over onto his back and brushed his tears away with the tips of my fingers.

"You're never going back there," I murmured, and rolled my body on top of his. I could feel him grow hard beneath me and knew this was a small way I could give him comfort, could take his mind away from the mines and the new job in a strange new world. I was terrified he would hate me for bearing witness to his humiliation, so I lowered myself down onto him and rocked my hips back and forth, finding an easy rhythm that pleased us both. My husband stared at me in scared surprise as if I were the Madonna come to life, but his tears were gone. I continued to move, closed my eyes, and tried not to think of Marco's soulful eyes or the way his rough knuckles brushed up against mine when he handed me the envelope.

It was only a minute before I felt Gio's wetness between my legs. He sat up and buried his face in the crook of my neck and whispered, "Thank you." It was the first time since we'd been married that I felt I had done my duty as his wife.

My husband had already crossed the strait toward Calabria by the time my stomach started to swell again.

FIVE

SARA

When I was seven and Carla was nine, we spent the first of six entire summers in Scranton with Aunt Rosie. Mom said it was because she worried Rosie was lonely, but we both knew it was because my parents' marriage was falling apart. Dad had recently taken up with an Outback Steakhouse waitress named Vienna, and Mom and Dad needed space to figure their shit out. Aunt Rosie loved the story about Dad and Vienna, not because she wanted to see my parents break up but because she was dying to know whether the twenty-two-year-old who served Bloomin' Onions and had stolen my father's heart was named after the city or the sausage. "Definitely the sausage," she insisted.

Rosie was well into her seventies by then, still working as a substitute when the school needed her. She didn't think twice about leaving Carla and me to fend for ourselves. To keep us occupied, she devised elaborate scavenger hunts that took us through the woods, over the creek, and down to Main Street, where we had to perform chores for the store proprietors in exchange for candy or sometimes our lunch. Each morning she'd drop us off at a new destination, driving with her hand out the window, chain-smoking Kools, and listening to Howard Stern. She thought Robin Quivers was the funniest woman on the planet. She'd give us a list of things to find and do for the scavenger hunt and we'd be on our own.

Those summers were the happiest memories of my childhood.

As a grown woman I would wonder whether those treasure hunts were just Rosie's way of keeping us occupied or whether she was trying to teach us much-needed lessons about how to maneuver in the world, a way of saying, *At the end of the day you're on your own, girls, and you've got to survive on your wits.*

Was this Sicily trip just another scavenger hunt to her, or did she actually believe there was some mystery to Serafina's death?

My heart cartwheeled in my chest as I read and reread her note while Pippo slowly made his way up the twisty road toward Calta-bellessa. I could practically hear Rosie whispering in my ear, the way she did when I was frustrated with a math problem or a riddle as a child. *You've fucking got this.* She thought nothing of dropping an f-bomb into my impressionable brain.

Within fifteen minutes the legendary village appeared in front of us. It was familiar, like a place I'd been before or visited in a dream, but also like nowhere else I'd ever seen. A single mountain rose above the low rolling hills. At its peak a massive, jagged rock jutted into the sky like the fin of a shark going in for the kill. Whitewashed houses clung precariously to the rocky cliffs and seemed to spill down from the tip of the mountain. If I squinted, I could almost see Daedalus's maze in the mess of streets. We finally reached the one-lane road that unspooled up to the village in a se-ries of perilous switchbacks. When a car came at us from the opposite direction, Pippo hit the gas. I let out a shriek and grasped onto the dashboard, but Pippo jerked the steering wheel to the left at the very last second, pulling us onto the gravel shoulder.

"Aren't there rules for who has the right of way on this one-lane road?" I gasped.

He shrugged. "You saw what happened. We figure it out."

We were hardly back on the road for a few minutes before he stopped again. A flock of thirty or so shaggy goats crossed from one olive grove to another, plodding over the broken concrete road taking all the time in the world. The sun blazed in the midafternoon sky by the time we arrived, which meant siesta had shuttered the town completely.

Pippo parked his Fiat in a lot outside the walls of the oldest part of the city, explaining that he needed a special permit to drive the narrow streets of the village. "We'll make our way on foot," he chirped. "It isn't far."

From the parking lot we climbed a passage of steep stairs. Then tiny alleyways brought us past a crumbling Roman tower to a small piazza. Flocks of pigeons and a couple of filthy dogs were the only signs of life until I noticed a few young guys slouched in the doorways of gated shops, smoking their cigarettes, staring at us through squinted eyes. Out of habit I picked up my pace. Around another corner two ancient men crouched forward on rickety folding chairs playing dominoes. One of them glanced up at me and murmured, *"Dovresti sorridere, bella ragazza."* You should smile, pretty girl.

I'm not pretty, not in any kind of traditional way. I've known that most of my life. One of the first things I remember hearing was my mom crooning over how gorgeous my sister, Carla, was, calling her a *pretty little angel* and a *beautiful babe*, words she never used to describe me. I was her *funny girl*, her *silly baby*. Never beautiful, never brilliant. With those off-the-cuff compliments my mom turned me into a goofy, overthinking perfectionist who was too often aggressively helpful. *Funny, silly, helpful.* I liked *helpful* the best. It made me feel needed and when I felt needed I felt loved.

Carla was the one who insisted I was beautiful in a "peculiar way" after she found a treasure trove of pictures of Anjelica Huston and Jack Nicholson from the seventies in Aunt Rosie's old gossip magazines that she kept stashed in the attic. "You look like her," my sister insisted. "The pointy chin, sensual lips, long nose, and the eyes that are sort of too far apart but in a really interesting way. She's so hot. And she was with the most unavailable man in Hollywood. Look how sexy the two of them are. I would make out with both of them."

It wasn't until I met my husband in my twenties and he was entranced by my height, my broad shoulders and odd features, that I ever felt beautiful in a man's eyes.

Pippo and I passed a stone church with a massive wooden door the height of at least two men. He made the sign of the cross. To the left of the church a rust-covered iron fence bore the sign CIMITERO.

"Is this the main cemetery here?" I asked him. He gazed up at the church and pulled a crumpled Google map from his back pocket.

"I do not know this town very good," he apologized, consulting the paper. After a minute he smiled. "Yes. It does appear to be the only cemetery in town. Would you like to visit it now?"

I wanted to sleep, to eat, to call my daughter again, but Aunt Rosie's latest request rattled around in my brain. *Find out what really happened to my mother.* Wouldn't Serafina's grave be the right place to start? Her headstone would, at the very least, confirm the date of her death, maybe more. As I walked down the path, Pippo gripped my arm with an unexpected intensity.

"Hey," I shouted, wiggling free.

"You cannot just walk in to visit the dead. We must ask permission."

"From the dead?"

"From the church." Pippo looked me up and down. His eyes landed on my bare arms and shoulders, on my tattoos, a pro-series meat cleaver on my left forearm and the La Macellaia flying pig on the right. He handed me two black scarves from his bag. "Cover your shoulders and hair as a sign of respect." He grabbed the handle on the massive door and pulled it open with no small amount of exertion. The church was empty and freezing. Gas lanterns perched in the nooks and crannies of the rock, throwing shadows against the wall that looked like angels. It was all grayish white stone. Stone walls, stone floors, stone altar, stone pews.

"The stone probably all came from inside this mountain," Pippo said, waving his hand around the room. A man in a dark cassock hunched over the altar. Pippo cleared his throat once, twice, and on the third the figure rose and turned to us.

The ancient priest moved like a wounded animal, dragging a leg behind him as he shuffled toward us. He said nothing until he was so close that I could smell him, the scents of incense, cigarette smoke, and decay. Pippo bowed his head in reverence. I did the same and felt ridiculous.

The hunched-over figure peered at us with rheumy black eyes, filmy like a dog's that was about to be put down. But when he spoke his voice was filled with fire and his eyes set on me with a profound weariness. I couldn't make out a word. When he stopped, Pippo translated his rushed dialect.

"He's mad that I brought an outsider into the sanctum without permission. This space is for those who live in town. I will tell him

64

you are not really an outsider. You have family from here." Pippo spoke and I heard the names *Marsala* and *Giovanni*, *Forte* and *Serafina*.

Smoke from the many candles and incense caught in my throat and I coughed, bringing the men's conversation to a halt.

"I just want permission to visit the cemetery," I stuttered in Italian. The priest rolled his eyes. The left one took its time rolling back into place. He stared at me as best he could and mumbled under his breath.

"Did you catch that?" I asked Pippo.

"He says you can go, but to be quick because there will be a funeral service right before sunset. According to him, your people are in row thirty-four."

"Wow. He knew that off the top of his head."

"It is a small village, Sara."

I asked the priest if we could leave my luggage inside the door to the church for a bit. He begrudgingly agreed with a nod and shuffled off. I considered bringing the box of Rose's ashes with me. After all, she wanted to be scattered close to the family plot, close to her mother. But I wasn't ready to part with them yet, so I left them with the rest of my bags.

The streets of the town might have been a labyrinth, but there was a meticulous order for the dead. The grounds of the cemetery were well kept and tidy. Small stone mausoleums ascended out of the dirt, each one bearing four or five names of relatives stacked on top of one another inside. We made our way to row thirty-four and as the priest had promised it was filled with my ancestors. *Quintu, Manfredo, Miceli, Luca, Giovi, Adianu, Santo. Enza, Ireni, Gianna, Lia, Itria, Talia, Valentina.*

I tried to remember the year Giovanni came to America, the

year Serafina died. Was it 1925? The dates on the headstones were mostly in order.

But she wasn't there.

"There's no grave for Serafina Marsala or Serafina Forte," I said to Pippo, even though he must have realized the same thing by the way he was backtracking and inspecting each headstone.

"It would be Serafina Forte on the gravestone. Women do not change their last names when they marry like Americans usually do. They keep their father's name. Like you kept yours." He attempted to make sense of the missing grave. "Perhaps because she died before her husband and because he had already left for America, maybe they buried her with her own people, with her mother and her father. We can go back and ask the priest. There is probably a record of the wedding and a recording of her death. It is all written down in a big book in the rectory I'm sure."

The priest was even more chagrined to see us when we found him in his small office, tracing his fingers along the text in a massive book that resembled some kind of registry. Once again I let Pippo explain what we needed while I tried to make myself shrink into the veil covering my hair.

"Serafina Forte, husband Marsala?" Pippo repeated the things he'd said earlier in Italian. "Died close to 1925. Is there a listing for her in your records?"

The priest glanced back down at his book and then rose with painful effort and shooed us out of his office with all his energy.

"*Lei non è qui,*" he nearly shouted. She is not here.

"What do you mean?" I asked.

Once he had gotten us outside, he repeated himself and this time he lunged toward me and spit on the ground.

"*Quella donna non è qui. Non seppelliamo donne come lei.*"

I turned to Pippo. "Did he say the church doesn't bury women like her?"

Pippo gripped my arm again. "Sara, we should go."

The priest glared up at me and pointed at the gate with a long yellowed fingernail before limping back into the church.

I let Pippo collect my bags for me. We stayed silent until we were off sacred ground. "What was he talking about and what did he mean, 'women like her'?" I asked.

By the way he sped up it was clear that Pippo didn't want to answer my question. His response was cautiously polite.

"Priests will not bury someone who fell out of favor with the church, who they believe committed an unforgivable sin. For example, those who took their own lives are not buried in cemeteries. Those who have taken the lives of others."

"She died of an illness," I insisted, while Rosie's letter tugged at the back of my mind.

Pippo was apologetic now, but also at a loss. "I am sorry, Sara. I do not have any more answers for you. I wish that I did. The priest read through the church records and he clearly found something he did not like."

"Can we ask to see those records?" Even as I asked it, I knew it was naïve and stupid.

"He would never allow it. Privacy."

The entrance to Hotel Palazzo Luna was hidden a few doors down another alleyway so narrow the walls grazed my shoulders. It was a weathered but imposing yellow building with wide green shutters, five stories high and teetering on the edge of the hillside. Vines of electric pink bougainvillea nearly obscured the front door, which was locked. No one answered the bell, while Pippo kept checking the time on his phone.

"You need to leave?" I asked.

He nodded. "It took longer than expected to get here, and the time we spent in the cemetery . . . My wife is waiting for me."

"Go. I'm fine." But he didn't move.

"Seriously. I can wait for a hotel to open. I'm a big girl."

He checked his phone again and made his decision.

"You have my number if you need me."

I nodded. "Thank you for everything," I said.

"I am sorry you did not find what you wanted in there."

"I'm sure it's a misunderstanding," I replied, yet I couldn't get the priest's anger out of my head.

I paused for a second and wondered if I should ask about Serafina one more time, but instead I simply said, "And thank you for being a friend to my aunt."

Pippo kissed me on both cheeks and brought me in for a hug.

"You will be safe here alone?"

I brushed off his sincere concern. "Go!"

"*Allora*, Sara. I know you have much to do. You will call me if you want to take a tour out of the village. There is much I can show you. And Rose already paid me to bring you back to Palermo when you are ready to go to the airport next week. We will see that *teatro*!"

Alone, I sat on the stoop of the hotel and stared at my phone. No service. I rang the bell again and then leaned my head against the cool yellow exterior, closed my eyes, and dozed off. It could have been twenty minutes or an hour later that the door opened, and I was startled awake. A tiny woman with a heart-shaped face and a mess of disheveled black curls emerged from the front door of the hotel. She was probably a little older than my sister and dressed like a Russian assassin or a lippy soccer mom from New Jersey with her curled bangs and bright pink Adidas tracksuit. She made no indication that she had heard me ring the bell twenty times.

"*Ciao, ciao.*" She looked me up and down like she was inspecting a mangy stray.

"*Ciao.* I'm Sara. I think someone booked a room here for me."

"*Sì. Sì.* The American. I have been expecting you. You come with me. I'm Giuseppina. Giusy." She pronounced it *Juicy*, in a way that was unexpectedly luscious even if her voice sounded like she smoked twenty Camels a day.

The inside was cool and dry from being shuttered for siesta all afternoon. The front room was massive with ceilings at least fifteen feet high. Giusy rummaged around the front desk to find a key while explaining that I would be on the second floor and that the door was probably already unlocked, so I didn't actually need the key because hardly anyone was staying at the hotel. I said I'd like the key if she could find it, which made her sigh in annoyance.

"Your room is clean, but do not expect too much," she answered when she found it, showing no interest in accompanying me, just shooing me upstairs with a flick of her wrist before mumbling something about needing to shop.

My room, really the entire second floor, was a riot of curiosities, lavishly decorated in the manner of what I imagined a nineteenth-century bordello would look like—massive canopy bed, green velvet curtains, a painting of a menagerie of mermaids, griffins, and angels cavorting on the ceiling. It could also have been a storage space for things someone had bought by mistake at a Sicilian garage sale. A boulder-size bust of Julius Caesar smirked from a corner next to a lamp that at first seemed askew but on second glance was merely carved in the shape of the Leaning Tower of Pisa.

I snapped a few photos. My phone service sucked, but I texted them to Carla anyway. Then I did something ridiculous. It wasn't the first time I'd done it in the past few weeks, but it felt more absurd every time I pushed the buttons. I texted the photos to Rosie's phone along with a message.

Wish you were here.

Whenever I sent it into the universe, I expected an instant response, one of the stock ones she always sent.

Have a great goddamn day sweetheart.

Grab the world by the balls!

The shower stall was tiny compared to the size of the claw-foot tub on the other side of the bathroom, and the spigot was way too short. I ducked beneath it until all the hot water ran out. Hotel Palazzo Luna only provided one tiny bottle of shampoo that might as well have been dish soap but I massaged it into my scalp anyway.

Finally clean, I collapsed onto the oversize bed and passed out. It was dark when I woke up. I fumbled for my phone but it was dead. There was no clock in the room, so the only option was to dress, go downstairs, and try to figure out the time and where I could get food.

The woman who wanted to be called Giusy was downstairs at the front desk playing Candy Crush on her phone.

"Is the driver coming back to take you for dinner? We don't serve it on Tuesday nights," she said without looking up.

"I don't think so," I replied.

She fixed me with a curious stare. "You are hungry."

It wasn't a question, but I answered it anyway. "A little."

"You look like a starving goat."

"What does a starving goat look like?'

"Exactly like you. Like you could eat another goat."

"A goat would eat another goat or I would eat a goat?"

"You need food. You'll need me to take you to dinner, then?"

"No. No. I can go on my own. But if you have some place to recommend that would be great."

She ignored me and rose. "I will take you. Give me a minute." It was way longer than a minute when she finally returned, now clad in a canary-yellow blouse and jeans that appeared spray-painted onto her ass.

Giusy walked with a dark ebony cane even though I could see no sign of a limp. She said hello to everyone we passed in town as we strolled to the restaurant.

"This is Sara. She's the American," she introduced me. Not *she's* American, but *the American*, as if everyone in the village was already talking about me.

Every couple of meters she stooped to pet one of the stray cats that had formed a kind of parade behind us. "The cats keep the souls of the dead," she remarked to me with a deadpan glare. "Be kind to them."

We wove through labyrinthian alleys and archways so low they touched the top of my head. The difference in the town after siesta was striking. Even the stone walls vibrated with a newly awakened energy. A trio of little girls chased after us with sparkly fairy wands as we emerged into a raucous square filled with tables and chairs, each of them crowded with smartly dressed people eating and drinking. Every door and window overlooking the piazza was flung open. Waiters in crisp white shirts and black ties scurried around with trays of orange cocktails and maroon wine.

"This can't be real," I murmured.

"It isn't," Giusy scoffed. "They set it all up because they knew you were coming. Ha! Come."

In the middle of the piazza a large fountain gurgled around a statue of a woman holding a child. Giusy flicked a coin into it and then leapt up to walk around its edge, holding her cane horizontally for balance. Suddenly I was surrounded by a pack of beautiful teenagers dancing to ABBA's "Waterloo" on a portable speaker, singing all the wrong words. A boy, no older than thirteen or fourteen, grabbed my hand and twirled me into the melee. I nearly bumped into an older man, sketching at an easel. He had a finely trimmed beard that matched the fuzz of white hair on the top of his head. His immaculate cream-colored suit was impressive given how dusty everything else was on the mountain.

"*Ciao, ciao.*" He looked up at me as I steadied myself. Giusy leapt down from the fountain and kissed both of his cheeks. They rambled in dialect while I stood there stupidly. When he squinted at me, I swore his smile contained a hint of recognition before he leaned over to hug me. Everyone in this town was certainly touchy-feely. I accepted it with stiff arms, since I'm not usually that affectionate with strangers, but I also didn't want to be rude. Once I was out of his grasp, he grabbed a chair from a neighboring table and placed it in front of his easel. He was older than I had initially thought and his movements were jerky and slow. He gestured for me to sit. I shot Giusy a questioning glance.

"He wants to sketch you. He says it should only take a minute."

"Oh, I don't know if I have enough cash on me to pay him anything. I probably only have a credit card," I said, hoping to get out of it.

Giusy tutted and shook her head, pushed me toward the chair. "He doesn't want your money. Just your face."

So I sat.

"I'm Sara." I extended my hand, but the man was busy sketching.

"He's Nicolo," Giusy replied for him.

I can never sit still, and I had no idea what to do with my hands. I folded them in my lap, but within seconds they flew up to tuck a piece of hair behind my ear and then to scratch my nose. I picked at a zit on my chin and then got mad at myself for picking at my face and clasped my hands together so I would stop. Eyes were on me from all over the square. I could feel them on my skin like mosquitoes landing with the lightest touch and staying much longer than welcome. The audience didn't bother Nicolo in the least. He focused on the paper in front of him, eyes flicking up only occasionally to glance at me as though he already knew the contours of my face and simply needed a quick reminder.

I met his gaze the next time he looked up and smiled. He gave a slight shake of his head, so I frowned, trying to take direction. This made him laugh, so I did too, and then he began to sketch so furiously I worried the exertion might give him a stroke.

It took maybe five minutes from start to finish, though it felt longer. When he was done he beckoned me to the other side of the easel. I stood, walked to him, and gasped.

I never looked like that when I saw myself in the mirror. The vision he saw was glorious. My skin was smooth, my eyes were bright. I looked happy and alive. I desperately wanted to be the woman in the drawing.

"Lo adoro," I whispered. I love it.

He ducked his head in a small bow and mumbled. The syllables sounded almost like *Serafina*, but I knew that was impossible. He grabbed a phone from his pocket and took several pictures of the portrait before handing the piece of paper to me.

"*Grazie*," I said.

Giusy looked over me at the piece of paper, resting her chin on my shoulder like we were already good friends. "He is a wonderful artist, yes?"

"I love it. I feel like I should pay him."

"I promise he does not need it," Giusy insisted.

Nicolo was already back in his chair, a blank canvas in front of him as he studied the scene in the piazza once again, and started something new. I thanked him one more time and clutched the drawing to my chest. I wanted to take it back to the hotel to keep it safe before we stopped to eat but Giusy was already walking in the opposite direction.

We took a left on the other side of the square and finally stopped in front of a rough wooden door with a bold brass knocker in the shape of a dragon's head.

A tricolor Italian flag shuddered in the breeze from a pole above the door, but a much larger Sicilian flag eclipsed it. I gazed up at the billowing yellow and red fabric.

Giusy smirked. "I love that the head of Medusa is on our flag. Don't you?"

"She was a monster."

"Was she? Or was she a brilliant woman with the ability to turn men to stone when they abused her or tried to take everything away from her?"

"I never thought about it like that."

"Life is all about perspective, American."

Giusy placed both palms flat on the door and pushed. The waiter standing just beyond the entryway was so handsome I stumbled a little as I followed him through the crowded room to the one empty table. Giusy caught me and pinched my hip.

"I get it. It is hard to look at him," she whispered. "He is a beautiful, sexy boy. You'd think he'd leave this town already, but he has a sick mamma and a slutty sister and nieces and nephews with no papas. They need the money and a man to stay with them."

The beautiful, sexy boy pulled out both of our chairs and whisked away the centerpiece, a bowl holding absurdly large plastic fruit.

"What do you want to drink?" he asked.

"A cappuccino?" I replied.

"No!" Giusy exclaimed sharply, horrified. Then in a lower voice that only I could hear, "Cappuccino is only a breakfast drink."

"Espresso?" I tried.

"We will have wine," she said, shooing the waiter away. "There is no menu. He'll bring things." Giusy placed her elbows on the wood in front of her so she could lean closer to me. "You are from Philadelphia. I have seen things on the Internet and in movies about your city. You have Rocky Balboa, who runs through the market with the garbage cans on fire. Your sports mascot is called Gritty. Your fans throw frozen batteries. It is certainly sunny there like the TV show claims."

Her sarcasm made me like her right away. Giusy was the town gossip and travel guide you always wanted to meet on a trip. With her everything was either insanely beautiful or a terrible disaster. Sicily's beaches were the most gorgeous in all the world but too crowded with fat tourists and trash washing down from the filthy mainland. They also had the most magnificent beach clubs if you didn't mind dancing with a bunch of coked-up Brits. I absolutely had to visit the cursed village ten miles to the north. A priest recently performed an exorcism by helicopter to save all ten thousand souls who lived there from their utter depravity. She claimed that the ruins at Agrigento were better than the ones at Segesta because there were fewer stray dogs and therefore less dog shit in the temples. Her transitions were sudden and unexpected and I struggled to keep up. The island of Sicily is "God's kitchen," she insisted, but I should only eat in the restaurants that write their menus on the chalkboard on the wall each day. A printed menu meant they were buying frozen food from the supermarket to cut costs. I should also always ask where a restaurant got their tomatoes. If they came from Naples they were probably poisonous because the Camorra, the Napolitano Mafia, got a government contract to bury waste in the foothills of Mount Vesuvius, which made the produce grown there toxic, but not too toxic to export. She told me their own small village was the most gorgeous village in all of Sicily, but also rotting from within like a neglected corpse. Then she got up to go to the bathroom.

While she was gone the lights dimmed and the restaurant went silent. Suddenly our beautiful waiter was illuminated by what looked like a large flashlight being held by a child. He began to sing. Opera?

Before I knew it, Giusy had returned. She stepped on top of our table with the same ease she'd used to leap on the edge of the fountain, carefully planting her feet between the dishes. She finished his aria with a great flourish. The room exploded in applause.

"Wow. That was incredible," I told her when she was back in her seat. "Was that Verdi?"

"Pah. No. Bellini. Vincenzo Bellini, the Swan of Catania. A genius. Sang his first solo at eighteen months old, composed an opera at six. A real Sicilian. Verdi was a second-rate Italian bastard from the north."

"Don't mince words."

"I never do." She snapped her fingers in the air and a carafe of house wine appeared. The beautiful, sexy waiter winked at Giusy when he poured it into her glass.

"He likes you."

"I am very finished with men," Giusy declared. "I was married to one once. That was enough."

"Are you divorced now?" I couldn't help asking. I enjoy women who have more problems than I do. I was also enjoying our easy rapport, how quickly we seemed to have fallen into an amiable rhythm. I'd been terrible at cultivating female friendships in my adult life. My two best friends were my sister and my dead aunt.

Giusy didn't mind my question. "Might as well be divorced. My husband is gone. Who knows where. What about you?" she asked me.

"I'm not married." Not entirely true. Not legally, at least, but that was just semantics.

Giusy didn't press me. Instead, she shifted the conversation to why I was in Sicily in the first place.

"My aunt wanted her ashes to be scattered here when she died." I opted for the simplest explanation.

"We get a lot of that. Also, all the people looking for their distant relatives. Everyone comes looking for cousins. What do they hope to find? A missing piece of themselves. Like we are the answer to all of their problems. We can't even take care of ourselves. Also a lot of people come here looking for Don Corleone or Tony Soprano or the funny guy from *Goodfellas*. The little one. With the voice. You Americans love your clichés and your drama."

This coming from a woman with the theatrical flair of Liza Minnelli.

"They think the Mafia is all shiny suits and machine guns and cars getting blown up in the piazza. Ha! They don't want to see that guy." She pointed to a dopey-looking dude in his thirties with large ears and a weak jaw, sitting in the corner of the restaurant and muttering into a wireless headset with four smartphones littering the table in front of him. He looked bored, or maybe stoned.

"That guy. That guy's one of the biggest *mafiosi* in town. And look at him with his big ears and little dick. Always doing all his work on the phones. Chit, chit, chit, chit, chit."

"What's he doing?"

"Drugs. Moving cocaine and heroin from the port in Sciacca, switching the drugs between the African ships and the European ships, paying the right guys, messing up the right guys. He does it all from his phone while he sits at that table. And then he goes home and plays with his small dick."

"He's a friend of yours."

"He is my cousin."

"Why didn't you say hi to him when we came in?"

"Because we despise each other." She turned to holler at the man on the phone. *"Mangia merde e morte!"*

When he looked up she flicked the backs of her fingers beneath her chin, a gesture known the world over as the Italian fuck-you. He returned the sentiment with a raise of his middle finger, thus concluding the familial exchange.

More wine arrived. Giusy explained that the Nero d'Avola from Sicily is the most delicious grape in the entire world, but it may not be for long. The climate is expected to change because of the forest fires.

"You had forest fires?"

"You do not know about the terrible fires here? Do you not get the news?"

"We get too much news in America. It's hard to keep track of everything. Tell me," I insisted as the waiter brought over another carafe.

"OK. So this is a Mafia story. I know you Americans love those. And, also, a story of things being lit on fire like they do in your city. Get yourself ready. The government is always saying that they are cracking down on the Cosa Nostra, but the Mafia here is in our DNA. It is a parallel state. It exists in every level of Italian bureaucracy. But the government and the police say they are fighting it. A lot of the big bosses went to prison. A lot of government contracts with firms owned by the Cosa Nostra were canceled. So a few years ago the bosses got into a new business. Forestry," Giusy explained.

"Forestry?"

"Replanting forests, growing trees. The problem was that no forests needed any replanting."

"Seems like a crappy business plan."

"It was. Until they burned them down."

"The forests?"

"The *national* forest, nearly the entire thing. The Cosa Nostra burned down all of the trees in the Madonie Mountains so the government would pay them to replant them."

"How long ago was this?" I assumed it was at least many decades.

"It just happened. But that's not the worst thing. Who cares about a few trees? They'll grow back." Giusy had a twinkle in her eye and I could tell she was excited to tell me the part that came next, the worst thing. "It is how they did it."

"How?" I took a sip of my wine and remembered how jazzed Rosie used to get over the punch line to a good story. She would have thought Giusy was a real trip.

"Cats. They greased up stray cats in kerosene, lit a long fuse on their tails, and sent them into the woods."

The wine ejected out of my nose and onto the table.

"No, they didn't."

"They did. It was in the national newspaper. They found the corpses of at least a thousand cats in those burned-up forests."

I didn't have words, but Giusy did.

"They'll get theirs. You don't fuck with the cats here."

As Giusy promised, the food began to appear. No one asked if we had preferences or nut allergies or gluten-free diets. I loved it. The waiter brought platters of anything he wanted from inside the kitchen, eggplant prepared three different ways, stuffed cuttlefish, and anchovies fried in crispy bread crumbs. A busiate pasta with boar ragù and black truffles, spaghetti with black squid ink and toasted almonds.

By the second carafe of house wine Giusy revealed that sometimes she steals little things from guest rooms, never anything valuable, just items that would be annoying for their owner when they went missing: earring backs, a tube of concealer, once a diaphragm. She sort of blushed when she said it but she also looked proud of herself.

"Why are you telling me this? I'm a guest, aren't I? Now I know what happened if my birth control goes missing."

"I thought you'd appreciate the story."

She was right. I did.

"My favorite was a fancy face lotion that claimed to be the fountain of youth in a bottle. It had real flakes of gold in it. Made my cheeks as soft as a baby's ass." She reached out a hand to stroke my cheek. "You have beautiful skin. What do you use?"

I blushed and admitted I never used anything. I usually forgot to even wash my face before bed. "It's from my work. I used to run a steak house. I'm a chef and a butcher. The fat and lanolin from slicing up the meat ends up all over any piece of my exposed skin when I'm breaking it down. Butchers tend to have glowy skin. I once apprenticed under a ninety-year-old Brazilian who was as well-preserved as a Kardashian."

A platter of what looked like a deconstructed cannoli, a pyramid of cannoli shells separated by thin layers of amaretto cream and smothered in a dark chocolate sauce, had barely graced our table when a new guest pushed his way through the beaded entryway. He had to duck as he entered and shift his body sideways because his torso was as wide as two men. The man didn't just fill the doorway, he filled the entire room.

The waiter led him to a table in the corner on the opposite side of the room from Giusy's criminal cousin.

"Now, that's who you need to talk to." Giusy nodded in the man's direction.

"Huh? About what?"

"He's in charge of the local police."

Her words startled me. I glanced nervously over at him.

"Why would I need to talk to the police?"

"Non solcare la fronte. Stringerai il tuo buco del culo." Don't furrow your brow. You'll clench your asshole. No one wants to walk around with a clenched asshole.

I'd had too much wine and it was scrambling my thoughts. But when Giusy looked at me her gaze was sharp, like something inside her brain had just decided to wake up, and I grasped that I was much, much drunker than my host. I was a woman alone in a strange country without a full grip on all my faculties. I cursed myself for always making such bad decisions, while Giusy kept talking.

"You go over there and talk to that man."

"I don't understand what you're saying."

When she spoke again, I realized Giusy knew much more about me and why I'd come to Sicily than she'd previously let on.

"Who else are you going to ask about your great-grandmother Serafina's murder?"

SIX

SERAFINA

1913

I clung to Cosi like my life depended on it. The little boy, completely unaware of my terror, was delighted that I had waded waist-deep into the ocean with him. I was ashamed I didn't know how to swim and knew it was ridiculous, dangerous even, to take my boy into the sea. But I'd been promising him this for a year. Promising myself too.

When I cupped my hand over my eyes to blot out the sun, I could make out Cettina on the beach playing with Santo. My second son, the one I named after my father, who had passed away suddenly from a tremor of the heart earlier in the year, was nearly two. Cetti raised Santo's pudgy hand in a salute, followed by a floppy wave.

"I see the fish, Mamma," Cosi said, and giggled, his mouth in my ear.

"Count them for me, little lion." He counted all the way to twenty just like I had taught him.

Once we were back on the sand, relief flooded through my body. With it came a kind of satisfied exhilaration that I'd taken my child out into the sea and both of us had survived. There were brief moments like this one when mothering presented the same challenges I'd been given in school and rewarded me with the same small pleasures. Cettina poured me a glass of pear juice. "Your belly is getting big again." My sweet friend glanced away. "It's not fair. Gio looks at you and you get pregnant."

"I promise that is not how it happens." I took the drink from her. But wasn't it true enough? I'd spent less than six months with my husband since we had been married and soon I would have three children. Getting pregnant was not work for me, not like it was for Cettina.

Cettina and Liuni had the largest wedding Caltabellessa had seen since the mayor's daughter got married. It wasn't that their families were particularly wealthy or important. The village simply loved the two of them. Cettina had perched sidesaddle on a mule for the hour-long procession up the entire mountain, her long wedding train dragging through the dirt behind her. The old women and men sang, wailed, and banged on goatskin drums and tambourines as the rest of us tossed wheat at the bride to wish her prosperity and fertility. For months before the big party Cettina talked of nothing but making babies and how my children would soon have playmates that we would raise as cousins. But it did not happen that month, or the month after. For the first year Liuni dutifully came home from Palermo every time the witch told Cettina that her body was ripe. She drank and ate everything the old woman gave to her, including the placenta of a goat right after it had given birth. None of it helped her conceive a child.

"He is going to leave me," she wailed after a year. "He should leave me because I am barren and I will never give him a family." I grieved with her each month when she began to bleed, but Liuni, sweet little Liuni, with his different-colored eyes and soft belly and pretty hands, would never leave Cetti. He did, however, start to come home less and less. But it wasn't because of Cettina. He was busy in his last year of studies at the university in Palermo. He tried to get Cetti to join him in the city, but she had no interest in leaving the village.

"The city is poison. It is like a nasty prostitute that leads you down a dreadful road with her charm and then stabs you in the eye," Cetti said. "We have everything we need here. This village is a small slice of paradise."

It was not. There was less money than ever to go around. Every promise made to us by the government was broken. We were told by the mayor that all our homes would be given running water, but that never happened for most of us. We went to the public wells and springs and protected every drop like it could be our last.

The criminal brotherhoods, the ones who liked to be called "the men of honor" instead of the *mafiusi*, had fixed our wells when they first broke down and the government did not come to help us. But a year later the so-called men of honor took the wells over completely and charged us enormous fees for our water. No one in Palermo bothered to stop them. When crops were weak, the *mafiusi* gave out money and extra food to peasants and farmers while the government let us starve. But a year later they would turn around and charge us double what we used to pay for the food and then they would demand protection money from the same citizens to keep us safe from bandits who were probably on their payroll. When it went unpaid, barns were burned to the ground, or worse.

My own brothers, still boys, had set off for *il continente* to find work and support my mother after Papa died. But for Cetti, despite her struggles to bear children, the village would always be more than enough. She loved it with the same passion I once had to flee it.

I prodded her. "You are a crazy person for not going. I would give anything to live in Palermo."

"You could join Gio on the mainland."

"You know that he has never asked me to come there, and he never will. He lives in one room with six other men. They sleep in bunks. There is no space for a wife and two, almost three, babies."

Santo began to whine. "I go in water?"

"Shhhhh. You're too little." Cettina wrapped her arms around him and began to cradle him like a little baby. "You are not big yet. You are still my baby. My teeny-tiny baby."

I rubbed my belly as Cettina tenderly kissed my child on his cheek and neck and each of his ears.

"I wish I could give you this new one." I chuckled as I said it, though it wasn't entirely a joke. With each of my pregnancies, I felt more and more hollowed out, like another piece of me was being carved away, taking me further from the person I had wanted to be, that girl who would go to school in a city by the sea. I had once wanted to read great books and write down all my thoughts. I wanted to debate big ideas and understand why our small island, so rich in so many ways, remained so poor in all the ways that mattered to the rest of the world. Since becoming a mother, I barely had time to remember all the things I once wanted, all the lives I hoped to lead, but sometimes the desire all flooded back and I felt a small death.

I thought joking about surrendering my baby to Cettina would make her smile, but it had the opposite effect.

"Do not say something like that. You could not give away your own child."

"I meant you would be such a good mother. And if I could give you a baby I would. I wish my baby could be your baby."

"Your babies *are* my babies. They might be my only babies."

"You will have your own little boy one day."

Cettina ignored me and nuzzled her face into the chubby folds of Santo's neck. "How do you know it is a he? You could be having a little girl this time. Wouldn't that be nice? We can braid her hair and put her in little dresses."

I didn't have the words to explain how I felt about bringing a little girl into our village. No part of me had any desire to raise someone who would only be able to grow up to be a wife and a mother.

"I love my boys. And you love my boys. But soon you will have one of your own. I know it."

"It doesn't help that Melina makes babies even faster than you do." Cettina rarely said nasty things and she never met my eyes when she did it. Instead, she let the words float out to the sea. Melina was her sister-in-law, Marco's wife. In the seven years since Marco had been married to Melina they had welcomed four babies and now she had another on the way. Melina told anyone who would listen how she planned to give Marco ten babies, maybe more.

Cettina and Melina quietly fought one another for their mother-in-law's affections. Cettina took Liuni's mamma to mass every Tuesday and Thursday night. She cooked Sunday lunches even when Liuni was out of town and brought her warm bread fresh from the baker on Monday mornings. But companionship was never enough to raise Cetti to Melina's status in her mother-in-law's eyes and everyone gossiped about it. Cettina knew that Melina pitied her. Her sister-in-law came from wealthy people. Her father collected taxes and was rich as a pig. She flaunted her family's money with nice clothes, braided corsets of red and gold that she would pass on to Cettina only when they became threadbare and ripped. One day Cettina overheard Melina telling Marco and Liuni's mother that it was not a problem if Cettina was barren because she would give her all the grandbabies she would ever need.

"Melina is a nasty beast who is not fit to carry your shoes," I had told her over and over. "I don't even know how Marco can stand to be around her. He's so kind and wonderful and she is truly wretched."

Cettina pulled the end of her braid into her mouth and sucked on her hair the way she did when we were small. "She is a better wife than I am and God has not sent her the misfortunes that he has sent me."

Cettina's certainty that motherhood made Melina a better woman made me want to rip my own hair from my head, but I never answered when she said ridiculous things. Instead, I poured us both more to drink and lay back on my towel, letting the two little ones climb all over my body, the sand scratching at my skin, the sun burning my face. In the moment, it was a life I could love.

Weeks later Cettina banged on my door in the middle of the night. "Melina is sick. Her baby is coming. He is killing her." I glanced at my own children, curled up together on a cot in the corner, Cosi's arm wrapped protectively around Santo. They would be fine alone for an hour. My mother across the alley would hear them if they cried out.

It was so early in the morning the streets were dark except for a single floating wick lamp lit in the bakery.

Melina was nearly gone by the time we arrived. There was hardly a pulse. Her breath was ragged and deep, but her baby kept coming.

It was much too early. Marco was sent away from the room. He screamed and fought, but his mamma and sister shoved him out the door. "This is no place for a man," they said.

Our job at the bedside was to pray, but I couldn't simply bow my head as *la strega* worked. "Let me help you," I said. "What can I do?" She calmly told me to slide Melina's hips off the bed and support her in an upright position. The woman's body was limp by then. The witch moved one of my hands to apply pressure on Melina's abdomen while she coaxed the child from her body.

The baby was very small but alive. The witch tied him to her own body with a scarf and took him away.

"She will try to make him well," Cettina whispered, choking on her next words. "But the baby came after Melina's last breath. The baby was born to a corpse. That means he is cursed." She only breathed the last words but every woman in the room heard her and they nodded their heads in agreement. There was no way this baby would live. And if for some reason he did, they all believed he was destined to become a monster.

But I didn't take to those kinds of things, the curses and superstitions. I had even stopped whispering my secrets in the dragon's ear and I skipped the confession box as often as I could. "Stop it," I insisted to Cettina and to the entire room. "He is not cursed. He is a miracle." But I didn't think that was true either, because when you stop believing in curses you also stop believing in miracles.

Cettina never mentioned any curse again and it was clear she regretted ever thinking it. Instead, she visited the witch every morning to see the baby. Melina's own family refused the child they believed killed his mother. They were content to leave him on the edges of town with the old woman. Marco and his mother wanted to see the boy, but Cettina assured them that he should heal before they took him back. She worried that if they saw him when he was still so sickly and weak they would also believe that the child was not right for this world.

Every day the witch instructed Cettina to strip down to her underwear and hold the baby to her own skin for several hours. This, she told her, was part of the cure.

"He is getting stronger," Cettina told me the day she invited me to come along with her. "He is drinking more milk from the goat. We mix it with cinnamon to help warm his insides. And yesterday he clutched my hand and opened his eyes. He looks just like Liuni. That is what I am calling him."

Cettina's affection for her brother-in-law's child was a dangerous thing, but I agreed to visit him anyway. As soon as we arrived at the witch's house Cettina bared her chest in front of the fire, the baby to her breast, not suckling, but nuzzling his head against her nipples as though he wished he could. His head was no larger than an apple and it flopped up and down like he was a dying fish. My heart ached for my friend. This should be her own baby rooting for milk, not the child of a dead woman. But Cettina fed him anyway, using a rag soaked in milk. She was so distracted she often forgot to eat herself and I would need to force an egg or a bit of pastina on her.

"No good can come of this," I whispered to the old woman, who sat quietly at her polished wood table chopping green nettle and parsley with a massive knife.

The witch released a long sigh that sounded like wind whistling through the eaves of an old barn. "What else can we do? There is nothing wrong with him that I cannot fix. It is not his fault he came into the world early. He did not choose to do this to the mother. Someone will need to care for him."

"But that someone cannot be Cettina. There are orphanages in Sciacca we could take him to."

"The orphanages in the cities are too full and they cannot give him proper care. He would not survive there. Why can't it be Cettina? She is his family. His aunt. She loves him. Someone will care for Melina's other children. Someone needs to care for this child. It can be her."

The plan seemed so reasonable. The baby was Liuni's kin too. It wasn't unheard of for children to be raised by relatives under dreadful circumstances. Liuni would never object if Marco didn't want this child and Cettina wanted to raise him. I walked to the fire and took off my shoes, stretched my bare feet close to the flames, and rubbed my own stomach. I'd soon have another infant squirming in my arms. Santo could finally walk, and I no longer had to carry him everywhere I went. He could reach for things on his own, feed himself even. But soon, I'd start all over again with this next one.

Melina's tiny one sputtered like a drunk kitten and Cettina sighed with a kind of pleasure I'd never heard from her lips. I knew then that the old woman was right. This baby was Cettina's. She was his mother for better or worse.

Days later, when the news came about the terrible thing that happened to Liuni, that baby was the only thing that saved my friend's life.

They found Liuni's body in the trunk of a burned-up car in the piazza of Piana dei Greci, a village close to Palermo. He was identified by the Saint Antonio medallion Cettina had gotten him on their wedding day and the fact that the car belonged to the town's administrator, Franco Cucciamo, whom Liuni was supposed to be meeting with that day.

"They were after Cucciamo. Not Liuni. It was a mistake. Liuni wasn't mixed up in all that," Cettina insisted even as she was paralyzed by grief. But we eventually heard the opposite, mostly from Maestro Falleti, our old teacher who could never hold his drink or his tongue. Liuni *was* mixed up in *all that*. He'd moved on from labor organizing and joined forces with the politicians trying to take down the Mafia. Liuni had been delivering messages between Franco Cucciamo and the men who were trying to dismantle the crime families. It was dangerous work. Retribution often included the brutal murder of inconsequential men like Liuni to send a message.

The whole village cried for days on end. But soon Cettina's and Liuni's families figured out what would be best for everyone to move forward from their grief: Cettina would marry Marco. It was not uncommon for the brother to take in the widow. He needed a wife, and his children needed a mother. She was already caring for his youngest child and somehow a marriage, a blessing from God, would release the new baby from the dire consequences of how it entered the world. Marco never proposed marriage to Cettina. Her mother-in-law did.

Cettina and Marco didn't have a wedding reception. They didn't even go to a church for the ceremony. The priest came to their house. In the uncomfortable silence between the vows I gave Marco a reassuring smile. He was doing his best. They all were. He missed his wife as much as Cettina missed her husband. Instead of kissing her on the mouth when it was all over Cettina's former brother-in-law, now husband, gripped both of her hands in his and said, "I'll keep you safe and honor you for the rest of our days."

I found Marco in his mother's kitchen later that night. "You meant what you said, yes? You will take care of her?" I asked. He fixed his eyes on mine. "Of course. I love her as my sister. I will care for her until I die." I knew that he meant it, both the part about caring for and protecting my friend and the part about loving her as a sister. I understood even then that Marco would never be able to see Cettina as his wife.

Everyone in town whispered about the way Liuni had been murdered and whether Marco would continue his own work in politics. He told anyone who would listen that it was more important than ever for him to take over the job of mayor of Caltabellessa after Accursio Romano retired in the spring. "I am not afraid of the politicians in Palermo or the crime families, and I won't let anyone in this town fear them either," he said during a speech in the piazza.

"Silly men and their politics," Cettina said, rocking baby Liuni to sleep. Marco's other children sat bathed and composed at her feet. "Nothing good comes from trying to fight them."

But some things were changing, all of them for the worse. The boatyard in Calabria had laid off all workers because there was no one to buy the boats. It had been six months since Gio had been home. He felt more like a stranger than ever before. My husband hadn't even met our third child, a son named Vincenzo.

The day I thought Gio was returning from Calabria I spent hours scrubbing the floor and cutting the boys' hair. He never arrived. I waited the day after that too. By the third day I almost forgot my husband was supposed to return at all and went about my regular routine. Then came the knock on the door. It was strange, but also right that Gio should knock. This was hardly his house anymore. I took a breath to prepare myself before flinging open the door.

But Gio wasn't there. His cousin Francesco stood on our stoop with his hat over his heart. I was certain he was about to tell me that my own husband was dead. But when he saw me with my newest child thrown over my shoulder he smiled and cleared his throat. "Gio has been delayed in Palermo. He is working to get papers there."

"Come in." I stepped aside to clear a path to my kitchen table. "Does he need papers to go back to the mainland now? What kind of craziness is this?"

"No, Fina. He is not going back to the mainland. I should let him explain when he returns. It could take all of this week for him to get what he needs though."

I brought out an *arancina* I'd prepared for Gio and began to heat sauce on the stove. "You can explain it to me now," I said to Francesco with more authority than I'd expected. My tone made him straighten in his chair even as I bustled around the kitchen preparing to feed him.

"Gio will be going to *la Mérica* to find work."

The words were not a shock. This had always been a possibility. So many of the men had already left. It was almost like a war had conscripted them to another life. Gio's brother had already gone to *la Mérica*. He worked in a factory in a big city there. I couldn't remember the name of the city or what they made.

The United States would be different from the Italian mainland. Instead of months going by without seeing my husband it would be years. Other men had left the village for the new country, too many of them to count, and some had never returned. Some sent checks dutifully home to their wives, and others completely disappeared. But did it even matter? My husband had always been a stranger to me. Since that one night years earlier when he'd cried in my arms, I had never had a single glimpse of his soul. We never had the time to develop grievances with one another or even opinions of one another. He had become less familiar to me than any of the other men in the village and frankly our little family had done fine in his absence as long as he continued to send the money to keep us clothed and fed.

But there was one thing I knew for sure: Life was many times more dangerous for a woman whose husband had left for *la Mérica*, and I would be no exception.

SEVEN

SARA

When I woke up the next morning my mouth felt like the inside of a toilet. I barely made it to the bathroom before throwing up deep violet chunks and melting onto the floor. All of my previous night's admiration for the house red wine disappeared. I needed to get something into my stomach but the idea of food made me lean over the bowl again even though there was nothing left. I lay down on the bathroom floor, letting the cold from the tile seep through the T-shirt I'd managed to put on before I went to bed.

I needed to piece together what happened last night.

I'd laughed when Giusy first mentioned the word *murder*. It was a completely inappropriate response, but I'd actually snorted so loud the waiter nearly dropped his platter of shellfish. Giusy remained deadly serious as she poured me a glass of wine so full it seeped over the rim and stained the white tablecloth, the liquid spreading like blood.

"How do you know my great-grandmother's name?" I'd asked, tracing the red stain with my fingertip. "I didn't tell you."

"Rosie told me," Giusy had said. I shouldn't have been too surprised. Rosie had told me in her letter she'd done her own research. But I also knew Giusy should have mentioned their familiarity to me earlier.

"Huh. Why didn't you tell me you'd talked to Rose?"

"I wanted to see if I liked you before I told you things."

"You told me that your husband once slept with your cousin."

"That's just gossip." She toyed with a bejeweled vape pen hanging from her neck.

"So I passed your test?"

"You did. You're fun." Her gaze held a modicum of respect.

"Thanks a bunch. Look. I don't know what the hell is going on but it's not funny. I just lost one of my favorite people in the world. I'm exhausted. All I want to do is what I came here to do and get back home to pick up the pieces of my shitty life, which will still be falling apart when I return." I threw back a gulp of the wine, knowing I shouldn't, knowing that once I passed a certain threshold the lights would go off in my brain.

"But didn't you come here to find out what happened to Serafina?" Giusy asked me. "That is what your aunt wanted to know. That is what she kept asking me about."

"Why did Rose reach out to *you* about her mother?" I tried to listen, tried to keep it all straight in my head.

"I've worked with other tourists to find their relatives. I know everything about this town. I have also done work in the local archives and in the library. She found me on the town website and asked me to help her research her mother. It was also helpful that I had the hotel where you could stay."

"How often did you talk?"

"At first we emailed and then we talked on the phone. Sometimes text. She was so interested in this town and she wanted to visit. She was planning the trip for the two of you. I told her all about the hotel. That's why you are staying with me."

"You really should have told me all this when I first met you."

Giusy shrugged.

"Did my aunt know that her mother was murdered? If that's even true? Did you tell her?"

"I didn't."

"Why not?"

She sighed. "Let's get more dessert."

"What?"

She flagged down the waiter with a wiggle of her fingers and nodded, a code informing him to bring more food.

I repeated myself. "Did Rose know about her mother?"

"Your aunt was an older woman. I didn't want to alarm her."

"If this really happened. And it's a horrible, horrible thing if it did, but if it did it happened nearly a hundred years ago. What good is it to dredge it all up now? My aunt, God rest her incredible soul, is dead and I'm not here to solve a mystery."

"But I think you are."

Then my memory got foggy. I could remember Giusy pulling a crumpled piece of paper with text on it out of her pocket. I remembered a platter of tiramisu coming to the table, the waiter plunking it down on top of the words. Giusy asked me if I knew what *tiramisu* translated to in English. I told her I didn't.

"Pick me up, or cheer me up."

"Is this supposed to cheer me up?"

"That's up to you. It is delicious."

She was about to show me the piece of paper again when two espressos arrived. The chief of police stood up and made his way to our table. He leaned down to kiss each of Giusy's cheeks.

"You two look up to no good," he said in Italian.

"Always up to no good," Giusy replied with a flirtatious wink.

"Introduce me to the American," he'd said. I gulped down my glass of wine. The officer started massaging Giusy's shoulders with his meaty fingers. It all got even blurrier. We sipped some shot glasses filled with a fortified sweet marsala wine.

"It is your namesake!" Giusy kept saying. "You and this wine are like one." The subject of Serafina's death was dropped. We went to another bar or maybe it was someone's house with a bar. The three of us traipsed back through the streets arm in arm singing "Volare."

As we stood outside the hotel Giusy fumbled for her keys and went through the door first. I sort of remembered the police officer leaning close to my face, his tipsy smile turning brutish in a flash as he whispered in my ear, "Go home, little girl."

Maybe he didn't. Maybe I imagined it. But hours later I could still taste his hot stale breath on my lips.

I hated myself for getting so drunk. I'd stopped drinking too much after I opened my restaurant and had Sophie. I couldn't handle the hangovers and the responsibility of keeping two fragile things alive, but lately I'd been reckless during the times when Sophie was with Jack, drinking more than I had in my early twenties. The night before had been no exception.

I needed to find that piece of paper. I needed to find Giusy.

But first I had to get myself upright and clean. I crawled into the shower and turned on the water, letting it run over me as I sat with my bare ass in the basin. Somehow, I made it out and into a vaguely presentable outfit before heading downstairs.

Despite the small number of guests staying at the hotel, a buffet worthy of a royal visit was laid out in the dining room. There were five different kinds of cake alone, each labeled with a little card, a *torta ai cereal*, a *torta mele*, a plum cake *cioccolato*, a *torta al cacao e caffè*, and finally a *torta al cocco*. The only other visitors, a German couple in their fifties who looked like Victorian fossil hunters in matching khaki shorts and thick-soled loafers with knee-high socks, gave me stiff nods as I walked over to the buffet to make up a plate of salty cheese, salami, olives, tomatoes, fluffy scrambled eggs, and stubby sausages in the shape of little thumbs. I lathered a flaky *cornetto* with pistachio cream jam and local honey. It took less than five minutes for me to scarf everything down before Giusy emerged from the kitchen looking no worse for the wear from the night before, wearing a tight black bodysuit under jeans that hugged all of her curves. She'd piled her hair on top of her head in an elaborate braided topknot. Gold hoops hung from her ears, so massive they practically grazed her shoulders.

"You almost missed the food," she said when she reached my table with an espresso and a glass of liquid the color of a sunrise with a glistening orange blob floating in it.

"What the hell happened last night?" I whispered.

The polite expression on Giusy's face didn't flicker. "I think our Sicilian wine might be a little too strong for you and you drank all of it."

"Are you messing with me?" The German couple looked over with disapproval. Giusy smiled at them with a roll of her eyes as if to say, *Americans, aren't they always the worst?*

"Let's not bother the other guests. Take a walk with me after breakfast?"

I dropped my voice even lower. "Do you remember telling me that one of my relatives was murdered last night?"

"Let's take that walk when you're finished eating. Wear comfortable shoes, OK?" She patted me on the head in a way that would have been condescending if it weren't so motherly.

I had no choice but to sip my coffee and eye the neon fluid in front of me while Giusy attended to the Germans, who had pulled out a dog-eared guidebook and were pointing to some landmark.

Giusy only stopped by my table again briefly to nod at the concoction. "Drink the entire thing and you'll feel like a better woman."

"What is it?"

"Blood orange juice and some other things it is best you don't know about."

I raised it to my nose and took a whiff. Even though it smelled like something died in the glass I did what she said, swallowing so quickly I hardly tasted it, but still gagging at what was definitely an egg yolk slipping down the back of my throat.

The German woman nudged her husband and shot me another look.

I returned to my room to put on sneakers and sunscreen, having no idea where we might be walking or if a "walk" was code for something else.

"Let's go!" I heard through the door.

Giusy was halfway down the stairs by the time I grabbed my backpack and made it into the hallway.

The German couple was sitting in the salon with their guide-book and walking sticks. Giusy picked up a picnic basket from behind the front desk and smiled angelically at them. "Have a glorious picnic at the Segesta ruins. I will make your dinner reservations for tonight but do not worry about rushing." She beckoned me out the front door.

"Germans make me want to stab my own foot," she exclaimed, pulling out a cigarette once we were a block from the hotel. *"Amunì."*

We wound our way through town. It was quieter than the night before, but not as silent and deserted as during siesta.

"During the week many men leave go to work in Sciacca or Palermo. There is little for them to do here. For anyone to do here."

An overfed man zipped past us on a motor scooter with a broken muffler and smacked Giusy squarely on the ass so hard it had to have left a mark. Giusy didn't cry out, merely bit her thumb and mumbled, *"Faccia da culo."* Face of the ass.

He called out over his shoulder, *"Puttana a buon mercato."* Cheap whore.

"What the hell, Giusy?" I said, enraged on her behalf.

She shook her head. "Many men here think they can treat me like shit because they know I live alone."

The further we walked from town the more rustic the homes became. Some of them were embedded into the rock and seemed to be merely caves with doors and windows added much later. The streets gave way to stairs carved directly into the cliffs. I stumbled, but Giusy never faltered. I rushed to catch up to her, but there was no room to walk side by side. Instead, I ended up behind her, close enough that I could hopefully grab onto her waist if I slid again.

She must have felt how close I was because she started talking again. "Do not feel bad for me. I am used to it. It is the way it is here. I don't know how it is back in America, but in Sicily we have very . . . I don't know how to say it. *Pazzi* . . . crazy . . . absurd . . . ideas about how a woman should be. Ideas that don't always agree with one another. It is hard then to know how to act in the world."

I tried to reach for my own words to explain that I got it, but I was wheezing from the hike. It was the cigarettes and the fact that

I hadn't done any form of real exercise since having a baby four whole years ago. We turned a corner, and the stone walls of a massive castle came into view, but Giusy walked in the other direction.

"Can I sit for a minute?" There was a stitch in my side and a piercing cramp in my stomach. "I feel like I ate a horse for breakfast."

"You didn't." She paused. "Maybe there was some in the soup last night." She didn't get my joke or maybe she was making her own. "Keep going. Only a little further."

In a couple of minutes, we arrived at the entrance to a small cave. Outside it a grove of palm trees perched on a cliff overlooking the pastures below and beyond them the sparkling sea. Giusy settled down on the grass, sitting cross-legged like a child and pulling items from her basket: a crusty loaf of bread, some cheese, and a perfectly ripe avocado.

"I can't eat another thing."

"I can." Giusy tore a piece of the bread apart and smeared the creamy cheese on top of it. "I haven't had breakfast. I've been serving it all morning."

Heat spread up my neck and across my cheeks while shame stuck in my throat for ignoring her labor. I sat next to her and grabbed a plastic bottle of water that she had thoughtfully packed while I stuffed my face with her food earlier. I knew what it was to serve people. I also knew how invisible a woman could be when she was providing a service. I let Giusy eat.

Her bites were fast and furious and she scowled in between them. She was probably still pissed about that guy slapping her ass.

"Did that hurt? When the guy hit you? The one on the bike?"

"It was nothing. The men in town treat women like whores if there is not a husband around. We cannot escape it."

"Was your husband from here too?" I asked.

She swallowed what was in her mouth. "No. I met him down in Sciacca when I went there to study at a *liceo linguistico*. Orlando was a bouncer at the beach club and a low-level goon for some crime boss. I was very good in the school. High marks. I wanted to be a translator, so I studied English, German, French. Translator is a job they pay good money for on the mainland. But there was no money for college. Then my parents died within two weeks of one another the summer I graduated from school. The hotel was passed down to me."

"At least you got the hotel. And an old palace at that?"

"Ha! I added *palazzo* to the name because you foreigners will pay twice as much. I just got the building. No money, lots of debt. I wasn't even allowed to own it alone because I was a woman. I had been seeing Orlando on and off for most of school. He married me and his name was put on the deed. It worked for us. But he was an idiot. When the hotel made any money he spent it, so I told him to go away and let me manage things on my own."

"He listened to you?"

"He listened to me so he could be with his girlfriends down by the seashore."

"Sounds like my dad." I tried to commiserate, to bring back some of the camaraderie we'd shared over dinner.

Giusy snorted. "Sounds like most men. My idiot husband left for longer and longer and then for good. I made sure he left for good."

There was something ominous in her pause after that sentence and I nearly followed up with a question, but then she began to speak again.

"I thought if he was truly gone the hotel would be mine and

mine alone, but everyone always tells me Orlando is the real owner when I try to sell it. I've done my best with the hotel. I got smart on the Internet. Taught myself the SEO. It was good for the town too, brought more people here, not that they ever thanked me. I made enough to send my own kids to Sciacca for school."

"Where are your kids now?"

"Grown. I was pregnant at seventeen. I was a baby."

"Do you regret it? Getting pregnant so young?" I asked it even though I knew it was also rude and taboo to say you wished your children didn't exist, that you wished you'd had a different life.

"You can't regret your children. But yes. Of course I do sometimes. I wouldn't want to not be their mother. Not exactly. But I do wish I'd been able to do other things instead of mothering them all those years, having to make money to support them, having to give up what I wanted. Do you regret it? Rose told me you have a little girl."

"I love my daughter." The question overwhelmed me. Nearly five years into it motherhood remained a mystery to me. There was more I could say. I could tell Giusy how sometimes I wondered whether my restaurant ultimately failed because I took too much time away to be a mom or whether I was always failing at motherhood because I worked too hard on my business. The gnarled shame shifted every day, but the common thread was always my failure at something.

All I knew for sure was that at the end of each day I felt the crushing weight of wishing I'd done better in both of my roles, never mind trying to be a decent wife to Jack.

I could tell her how desperately Jack wanted to grow our family at the same time that I desperately wanted to grow my business. Jack had loved how ambitious I was until it got in the way of our life together. Then, according to him, I was aggressive and selfish when it came to making time for work.

I could tell Giusy about the positive pregnancy test I thought I buried deep enough in the trash can that Jack wouldn't find it, but he saw it later that week when he was taking out the trash because he always took out the trash and was meticulous about plucking the soda cans out and getting them into the recycling bin. By the time Jack saw the test it was too late, I had started bleeding anyway. It was just a chemical pregnancy, but he was hurt I didn't tell him right away. I also didn't tell him when I got back on birth control either, and then he saw that on our insurance statement. That was the real betrayal. We'd talked about how many kids we wanted when we first got married. Jack said five and I said one and we settled on two. After we had Sophie we said we'd roll the dice and I wouldn't go back on the pill. But then I got nervous. The restaurant was taking off and a new baby would require full-time child-care in addition to the expenses of the child we already had. Jack was working long hours in the DA's office. Both of us had jobs that looked successful on paper but there was no cash to show for it. A nanny was out of the question and Sophie's day care that billed itself as a "preschool" cost more than our mortgage. We couldn't afford another child if both of us kept working. But that was the rational math of it all. What was harder to explain was that I couldn't afford another child, not yet, maybe not ever. I couldn't return to the months and months of little to no sleep. As a newborn Sophie had screamed uncontrollably for hours every time she woke at night to feed. Jack had to be in court first thing in the morning. I had to be at the restaurant too, but somehow court was more important, so I had always let him sleep, though I resented him for it. The lack of sleep ate away at my brain. One day after I'd passed

Sophie off to my mother, I had tried to quarter a dozen game hens and cleanly sliced off the tip of my index finger instead of the chicken breasts. The top of the digit couldn't be saved. I was slow and sluggish even as I made my way to the emergency room on my own. The stump still tingled each time I picked up a knife.

Having Sophie had broken my heart and brain open in ways I appreciated with time. I found new things to love about her every single day. But I had to let things settle, keep easing into the terror and newness of motherhood. Another seismic eruption of our life would have ended me. But that didn't even make sense to me, so how could I say it to Jack, my ever-optimistic husband who doted on everything our daughter did, who took on much less of the mental load and just assumed that all parental love was exponential.

"What do you need to make it work for us to have another baby?" Jack had begged me.

I choked out a laugh and tried to joke like I always did when things got tense. "We need a third parent," I said. "I want a wife."

He looked me dead in the eye. "I want a wife too."

I said, "Fuck you," and that was that.

I definitely wouldn't tell Giusy about how it was the final straw for Jack.

A pain seared behind my eyes. Hangover or memory? Both. I rooted around in the picnic basket, finding a pack of cigarettes and a lighter. We sat in silence. I smoked. Giusy ate. Then she smoked. She opened a bottle of white wine despite the fact that it was an hour before noon. I took a cup, hoping the hair of the dog would work better than the egg yolk I'd swallowed an hour earlier.

"Do you see that cave behind us?" Giusy pointed to the jagged opening in the mountain. "That is the cave of the terrible dragon who tried to destroy our village. He feasted on the children of Caltabellessa for centuries and the peasants believed that they could protect their good children if they sacrificed the bad ones. The women would bring their wicked children up here and let the dragon take them in order to keep the others safe. That smooth part of the rock over there. We call that the dragon's ear. We whisper our secrets into it. Anything you want to tell it?"

I waggled my head no. What would I say? I couldn't stand the person I'd become? I was a failure? None of that was a secret. But something about the story was familiar.

"Aunt Rosie used to tell me this story. Or some version of it. She heard it from her father. It used to scare the shit out of me."

"Most of the stories we pass down are terrible ones." Giusy blew smoke rings into the air. "But this one has a twist that I bet you do not know."

"In the one I know, Saint Pellegrino slays the dragon and saves the village."

"That is the version the men love to tell. It's a silly story. Of course there was never a dragon. The myth was invented by the women of our village as a way to keep this cave, this place, just for themselves. A long time ago women would gather here and talk away from the ears and eyes of men. The story of the dragon kept people away. The story of the sacrifice allowed them to rescue young women and girls from the village who needed to escape from abusive fathers or priests. They said they fed them to the dragon, but really they took them away to another village and kept them safe."

"Is that pretty well known?" I asked.

"No. Not at all. I learned it from a friend who works at the university in Palermo, who studies the history of women. She discovered it in her research and I love it, how the women helped one another, protected one another, found secret ways to cooperate. I want to help you, Sara."

Her left turn took me aback.

"Can I show you something?" Giusy asked.

"Is it what you were going to show me last night?"

"Yes."

"I've been waiting all morning for it."

The piece of paper she had brought out at dinner was now stained with tiramisu and espresso. It was a photocopy of something that looked like a police report all scribbled in Italian. Official-looking type marched across the top—*Polizia di Municipale, Commune di Caltabellessa.* Thick lines redacted entire sections.

The words swam in front of my eyes. *18 luglio 1925, Omicidio.* Murder. I sucked in deep breaths trying to calm the intense emotions welling up inside of me.

"Do you want me to translate it?" she asked.

"I can do it." I focused harder on the page and translated in my head. I didn't want to hear the words out loud.

I read about an unnamed witness who discovered the female victim approximately half a mile from town. A hand-drawn map had an actual *X* marking the spot. According to the witness, the woman's body was tied by the neck to a stake outside the entrance to a small cave. *Come una capra ha portato al massacro.* Like a goat led to slaughter.

I couldn't stop until I reached the end. As Aunt Rosie used to say, *When you've stepped in the shit you've got no choice but to keep walking until you get home to clean yourself up.* I kept reading.

She was naked from the waist down. Her left ankle was shattered with something heavy, possibly a rock. There were slash marks from a dull knife up the insides of both of her thighs. Her midsection was partially sliced through, purple bruises on her neck, a smashed windpipe. *Strangolamento?* Strangulation, followed by a question mark.

Whoever blacked out the document did a piss-poor job. The name of the victim was missing from the top of the page, but not the bottom.

    Victim Age: 32
    Name: Serafina Forte

EIGHT

———

SERAFINA

1914–1917

The men kept leaving Sicily. Thousands of them, hundreds of thousands, maybe even a million. During our years of scarcity, our men heard about the opportunity to make more money in a year in *la Mérica* than they could make in a lifetime at home. Wages for laborers were thirteen lire a day in New York City compared to just one or two lire in Sicily. For years American businesses had been running advertisements in our national newspapers with headlines screaming: HOW TO BECOME A MILLIONAIRE IN THE UNITED STATES and YOUR DESTINY IS IN YOUR OWN HANDS IN AMERICA. The ads came from factories, coal mines, and construction companies. Brothers followed brothers, nephews followed uncles. Many said that the enchanted land enticed them like a seductress. They scraped together money, two hundred lire, to book passage on ships called the *Sicilian Prince*, the *Saturnia*, the *King Albert*, the *Archimede*.

The exodus came late to Caltabellessa. It had been happening in the provinces around us for decades. And from those towns we had heard the horror stories—the men who refused to come home, the ones who disappeared. We heard of Sicilian politicians begging men to stay, putting the fear of God in them by telling them they could never protect their family's honor from an ocean away. When platitudes didn't work, they started rumors of cuckolded men and their wanton wives who sought solace in another man's bed the day after a husband's ship crossed the Atlantic. Priests preached that wives and daughters left by their husbands and fathers would turn to prostitution. But still the men left.

In Caltabellessa we didn't weep when the men left. We didn't complain. We believed the stories from other villages were myths or exaggerations. The hope for a better life, a life with some money in our pockets, allowed us to turn a blind eye to the warnings. That is not to say things didn't change for us. Everything changed. Before long there were so many men gone that women had no choice but to take on the jobs they had left behind. When Carmelo the baker sailed across the Atlantic his wife, Paola, simply took over baking and selling the bread. And so it went with the cheesemonger, the ferrier, the cobbler, even the gravedigger.

The leaving was gradual, until one day the women looked around and realized we outnumbered the men. The old men remained. One of my favorite proverbs rang truer than ever: *With old men and flowering cabbages . . . there is nothing left to do.* The younger men who worked for the criminal families stayed. They took even more control over the local citrus farms because there was big money in lemons and limes, allegedly from the British and American navies, which had more ships than ever before and more sailors to keep healthy. The *mafiusi* also continued to purchase all the foodstuffs and the medicine in the nearest cities and then sold it back to us in the village at enormous black-market prices.

When the Great War came to the continent we Sicilians were

slow to get involved. Some of the remaining men fled to the Nebrodi Mountains and hid from the generals who came to the smaller towns looking for recruits. The men who had already gone abroad to *la Mérica* were making more money than ever because they stayed and worked in the factories when the American men joined up with their army. Our lives in the villages were impacted little by the continental war. It is terrible to say, but if anything, we were better off because the money kept coming in.

Marco was one of the few honest men who stayed in Caltabellessa. There were grumblings that he was soft for not avenging Liuni's murder, but he remained steadfast in his belief that violence was no answer.

"I will avenge my brother's death by making lives better, not by taking them," he insisted. "Sicilians too often cover our fears and insecurities with violence and it does us no good."

He became mayor, replacing Accursio as everyone had expected he would. Soon he was one of only a handful of men between the ages of fifteen and fifty left in the village.

Gio's money came to me every month along with short notes about his life in the big city. With him gone I was free to spend my days as I wished. My children were no longer babies. I had more time to read the books that Maestro Falleti had borrowed for me from the library in Sciacca, to care for my mother as much as she would allow me, and to accompany Cettina when she took little Liuni to the witch for his treatments. My life was quiet and simple and often terribly dull.

At four years old Liuni remained small and sickly, but he got better with each passing year. Cettina doted on all her stepchildren, but Liuni the most. When Cettina came down with an illness that kept her in bed for a week I offered to take the little boy to the witch on my own. Cetti was so weak she agreed with a small nod and no words before falling back to sleep.

I ran into Marco on my way out of her house, our bodies colliding with one another. We both laughed and he offered to walk me and his son to the edge of town. Even though the rest of the village remained wary of little Liuni, often making the sign of the cross at the sight of him, Marco never treated him any differently than he did his other children. He lifted the little boy onto his broad shoulders and tickled the bottoms of his feet, making him squeal with delight as he held on to his father's thick hair like the reins of an ox.

It was one of those perfect summer days when the sandy African winds skipped up the mountain from the sea, filling the air with the sweet smell of brine. Marco chatted easily with me about the town's affairs, about how frustrating politics continued to be in Palermo and on *il continente*. He spoke to me like an equal, like I was a man. I envied Cettina for having such a thoughtful and intelligent husband even though I knew she never saw him as that kind of partner. As far as I knew the two had never consummated their marriage. Cettina told me she once tried to seduce him out of a sense of duty, but he gently rebuffed her and she never tried again. They lived as brother and sister, and Cettina did not care because she got to become the thing she desired most; she got to be a mother.

Marco said goodbye to me when we reached the dragon's ear. "I don't think I'm allowed to step beyond here," he said with a smile.

He leaned down to kiss my cheek goodbye, his stubble grazing my skin, scraping my cheek in a way that sent an unexpected thrill through me. Did I imagine that his lips lingered a second longer than usual? I rarely thought about men, about their bodies, their hands, their lips. But suddenly every part of Marco was incredibly interesting to me and I could feel the heat moving from my cheeks down my breasts. I pulled away and thanked him for walking us this far, helped Liuni off his shoulders, and hurried to the witch's house.

I must have been flushed when I arrived because she quickly offered me a glass of water before laying the boy on her bed for his treatments. While she did her work, she instructed me to chop the herbs on the table and then grind them into the olive oil to make a salve.

"Come here," she instructed once I was finished. "I'll show you how I rub this into his body." She lathered the boy's back and buttocks in the oil and then placed her hands on top of mine as she demonstrated how to knead it into his skin.

"The system that moves the blood around his body is still weak. It's called his circulation," she explained. "The massage helps get more blood to his muscles so they will grow stronger. You see, like this."

Her hands, gnarled and knotty, were powerful on top of mine and I felt a similar exhilaration to the one I'd felt when Marco kissed my cheek. I enjoyed the small power of being able to help heal this child, to help him be able to move a little bit better in the world.

She left me to the massage while she went to check on a broth she was preparing over the fire.

When she returned, the boy was so relaxed he'd fallen asleep. His little tongue lolled out of the side of his lips.

"You are a natural," the witch whispered as she watched my hands move across his limbs on their own. "I have thought this about you for a long time, since you first came to me as a girl when you lost out on the opportunity to go to the upper school, which you very much deserved. I knew that meant you were driven, but I also felt something when you helped me as Melina was dying. I believe you have a gift. Would you like to learn more?" the witch asked as she flipped Liuni over onto his back.

Yes. I couldn't make my mouth form the word, but I was able to nod. Saying it out loud felt like a sin. *Yes, I want to learn everything.*

"Good." She gripped my hands in hers and laid them on the little boy's soft tummy and together we massaged him in a circular motion from his groin up to his chest and around and around again.

I kept kneading the boy's belly, now feeling each of his little organs beneath my fingers but not being able to identify anything I touched. Still I knew I was doing some good.

I went back many times without the child. Cettina, delighted I finally found something that brought me joy, offered to watch my own children for me. What were three more when she had a whole house of them. Every time I visited the top of the mountain the witch taught me a bit more. I learned that ergot fungus mixed with parsley oil could help to push forward a woman's labor when it stalled and also that it helped to stop the bleeding after a birth. But the amounts had to be carefully measured because even slightly too much caused a burning sensation of the limbs and more than that could be fatal. The juice of leeks dissolved in warm water and another woman's breast milk could also speed up a delivery. I learned how to crush pennyroyal and mix it with pomegranate pulp and willow leaf to help hasten the menses for women who did not want to become pregnant and how much to deliver in the first month or two of pregnancy to open the womb.

"How do you know so much about healing?" I finally got up the courage to ask *la strega* one evening after we had coaxed a stubborn child out of its mother's womb. The baby was in an unnatural position, and I'd helped the old woman turn it so it was facing the mother's back and could be pulled out by its tiny ankles, much the way she had done for me with my first pregnancy.

"I was taught by my mother, and she learned from her mother before her. She always told me there are some things women know intuitively, especially poor women, the ones who are the most underestimated. We know our bodies better than anyone, but we are often afraid to embrace that knowledge. I also learned things, different things, from a man in Palermo whom I lived with for many years. The women from my family taught me the old ways and he taught me the new."

"Who was he?"

"A doctor. I was sent to cook and clean for him when his wife died. My family sold me to him to be his house girl. He kept me maintained and gave me a fine room. But he noticed something in me, much like what I noticed in you. He began to teach me to read and to write, and when I excelled at both he taught me Latin. After that he taught me everything he knew about healing. In return I gave him what he needed. I made his meals and kept his house free of dust. When I got older, I took to his bed with him when he asked. He explained to me the real names for the systems of the body and how to use modern medicines, even though many of them are not as good as what I can make on my own." She twinkled a little at the memories. "He showed me how to cut the body and how to seal it back up."

"So, he taught you to be a doctor?" I asked.

"He taught me knowledge. I would not call myself a doctor. We must be careful what we call ourselves. When he died, I could not stay there. I was not his kin. I did not want to be a servant to anyone else, not after what he had made me into with all of his teachings. I came home, but there was nowhere for me to be in town because I had no family left and I was a strange unmarried woman. I moved to the outside of the town, and I did what I do today. I treated women and children when the midwives and doctors could not. The village never accepted me, but they would take what they could when they needed it."

I could not believe I had never asked what I asked her next. It had simply never occurred to me and that felt like a wretched sin.

"What is your name?"

She hesitated. Perhaps it had been a long time since anyone had asked her this. "Rosalia."

"After Saint Rosalia?" My favorite saint. We also called her *Santuzza*, or the "little saint," because she was tiny, a dainty woman born to rich parents who chose to live as a hermit inside of a mountain in order to pledge her life to Jesus Christ.

A smile danced on this Rosalia's chapped lips. "It is fitting, no? The little saint who lived and died in a cave? The patron saint of those infected by the plague."

Rosalia. Would I ever be able to call her that? Would I ever be able to think of her as anything but *la strega*? She must have been able to read my mind.

"I do not mind what you call me, what anyone calls me. You may call me the witch. There is probably a truth to that too. The things we have to do to save lives feels like magic every day."

"I would like to call you Rosalia."

The ends of her mouth twitched upward. How long had it been since someone called her by her name?

"Someone will need to take my place when I am gone. I think you can be of service to the women in the village, and unlike me, you can do it in the light of day because you are a wife here and a mother, a woman with honor."

We worked in comfortable silence for the rest of the day and for many days after that. It was the start of something, but also the end of something else. If I'd stayed ignorant, remained in the darkness of my simple life, could I have kept myself safe?

NINE

SARA

"Where the hell did you get this police report?"

Giusy stared at me with an abstracted air, as though my question about Serafina's murder was absurd and unreasonable. "It is in the town records. I have many friends in the *polizia* and the *carabinieri.*"

Of course she did.

I had no idea what a police report should look like, much less one from a hundred years ago. This document was probably real. Regardless, everything about the situation was completely insane, both Giusy giving me the information and the fact it existed at all.

"Why are you showing me this?" I asked.

"It's proof."

"Proof of what?"

"That Serafina was murdered. It is what your aunt wanted you to learn. I have solved your mystery for you. You are welcome, American!" She had the nerve to make jazz hands.

I massaged my temples with my index fingers. The unease that always accompanied my hangovers doubled and the tendons in my neck and behind my eyes tightened. Despite what my aunt had asked me to do in the letter I couldn't worry about this generations-old mystery Rosie had started to piece together before she died. I needed to focus on my life, my miserable, ruined life, and in order to fix any of it I needed money, the money I might be able to get if I could sell my family's land. That was what I needed to be working on.

"Giusy. I don't know what you want me to say. What is in this report is terrible and disgusting and . . . I don't have words for it. But it happened a long time ago."

"To your grandmother."

"Great-grandmother," I corrected her even as it felt like a tight fist was closing around my throat. Serafina. The woman I was named for. Tortured. Beaten to death.

"She is your kin. Your namesake, the mother of your aunt who you loved so much. What they did to her is a sin."

"Who is 'they'?"

"I do not know. Her murderer was never caught. It is like the most famous unsolved crime here in Caltabellessa. That is what I thought you would want to figure out. I thought you would want to bring justice to her."

Her words made me queasy. That this story was the town's public property. "Bring justice to her? Who do you think I am? Whoever did this has been dead for a long time."

"This is what your aunt Rosie would have wanted. Didn't she ask you to find out what happened to her mother? It may seem like a long time ago, but time means nothing here." Giusy exhaled with intention. "People in our town still talk about Serafina."

"They talk about a woman who was killed a hundred years ago? Why?"

"Because she was murdered out of revenge and because they say she was wicked, because she defied the conventions of the town and she was punished for it."

"Revenge for what?"

"For the things she did."

"What things? Stop talking in riddles, Giusy."

"It's a story we all know, our grandmothers knew and told our mothers, who told us. We all knew her name, Serafina Forte, one of the women left behind. Her husband worked hard in America and sent money home and she betrayed him. She found other lovers. She practiced dark magic. She was a witch and whore. That's what happens when a woman is left to her own devices and she was killed for it. She's a cautionary tale here."

I quickly realized how little I knew about Serafina. "None of this is right." I laid out what I believed to be true. "What I know about my great-grandmother is the opposite." I explained how my family had always talked about Serafina. Serafina the matronly saint. Serafina the dutiful wife. "You have her confused with someone else. And even if you don't, come on. Witch? This may have happened a long time ago, but it was still the twentieth century not the Middle Ages. And besides, even if people here believed she was a witch then, they couldn't possibly believe it now. And if they do, I'm not here to change anyone's mind about century-old gossip." But the names Giusy called Serafina wormed into my brain. *Witch* and *whore*. Didn't I know something about how rumors and lies could be spread by those wishing to hurt you and damage your reputation?

"You'll never sell that land if you don't."

That one sentence sent a chill down my spine despite the glare of the sun on my shoulders. Yet another thing Giusy knew about me that I hadn't told her yet. She knew about the deed Rosie gave me.

"I don't know much about the land that Rosie left me, but I can't imagine selling it would involve solving this crime," I said.

"You are wrong and dumb. People here still question how Serafina got the land, whether it belonged to her or whether she tricked a man into giving it to her. If she did, if she cast a spell on him, or blackmailed him, then the land doesn't belong to you. There are men here who will fight you for it and the town elders will be the ones to decide what will happen."

It was too much information all at once. "Giusy. I am so confused. I'm not clearing anyone's name. I'm not Nancy Drew or Jessica Fletcher. I'm a broke-ass woman who has to go home to the US as soon as possible to fill out unemployment forms for my twenty employees whose livelihoods I've taken away and then battle my husband for custody of the daughter I can't afford to raise."

Her expression hardened. "You are ungrateful. Everything you have in America is because of that woman. You were allowed to run your own business in America. You were famous on the cover of magazines. And now you whine. You are an American. People will listen to you if you speak up about Serafina."

"I know nothing about her."

"I have things I can share with you. I have learned there is more to the story. I have heard it from some of the older women in town. I do not believe she was actually a witch. I believe Serafina was a healer like a doctor."

"She wasn't a doctor. She was a housewife. You definitely have the wrong woman."

"No, I do not. You have the wrong information. You are an asshole, Sara Marsala. You know that?"

"I've been told that a time or two," I admitted.

"I promised your aunt Rose I would help you, but she also promised me something."

"What?" I asked through my exhaustion.

"She told me if I helped you I could get a little bit of the money, a small percentage of the sale from your land. I need that money. My hotel is in debt. I have to sell it, but to do that I need to hire a lawyer and a good real estate agent and I need cash. I've been counting on helping you."

Giusy's information seemed tenuous and yet she was so earnest and passionate about all of it.

I softened my approach. "I'll look at the report again when we get down the mountain. Back at the hotel. I can't make any promises. But I will read it again. OK, Giusy? But everything you said about selling your hotel and finding a lawyer and a real estate agent. I need to do that too to talk about the deed and the land and whether any of it is real and if my family still owns it after so long. Can we just head back?" The sun was climbing higher in the sky and I was sweating out the dregs of last night's wine. "I don't even know what the land is worth. It could be nothing."

"It's a big plot of land at the base of the mountain. It's been used for grazing by the farm next door. But lately there has been a foreign developer sniffing around. He wants to build a big classy resort down there with a golf course and swimming pools and a fancy restaurant. You could get good money, but only if you can prove you really own it, that Serafina truly owned it."

Giusy knew she had my attention with all this money talk. She quickly packed up the picnic basket and started to walk down the mountain, forcing me to follow.

I grabbed her arm. "I want to do right by my aunt and my family. But I thought I was coming here to find a nice place to spread

Rose's ashes and say some prayers to a god I don't believe in and let her rest in peace." I didn't realize tears were rolling down my cheeks until one of them landed on my bare arm. "Please, help me do that."

"The money won't hurt you either." She turned to face me head-on. "You need it."

"No, of course it wouldn't hurt." Why mince words? "But it still makes no sense to me why a generations-old grudge against my relative has anything to do with the sale of land right now."

"Welcome to Sicily. Holding and maintaining grudges is our national pastime. It's our golf." She sped up on the trail ahead of me.

The way down was much faster than the way up and the town had fallen asleep by the time we were back. Siesta was something Rosie would have approved of, a mandatory nap in the middle of the day, a public edict to rest for an entire afternoon. Whenever Carla and I were cranky as kids she always told us, *You just need a nap, a crap, and a snack.*

Once we were close to the hotel, I checked my phone for service, but it was barely at one bar. I hadn't talked to my daughter since I'd arrived and I needed to find a way to get in touch. I also needed to call my sister so Carla could do her Carla thing where she said all the right words to help shove my anxiety back into a box.

But first I reassured Giusy: "Let me think this through, OK?" She nodded, suddenly speechless, maybe recalculating her plan. I had no doubt that Giusy was a woman who always had another plan at the ready. She disappeared through the door behind the check-in counter.

I couldn't worry about her feelings. I hardly knew her. I tried to push her and everything she'd told me out of my mind as I walked back out of the hotel to take a short stroll to try to find phone service. In the piazza the *pasticceria* door was slightly ajar, though the windows were still shuttered. I knocked, pushed it open slightly, and begged for an espresso from a bored old woman who perched on a stool behind the counter. I sipped it quietly on a bench, my phone still useless.

Back at the hotel I climbed the stairs to my room, grasping the handrail for dear life as I wobbled up. My legs shook from the day's exertion and the hangover still dripping out of my body. I once read an article that explained that hangovers came on in waves, peaking exactly twelve hours after you stopped drinking. Surely the last wave had already passed.

Someone was rushing down the stairs ahead of me. I heard them before they slammed into me, knocking me hard into the wall.

"Hey," I yelled.

By the time I got my bearings there was only a shadow at the bottom of the stairs. It was definitely a man, so slight he could have been a teenager. He wore a dark jacket with a hood pulled over the top of his head. The front door of the hotel slammed.

The door to my room was slightly ajar. I nudged it open with the toe of my sneaker and gasped at the scene in front of me.

The place wasn't exactly spotless when I left, but now it looked like something out of a movie where a room has been ransacked by the FBI. The floor lamp next to the bed had been tipped over, the bust of Julius Caesar was shattered on the floor, the television had been smashed, and my suitcase had been flipped upside down. My clothes covered every available surface. A well-worn bra hung from the chandelier, which felt a little too theatrical. I perched on the edge of the bed to survey the damage and started to cackle. Everything about the past twenty-four hours had been ridiculous. But then the laugh caught in my throat, and I slid off the comforter onto the floor. I crawled to the armoire, my heart pounding.

It was still there. The relief felt like a drug. But then why wouldn't it still be here? Who would steal a cardboard box full of my dead aunt's ashes? I gnawed on my lip to keep my tears at bay as I placed my hands on top of it, and again, I swore it felt warm to the touch.

"What have you gotten us into, Rosie?"

There was nothing worth stealing in this room. I checked my backpack and felt the bulge of my wallet. I didn't bring a computer and I had my cell phone with me.

"Shit," I whispered as the possibility hit me. "Shit. Shit." I scrambled to my overturned suitcase and reached into the interior pocket. My passport was gone.

How could I have been so stupid to leave behind the one thing I needed to get home?

"You're a world-class idiot, Sara. Goddamn it," I yelled out loud, and laid back down on the floor, wishing the thief had taken my credit card instead, the one I'd probably have to default on when I got back. I reached for my phone to Google *replacement passport Sicily*, but the Wi-Fi wasn't working and the cell service was still terrible. I had to find Giusy and ask for help.

I picked up the box from the closet, clutching it to my chest as I hurried down the stairs.

Giusy was arguing with someone on the phone, too fast for me to understand her. The only words I could make out were the curses. Suddenly she slammed her hand onto the marble of the check-in counter with the intensity of a judge banging a gavel, and then silence.

She fixed her eyes on me once I made it in front of her.

"I'm sorry I was an asshole on the mountain," I said, echoing her earlier comment about me.

"Don't apologize. It was a lot. My entire life, people have told me I am a lot to handle. Would you like a coffee? Why are you carrying that box?"

"My room," I started. The sentence caught in my throat. "Did you see a man run out of here when I came in?"

Confusion clouded Giusy's face as she shook her head.

"I assume it was a man. Or a boy. He banged into me in the hallway and when I got to my room it was a mess. He broke things. But that seems like maybe it was a distraction because the only thing he took was my passport."

"Your passport is missing?"

"Did you see him?"

"I did not see anyone." She repeated her question. "They took your passport?"

I nodded. "What do I do? I need to call the consulate, right? Do I have to report it to the local authorities? Has anything like this happened to your other guests?"

"Come with me. Let's sit. Let me think." Giusy opened the heavy door behind the desk.

This must be where Giusy lived. It was an entire house on the other side of the wall from the hotel. I almost bruised my shin on a canister of canes next to the door. Canes in all colors, shapes, and sizes, though I had still witnessed no actual limp in either of Giusy's legs. She had scurried up the mountain like a champion.

The decor couldn't have been more different from what was in the hotel. The walls were painted bright blue and electric orange.

They clashed terribly with the red Turkish rugs covering the floor. Giusy pulled out a bottle.

"A splash of wine?"

Screw it, I'd been robbed and presented with an ancient police report detailing the grisly murder of a long-dead relative. I held up two fingers in a little pinching gesture to indicate I wanted only a bit.

She poured us two juice glasses full. Suddenly I felt so incredibly grateful for her, for someone to take care of me, and I nearly forgot the tension between us this morning.

"Should we call the police?" I asked. "I don't have any phone service. I haven't been able to call anyone or check my messages. I have no idea what is going on back home, what is happening with my daughter. We don't go this long without talking."

She nodded. "I will try to reach my friend who works with the police. Let's go sit on my roof. You will get phone service up there if you want to check in with your family."

We walked through her kitchen. I noticed a cut of meat thawing on the countertop, spring lamb rump from the shape of it, the kind you hardly need to season if you roast it straight over an open fire. The different cuts of meat once called out to me, as strange as that sounded. I could carve them with my eyes closed and sometimes I did. But I hadn't picked up a knife since we shut down.

Giusy led me up a narrow staircase. On the top floor we walked to the end of the hallway and climbed a short ladder to a trapdoor in the roof. Giusy flung it open, and I followed her through the hole of blinding light.

I squinted into the sun and saw a few lounge chairs, a rickety side table, and an overflowing ashtray. Lines of laundry flapped in the wind.

"Welcome to my office." Giusy spread her arms wide.

"Now this is the million-dollar view," I said. You could see the entire town from here, up to the castle at the top of the peak and down to the sea on the horizon.

"I know." Giusy lit a cigarette with one hand and pulled dried sheets off the line with the other. "It is nice to look at, but I would rather get money for it and leave it behind. Right now we are on the roof of my house. That roof next door is the hotel. I want to sell both of them and be done with it all."

She blew a ring of smoke up into the sky. "You will get phone service up here."

I pulled my phone out of my pocket and realized she was right. Text messages from Carla and Jack flooded in.

"There's a cell tower on the top of city hall and it is a block away." Giusy offered me a cigarette and I sank onto one of the lounges with it. I ignored my sister's messages for a moment and checked the ones from Jack. They were clearly from Sophie. She'd been able to send text messages since she was three. These were mostly emojis and photos of her grandparents' dog and her toes and half of her face that I assume was an attempt at a selfie. They made me woozy with longing for her. I dialed Jack's number but it went straight to voicemail and I remembered that he had said he'd have bad service for most of their trip too. I dashed off a video message for Sophie in the hopes that it would eventually go through, before googling *missing passport and Sicily* to find an official-looking page from the Department of State that said to report the theft to the police and go to the nearest consulate armed with a photo ID and a copy of my passport or my birth certificate. My expired driver's license was safe in my wallet. I definitely didn't have a copy of my passport. My mom probably had a copy of my birth certificate but I doubted she had a clue where it was. She wasn't the kind of mother who kept meticulous records of our lives. Jack used to keep track of all our personal documents, but I couldn't tell him I lost my passport just twenty-four hours into my trip.

"Christ." I exhaled as I thought about all the bureaucratic bullshit that lay ahead of me.

Giusy tossed her half-smoked cigarette onto the ground and stubbed it out with the toe of her pristine white sneaker. She leaned down to pet a cat eating out of a yellow ceramic bowl. More dishes dotted the roof. Giusy was feeding all the town strays. The tabby beneath our feet had a bit of egg hanging from its beard.

"That's not cat food," I said. "What are you feeding them?"

"Leftovers from breakfast. They deserve a nice feast," she said as she walked over to the trapdoor, tripping a little on the bundle of sheets hanging from her arms. "I'm going to go down to check on the Germans. You want to stay up here for a while?"

"If it's OK."

"It is OK."

She disappeared down the hatch. I waited for a few minutes and wondered if she was just behind the door listening for me to make a call. Why did that make me nervous, her eavesdropping on me? Instead of getting on my phone right away I stared at my sneakers. Black Chuck Taylors, old as hell. I found them in the guest room closet when I went to Scranton for Rosie's funeral. Carla's Chucks were there too. We had lots of matching clothes. At first it was our mom who liked to dress us like twins, despite the age difference, but we kept it up when we were teenagers because we thought it was weird and we liked being weird. One day we'd grabbed a bottle of Wite-Out and another of red nail polish and wrote song lyrics and the dirtiest words we could think of on the sides of our shoes. Mine read, *Motherfucker ass clown*. Most of the letters were faded now so *ass clown* was the only thing still legible. I couldn't remember what we wrote on Carla's shoes.

I opened the messages from my sister.

WHERE ARE YOU?

CALL ME

ARE YOU DEAD?

IF YOU'RE NOT DEAD AND YOU'RE IGNORING ME I AM GOING TO BE SO PISSED.

UNLESS YOU MET SOMEONE. YOU DESERVE A LITTLE FUN. IF YOU MET SOMEONE IGNORE MY LAST MESSAGE. I'M NOT PISSED.

I HOPE YOU'RE HAVING SEX.

CALL ME.

She answered right before voicemail picked up, but her voice was a low whisper.

"In a meeting with some real dildo IP attorneys. Can't talk. Call you back in an hour. Love you. Miss your face."

I missed my sister too. I missed my daughter. I missed my aunt.

I walked to the edge of the building to take in the view, letting my toes creep too far over the edge. It had to be a hundred-foot drop down a sheer cliff. I teetered back and forth, my muscles taut. I could do it. Just tumble off the edge and end all my misery. It wasn't the first time I'd had such terrible thoughts. As my problems piled up, so did my anxiety, until the darkness threatened to overwhelm me entirely despite everything I knew I had to live for. Sometimes I imagined life would be easier for everyone if I was gone.

Power swelled in my chest. The wind picked up at my back.

I began to wobble just as I felt someone breathing right behind me, grasping my arms, shoving me forward. I was at the mercy of gravity. The decision to jump was no longer mine.

TEN

SERAFINA

1918–1920

The years passed easily without my husband. As my children grew, they needed me less and less and I had more time to devote to learning new skills.

One day the doctor from Sciacca simply stopped coming to the village for his weekly visits. There were rumors that he too had left for *la Mérica*. Because Rosalia did not want to come into town except for an emergency, I began doing small things that the doctor would have done. I applied salves to burns and bandaged wounds. I mixed tonics for stomach ailments and packed gums full of herbs for toothaches. When Accursio Romano's prized and only mare fell to her knees in the piazza I felt around on her belly and found that her foal was sideways rather than head or ass first. I hesitated before reaching inside the groaning horse's body to attempt to turn the animal. It was not my place, but we no longer had an animal doctor either and I could not let the beast and her child die, not while I watched. The foal was stuck and every movement caused its mother more pain. I called for the butcher, or rather I called for Saverina, who had been running her father's butcher shop for more than a year since his hands had become shaky and her brothers had left. I asked her to bring me the sharpest, thinnest blade she had. I sliced the mare's stomach right there in the square and plunged my hand into the hole to twist the tiny legs behind the foal. Once freed, it slid right out of the womb, diving headfirst into the dirt. I managed to stitch the mother's flesh even as she licked the blood and dirt from her baby. Saverina, no stranger to the insides of animals, looked down at me in awe. Accursio Romano looked on in horror, or perhaps fear, but thanked me profusely when his mare stood and nudged her child to do the same. That was when the remaining men in town began whispering about me behind my back. *Witch*.

It wasn't only Saverina and me. Many of the women worked now. We worked because someone had to with the men gone.

Our children ran ragged through the streets as they always had. The most noticeable difference in the town with the men away was the absence of large bellies ripe with child. Not that some husbands didn't return. Some of the men had merely gone to the mainland and could come home every few months. When they returned, their wives asked me for a female wash made of olive and cedar oils that Rosalia had taught me to prepare that would make it more difficult to become pregnant. I was also entrusted with the secret for the tonic, the quinine and black hellebore, that I had asked the witch for years earlier, the one that might have safely stopped my pregnancy if it weren't so far along.

These were things we didn't discuss openly. A woman would merely tell me, "My husband will be home in September," and I would prepare what she needed.

I rarely heard from Gio but knew he was working in a factory in New York City and his money somehow made it across the ocean when it was supposed to. Marco was kind enough to pick it up at the bank in Sciacca when he went to the port for business. I was one of the lucky ones. Carmela Planeta's husband went away to work in coal mines in a place called Alabama. At first, he sent money but then six months passed with nothing. Carmela asked Marco to find some way to contact the Italian consulate. It took many more months for Marco to discover that Carmela's husband had at first fallen ill and been unable to work, and then, when he was healed, he took to drink and never went back to the mines. Carmela was essentially a widow without a dead husband, a purgatory of sorts. "I wish he'd died in the mine," she said. We all understood her words even though we thought she would be damned for letting them pass across her lips.

Gio did well. Much better than he would have in Italy. He finally saved enough to purchase a narrow three-story house on via Benfari, a house with a proper *cucina*, including a tile stove with a closed hearth and a flue. The kitchen was twice the size of my mamma's and our bedroom had an iron balcony overlooking the small *giardino*. I was tending to my vegetable patch one morning when Marco knocked on my door.

"Can you come with me to the port?" he asked. Our paths did not tend to naturally cross despite his marriage to my best friend. Marco was always busy with meetings in town or in Palermo or Sciacca.

Although we did not often speak, I still saw him, watched him. I glimpsed him walking through the piazza in the mornings in his three-piece suits, sweat glistening at his temples. I spied him in church in the second pew with Cettina and their children. And then I saw him in my dreams, the ones I told no one about. He visited me there more than my husband did, which I convinced myself made sense because I saw Marco in real life, and it had been two years since I had seen Gio.

Being face-to-face with Marco was a different thing than watching him from a distance, and my heart sped up as I asked him why he needed me down in the port.

"I think you can be of help," he said. "There is an outbreak of something among the children who live near the marina. They have sores on their bodies that aren't healing. The doctor in Sciacca is nowhere to be found."

"Why do you think I can help them?" I said, not meeting his eyes.

"You have done so much good work here."

I flushed at the recognition, knowing I should not let myself be proud.

"I am not sure how much I can do but if you need me to come, I will come. Let me see if Cetti can mind my children after their lessons. Will we be gone all day?"

"Most of it," he said. "I will feed you while we are gone." He smiled, an inviting grin, the kind that could undo a woman, and I considered telling him that I had reconsidered. But before I could say anything, I had turned and was walking to Cetti's house to ask her to take my children.

She said yes, of course. "Tell Marco we need tuna for the feast on Sunday. He won't remember to do it on his own, and get me some *polpo* too."

There was no time to change my dress from the rough checkered smock I had worn that morning as I made the rounds of the village, the one stained in blood and vomit and everything else that could leak from a human body. Maybe I wore the smock as armor. Who would look at me dressed like this?

As soon as we were in the car on our way to Sciacca Marco peppered me with questions. How was the health of our small village, were the children strong, what could we be doing better, what did we need more of? This was his job as the mayor, as our leader, to identify the problems and find solutions. He truly cared about the answers, and I provided them as best I could. I told him the town's children were strong and that I had seen much less sickness now that fewer men came back and forth from Sciacca and *il continente* on a regular basis.

"They brought the sickness with them," I explained to Marco. He nodded as if he understood even though none of us completely knew how a disease made its way from one body to the next. I told him I had read about the transfer of germs in an old medical journal.

"Of course you did. You were always the smartest in all of your classes." I was surprised he remembered this.

"Cetti was smart too. She never should have left school," I replied. It was the truth.

"Yes, of course. She is very intelligent. I have been meaning to tell you it brings me joy that she has a friend as close as you. Melina did not have that and it made her perpetually unhappy."

"Cetti is like my sister," I said, suddenly conscious of the wind whipping my hair around my face in the open-topped car and how ridiculous that must look.

"We both miss my brother, Liuni, very much," Marco said. "I think about him every day."

"I know that she does too." I did not think I was betraying Cettina's confidence to reveal this.

"It makes sense for the brother to care for his own brother's wife if he passes, but it is also strange, don't you think?"

For most of my life no one had asked me what I thought. It was happening more and more lately, but I did not know how to answer his question. It was strange in some ways, but it was also the way things had always been done. And in their circumstances, Marco and Cettina's terrible, terrible circumstances, it was the best possible solution. I had, of course, thought about what would happen to me if Gio passed. All of his brothers were gone, off in America with him, so if Gio died I would be a widow, which came with its own rules and restrictions, but I would not be promised to another man. Still, being promised to Marco, even if not in love, seemed to me a blessing. But I was not going to say all of this to Marco either.

"Isn't all marriage strange in its own way?" It came out of my mouth before I'd had time to process it. "There is always an obligation. Gio and I have been married for years, but I hardly know him. He lives on another continent and yet I call him my husband and I am connected to him forever."

Marco considered this thoughtfully before he replied. "I loved Melina when we married, but we were very young. Maybe I also loved how much she loved me. I still think about her now. I miss her, but I miss the way I was when I was with her too. I was young and idealistic, impressionable. I thought I could change the world with big ideas. I had no idea how much work lay ahead of me. I had no idea how tired I would be."

I had never spoken like this with anyone but Cettina. I was hungry to hear more and hoped my silence would compel him to continue.

"Melina was so eager. She wanted nothing more than to please me. I suppose that is intriguing for a man."

"And a woman," I added with a smile. I knew my response came with a hint of flirtation I needed to keep at bay.

"Yes. Very true. Do you miss your husband?"

"Of course."

"You can speak freely with me."

I felt that this was true even though it also felt dangerous. I sat with it for a moment and pretended to fix my hair with a piece of twine I kept wrapped around my wrist. The truth was I did not know my husband well enough to miss him. I considered what to say for a moment longer. "Life is easier with him gone. When he returns it is another person to take care of. And he is a stranger in our home, a stranger to our ways and our routines. My children do not know how to behave around him. They want to love him like a father, but they tiptoe around him and often make themselves scarce. They are scared to disappoint him, I think."

"But are you lonely when he is gone?"

"I have three boys and Cettina and the women of the town."

"And the old woman beyond the town."

"Rosalia." I said her name. "She has taught me everything I know about caring for people."

"I feel badly for her. We would never force a man to live out of the village for not having a wife and a family and it is wrong that the town did not welcome her back when she returned from Palermo, that she was asked to live beyond the edge of the village like a leper."

"Do you remember that time?"

"No. It was before both of us were born, I think. But I heard that it was the priest who demanded her exile to the top of the mountain."

"I do not know if she minds," I tried to explain. "She likes her quiet life. I don't know how well she would do in the center of town with all the people."

"Maybe so. But she still deserves more of our respect."

"You are not wrong. She deserves everyone's respect."

When we got close to the marina, I pulled a swath of linen out of my bag and tied it around the lower half of my face like a mask and then handed a second one to Marco.

"Rosalia explained to me that this will help us from getting sick when dealing with those who are ill. We also must make sure to wash our hands and not spend too much time indoors with them."

We left the car on the side of the road and walked in easy silence down to the filthy dwellings close to the docks. Vendors sat on the side of the road selling half-rotted watermelons and brightly colored scarves covered in dust. We had to step over a man, a sailor from the looks of his uniform, who was passed out on the side of the road, likely overcome by drink the night before. I heard the cries of the sick children before I saw them and felt each moan deep within myself. Since having my own child, I could not help but be pierced by the cries of another.

The ill ones were collected in one room on the second floor of a wooden building that looked as though it were about to collapse into the sea. We were greeted by a young woman, younger than me, who introduced herself as Lucia. Her skin was very pale, and she was painfully thin. Her cheekbones protruded out from her face like arrowheads and her hair was matted and unwashed. Three other women rushed about the room, applying cold compresses to the skin of a dozen little ones from ages one to ten. They were all deeply uncomfortable. Bursts of red pustules appeared on some of the children's faces. On others, the rash was confined to the body but their faces were red from screaming and streaked with dirt and tears. Some had itched the red spots open, causing bleeding, scabbing, and the oozing of a yellow pus. I asked one of the women if I could get closer to a small boy of two or three who howled with pain and itch. The rashes looked familiar even from a distance. I thought I had seen something similar in one of Rosalia's books, but never in person.

Marco hesitated in the doorway. I held up my hand to let him know he should stay where he was. As I got closer, I saw tiny trails, thin red lines, between the bumps on the children's skin, tracks that told me what I needed to know.

I questioned Lucia. "All of these children had fathers who were recently out at sea?"

She nodded, her enormous brown eyes filled with pain. "Our husbands came back on a ship from Tunis two weeks ago."

"And do they have this rash? Your husbands?"

Lucia nodded.

"Did they bring anything into the home with them? Blankets, rugs, pillows." The first two women nodded.

"I do not think it is an illness," I explained to them. "It is a bug, an infestation and not an infection. A tiny bug that burrows beneath the skin like a weasel burrows into the dirt. It can travel through human skin or in fabrics. We will need to bathe these children in an antiseptic and burn their clothes and sheets." I turned to Marco. "Can you get me mercury from the *farmacia*? As much as they have? This will spread to the whole family and to other children if it is not contained."

He nodded, pleased to be given a task. I had learned this about men. As headstrong as they could be, they also liked to be told what to do as long as it didn't question their own intelligence. Men needed to feel useful in a situation they could not control.

"Your children will be fine," I assured the women as I went about boiling as much water as possible while they stripped their little ones naked and tossed the infested clothes onto the flames in the hearth. I instructed them to burn their own clothes as a precaution and any other cloth in the room. They observed me with suspicion, as though I had asked them to toss their children into the fire. Clothes and sheets were not inexpensive, and these women were poor. "I will ask my friend, the man I came with, to find you new linens. He is the mayor of a town up the mountain. He can talk to the officials here and get you help." I did not know if this was true, but I promised it anyway. "Your husbands, where are they?"

"Gone again," they all murmured. God help whoever was on the ships those men went back to. I went downstairs to meet Marco and fetch the items he returned with, sparing the women his presence in their nakedness. I asked if he could search out clothes and sheets. "Maybe the sisters at the monastery could help."

"I will go right away," he said, and promised to return in a few hours.

I was in constant motion for those hours, getting everyone comfortable, soothing the wounds, binding their bodies with gauze. Once no one needed me, I took my leave of the women and children and walked out toward the sea, careful to wash my hands and dip my own smock in the hot water before I left. The fabric was damp when I put it back on, but the moisture felt good after working in the fiery room choked with smoke.

As always, I was drawn to the waves and the rocky sand. I carefully removed my shoes and left them where the road met the beach. The sight of the ocean never ceased to bring me delight, the vastness of it, the possibilities if one was lucky enough to cross it and go somewhere new. I pictured myself heading across the horizon on my own, leaving everything behind, letting the currents carry me wherever they may. I must have closed my eyes because suddenly there was a hand on the small of my back and I startled with a small yelp.

"It is only me. I am so sorry. I did not mean to frighten you. I saw you here as I was leaving the house. The sisters were generous. They had many donations to share with the families," Marco said, quickly moving his palm away from my skin. I missed it the second it was gone. I was suddenly aware that my wet smock clung to my curves like a second skin, the white linen slightly opaque even with the sun starting to slip below the horizon. I blushed at what Marco might be able to see. He was ever the gentleman and never took his patient green eyes from my face.

"Shall we return home? It is getting late." My shoes dangled from his fingers. "I know I promised you a meal but we need to get back."

I nodded even though I was starving.

We settled into the car. "I still do not entirely understand what was wrong with those children," Marco said. "And can whatever it was infect us? Will we be taking it home?"

"Probably not. We were not there long and we took precautions. It is not a sickness. It is a tiny bug. Think of a nasty ant, but smaller. It spreads in close quarters, like ships, but also in homes with many people. It is tiny. The eye cannot see it."

"Then how did you know it was there?"

"It moves under the skin, creating little trails between the rashes. I saw the lines."

"But how did you know to look for them?"

"Rosalia has books written by doctors from Palermo and from the mainland, from all over Europe. She brought them with her when she returned, and she gets more from Cettina, and Maestro Falleti fetches them when we ask. They have drawings of things you couldn't even imagine."

"So you read all of these things?"

"I do."

"You are a doctor." He said it matter-of-factly.

I remembered saying these very words to Rosalia and her response. I echoed what she had told me. "I am just a woman."

"Those children are healed because of you."

His admiration was like a balm for my exhausted and weary

soul. I loved the work of healing, though I often took in the pain of my patients.

Marco did not take his eyes from the road when he said his next kind words. "I think about you before, from years ago. Your mother taking you out of school. All that wasted ambition. Are you happy now that you can do this work?"

What a complicated question. I was not unhappy in those years before I worked with Rosalia and healed the villagers. I was too busy with the work of being a new mother to be unhappy. Instead, I felt like I did not exist. I lived and moved only to keep my babies alive. Children, chores, and church. Church, chores, and children. The days passed without my noticing them and with no one noticing me. Some of this came out of my mouth. "I don't know. It was as if no one saw me."

"I saw you."

He smiled over at me, removing his eyes from the road for a second too long.

Suddenly my head slammed into the panel in front of me and I saw nothing but a flash of white light. There was the screech of tires and shattering glass. I could have been out for seconds or for an hour. Marco's hands were on me, feeling my arms and my legs. "Fina, Fina, are you OK?"

I grunted some kind of affirmation. My head ached, but nothing else. I could move my fingers, my wrists, my legs. My voice returned to me. "What did we hit?"

Marco slowly emerged from the car, and I tried to follow him despite a wave of dizziness. The front was dented; a rusted bicycle was crushed beneath the front tire. I groaned as I imagined the rider beneath the car, but then I heard a sound behind me in the brush.

It was a man, practically a boy. He'd been thrown clear of the car and into the ditch on the side of the road. By the time we reached him he was starting to stand.

"It is a miracle," he declared as he looked down at his own two legs supporting him. "I was flying through the air, certain I was a dead man, but look at me. I can walk. Nothing hurts."

Something must have hurt because blood was dripping down his temple and I worried that he was delirious and damaged in the brain. "Please sit. Let me check you," I said.

"She is a doctor," Marco insisted. I gave him a sharp look.

The blood came from a cut that must have split open when the man landed, but wherever he landed had to have been soft mud, because the wound didn't look very deep, and he did not appear to have any other injuries. "It does seem like a miracle. But why did you ride in front of the car?" I asked.

A sheepish grimace crossed his youthful face. "I was not watching out for cars. I did not even see you coming. I was looking behind me, checking if . . . No, it is stupid of me . . ."

"Checking if?"

"I was hoping this girl had followed me down the road. I was calling on her at her mother's house and invited her to come to my father's restaurant and I was looking behind me hoping to see her and I did not notice your car when you turned onto the road. I was stupid."

Marco returned to the driver's seat and tried to start his car. It sputtered once and twice and then groaned into silence.

"I can have this fixed for you," the boy insisted. "My cousin fixes things, even cars, though we do not see many. He can come out to do it first thing in the morning if we can get the vehicle off the road for now. The accident was my fault. Please let me take care of you for the night. Come back with me to my home. It is down the road. We will feed you. It is the least I can do. We have empty rooms where the two of you can stay."

Marco tried to start the car again and was met with silence. His hands gripping the wheel were white with tension. Neither of us wanted to stay the night in Sciacca, but it was getting dark and there were no good options for returning up the mountain. We could have perhaps paid someone to take us, but the price would have been high and the danger of being on the roads so late with a stranger would not have been worth it. There were still many desperate men out of work, all of them looking to find money, to take money, and it would be too easy for the brigands and highwaymen to attack us in the darkness when they could not be easily identified.

"We will need two rooms," Marco said. "And do you have a telephone?"

"We do not, but there is one not very far from here."

One public telephone line had recently been installed in our village inside the shop that sold wine and liquor and tobacco, the most visited store in the village. I felt relieved that we could tell Cettina what happened to us.

"Let me get my father's carriage." The boy ran off, leaving the two of us alone on the side of the road.

"Wait here," Marco said. "I always bring something with me in case of an emergency."

He went to the auto trunk and pulled out a small leather satchel. I assumed it was a gun for our protection and I shivered as he reached into his bag. I'd never seen a handgun in person, and I had no interest in seeing one now even if it was meant to keep us safe. The night was so black I could not make out what was in his hand as he approached me. I shied away from him.

"Have a piece?" he insisted.

In his hand he held a small bar of chocolate. I laughed at how frightened I had been only moments before.

"Yes, please." The chocolate was hard and difficult to break with my hands.

"Just take a bite," he encouraged me. I scraped my top teeth along the thick bar of sweetness, letting a piece break away and fall onto my tongue. The explosion of flavor inside my mouth was unlike anything I had ever tasted. There was a spice in the taste, a hint of cinnamon. It was not buttery like the chocolate I'd had before. Individual grains of sugar dissolved on my tongue. I allowed a low moan of pleasure to escape my lips and even though it was too dark to see Marco's face I knew he was smiling at the sound.

"It is good, yes?"

"Better than good." I took another bite, sure I would have a stomachache if I ate too much and not caring.

"It is a special chocolate. All the way from Modica on the southeastern part of the island. They make it differently there than anywhere else in the world. They do not use cocoa butter, or so I have been told, I am no expert in the making of chocolate. But they say it is an ancient recipe passed down by Spaniards who lived in eastern Sicily hundreds of years ago. It was taught to them by the native people in Mexico. I have a friend who works with the mayor of the city of Modica and when we meet in Palermo he brings me bars and bars of this. I hide them from my children. Am I a terrible father for keeping them all to myself?"

"Not at all. I am honored you shared them with me."

"After today and tonight we deserve a little enjoyment."

I nearly choked on the last bit of chocolate in my mouth, wondering if there was more to the meaning of his words than just the sweetness of the candy.

There was a rumble in the road. We stepped out of the way of the cart that was barreling toward us.

"I am Enzo," the boy said when we settled next to him, "and my father is grateful that you did not kill me even though he says I deserve it. He wants to feed you and thank you in person. He said not to worry about your car. He has asked his brothers to come and push it to the shop and they will fix it in the morning when the sun rises. It will be good as new. Maybe even better."

Back at Enzo's home we were greeted by his stern-looking father and fat mamma, who sat us down by their fire, poured us generous cups of wine, and immediately placed plates of roasted goat in front of us, meat that had just fallen off the bone after soaking in broth all day. I ate it faster than I'd eaten anything in my life. I drank the entire glass of wine and let her fill it up again for me. I hadn't been drinking much wine since my babies were born. It often gave me a headache, but I welcomed the lightness it brought me. I felt even more relaxed when Marco assured me he had reached Cettina on the phone and all of my boys were safe in a bed in their home waiting for me to return tomorrow.

"Do not forget to get the *polpo* and the tuna." I suddenly remembered. "We must return to the fish market tomorrow. We nearly forgot and Cettina will be so angry with me if we don't bring it back."

"I am a bad husband. I cannot believe I forgot."

"You are a wonderful husband. A wonderful man." I meant it, but the wine was making my tongue loose.

When Marco sat back down, he was slightly closer to me, so close our thighs were nearly touching and I knew I should slide away, but I did not want to. At that moment I wanted nothing more than to feel his skin right up against mine, to lean into him and see what might happen. But no sooner did I have the thought than he stretched his long arms over his head and yawned again.

"We should get to bed."

"We should," I agreed.

I felt his eyes on me as I took the stairs in front of him and wondered if he was having the same thoughts I was having. I'd had too much wine. He was married to my best friend. I was married to a man who was across the sea. And yet, feeling his gaze ignited something inside me. I paused at the door to my room and turned to him in the small hallway, knowing there was hardly enough space for the two of us to face one another. What if I wrapped my arms around his neck and pulled him into me? My heart thrummed against my rib cage. I was certain he could hear it, maybe even see it through my thin smock. The fronts of our bodies were nearly touching as he lowered his head and brushed his lips across my cheek.

"Good night, Serafina," he whispered.

His mouth lingered on my face longer than a typical good-night kiss. It was slightly closer to my lips than it should have been. My skin burned where his lips parted slightly and his warm breath settled on my cheek.

I turned away and walked into my room.

I climbed into bed. I went to sleep.

But that wasn't what they would all say happened that night. From then on we were watched and even though I was completely innocent that night, no one would believe me. Everyone whispered behind our backs.

Witch. Whore.

ELEVEN

SARA

For a brief moment I was weightless. I was free. I was resigned.

Suddenly I was yanked away from the precipice with a single jerk, sharp fingernails digging into my biceps, hurling me backward onto the hot slate rooftop.

"What the hell is wrong with you? You're mental. *Pazza*. Totally *pazza*." Giusy's face was bright red from the exertion of pulling me back from the edge.

But I had felt someone shoving me forward. I knew that I had. I could still feel the force of it. The wind swirled in my ears, and nothing made sense.

"I wasn't going to jump!"

"Like hell you weren't!"

"You pushed me?"

Her face contorted into disgust. "I saved your life. You were about to go face-first down into the valley if I hadn't grabbed you." Sweat poured down her cheeks. She was as terrified as me. Three of her red nails were ragged. They broke where she dug them into my skin. She followed my gaze to her hands and peeled off the remaining acrylic, revealing the rough yellowed nails beneath. "I came up here to tell you I called the police for you and then I found you like this, doing this!"

"I wasn't . . ."

But she didn't let me finish. "Whatever. Thank me later, American." She gazed out over the edge of the roof and caught her breath. "We can go to the police station and officially report the stolen passport tomorrow morning. I also reached out to the *notaio*."

"The who?"

"The *notaio*, the person who handles land sales and purchases and deeds and all the things. He will determine whether you have a real legal claim to the land and figure out the next steps." Giusy said this like she was explaining something to a slow child.

I nodded and sat in silence for a moment, brushed the dust and grime from the rooftop off my legs and pulled in a couple of deep breaths. "Thank you."

"It's the least I can do. You were robbed in my hotel." Giusy lit her cigarette with shaking hands, as unmoored by what just happened as I was but clearly trying to regain her composure. "Your aunt trusted me to take care of you. We're lucky. Appointments with the *notaio* can take months to get."

"What do I need to bring?" I asked her. "He'll probably want some form of identification besides my expired driver's license, and I still don't have my passport. I need to drive into Palermo to apply for an emergency document with the consulate."

She produced a folded piece of paper from her pocket. A photocopy of my passport.

"From when you checked in," she said, like it was obvious all along that she had this copy of my missing identification.

"And you have the deed?" she said. I wondered if she had a copy of that too.

"I do." It was in my backpack along with Rosie's letters.

"Why don't you rest for a while? We will go first thing tomorrow." She looked me up and down. "And dress nice, Sara. Maybe wear something that shows off your boobs. It never hurts."

———

"It isn't the first time we have been broken into," Giusy admitted as we walked to the office of the *notaio* the next morning. "Petty theft. Crime. It is worse now, but I cannot blame them, the thieves. We are all poor. In hard times we turn on one another. It has always been that way. At least for the men. There are few jobs. Palermo and Rome have been cracking down on the illicit organizations and the crime families so there is barely any money left even in illegal activity, even the drug money has started to dry up because the Cosa Nostra has gotten lazy in their work."

"How so?" I asked, genuinely curious.

"The Sicilians and Calabrians used to control much of the cocaine and heroin coming in from Europe. Now the syndicates from the Balkans and old Soviet countries are taking over. They're smart about things like technology and cryptocurrency and they're more organized."

"How do you know all this?"

"I read the news. I am very informed."

"Of course. Right."

But then she added almost shyly, "We're all a little obsessed with the Cosa Nostra. The Brits have their royals. You Americans have your reality television stars and the Aniston to gossip about. We have the Mafia. Don't even get me started on what I know about their wives."

"But the Mafia didn't steal my passport?"

"No, no. Some young dumb boy probably did. People are desperate. Passports can be sold to the migrants for a lot of money these days, especially someone who looks like you with dark hair and dark eyes."

I thought about whoever was desperate enough to pay for my identity and the disappointment they'd face once I reported it missing and they got arrested at one of the borders.

We strolled past whitewashed cliffs with small squares cut out of them, almost like windows.

"What are those?" I pointed to them.

"Tombs," Giusy said. "Sican *necropoli*. The Sicani were the first people here. Our first people. They dug funeral cells into the rocks to suspend the dead above the earth, keeping their bodies in the void between here and the other place."

"There's bodies in there?"

"Everything buried in those holes is long gone, eaten by animals, pillaged by looters. They are empty."

"That's sad."

"We all disappear eventually."

I thought of teetering on the edge of the roof; I thought of the cemetery, of Serafina's missing grave, and mentioned it to Giusy.

"They wouldn't have buried her in sacred ground," Giusy said with certainty. "She was believed to be both an adulteress and a witch, a pagan. I don't know which was worse in the Church's eyes."

"So what happened to her body?"

"I couldn't tell you," Giusy said. "I don't know what they did with bodies of heretics back then. Burned her, fed her to the animals, threw her in a cave."

My stomach roiled at the nonchalance in Giusy's tone.

"I am sorry, Sara. That was rude. I honestly do not know. I wish that I could tell you more."

"Do you want to be buried there? In that cemetery by the church?"

"I once read a story about a company who will send your ashes on a rocket deep into the ocean," Giusy said. "Maybe I want that." She paused. "Sometimes I want to be as far away from here as possible. Other times I want to crawl into this earth and stay forever."

The two of us turned a corner to find a small business district, a path lined with shops.

"The office is in here."

We entered a narrow storefront wedged between the *pasticceria* and a tambourine shop.

The first thing I noticed about Signor Raguzzo, the *notaio*, were his braces. It was impossible not to stare at them. They were the kind of ancient metal braces that Carla and I had as teenagers, not the near invisible modern version that kids and vain housewives get today. He was my age, maybe slightly older, and didn't seem at all shy about showing off his mouth full of silver as he smiled wide when we walked in.

"The American!"

"Indeed." I tipped an invisible brim of an invisible hat to him.

He chuckled at this. "Sit, sit, sit." He cast a nervous glance in Giusy's direction and then pointed a finger at her. "Are you sure you want her to be here, or would you prefer to talk alone?"

Giusy's chest puffed out as she sighed with irritation. "I am helping Sara with this process. I told you that on the phone."

Raguzzo rolled his eyes before he addressed me again. "With situations like this you need to make sure to surround yourself with people you can trust."

I didn't totally trust Giusy, but I needed her help.

"Giusy stays."

Raguzzo accepted my answer and moved on. "It is up to you. I have reviewed your deed."

Clearly Giusy *had* obtained a copy of the document at some point and had given it to this man. For all I knew Rose had sent her a copy months ago. Raguzzo pulled out a crisp pile of papers from the drawer in the middle of his desk and donned a pair of clear-framed glasses, the kind hipsters in America took to wearing a few years ago but that I imagined never went out of style here.

"This land was absolutely deeded to a Serafina Forte, who I have been told is your great-grandmother. Her name and her name alone was put on the documents . . . no husband's name on the paper . . . which was rare for the time. It's rare now." He snorted like it was still completely absurd for a woman to own property on her own.

"Why wouldn't my great-grandfather's name be on the lease?"

"It was never his land," Raguzzo said. "Here is what I could find. Giovanni Marsala owned a house here in town. His wife sold that in 1925. She sent the money to her husband in America shortly before she . . ." He paused. "Before she died." It was obvious he knew *how* she died.

"This land was deeded to her by Marco Domenico. He was then the mayor of the town. There is a note in the transfer that says it was given to her in gratitude for her service to the village and that it was intended to be used as a place of care for the infirm. A clinic."

I pressed Raguzzo for more. "And this land. It's been vacant all this time? For a hundred years?"

"Not vacant. It has been in use by the neighboring farm. This is not unusual. There was no one here to claim it for themselves after Serafina died. You know that her children went to America. They would have been the ones to inherit it, but they never returned. Her own parents had passed. Her siblings left. So for all intents and purposes this land was abandoned even though it appears that the estate of Marco Domenico left money for the payment of property taxes." The sunlight from the large window in front of his desk glinted off his mouth full of metal as he spoke. "And there are unspoken rules here about land abandonment. Why should a parcel of land go unused when it can be used for growing and grazing? The neighbors of the land tended to it and cared for it, so they do have some claim to it. We call it *usucapione* here, adverse possession. I think you call it squatter's rights in America. The land next to the plot is owned by the Puglisi family."

He paused and looked pointedly at Giusy, who just made a gesture for him to continue. Raguzzo rolled his eyes as he did. "The Puglisis have an olive grove and a sheep farm next to it."

And recently there has been some interest from a foreign buyer in purchasing the land. The owners of the farm next door have been in negotiations with a developer, the same people who built that fancy resort and spa and golf center over in Mazara del Vallo, the Giardino, the one that uses a helicopter to get the people from Palermo. Five-star deluxe. He leaned forward. "And, well I really shouldn't be telling you all this."

There was no doubt he was going to tell me all this.

"But the potential buyers have allegedly already done tests on the land. Your family land is set up for access to the kind of water that they will need to keep something like a golf course in the condition that it needs to be kept in. So I expect they, all parties involved, do not want you to come and claim this land."

"I'll sell it to them," I said too quickly. "What is it worth?"

He pulled out an old-school calculator, the kind that my sister and I used to play with when we were younger. We'd punch in numbers and flip it over so that it read BOOBIES on the screen, the most hilarious joke I knew at age six. Raguzzo tapped in number after number, consulting the papers in front of him several times.

"Maybe $300,000 from the right buyer."

It was life-changing money for me, enough to put a down payment on a new restaurant and pay off my old investors so I wouldn't be beholden to anyone. The idea excited and terrified me in equal measure. For as much as I loved my restaurant, I hated what it had turned me into. I'd become careless, sometimes selfish. I'd been overworked and burnt out. But the money was also more than enough to hire a lawyer to get me primary custody of Sophie and pay for her preschool, a prospect that mattered so much more. I was grossly eager in my response.

"And these resort people? They are the right kind of buyer?"

Giusy grunted. "They're Arab princes. They have more money than God."

"You're screwing with me," I said back to her. "They're not Arab princes."

Signor Raguzzo gave Giusy another one of his looks. "We don't know much about them. They may be connected to the royal family of one of the Emirates. There has been a lot of interest in Sicily from the Gulf States."

Giusy chimed in. "And we need the tourists. We will never get the kinds of tourist money the mainland gets. Sicily is still the sad forgotten stepbrother of Italian tourism. Americans all want to see the canals in Venice even though I have heard they smell like a pig's ass. They want the Colosseum and that stupid tower that is not straight."

I barely heard her at all because I couldn't stop thinking about the money. It suddenly felt like it could be easy. Like something could finally be easy. "OK. OK. I think I want to move forward. What do I need to do?"

Raguzzo took a very long breath. "The owners of the land next door do not want to admit that the land is yours. This is a small village. Word travels fast. They are not happy about you showing up here the way that you have. And there are many things working against you. First there is the fact that the land has been abandoned for a hundred years. The people next door think they have a right to it. Second there is the problem of a woman owning the land back then in the first place. Was it even legal for Serafina to own it? And third there is the issue of why Marco Domenico gave Serafina that land. What did she do to him that forced him to give it to her?"

"Do to him? You just said he gave it to her as a clinic. A place to treat sick people." I was finally coming around to the idea that Serafina might have been some kind of healer, probably because of its benefits for me. "Also, who cares what she did?"

Raguzzo coughed. "There were stories about Serafina Forte. Not all of them were kind. And people believed she had special ways of compelling people to do things."

Giusy piped in. "I told you everyone thought she was a witch."

"I didn't say that word," Raguzzo said.

"You don't have to say it. No one thinks she was given that land fair and square and everyone here thinks she was a witch. My grandmother and aunts told stories about her when I was a little girl. It was a warning. Go to church. Be a good girl. Listen. Do not be a whore. You could end up like *la strega* Serafina Forte."

This time Raguzzo chose to ignore her, so I did the same and let him continue.

"You'll need to get your identification documents in order. A copy of your passport will not be acceptable. You will need to get a new real passport in Palermo. Set up a local bank account. The money from land transfers can only be done through a local bank and you'll need a real passport to create the account."

"Do I need a lawyer?" I asked.

"I do not think the neighbors next door want to take this to the official courts in Sciacca. They are not the kind of people who love the law."

"What do we do next?" I asked.

Raguzzo considered this by pulling a toothpick out of his desk drawer and picking at the jewels in his front teeth for several minutes in silence.

"This is a matter for the town council to decide. It is how things are done here. There will be a municipal meeting."

"When?"

"Maybe this week? Maybe next. You never can say when things will happen. They happen when they happen. In the meantime, I will try to get the surveyor out to assess the land independently, the capacity for water, the property boundaries. You will want your own information."

"And what is your fee?" I asked. I had learned enough about real estate deals gone wrong to ask everything about money in advance. But Raguzzo waved his hand.

"We can discuss that later. We are all friends here."

But we weren't. "I'd like to discuss it now if possible."

"You Americans always think about the money. My fee for a successful deal is five percent. Something like that. Give or take. Like I said, we are all friends here."

I stopped myself from saying that we literally just met.

"Ten percent is what you told me when I asked you to help me sell the hotel." Giusy fixed her glare on him. "Plus a big retainer up front."

"Ahhh yes, but that is more complicated because your husband's name is on the deed and no one has seen him for years."

"Only because they wouldn't put my name on the deed alone."

Raguzzo threw his hands up into the air. The toothpick flew out of his fingers and landed on Giusy's lap. We all ignored it.

"It's not how things have been done here. But precedent matters. Let's see what the town says about Serafina's old deed and about your friend here, Sara, having *her* name on the deed for this land. Look at you women doing all these big things. Making changes. And of course, Giusy, your husband will still have to return to relinquish his rights at some point and then maybe we can move forward with selling your hotel. Or you can take my other advice and hire yourself a fancy lawyer from Palermo to come fight with the town council."

"My husband is probably dead in a gutter somewhere and you know it."

Raguzzo chuckled like this was a truly hilarious joke. "Well, then let's find a body. I have another appointment outside of town, so I will need to leave you ladies. We can see one another before the town hall meeting to discuss the surveyor's results and until then, stay safe."

The last two words sounded more like a warning than a platitude. Giusy flicked the discarded toothpick across the room with her thumb and index finger and mumbled something under her breath as she stood and flounced to the door.

On the street I grabbed her arm to get her to stop walking. "Thanks for what you did in there. You were a big help," I said.

"It was nothing."

"It was a lot and I'll make sure you get some cash if we pull this off and who knows maybe this whole thing will help you. You know, with selling your hotel."

"Maybe." Her gaze was faraway. "If you're ready, we should get to our next meeting."

The door to the police station in the town square was locked. Giusy jabbed at the bell with one of her broken fingernails and hollered into a speaker, "Giusy here. *Ciao. Ciao.*"

She looked over her shoulder at me. "They know we're coming."

I wasn't sure who I expected to answer the door, our karaoke buddy the chief of police maybe. It certainly wasn't a striking young woman a few inches taller than me. A very young woman. She couldn't have been older than twenty and yet the crisp navy blue and red-trimmed uniform of an officer fit her well. She was formidable. The late-afternoon sun gleamed off the gold eagle insignia on her cap. She greeted Giusy with a tight nod as if she was indeed expecting us. The police station appeared empty, and the woman officer led us past the front desk and into a small but neat office. She gestured to the chairs and then shut the door behind her.

"You were robbed?" Her English was heavily accented.

"I was. Someone broke into my hotel room."

"At the Palazzo Luna?"

"Yes."

"Did you see them?"

"Maybe. I don't know. I think it was a man who did it. I saw a guy wearing a black or navy blue jacket with a hood pulled over his head running down the stairs when I was going to my room and that's when I noticed it had been broken into."

"Did you see their face?"

I rubbed my shoulder where he had slammed me into the wall.

"I didn't."

"How tall?"

"Definitely shorter than me."

The officer addressed Giusy next. "Who is staying in the hotel right now?"

"Just Sara and an old German couple."

"I have seen them around town, these Germans. They did not do it." The officer opened a desk drawer and brought out a form. "What did they take? The thief."

"Just my passport."

"How do you spell your name? Giusy said you were called Sara?"

"It's short for Serafina. My name is Serafina on my passport. Serafina Marsala," I said.

"My name is Serafina too," she replied quietly. "But everyone calls me Fina." The officer sighed and looked up at me. "There are some things that are better left forgotten. There are wounds that stopped bleeding long ago. Now they are bleeding again."

I shook my head. "I don't understand." But part of me did. I thought back to the terrible police report that Giusy showed me. How she got it from a friend who worked for the police. Fina had to be that friend. I suddenly realized that I was at the police station for reasons other than my missing passport.

"You're not safe here. And now that you're here, now that the wounds of Serafina Forte's murder have been reopened, none of us are safe. Your stolen passport is only the beginning."

TWELVE

———

SERAFINA

1921

The first time all of us women really talked about the work we were doing was an accident.

Actually, it was a funeral.

Stefano Parlate, the town's oldest citizen, passed away the day after the Easter feasts. No one knew how old he was. Some said a hundred, some said a hundred and ten. His first wife, the only one who might have been able to verify such a thing, was long gone and he was on his third when he keeled over in the middle of the piazza while playing dominoes and smoking cigars with Brunu Favata. When Stefano's heart expired, his cigar was still lit and his left hand was still tucked into the top of his pants, scratching his testicles. Everyone at the funeral commented that it was exactly how he would have wanted to go.

By then most of the men left in town were elderly, like Stefano, the ones older than fifty and useless to the American factories and mines. Or they were children, younger than thirteen and not yet men at all. Only a handful of working-aged men remained, mostly those tied to organized crime. They had plenty of money coming in from protection rackets and blackmail despite the poverty in the rest of the country and no reason to leave unless they were summoned to Palermo for their work.

Then there was Marco. I hadn't seen much of him since we returned from our night in Sciacca six months earlier. He had been away from the village for various political meetings, but I knew he would be in town the day of Stefano Parlate's funeral and perhaps that was why I took extra care with my hair and dress as I prepared for the procession through the village.

The old ladies wailed and groaned the requisite mourning cries and once we reached the town square Marco gave an eloquent speech honoring Stefano's life that was mostly lies because everyone, especially his third wife, Gaetana, hated Stefano. We all loved Gaetana, who was closer to my age than to Stefano's. Though she despised her deceased husband, Gaetana had considered herself lucky to be married to the old man since she was terribly ugly and missing three toes on her left foot from a wheelbarrow accident when she was a girl. The missing toes made her hobble and her lazy eye made it seem like she was never paying you much attention, which most men found unnerving, but she was the loudest and funniest woman all of us knew and we adored her. We walked behind the open casket from the piazza to the church for a mass and then to the Parlate house, where the coffin would remain open for the night so that Stefano's soul could exit the home and make his way to heaven of his own free will.

By the time the sun had set, it was just us women left in Gaetana's parlor. Us and Stefano's body, his skin waxy and yellow, pooled like the folds of a curtain below his chin. His eyes were blessedly closed but his left hand remained tucked into the fold of his pants.

"I would close the wooden box, but then I fear his nasty spirit may be trapped in this house with me forever." Gaetana scowled down at his body. "Get out of here," she instructed him like she would shoo away a stray dog. "Leave me be."

We all laughed when Gaetana bowed her head in mock prayer. When she stood she flicked a fly from Stefano's forehead before she brought out the good wine and poured us all generous glasses. We sang the old songs while Gaetana accompanied us on the cylinder piano. Paola brought out delicious little *collorelle* pastries and we dipped them in a brandy she'd been saving since her wedding day.

"We deserve a treat," she declared. "Let's put this liquor to good use in our bellies."

All of us wondered why we didn't do this more often, why we gathered like this only when someone died. The answer was that we never had the time. We had our children and now we had our work, the butchering, the bricklaying, the baking, and, for me, the medicine.

It was the first time we addressed the men's absence and our new positions in the town so openly.

With the wine flowing we could say it—we were essentially running the town. Because it had happened slowly, over the course of several years, it had at first seemed unremarkable and also temporary. We had spent our entire lives doing work inside the home, work that was rarely acknowledged. Many of the women had also helped their husbands in their trade, but never in a particularly visible way, always far behind the scenes. But now most of the women in the room were doing all the work out in the open. And for the first time we allowed ourselves to express the proper amazement at this development.

Paola stood. "I make wonderful bread. Better than my husband ever baked. I love running the shop. I also love going to Sciacca for ingredients and getting to see the handsome fishermen coming in from the ports."

"I like feeling useful outside of my home and you know what?" I chimed in, my tongue loose but not regretful. "I don't miss my husband." The room grew deathly silent. I met Cettina's eyes and she gave me a glimmer of a smile and then looked away. Perhaps I had crossed a line.

Suddenly Gaetana raised her glass high above her head and then smashed it against the floor. "I am so happy my husband is dead." And everyone laughed and nodded because how many times had we wished for the same forbidden desire.

One by one every woman rose and talked about what was bringing her joy. And to each woman we raised a glass and made a toast or gave a blessing. *Salute!* and *La speranza è l'ultima a morire.*

Cetti was the only one who stayed silent, blinking dumbly into the flickering fire. She was separate from us in this, the only one in the room who still had a husband here in town. She devoted all of her time and energy to caring for him and their household. Her brothers had also stayed. They owned many of the grain fields and lemon and olive groves surrounding the village and they needed to stay close to the land to keep it safe, to manage the crops and to deal with the *mafiusi*, who were now being called by a new name, the Cosa Nostra. Landowners often had to work closely with organized crime or face consequences like torched crops or murdered animals. The *mafiusi* controlled who bought goods and at what price. They controlled the ships. And because of this they now controlled the men who grew the good golden grain, the lemons, and the ones who made the olive oil, the men like Cettina's brothers. Cetti was separate from them because of her marriage to Marco, who despised organized crime and everything it represented. Cetti's father had never been a part of it either. He managed to work their land and protect it without joining any of the syndicates. He was loved, but more important, he was respected and also perhaps a little bit feared. But when her brothers took over the business, they had none of the same grace and they quickly found allies among the criminals to help protect their fields, to sell their products for unforgivable prices and help them make extra money on the side.

Their alliances represented everything Cettina's first husband, Liuni, had died fighting against. I always wondered what her brothers thought about her two husbands, both of them idealists who wanted nothing to do with the crime families, but somehow they all managed to keep it separate.

Even though Cetti's life was different from many of ours, she was happy. But that night amid the laughing and drinking and all of the toasts at Gaetana's I could sense that she felt left out.

I scooted closer to her and slung my arms around her. She leaned her head onto the hollow of my shoulder and whispered, "I should go back to the children."

"Is Marco home?" I asked.

"He is."

"Then they are fine."

"I suppose." She yawned. "I am also tired. And boring. I don't have anything to say."

"You don't need to say anything at all." I remembered that feeling, that sense that I was completely uninteresting. I moved behind her and began braiding her hair. One of my favorite things to do was run my fingers through her profusion of thick black curls. When we were small I would do it for hours, twisting the silky strands around each of my fingers and then letting them spring free before doing it all over again. Cetti sighed with pleasure and relaxed her body into mine, content for a minute more.

It was Paola who had the idea of "the Ask." It started because Paola needed help hauling all the flour and salt up from Sciacca each Friday for the bakery. "If I had another set of hands I could bring twice as much and make twice as much bread and then sell it in Sciacca too and make more money. I am getting less money from my husband, and it would be very helpful."

The widow Gaetana immediately volunteered. "I have a Stefano-size hole in my time now. I no longer need to help him out of bed and wipe his ass and make his breakfast, praise the Virgin. I will come whenever you need me."

It was a bright and radiant thing, this meeting of needs, but also not entirely new. It was similar to what we all used to do to manage our domestic labors. I will take your child if you are ill. I can nurse your baby for you if your own milk runs dry. I will put your laundry out if you need to go help in the fields during the harvest. I'll walk your mother-in-law to church if your monthly cramps keep you in bed. We always did what needed to be done. We did other things too. We ushered girls out of the village who were being beaten by older men in their families. We took the unwanted babies born of incest or infidelity and gave them to our infertile cousins in villages many kilometers away. We did what was necessary to maintain a sort of silent social equilibrium. But these asks were business.

Does anyone have a truck I can borrow to obtain new goats from Trapani?

Do you know a banker who will let me purchase land without my husband present?

I need lessons in basic math to get the accounting at the shop right. Who can help me?

And a final toast.

It is on friends that one depends to get along in life.

A flash of lightning lit the sky outside of Gaetana's window followed by a crack of thunder slapping the clouds. A warning.

We all glanced into the coffin, but Stefano's eyes were still blessedly closed. Gaetana rose and finally shut the wooden lid with a dull thunk. "I think he has left us by now. And I no longer want to stare at his shriveled old face. It only reminds me of his shriveled old balls."

Another slash of fire turned the sky a violent mix of orange and purple and I felt Cettina stiffen in front of me as she bowed her head and trembled her fingers in her lap. Was she making the sign of the cross? Did she think what we were talking about was sinful?

My own body tingled with a strange excitement as I walked to the window to breathe in the sizzling air. I looked down at the courtyard, expecting it to be deserted except for the stray cats looking for shelter from the rain, but there was a shadow striding toward the house. For a brief moment I imagined it was Stefano resurrected from the dead, returning to shame all of us for our joy at his funeral, one fist raised in anger, the other shoved down his pants.

But then Marco stepped into the weak glow of the gas lantern outside of Gaetana's door. His shirt was plastered to his broad chest, his hair long and slick on his cheeks. When he looked up, our eyes met. I considered sneaking down the stairs to greet him, to return to that moment in the hallway when our bodies were so close, when his lips grazed my cheek. What would it feel like to slip into the dark alley alongside the house and let him pin me against the stone wall? To feel his lips move from my cheek, to my mouth, down my neck?

These thoughts visited me often when I was half asleep and alone in my bed. It felt more illicit to have them when only a flight of stairs separated the two of us.

I forced myself to turn away first, to grab Cetti's sweater and tell her that her husband had come to walk her home.

A look of relief overtook her features as she stood, smoothed her dress, and said her goodbyes, raising her voice to be heard over the raucous conversation. As she prepared to walk out the door, I grabbed her arm. "Do you want me to come with you?"

She considered it for a moment before glancing out the window at Marco. "No. I do not think so." I thought I detected an edge in her voice, but I dismissed it as my imagination, as my own guilt for the wicked thoughts that traipsed through my mind as I stared down at her husband in the rain. We both knew there had been whispers over these past months. The old gossips wondered why Marco and I had to spend the night in Sciacca. When we returned to the village in the morning Marco's car looked practically brand-new, as Enzo had promised. The boy's cousins did good work, which made our story about an accident seem almost ridiculous, but doubting Marco was like doubting Jesus Christ himself and whispers were whispers. A small village loves nothing more than gossip because what else did we have to keep us amused and connected to one another?

There were other rumors about me, about the work I did. Rosalia had warned me that practicing medicine in the public eye would bring both gratitude and scrutiny. "They will be thankful for your work but afraid of your power. Choose who you heal and how." So I was careful. When we learned that the children I treated in Sciacca had been healed, I explained it was a consequence of the good sea air and a blessing from the Lord. Just the other day I did the same when I was accidentally called to an exorcism. As I walked to my appointment I fell into step behind Father Caputo when I realized we had both been asked to the same house to heal the same girl.

I deferred to him as we walked through the front door. I nodded to the mother of the home, the one who had summoned me. I tried to silently express that the priest should take the lead, should take over. I couldn't exactly disappear, but I also couldn't do my work. The priest was led to the bedroom of a teenage girl while her father insisted she needed a purgation. She certainly looked possessed by something as she moaned and screamed, writhing in a pool of her own sweat. Her wails echoed off the walls of the small room.

The priest wasted no time falling to his knees at her bedside and thrusting a crucifix in her face. He out-screamed her yowls, "I am talking to you, Satan, Prince of Darkness. I curse you, I chase you out of this child." Then he reached into his pocket and threw raw flour into the girl's face. Her sneeze would have been almost comic had she not clearly remained in pain. He slapped her across the face. Her head snapped to the side and the screams stopped as she lost consciousness.

The father thanked the priest and slipped some money into his palm. Only once he was gone did I dare sit next to the girl and gently pull up her dress to examine her as she slept. Her rapid breathing assured me that the slap had not done permanent damage. She would wake up in time and still be in pain. The mother had told me that the child's urine ran thick with blood and she was tortured with discomfort. I'd experienced some form of this illness myself, all of the women had. I treated her with a solvent to cleanse the vagina and then slipped an opium tincture into her mouth.

"It is an infection of the urinary area. Give her all the water she can handle. Keep her asleep. Time will heal it and the opium will help with the pain."

The mother kissed my hand, but I pushed her away. "If she is healed then let everyone believe it was an act of God. The priest did his duty. I did nothing." I was learning how to protect myself with humility and silence.

Cettina was nearly out the door of Gaetana and Stefano's home when she returned to embrace me again. The corners of her mouth turned downward. "I do think you should leave here soon. This is not . . . It will not end well."

She wasn't wrong. There was much for every woman in that room to fear. But what did Cettina know of our future? What did she see? Maybe nothing at all, or maybe everything. Maybe she was the only one of us, being separate from our new freedoms, who could see the dangers. Because in the end, she was right.

It did not end well for most of us.

———

Eventually, they would all say that I killed the man. Some called it murder, said that it was intentional, that I did it in cold blood, that I was a monster with dark thoughts. But all I was trying to do was save his life. I did not let him die with any intent or malice. I should have walked away and let him bleed out into the dirt. At least then it wouldn't have been my fault.

The man who died beneath my hands was a visitor to our town who had been staying with Cettina's brother Carmine on their land below the village. A tall, ugly man, only slightly older than me, he strutted around Caltabellessa like he owned it, grabbing at women and even the teenage girls. There were whispers that he was a money

173

man for the *mafiusi*. The Black Hand, they called him. He had something to do with organizing the protection payments for the farms in our region.

Farmwork has never been easy or particularly safe. A hand or a foot is easily lost to a thresher or scythe. Horses bolt, tree branches break. Men drink on the job and everything becomes that much more dangerous. By the time I reached the farm there was probably nothing I could have done for the ugly money man after he was thrown from his horse onto the tines of a pitchfork left in a stack of hay. The spike pierced his back straight through the ribs and yet he was still conscious when I arrived. There was less blood than you might have expected given the grisly nature of the wound. Perhaps this was why Carmine was so certain he could be saved, why he called for me at Cettina's house in the first place while the two of us were having lunch. What I knew, the very second that I saw the victim, was that the thing that was killing him, the pitchfork, was also keeping the blood in his body. He had been rolled onto his side so that I could see the wooden shaft of the instrument emerging from the front of him like a lightning rod.

"Take it out," Cettina's brother ordered me.

"Wait a moment," I insisted as I scrambled to the ground and felt around the wound, causing the injured man to groan and cough. Blood poured from his mouth, another frightening sign of what was happening to his organs beneath his skin.

"Do it," Carmine barked.

I turned to face him, tried to explain what was happening in the simplest way possible. "I worry that his lung has been punctured and maybe one of the main pathways into the heart. If we pull the fork out we may not be able to save him."

"But you cannot leave it in," Carmine said. "I knew we should have called for the real doctor. We should drive him to Sciacca in the truck."

"I do not think you should move him."

"But there is no blood except for that." He pointed at what came from the man's mouth, now staining his shirt and pants, covering my hands. The injured man's eyes lolled back in his head. We were already losing him.

"You cannot move him without shifting the tines of the fork and we don't know where they will go inside his body. I do not think that is a good idea."

"What the hell do you know anyway? You are not a doctor."

"No. I am not," I whispered.

"We need to take this fork out of his body. He is not even badly injured," Carmine said.

"We should not remove it yet," I said. "I can make an incision near the wound to try to see where exactly the tines are in his body. But if they are in his lungs or close to his heart, when we remove them the blood will fill his lungs and he will suffocate." I did not know why I was begging to save this wretched man I hardly knew, only that it was the right thing to do.

Carmine growled. "I will get a car so we can take him to the real doctor."

"I am going to make one cut. And then we can put this gauze in the wound." I held up the cloth as evidence of my plan as I swabbed the area around the tines with an antiseptic. "And that should help get him to Sciacca." *Where the doctor won't be able to do anything*, I thought.

Blood oozed from the incision as I tried to widen it enough to see where the tines had gone. As I cut, more blood bubbled over the wound.

"Stop, you are killing him. I told you not to cut, you ignorant bitch," Carmine yelled. "Take the fork all the way out and bandage the wound and the real doctor will fix him."

He loomed over me, his massive shadow darkening both of us. The blade of his machete gleamed against his thigh, his hands clenched into white fists at his sides. I knew I did not do what I did next out of spite, but it might have been out of fear. I also knew in that moment that Carmine would not hesitate to strike me if I didn't do exactly as he asked. I stood and gripped the handle of the fork and pulled it from the man's body. It slipped out easily, too easily. I felt it slide around the soft tissue of the lungs, right between the ribs. Blood pooled at the wound as I rushed to wrap a bandage around the chest cavity and stop the bleeding. But the damage was on the inside. The man on the ground began choking, blood poured from his mouth, much more than before. As I suspected, the only thing holding his body together had been the pitchfork. He was drowning in his own fluids. I held on to his hand, hoping to give him some comfort, but his eyes bulged from his body as he gagged and was overcome.

Carmine cursed and spat at me. "Stupid woman. Stupid bitch." I heard the same words over and over again. Then something different. "Witch."

The man's soul had left his body, but I held on to him anyway, afraid of what would happen when I stood.

Before I could react, Carmine grabbed a handful of my hair and yanked me to my feet. I stared up at him, my eyes beseeching. When I looked into his sun-worn face I did not see the angry, desperate man. I saw the gentle teenager who had once whittled little dolls out of sticks for Cettina and me to play with, the young boy who wet his bed when there was a thunderstorm. Cettina and I had washed the sheets so no one would know. Desperation, the need for money, and the desire for power had changed him.

"You did this on purpose, witch." I felt blood on my scalp as the handful of hair ripped out of my skull, taking my skin along with it.

"Please. Please, Carmine. There was nothing I could do for him. It was a terrible accident."

"Look at him." When he released me I collapsed onto the ground, and he swiftly kicked me in the side with his boot. "When you arrived, he was breathing. There was no blood. Now this. How can I explain this? I cannot say it was an accident. No one will believe me. Do you know who this man's boss is? Do you know anything? They will think I did this, and they will come after me."

I did not know exactly who *they* were, but I had an idea.

"You can blame me," I said, desperate to get out of his reach. I slowly crawled away through the dirt for all the good that would do. I could feel that something was shattered in my chest, a rib.

"Like anyone would believe me. Believe that I called a woman to come to heal him. No, they will blame me." He was no longer speaking to me but rather up to the sky, perhaps to a God who would always favor men.

The sound of a motor saved me. Someone was driving up to the farmhouse. Suddenly Carmine lost interest in me, though he left me with a few parting words as he walked away to the house. "You will regret this."

I had no doubt of that.

When he was out of my sight I managed to get to my feet and walk off in the opposite direction, through the fields, away from the house, toward the road. I did not know how I'd make it home. After walking for an hour, I was so slow I was not even close to the village. I settled into the shade of the one giant ficus trees among the olives and lemons. Its massive roots supported my back as I lifted my dress to examine the damage. My entire left side was already turning purple. There was blinding pain with each breath. I knew that I should not be walking. The sound of another engine saved me. Stepping out to the road was a dangerous proposition. It could be anyone. It could be Carmine. It could be the men who employed the Black Hand. But I did not see any other choice.

The Virgin Mary was on my side. I saw her shrine as I stepped onto the dirt of the road. It had been built by Cettina's mother when we were children. Mamma Filippa took exquisite care in hand painting the beautiful features and the flowers lining the hem of her blue gown. Sunlight seemed to pour out from inside of the statue's ivory skin. I kissed her dusty foot as I stumbled into the road.

Paola was driving, thank the Virgin. I stepped out and waved my arm at my friend. The sheep grunted their annoyance as she stopped and pulled up next to me, leaping from behind the wheel and taking me in her arms.

"What happened to you?" I shook my head. I didn't know yet what story I would tell.

Paola took off her shawl and wrapped it around my shuddering shoulders. I inhaled her familiar scent of yeast, the strong amaretto she used to sweeten her sponge cake, and the pipe she sometimes smoked while she drove. She pulled me tight to her and kissed the top of my head like a mother.

"Take me to Rosalia," I managed before everything went black.

THIRTEEN

SARA

The police officer's long hair flew behind her like a banner in the wind as she drove the three of us down the side of the mountain on our way to the coast. In another life Fina the cop could have been a Formula 1 racer. She took the hairpin turns at a breakneck clip that shuttled me from one end of the back seat to the other.

Immediately after filing the police report for my missing passport, the two women asked me to decamp for a long lunch by the sea.

"It is not safe for us to talk about things here," Fina had insisted, and I was at their mercy if I wanted more information.

Before I knew it we were driving alongside the stunning ruins of what looked like a Greek temple.

"Selinunte," Fina said, waving her hand at the massive columns that reached high into the sky in front of the cerulean sea. It was as impressive as pictures I'd seen of the Greek Parthenon back in my grade school history books.

I took out my phone to snap a picture and got stuck on the lock screen before I pushed the button. My eyes stung looking at a family photo. Jack and Sophie and I all dressed up as planets two Halloweens ago. Sophie was Saturn. I was Jupiter. Jack was Earth. In this picture, which I couldn't bear to change, we were smiling like idiots with our arms wrapped around one another, a functioning solar system all our own.

The photo unsettled me, and I quickly wiped the moisture from my eyes before anyone could see. I unlocked the phone and toggled to the camera app to snap the photo.

"Are those Greek ruins?" I asked.

"Sicily was Greece and Greece was Sicily and all the good stories come from here and have been bastardized around the globe. You know the story of Persephone, yes? A maiden who lived in the fertile fields close to Enna in the center of the island," Fina explained. "This is where Hades, the king of the underworld, found her and abducted her, bringing her to be his queen down in hell. Persephone did not go quietly, a Sicilian woman never would. She went on a hunger strike and finally he had to relent and allow her to return for half of the year."

"Right, I remember reading the myth in lit class," I said, feeling slightly schooled.

"But you thought she was Greek. Persephone, the grain mother, is the reason we have such a fertile growing season followed by such a miserable drought. She was a rebel. She was a queen. She was a Sicilian woman!"

We didn't stop at the ruins, merely slowed. Soon enough, the olive groves and pastures gave way to squat concrete apartment buildings on the edge of the city. Strings of wet laundry flapped outside every window. Urban sheep nibbled at the detritus that collected in the gutters on the side of the road.

"Trash-eating sheep," I remarked.

"Sheep will eat anything," Giusy yelled above the wind. "They're like pigs. I saw one eat a condom last time I was here. A used condom. Filthy beasts."

Some of the buildings we passed were gorgeous, intricate beaux arts relics in various shades of faded yellows, oranges, and pinks. They were interspersed with brutalist monsters, concrete blocks with tiny windows. Even worse were the lots where it looked like something had gone terribly wrong, burned-out husks of former structures, some still black with smoke stains battered by the sea air.

It was siesta time, and like in Caltabellessa, most businesses in this city were shuttered, lending everything an abandoned and menacing air.

"Merda!" Fina cursed at herself and did a U-turn in the middle of the road, hardly checking for oncoming traffic. "Missed it."

Within minutes we were on the coastal road, the sea so close it felt like one deep pothole in the concrete could careen us straight into the water. Ancient-looking wooden rowboats were tied to thick metal stakes pounded into the concrete lining the shore.

We drove up a low hill and finally parked in a field across the road from the ocean.

"Mangiamo," Giusy shouted as she slammed the car door shut. She transformed into a different person outside the walls of her village. There was new color in her cheeks, and she had this fiendish smile. It clearly had something to do with the presence of Fina, who giggled easily with her friend despite her ominous warning to me back in the police station.

The two women rushed across the street ahead of me holding hands. Suddenly they began to walk down the hill and out of sight.

I scurried to catch up and saw stone steps built into the cliff hugging the shore, leading precariously down to a white stone building with an orange roof.

Closer to the structure I could practically taste lemon and garlic in the air. I was starving. As dilapidated and abandoned as the place appeared from the outside, it was stunning once I passed through the entrance. An expansive teak floor stretched out toward the edge of the hillside. Below us the sea was a calm pool of aquamarine. Gold and silver lanterns hung from exposed beams on the ceiling. The interior was much more solidly built than the exterior, which now seemed like a trick, a facade to discourage those unwilling to see beyond the ruins. A massive and gleaming wooden table took up the center of the room, made of a single piece of wood with live edges and surrounded by at least twenty chairs. It was set for a feast, but only Giusy and the cop were sitting there, smiling strangely at me. I felt like Alice falling down the rabbit hole, confronting a pair of Cheshire cats, eager to screw with my head. Why were we on this strange little field trip? I'd have to sit to find out.

A grilled slab of bread was in the center of the table, surrounded by bowls filled with honey-covered figs and glistening artichoke hearts, crumbly white cheeses and roasted eggplants smothered in bright green olives and fiery red peppers. Before I could take a seat Fina stood. She'd taken off the top of her uniform to reveal a bright yellow halter beneath that showed off her smooth olive skin and her tattoos. The first one I noticed was the Medusa from the Sicilian flag etched into her left shoulder. In this design Medusa's thin lips from the flag cracked into a massive and gorgeous smirk, like she's in on the joke and you're not and that will not end well for you. On her right shoulder there was a second woman with the wings of an eagle sprouting from her back. Her face was entirely blank, no features at all. In her hand a curved blade dripped with blood.

"What's the name of this place?" I asked.

"Sicania," Giusy mumbled through a mouth full of bread. "The earliest recorded name of the island."

"Since we are talking of records, we should show the American what we brought her here to see," Fina said, reaching into a massive backpack she'd brought from the police station. She pulled out the largest book I'd ever seen, at least twice the size of the kind of books fancy people have on their coffee tables back home.

The pages were thin as parchment, the ink faded. "What is this?" I asked.

"Ecclesiastical records," Fina said. "Church records of births, weddings, baptisms, deaths."

The big book that had boiled the priest's blood back in the church. "Why do you have it?"

Giusy answered for her. "Fina has been given the task of matching the church records with the civil records, marriage certificates, death certificates. And she is putting it all in the computers. In a database. They let her borrow the books to get it done."

"It is exhausting," Fina said. "The work makes me want to set a car on fire."

"But it is lucky for you, American, because Father Silvano never would have let you see this book and there is interesting information about Serafina Marsala we can show you. Sicilians keep some of the best records in the world, you know," Giusy interjected as she opened the book, a thin layer of dust fluttering up from the pages and resettling on the table. It was all organized by year. Handwritten entries for every single event.

"How far back does this go?" I asked.

"This book is from 1890 to the Second World War," Fina said, carefully turning pages until she landed on what she wanted to show me. "First, we have Serafina's earliest record. Right here. You see. She was christened Serafina Forte in 1893."

The cursive was barely legible. She flipped forward a few pages. "And in 1908 she was married in the church to Giovanni Marsala."

I did the math in my head and gasped. "She was only fifteen."

"Very young," Giusy said. "Even younger than was common then. Most girls did not marry until after their sixteenth birthday."

Fina continued. "And here is the baptism record for her first child, Cosimo Marsala. Same year. Four months later."

It took a moment for the dates to click into place. "She was pregnant when she got married. Very pregnant."

"I imagine that the rumors about her began early because of this." Giusy cocked her head as she thought about it. "The whispers about when the baby was made and what that said about her honor."

"What else is there?" I reached out to touch the book again, but Fina swatted my fingers away.

"The pages are fragile," she warned. "I could get into much trouble for bringing this here. But I think it will help you." She wanted me to know she was doing me a favor and I wondered what I would eventually owe her for it.

"Then there are two more children," Giusy said. "They come quickly. Both boys."

"Three kids before she was twenty?"

"Three was not very many then. Most women had six or more. But her husband left for America, remember?"

"But what about my aunt Rose?"

"There's no record of her in this book."

"Why not?"

"We have to assume that she left before she was baptized."

I had no idea whether that was true or not, but it did beg some questions. "And Serafina's husband had already gone to America?"

Giusy nodded. "He could have returned for a visit. We do not know."

"And what about Serafina's death?"

"It is also not in here. Which must mean there was no funeral. Remember these are only events that happened in the church, not civil records."

No funeral. She had never been buried. But the priest must have read something between the lines, or known another piece of information about her that had made him so intensely angry.

Fina kept turning pages. "Look here. These are records of the location where someone received their last rites. There is no listing for Serafina. But there would not have been last rites for a murder. When I was trying to find it, I noticed something else. Look here; all of these. Hundreds were on your land. It really was a clinic. It proves the stories about Serafina treating the sick there." Fina's eyes were shiny with a childlike wonder and satisfaction at piecing together a puzzle.

"Won't you come to say hello?" A male voice wafted out from somewhere behind a wall.

"We should pay our respects to the chef." Giusy headed toward what I assumed was the kitchen. I grabbed a hunk of the bread and swiped it in thick green olive oil before following.

The kitchen was as well-appointed as the dining room. Steam rose from terra-cotta tagines perched on a massive industrial stove top. A long silvery tuna was laid out on a butcher block in the middle of the room and behind it a man wielding what looked like a razor-sharp machete was preparing to slice off its head and tail. He had his blade raised high in the air, blood already spattered across the lemon print apron on his belly. His hazelnut skin glistened with sweat and oil. When he looked up at us, I was nearly undone by his wide, sensuous mouth and eyes the color of a pond after a fresh rainstorm, light brown with a hint of moss at the edges. His facial features could have been chiseled in stone, made all the more delicious by his lazy smile. He met my gaze as his blade sliced clear through the fish's neck and the severed head fell to the floor.

"So dramatic, Luca. And I thought I knew how to make an entrance." Giusy strolled behind the butcher block to kiss the man on both of his cheeks. My pulse quickened and something shifted inside me as I walked closer, wanting to be near enough to smell him and inhale the air around him.

"Sara Marsala, meet our friend Luca," Fina said, making a little flourish with her hand.

"I wasn't much older but I used to babysit him," Giusy bragged, ruffling his hair.

He was definitely an adult now, maybe a few years younger than me. With another swift slice of Luca's blade, the fish was filleted from neck to tail, revealing its bright red, ribbed muscles. I was suddenly seized with a desire to feel the heft of Luca's knife in my hand.

"Sara is also a chef," Fina said.

"Was," I murmured, not yet meeting the man's eyes.

"Would you like to do the honors?" He offered me the blade and then thought better of it. "No, this is no good for the next bit. Hold on. I will find something smaller." He turned his back and rustled around in a drawer.

"How do all of you speak such perfect English?" I knew why Giusy's English was so good, all of her studying to be a translator, but Fina and Luca were equally fluent.

"We were raised on American music and television. Ross and Rachel and Chandler and Monica and Carrie Bradshaw," Fina said. "Also, Britney Spears."

Luca handed me a long, narrow fillet knife, the handle inlaid with a creamy white bone. "Wild boar skull," he explained as I examined it. It was perfectly heavy and the weight in my hands felt like sunshine running through my veins.

"Do you know what we call tuna here?" he asked me.

When I made the mistake of looking directly into Luca's eyes all of my insides turned to liquid.

"*Tonno*?" I answered.

"That. And also *il maiale del mare*. Pig of the sea. Because each cut of fish is valuable and used for something. The whole animal. This place used to be where they processed all the catches. A tuna fishing estate. A hundred years ago."

"And now you serve it. I appreciate the continuity," I said, as I crossed in front of Luca, placing myself between his body and the fish. He stepped slightly aside so he could watch and the idea of impressing him spurred me on. I let the blade slide in deep enough that I felt a slight resistance from the ribs and the spine before slicing along the bones.

Warm blood spilled over my fingers and I knew this fish came straight from the sea to this table. I bowed my head in a silent prayer and thanks to the animal for sharing its body with us. I'm not a religious person, but you can't help considering an animal's soul when you hold its bones and muscles in your hands and tear apart its flesh in order to nourish yourself.

"Did you catch this yourself?" I asked Luca without taking my eyes away from my work.

"No. I am a terrible fisherman. I've nearly drowned in that sea too many times. You need to be stronger and less afraid of perishing than I am to pull these from the water. The men who fish tuna here have been doing it their entire lives. They row out at dawn in those boats." He pointed to the wooden wrecks lining the shore down the coast, the ones that hardly looked big enough to hold two human bodies, much less a fish the size of a small cow.

"How is it possible to catch tuna in those little things?"

"Cooperation. They herd them together with nets into a *camera della morte*, a death chamber, and then they use the spears, piercing them straight through the heart for a quick slaughter. They return as the sun creeps over the horizon. I bought this one on the beach this morning."

I continued my cuts until I crafted thin slices of belly steak that pleased me. Luca smiled his agreement.

"Would you like to prepare it with me?" he asked.

I wanted nothing more, but I also wanted Fina to tell me everything else she knew about Serafina. The two women had disappeared from the kitchen while I worked on the tuna. I'd been so engrossed I hadn't even noticed. Luca placed the tuna in some kind of marinade and added a variety of spices.

"I should get back to the others, but I can't wait to taste whatever you make for us."

I wasn't ready to hand the knife back to him just yet, so I examined the handle closer. "It was my mother's," he told me. "She taught me everything I know. I never wanted to leave the kitchen. I used to be teased for it. People said I was doing women's work."

"Everyone always said I was doing man's work, preparing meat."

The words spilled out of my mouth in a jumble. It was true. Less than twenty percent of butchers in the world were women, even less than that if you took out the ones working for their husbands. Meat production was a physical job due to the sheer size of the animals and the need to be able to move their carcasses, but the carving of meat was a craft, an art, and brute strength could often be your enemy. For that reason, I always believed that women were better with a knife.

I didn't say this to Luca. Instead, I murmured, "But who gets to decide who does what?"

"Who indeed?" When Luca reached for his knife our fingers brushed against one another's. An electric current passed between our skin.

I uncurled my fingers from the handle. I had to get out of his kitchen.

"Take this with you." He handed me a platter of thick black pasta. I raised an eyebrow to ask what it was.

"Squid ink linguine with sea urchins." Luca moved quickly. He was already putting the tuna in the pan.

"Of course," I said, and carried the pasta into the dining room.

Giusy and Fina were still the only ones in the restaurant, sitting at the long table, sipping generous glasses of a dark orange cocktail from wide crystal tumblers. I put the pasta down and walked over to admire the view for a few minutes. When I returned, a sweaty glass waited for me along with a plate piled high with selections from the table.

"All of this is just for us?"

"Luca is a good old friend from the village. We were raised next door to one another, like siblings," Giusy said. "He likes to try out new recipes before he opens for the season so we come and we eat and we tell him how terrible his food is so he will keep

189

experimenting and inviting us down and sometimes we get too drunk to drive back up the mountain so we sleep at his apartment and make him feed us again in the morning."

"That doesn't sound so bad. Thank you for bringing me."

I slid a date stuffed with pistachios and a creamy white cheese between my lips and groaned in pleasure at the salty sweetness melting on my tongue.

"It is better than an orgasm," Giusy said. She wasn't wrong.

I took a sip of the drink. "What is this?"

"Amaro and Zibibbo sparkling wine."

"Zibibbo?"

"A sweet little thing of a grape that came here from Alexandria thousands of years ago. A bastard of Arab vines and Sicilian soil."

The two of them clinked glasses. *"Astarte!"* Giusy yelled, staring deep into Fina's eyes. They didn't invite me to toast with them. I'd never heard that word before. Before I could ask any more questions, Luca arrived with the lightly seared tuna and more bread fresh from the oven.

"Are you eating with us, Lulu?" Fina asked him, running her finger along the slick surface of the tuna steak and then licking the capers and garlic sauce from the tips of her elegant fingers.

"No, no. There is too much to do in the kitchen. I must do dessert."

"C-can't wait," I stuttered, and looked at the ladies to see if they noticed my nerves. Neither of them did a thing to hide their sly smiles.

Luca, thankfully, was oblivious. "Let me tell you what I've done with the tuna. On the top are the tomatoes, capers, olives, garlic, onions, pine nuts, and sardines as usual and I added some wild fennel tops."

There was nothing usual about that for me. I'd never had tuna smothered in finely chopped sardines.

"But I've also sweetened the fish with a brown sugar glaze. You will tell me if it works."

"I'm sure it will be delicious." I was so eager I hated myself and Giusy stifled a laugh.

"And wine. You can't have the Amaro with the fish. Hold on. Let me get you a different bottle."

"You can put your tongue back in your mouth," Giusy said to me once he was gone.

"Hmmmmm," I said, trying to fix my expression.

"I saw how you were looking at him."

Fina pinched Giusy on her biceps. "You cannot pimp Luca out to an American."

Her comment brought me back to the topics at hand, the land and Serafina. "Is that another problem with me claiming the land owned by Serafina?" I tried to bring the conversation back around. "I'm a foreigner?"

"They might use that." Fina nodded. "But that is not the main problem. There are many. It is why I showed you the book. To help you understand. According to the official records Serafina is not dead."

"But the police report said she was murdered."

"And the Church did not consecrate her death. If the Church does not believe she is dead how can she pass on the land? The Church and the state are very, how do you say, in bed with one another, entwined," Fina said. "The other problem is that many people in our village think that land never should have been given to Serafina in the first place. They think she got it because she tricked a man into giving it to her with her witchy magic."

"With her magic vagina," Giusy said, laughing, and Fina joined her.

I wanted to throw up my hands at all this nonsense. "A magic vagina? A witch? Seriously?"

"I heard she could catch a wild turkey with her bare hands, flip it upside down, and murder it with her gaze," Fina said.

"She used the cries of pigs to diagnose the health of the villagers," Giusy chimed in. "She made amulets for protection out of menstrual blood."

"She was a wild woman," Fina finished. There was something special about how the two women interacted, their easy intimacy, how they finished one another's sentences. It made me miss Rosie.

I thought again about how none of what Fina said coincided with my family lore. Our family stories never talked about how she was just fifteen when she got married, or how she got pregnant before then. They only detailed the dutiful and faithful wife and mother who waited for my great-grandfather to make his fortune in America. Patiently waited. She was Penelope waiting for Odysseus for twenty years. I mentioned this to the women and they scoffed. As Fina had said, the Greek myths were still very much alive in this ancient place where so many of them were born.

"I do not think Penelope stayed saintly and chaste while Odysseus was gone. I think Penelope fucked," Giusy said.

"For sure Penelope fucked," Fina agreed.

I should have known I could sidetrack them so easily. I tried to make sense of it all as I summarized it out loud. "OK, so I'm an American, a foreigner, and that could be a problem. And the woman who once owned this land, my great-grandmother, may have been a witch who was murdered under mysterious circumstances, which may make some people skeptical of her right to the land, and by proxy my right to the land."

"Also the fact that when the land was given to her, women didn't own land on their own. All of their property was their husband's property," Giusy said.

"It still belonged to my family then."

"True."

"So what is the problem?"

"Let us explain some things to you, American." Giusy pointed one of her still-broken fingernails at me.

This was exactly what I'd been waiting for. "Please do."

"We've always been a poor island. But our people never minded. If we were poor in the eyes of the world, we were rich in other things. We had good food in abundance. We had good families. We didn't need much. The island always provided for us. But the invaders who ruled us wanted money for their beautiful cathedrals and their wars. There were taxes and then more taxes. Only once we were taxed did we realize that we were poor in terms of money. The invaders and foreign rulers also bled our land dry. And then when Italy became one kingdom—"

Fina interrupted. "Especially when Italy became one kingdom."

"The north sucked away all of our resources. No poor Sicilians could make even a modest living. Eventually many of our men left for the mainland and for America to make the money to keep the land that we loved. So many men fled that entire villages were left to the women. A million men left this island."

Giusy raised her glass in salute to the exodus. "*Astarte!*" That strange word again. "It was glorious in many ways. You should hear some of the older women tell the stories they heard from their mothers and grandmothers. For the first time women broke free of the bonds of marriage and motherhood. They taught themselves to read and to write and do math and run businesses, all because they had to support their families and step in while their husbands were an ocean away."

Fina chimed in. "For the first time in their lives they were free."

"No one was getting them pregnant once a year. But it couldn't last. It couldn't last because eventually the men made enough money to bring their wives to America."

"Some returned," Fina added.

"Some men returned. Regardless of whether the husband came back, or the wife joined him in America, the women who had gotten to learn and work were forced to become wives and mothers again and nothing else. Everything they'd learned was useless. They were back in their homes."

"Having more babies."

"Cleaning and cooking."

"And miserable."

"But not Serafina."

Now it was my turn to interrupt. "Because she was murdered."

The waves crashed in a moment of silence. "Which is worse?" Giusy asked. "A life of servitude or death?"

"I'd say it was death." The answer was merely a reflex. But I thought about my own reaction when I learned I was having a second child I wasn't ready for.

"You could also say that she escaped a fate that would have been worse than death for her," Giusy said. "That she did not have to follow her husband to America and just be a wife again. Here in Sicily she was a healer and a landowner."

"OK. But how did Serafina get the land in the first place?" I tried to get us back on track. "Who was Marco Domenico, the one who allegedly gave her the land?"

Fina reopened the book and carefully searched for an entry.

"Domenico, Marco. Here is his first wedding to a woman named Melina Vitale. I have looked her up. She died very young. And then a second wedding. To a woman named Cettina. And here is his death. He was also young. Forty-five."

"What else do you know about him?"

"He was the mayor. He was a good mayor. He tried to fight for the rights of the village, tried to make the politicians in Palermo tax us less. Worked hard to get running water into the village. From what I have learned he gave Serafina the land. His family was not using it. Some say it was because they were lovers," Giusy explained.

The accusation lingered in the air as Luca appeared with another bottle of wine. He was happy and sweet and oblivious, like a yellow Lab just purchased from a country breeder.

"Enjoy it, beauties," he said as he hustled back to the kitchen to get the dessert.

We ate and drank in silence for a few moments.

"Do you think he was the one who murdered her?" I finally asked. "The mayor?"

Fina looked uncomfortable with the question. "I believe there is a strong chance she was murdered by members of the Cosa Nostra, that she crossed the wrong person. The way she was hurt before she died. It reeks of them."

Luca chose that moment to bring out a sugary sweet black currant granita.

"No matter what I bake, a granita is my favorite dessert," Luca said as I drank directly from the bowl to finish the dregs of the icy sweetness. "Centuries ago, it was made from snow dug up from ditches on Mount Etna, which meant you had to eat it moments after it emerged from the earth. I think about that every time it melts on my tongue."

"You should write a book on the history of Sicilian cuisine," I teased him.

"You should finish licking that bowl," he teased right back.

Luca was blissfully unaware of the gravity of our earlier conversation. He grinned and looked out at the sea. "It is a beautiful day. We could go for a swim."

Giusy and Fina were easily swayed even though all I wanted was for them to keep going, to keep explaining, to tell me more about these women who were left behind. But I wanted other things too, things I hadn't wanted in a long time. I wanted to be close to Luca, if only to smell his skin and stare at his delicious body.

We walked down a dusty path lined by squat, spiny palm trees, prickly pears, and electric-pink-and-purple flowers to the tiniest rocky beach inside a cove hidden by the cliffs, and without giving it a second thought I stripped off my shirt and slid out of my pants. As soon as I stood up in my underwear, I realized I was tipsy, but in a good way. I was squiffy and light, nearly weightless as I let my feet sink into the fine warm grains. A speckled lizard startled as I walked, escaping by skittering over the top of my foot.

The water was sun-warmed and calm, a gap between the tides slowed the waves. I didn't change my pace as I dove beneath them and swam out beyond the small breaks, surprised at how good it felt to be back in the water. How long had it been since I had had a swim? A year? More? The last time was that trip to Rhode Island with Jack, the house in Little Compton, morning swims in the freezing Atlantic, thick-cut greasy bacon and creamy scrambled eggs for breakfast afterward. Sophie burying the two of us in the sand. My tears at the memories mixed with the salty sea. I flipped on my back and floated on the waves letting my ears sink below the water so all I could hear was the pulse of the ocean. The past fell away and for the first time since my plane touched down I felt like I was on vacation, like I could relax and enjoy myself.

But suddenly something yanked me violently beneath the surface. The darkness swallowed me. I couldn't breathe. Salt water poured into my mouth and nose as I tried to kick my way back up. My foot hit something soft, flesh. I could see the sunlight through the surface of the water and I flailed toward it, finally breaking through, gasping, choking.

I was alone. No sign of who or what grabbed me, and I wondered if maybe I was losing my mind. But then a head of dark hair broke the surface, blood darkening the water around us. It was Luca, red gushing from his nose and I realized that nose was what connected with my foot down below.

"*Mi dispiace. Mi dispiace.*" Luca kept apologizing.

"What the hell was that?"

"I am so sorry. A joke. It was only a joke. I thought you heard me coming. That you knew I was messing around."

He cradled his battered face with his hands as his legs paddled furiously beneath the surface.

"I didn't hear you."

"I know that now."

"You can't pull a person under the water like that. I thought I was going to drown."

"I am very sorry."

"Your nose," I said, softening.

"It is fine. You didn't kick me that hard."

But I knew that I did. He was being kind. Still, I didn't know why he thought it was OK to sneak up on me and yank me below the surface. Was it a silly flirty prank or something more treacherous?

I looked back at the shore and realized we were further out than I thought. The current must have been strong.

"We should go back. Are you sure you're OK? Can you swim back?" I asked him.

Luca was sheepish, embarrassed. "I am fine. I am so sorry that I scared you. That was not my intention. I-I'm . . ." He was stuttering. "I'm clumsy."

That was the last word I would have used to describe him after watching him in his kitchen.

"Andiamo!" I started swimming back to shore, long, strong strokes. It was Aunt Rose who taught me to swim. Or rather we taught one another. No one ever bothered to teach her as a child, and in her seventies, she finally decided to learn, taking Carla and me to the county pool. The three of us started out with fat orange flotation devices strapped to our biceps. Rosie laughed the entire time, even as she struggled to stay afloat while Carla and I took off in a furious doggie paddle. But once Rose got the hang of it she never stopped, even joined the Scranton synchronized swimming team for ladies over eighty, the Chicks with Kicks. They came in second in the seniors national tournament a decade ago with a routine set to Prince's "Let's Go Crazy." When Rose did something she did it with every ounce of her body and soul.

Giusy and Fina had never made it into the sea. They were laughing their asses off when I returned to the beach, clutching one another and the bottle of orange liquor. I could see where the day was heading, and I wasn't into it anymore. The water sobered me up and I didn't want to drink myself senseless.

I asked Fina if I could drive her car up the mountain and pick the two women back up in the morning. She told me not to bother to come back down. They would find their way home. I was off the beach before Luca returned. He was still tending to his nose, or his pride, out beyond the waves.

My butt squelched into the driver's seat as my hair dripped a puddle around me. The sun was starting to slip closer to the horizon as I headed back to the mountain. I'd never felt less secure, but I also hadn't felt this alive since I found out we had to shut down the restaurant.

You notice things while driving that you don't see while being driven. I had the sudden urge to turn into each gravel tributary of the main road just to see what I would find. On the way up the mountain, I spied a sign I hadn't seen on the drive down—PUGLISI OLIO D'OLIVA BIOLOGICA. This must be it, the farm adjacent to my family's land. I pulled the deed from my pocket and examined the hand-drawn sketch of the area to determine I was right. Our land was the next parcel.

I parked when the shoulder of the road widened and walked along the fence line until I found a break, unsure where the Puglisis' land ended and ours began. I wondered when I began to think of it as "ours" anyway. There was a gap in the barbed wire fence that I thought I could shimmy under, next to a weather-beaten shrine to the Virgin Mary. She was a blue woman in a blue box, the paint peeling off her skin and face, her feet perched on what appeared to be a full moon. A lipstick stain graced her foot, the imprint of a mouth. It looked fresh.

I hesitated for a moment. It wasn't like me to wander onto

private property, but my curiosity outweighed my trepidation. I impetuously ducked beneath the wire, a sharp spur catching the skin above my left eyebrow.

The air was thick with the scent of wild lavender on overgrown terrace paths. An imposing stone tower rose above the trees in the distance, intact but crumbling amid a patch of lush meadow and windblown grass. It was attached to a larger building that was mostly just piles of rubble. Beyond it was a small terra-cotta cottage that blended into the orange brown of the earth. I approached the structures. There was no door on the tower, just a human-size hole in the ancient stone wall leading to a cool bare room with a dirt floor and a spiral of stairs going up to the top. I climbed without thinking. At the top of maybe a hundred stairs there was a waist-high wall that I leaned against while drinking in the view of the village; the mountain on one side and the endless expanse of pastures filled with a profusion of rollicking wildflowers painting a path to the sea on the other. The setting sun above the water turned the sky a chaotic swirl of pinks and purples and the air had a gauzy haze to it. You didn't even need to squint to make it the most beautiful scene in the world.

This tower was the highest structure for miles, and I felt both exposed and powerful. What if a small part of this sunburnt land was mine? I didn't need much, definitely not an entire farm, just a small patch of earth overlooking the mountain. I pictured Sophie here, running wild, always barefoot, whining in an Italian singsong for more gelato. The thought of Sophie had me dialing Jack's number. It rang this time, but he ignored my call. This was the longest I'd ever gone without hearing my daughter's voice. I didn't just miss her. I longed for her awe-filled childlike description of this place where I was standing. This tower would be a castle. The irrigation canals beneath it a moat. She'd be certain that a dragon lived over those cliffs and that the terra-cotta cottage belonged to a fairy. More than anything I missed seeing the world through my daughter's magical eyes.

I made my way down the stairs, out of the tower. I crouched low and dug my fingers into the dirt. I wanted to smell the soil, taste it even.

A large boom, like a thunderclap exploding directly above my head, nearly knocked me flat on the ground. When I turned my head, a snarling dog bared its teeth inches from my face. I scrambled back in horror and saw the animal was at the end of a short chain. There were two men standing there. The one with the dog and another pointing his gun at me, the one he just fired into the air above his head. They murmured back and forth in dialect, their voices low and angry.

It was almost dark. I was so stupid for thinking I could trespass like this. So classic American, never thinking about the consequences of any action on foreign soil. "You idiot," I chastised myself. No one knew I was here. The two people who could possibly vouch for me were miles away and probably heading toward a drunken blackout.

The first man turned his gaze to me and twisted his mouth into a sneer as I stood. He was a head shorter than me. A pair of expensive-looking sunglasses dominated the top half of his face despite the fact that it was nearly dark. His belt spelled out *Armani* over and over again. The bright gold buckle gleamed in what was left of the sun. There was something familiar about him, but I couldn't place it. The other guy was his exact opposite, a string bean with a mighty nose and a mop of hair that kept falling into his eyes in a way that made him look more innocent than he probably was.

"The American. We know who you are." Armani Belt glared at me.

I remembered something Aunt Rose said to me when I started dating in high school. "Men are easy to manipulate. You just have to know when to play the Madonna, when to play the whore, and when to play the broken bird. There was really only one part I could play. I thought hard about how to phrase what I needed to say in Italian.

Mi dispiace molto. Mi sono persa. I am so sorry. I am lost.

Per favore aiutami a tornare in paesa. Please help me to get back to town.

I begged and cast my eyes to the ground. The small one took pride in his appearance. If the belt weren't enough I could tell from the shine of his impractical loafers. The other one wore tight acid-washed jeans with dirty old Reeboks.

My eyes fixed on the gun dangling against his thigh. He kept tapping the barrel against his leg. Tap, tap. Tap, tap. I backed away slowly. He spoke in English.

"Why did you come here?"

"I'm lost. I was just taking a walk. It was so pretty. I wanted to see the tower up close."

"You shouldn't be here." I got the sense he didn't just mean here, on this land. He meant here in Caltabellessa. In Sicily.

"I'm a tourist on vacation. Please let me get back to town. My husband is waiting." News spread fast in this place, and they must have known I was here alone. But maybe they'd believe that my husband had only recently arrived, that I had a man waiting for me, a man who would come looking for me if I went missing.

I inched backward. "My car is right there," I said. "I am so, so sorry. I did not know I couldn't walk here." They made no move to stop me and I kept going, not taking my eyes off them. One step at a time.

"Have you been on our land before?" the little one suddenly

barked as he took off his sunglasses. When I met his eyes, I realized why he looked familiar. He was Giusy's cousin, the one from the restaurant the other night, the one she described as one of the biggest Cosa Nostra in town, the one with the large ears and the little dick. His voice was low and rough.

I didn't let on that I recognized him, that we would have any possible connection. I shook my head. "No. No. This is my first time here. Like I said. I was only passing by and now I need to get back to my husband. My husband is waiting for me." I'd never said the word *husband* so many times in such quick succession, not even when I had an actual husband. But here the word felt like a necessary shield.

They let me continue until my back pressed against the barbed wire fence and I could feel the sharp spikes digging into my spine. They approached me again. I could feel the dog's breath on my bare legs. Either man could reach out and grab me by the hair or strike me in the face.

"That is not your car." The tall one pointed over the fence.

"It belongs to Fina, the police officer."

"We know." He flicked his hand in a little shooing motion toward the ground. "Go."

The last thing I wanted to do was lie face down on my belly and shimmy under this wire, but they were giving me the option to escape, no matter how humiliating, and I had no choice but to take it. I tried to squirm my way through the barbs as quickly as I could, aware of my shorts sliding up the backs of my thighs and the men laughing. But once I was through, blood dripping down the backs of my legs, they made no further move to chase me. I didn't turn back again as I walked to the car, but I heard one of them grumble at my back. He said it in English to make sure I understood.

"Women like you disappear every day here."

FOURTEEN

_____

SERAFINA

I woke to the sound of women's voices all around me. They'd been coming and going since Paola drove me as far as she could up the hill to Rosalia's and then carried me the rest of the way.

"She is coming around," I heard the old woman announce as I tried to open my eyes. My entire body ached. When I tried to sit up a sharp pain stabbed me in the side, reminding me of Carmine's boot to my ribs.

"Be still, my girl," Rosalia whispered. I kept my head on the pillow and looked around the room. They were all there: Paola, Gaetana, Saverina, Leda, Tonina, Ninetta, Vincenza. Only Cettina was missing. Everyone sat around the old wooden table sipping from glasses and mugs, their faces stoic.

"We were so afraid for you," Paola said.

"Thank you for getting me here." I coughed out the words. It was not easy to breathe, but there was no blood.

"Who did this to you?" Paola blurted out. What was safe to tell her or to tell these women now? And why wasn't Cettina here? What did she know about what her brother had done to me? So many questions swirled through my mind. Chief among them was whether I would put my friends in danger if I told them what really happened. So I just shook my head. "Could I have some water?"

Rosalia lifted a glass of cool liquid to my parched lips. My intestines clenched in pain after I swallowed but I took it all.

"Three of your rib bones are broken," Rosalia explained. "And there is a nasty gash on your head, but I stopped the bleeding." She rose and fetched more water from the pitcher and looked me straight in the eye as I began to drink. "Did you fall?"

I knew what she was doing. She had always known things she could not know and now she wanted to protect me from revealing too much.

"I fell."

"Donkey shit," Paola said. "You didn't fall."

"I fell," I insisted, staring into Rosalia's eyes to search for more words. "I was birthing a foal, the mother was in pain. She kicked me in the ribs, and I fell backward onto a rock and hit my head." The old woman gave me this story, planted it in my head. I was certain of it.

———

Carmine went missing after the day he attacked me. And it was a long time before he would tell anyone of my involvement in the money man's death, a long time before he would assign me the blame.

I rested for a week and then went about my life. My bandaged ribs ached with every movement, but the bruises were hidden by clothes and they would heal in time. The missing patch of hair on my scalp disappeared beneath my scarf and I tended to the wound as best as I could late at night so the children wouldn't see it.

I waved to Marco on my way to the market one morning. He

appeared restless, uneasy. His lips parted as if he wanted to speak, but he stayed silent as I passed.

It was a surprise when there was a knock on my door later that evening, well after my boys were in bed. I was stretched out on the rug reading in front of the fire, a novel that Maestro Falleti had slipped me, something by a woman named Elvira Mancuso. A woman writer! *La Maestra Annuzza*, the story of a woman who chooses to forgo marriage to become a teacher. It read to me like a fantasy, and I was so absorbed in the story that the knock on my door startled me before sending a rush of adrenaline through my veins. I feared it was Carmine, or maybe the Black Hand back from the dead. I did not want to answer it, but a knock this late could also mean that there was a medical emergency, that someone, most likely a woman or a child, needed me. I pulled myself away from the warmth of the fire and glanced in the corner to make sure I had a bag packed with medical supplies. Then I wrapped my fingers around the handle of the carving knife I had left on the counter after preparing dinner.

Panic rose in my breast. I kept the knife hidden behind my back as I went to the door, gripping it harder as I peered through the tiny peephole.

"Marco?"

I ushered him through the door, taking care to look down the street for gossiping mouths. It was a Saturday night and laughter still rang off the stone walls from the piazza several blocks away, but our street was blessedly empty.

Marco gently gripped my waist, his hands brushing against the many bandages binding my wounds beneath my thin linen nightgown.

"Who hurt you?" he asked as I winced at his touch.

"Who told you?"

"Cettina. She has worried herself into a fever about it."

I wondered who had told her and why she hadn't come herself.

It was as if Marco read my mind. "She heard it from Rosalia this morning when she took Liuni there. But she's worried you must hate her now and she was afraid to come. It was Carmine who did this to you?"

I shook my head.

"You were on his land. You were with Cettina when he called for you."

That day at Cetti's home, the two of us laughing at her kitchen table, seemed very long ago.

Marco was insistent. "There was no injured horse, Fina."

Another shake of my head. But who was I protecting with my silence? It was the dead man I was most afraid of, the one with the powerful bosses. What would Carmine tell those bosses? Who would he blame when they asked their questions?

I answered Marco's question without answering it.

"I could never hate Cetti."

"You are more her blood than her brothers."

But this wasn't true. Blood was blood and nothing was stronger.

"Tell Cetti I will come see her tomorrow. I am fine. Thank you for coming here to check on me, but you should get home."

Neither of us moved.

"Your head is bleeding," he said faintly.

I cursed under my breath. The cut kept opening up and I had not been able to make it back up the mountain to have Rosalia stitch it for me.

"Can I help you?" he asked, and I said yes because I was so tired, and I needed another set of hands and eyes. I got the antiseptic and clean bandages from my bag and sat in the kitchen.

"You will need to tell me what to do."

His hands on my scalp were tender as he parted my hair to expose the gash made when Carmine ripped out the strands. I knew it was ugly and filled with pus. Before I could think, he went to get a warm washcloth and was cleaning the area around the wound. I could hardly feel the pain, my mind focused instead on his fingers massaging the place where my shoulder met my neck as his other hand cleansed my head.

"After the water you'll need to sterilize it with the alcohol," I whispered. "And then use the needle to stitch the skin together. If you can't, do not worry. Reapply the bandage and I will take care of it in the morning."

He pulled in a deep breath. "I can do it."

His hands shook as he threaded the needle through my skin. Stitches are not so difficult if you are used to sewing and mending the way all of us women have done since we were little girls. But a needle seems so small and useless in a man's big clumsy hands. Yet Marco managed to do what he needed to do. I explained how to reapply the bandage and then I rose to inspect his work in the glass of the window. It wasn't as good as what I could have done for myself, but it was still better than I expected. I knew he was more shaken over the blood and the needle than he would care to admit aloud.

"Thank you," I said.

"I am in awe of the work you do," he said.

"Thank you, not everyone is. But you know that already." A part of me wanted to tell him everything that happened to me on that farm.

"I thought I was going to die." That was all I needed to say, and he understood. He did exactly what I wanted him to do, which was wrap his arms around me. I hadn't realized how much I needed to be held and comforted until that very moment.

I was the one who kissed Marco first. I tipped my face up to his, ugly tears still streaming down my cheeks as I found his lips with mine. He kissed me back as I had known he would ever since that day we drove to Sciacca together and maybe even before that. My hands found their way into his thick hair. I'd imagined this moment before and yet nothing in my imagination matched what it felt like to have his lips pressed hard into mine, to feel his hands grip my body with a desperate need.

My children were asleep in the other room. I did not forget that. It was as though my brain were split into two parts, the mother and this woman who was being touched and desired.

We separated after only a few minutes and stared at one another. Maybe it wouldn't go any further, maybe we would simply press our lips together forever until the devil himself exposed us. But I wanted more. I wanted to feel him against me and inside me. It had been so long since my body was mine and mine alone to do whatever I wanted with. It had belonged to my husband and my children and my patients, but never to me and never to a man I truly desired as a grown woman.

I searched Marco's face for guilt or shame, but there was nothing but care and desire.

"Should I leave?" he asked, his voice uncertain.

"You should."

I kissed him again, opening my mouth and letting my tongue meet his. It lasted longer this time, both of us losing ourselves in the moment. He kissed differently than Gio, surer of himself, confident and strong where Gio was always fumbling like a boy. Marco scooped me into his arms, careful with my broken body, and carried me over to the floor in front of the fire. I groaned into his ear as his hands roamed over my body, my hips, the softness of my belly. He stopped just shy of my breasts and I placed my own hand over his and guided it where I wanted him to touch me, laying his palm flat against my nipple, needing his mouth to follow.

"I've wanted to do this for so long," he whispered into my neck.

"Me too," I managed through lips desperate to be kissed again.

A sound. A bump in the other room. I sat up so quickly that a sharp pain shot through my side. Marco was already on his feet and back in the kitchen, as quick as a wild cat. I hoisted myself onto a chair and into a more respectable position, listening to the sounds of the house. There was only silence.

But that bump, whatever it was, made me imagine my boys walking out of their room to find their mother sprawled in front of the fireplace, just inches from where they ate their meals, entwined with a man who was not their father.

"You should go," I said to the floor.

"I should go," he replied out the window, not looking at me either.

I stood and walked over to him, turned his face to mine. "Thank you for coming. Thank you for helping with the bandage. Tell Cettina I will be by in the morning with pastries and gossip."

I placed a hand on the small of his back to usher him over to the door and gave him a nudge. He was nearly out when I stopped him and handed over a bundle of mortadella and cheese to take home to his wife. "In case anyone wonders why you came. You were picking up a gift for my friend."

He took the package and, along with it, my hand. I worried he would kiss me again, and if he did I knew that despite this being my best friend's husband, despite what people would say, despite my own marriage vows and my children so nearby, I would not be able to stop. I would drag him back to my small room at the top of the stairs and never let him leave my bed.

"I do not regret it" was all he said, clutching my fingers and then brushing his lips over my knuckles before he walked out the door.

"This can never happen again," I whispered to his back. I knew he heard me, but I also knew that my words were wishful thinking. Of course it would happen again. We'd started something neither of us could undo.

FIFTEEN

SARA

I parked Fina's car outside the city walls and stumbled toward the hotel, sneaking glances behind me as I approached the medieval gate. Did someone follow me? There was no one in the lot, nothing at all except an overflowing dumpster, a few cars, and a mangy calico cat missing a leg.

I wanted to crash hard into my bed, but something made me pause next to the empty front desk of the hotel, at the door leading to Giusy's private residence. I grabbed the knob without thinking about it, assuming it would be locked, but the metal of the old brass turned easily beneath my palm.

Outside the hotel walls, a dog yapped, a baby yelled, a young woman shouted for her friends to join her for drinks. Sounds of the town awakening for the evening. Part of me expected Giusy to materialize as I waltzed into her home, but no one appeared to reprimand me. I flinched as I flicked on the lights, mistaking a coatrack for a tall, reedy man. My nerves were as taut as well-tuned guitar strings. Things could have gone much worse for me down in the olive grove. The adrenaline had finally drained down to my toes, leaving only a residue of exhaustion blanketing my entire body.

Giusy was keeping secrets from me. She should have told me her cousin owned that land. That much I knew. I pulled the handle of a drawer, which meant I was fully committing to snooping. It was stuffed so full of crumpled receipts that it opened only halfway and I shoved it closed again. Perfectly sharpened knives lined the back wall of the kitchen on a magnetic strip. I could see my reflection in the blades, dried blood dripping down the top of my forehead onto my cheek. The gash was gnarly enough that I should have felt more pain. I reached behind me and touched the sticky warm blood still coating the backs of my legs. I had to clean myself up.

There were no paper towels anywhere in sight. I looked below the sink but found only bleach and a gallon of white vinegar. Aunt Rose used to tell me that white vinegar could clean anything. She was right, but it also made everything smell like a sad desk salad. I went into the bathroom to wash up instead and wiped the blood away with some rough toilet paper that felt like sandpaper. The wound on my head was much bigger than I thought and was going to need some kind of Band-Aid to stop the bleeding. Surely Giusy had to have a first aid kit around for guests. I wandered up the narrow stairs to the bedrooms and let myself in to what I assumed was Giusy's room. A massive four-poster king-size bed dominated the modest space. Brightly colored clothes littered the floor like spilled Skittles.

A framed photo on her dresser caught my eye. It was the only one in the room. Giusy and Fina, their arms wrapped around their sun-kissed shoulders. Each of them beaming into the camera. They were clearly close, but what did this photo in Giusy's bedroom mean? Were they simply friends? Were they lovers? It felt like another mystery Giusy was keeping from me.

Every other inch of her dresser was covered in expensive makeup that I figured she stole from her guests. MAC lipsticks, Chanel eye pencils in every color of the rainbow, Yves Saint Laurent powder at least two shades too light for Giusy's skin. A part of me adored the idea of her pocketing these treasures that no one would ever truly miss but that she would covet. It also reminded me that she was a thief. An unwrapped Band-Aid curled among the detritus, along with a wrapped tampon and a half-empty dial of birth control pills. One Band-Aid wouldn't be enough, so I scanned the surface for another and noticed the end of a large one being used as a bookmark in a leather-bound book. The cover of the book was a deep bloodred, faded, scratched, mottled, and pockmarked with oil and water stains. It reminded me of the church registry, only smaller. Folded pieces of white paper fluttered to my feet when I picked it up. When I looked at the floor, I saw my own face staring up at me, a printout of the cover of *Philadelphia* mag. The queen of meat. The whole story was there, as well as every review of La Macellaia ever written, from the smallest blogs to the three-bell review from Craig LaBan in the *Inquirer*. There was even the Instagram account of the influencer who complained that once the restaurant expanded I didn't come out of the kitchen and greet the diners enough. It was highlighted where she called me an uppity upstart with a stick in my ass. The words on the pages blurred and then slowly came back into focus like a kaleidoscope being turned too quickly. Giusy had also printed out an online real estate report for our row home with the estimated price and square footage. There was a map with the location of Sophie's school and another of Jack's office. A wild rage rushed through me even though all of it was publicly available in a deep-cut Google search. I felt exposed. Filleted.

My hands trembled when I opened Giusy's diary to where the

Band-Aid was lodged. The lines were filled with tiny tight script. Curiosity replaced some of my unease. A bunch of pages had been ripped out, leaving ragged edges inside the margins.

I stopped at a date—1924. There was no way this book belonged to Giusy.

I flipped backward to 1918. Finally, I made it to the first page. Her name was written on the inside cover.

Goddamn it, Giusy. As usual she was so many steps ahead of me. Of course she knew much more than she let on about everything I was here to learn. I traced my fingertip, still wet with my blood, along the name.

Serafina Forte.

———

There are stories we tell about women. The same stories get retold over and over with different characters in different times, but all containing striking similarities. The story I knew about my family's matriarch was the story of a saint, a martyr, a mother, a wife. A stock character, really. A duty-bound woman who waited patiently for her wandering husband. How many of those kinds of women populate history books and great novels? A sexless being, free of passion. She was a vessel of purity who bore and raised strong children. For generations, we passed down the parts of her that the storytellers found appealing.

But none of that was true. Or all of it was true, but it was only part of her story.

These myths rarely define a woman by what she does or produces or how she contributes to the world. What really defined Serafina? Before I began reading her diary, I tried to drop myself into her life a hundred years ago. It wasn't so hard since, for the most part, this village remained largely unchanged. At first, I imagined her as incredibly lonely with her husband far away in *la Mérica* as she wrote it. But once I began reading, I saw no trace of loneliness in her words. She wrote in dialect, which I discovered was much easier to read than to understand when someone was speaking. Her diary revealed a life full of friends and work. She mostly described the things she did to heal people, a part of her life that no one in my family had ever talked about. She delivered babies, both human and beast. She healed burns and scars, strange diseases. She wrote down recipes for ointments or tinctures. There was a list of ten children, none of them her own, who had been lost to a particularly violent strain of the flu.

The words she used to describe her passion for healing tugged at something in me. She loved her work as much as I had loved mine. Her pride was palpable in every sentence.

I collapsed to the floor in awe the first time I held the small frame of the infant as it gasped its first breath. I shouldn't be allowed to do this, I thought. I don't deserve this honor.

It's how I always felt about feeding people, about nourishing them.

And then there was Marco. I blushed when I read the passages about Marco. They were imbued with a passion that Serafina never once used to describe her husband in the one or two lines where she wrote of him at all. Gio, as she called him, was nearly a ghost in her story. I could picture Marco from Serafina's many descriptions— his raven-black hair, his broad chest, thick lips. It was more than that though. It was his kindness that truly stood out, the things he did to protect his people. He refused to tax the citizens of Caltabellessa at the rates Palermo asked for. He found ways to get excess food stores to the poorest among them. According to Serafina, he wrote long letters to the husbands who went to America reminding them to send money home to support their families.

And yet despite what Giusy had told me about Serafina being an adulteress, there was no proof in Serafina's written words of her actually committing to anything besides a fantasy. But, there *were* pages missing, ripped violently from the worn leather binding.

The most striking entries were the ones about her friendship with a woman she referred to only as C., about the intense love and devotion she felt for the other woman. Their friendship was a refuge of care and support, salted through with moments both tender and violent. Serafina wrote of pulling C. out of her young husband's grave as C. sobbed that she would rather be buried alive with his corpse than live without him. C. was there for the birth of all of Serafina's children, sleeping in her bed to care for her and the babies in the postpartum weeks. My only parallel to that kind of devotion was what I felt for my sister, or for Aunt Rose. I'd worked so hard to be successful in a world dominated by men that meaningful connections with women fell by the wayside. I'd never had many close girlfriends, something I regretted only now, as a grown woman, when I could use more witnesses and confessors to assure me I hadn't made all the wrong decisions.

As I devoured Serafina's moments of joy, as her words turned her into flesh, I tried not to think about what else I knew about her, about the police report detailing her untimely end. Her neck would be tied to a stake, her bones would be shattered, her skin would be slashed. I tried to keep those images out of my mind, but it was impossible. The end of her story haunted every page.

———

When I woke up the next morning the diary was splayed open on my chest. I tucked Serafina's book in between my mattress and the box spring and headed down to breakfast.

In the dining room Giusy appeared in front of me with a steaming cappuccino and a slightly amused expression on her face. She leaned in and kissed me on both cheeks. Her easy intimacy disarmed me.

"You slept in," she said.

"You must not have slept much."

"I do not need more than a few hours. *Il mattino ha l'oro in bocca.*"

"The morning has gold in its mouth?" I translated the jumble of words.

"How do you say in English? It is like the importance of waking up early to catch the worm."

"Yeah, but the worm makes sense."

"It's disgusting. Wouldn't you rather have gold in the mouth than a slimy filthy worm?" She laughed, baring all her teeth.

I looked at her carefully, wondering when she returned from Luca's restaurant and if she noticed that I had been in her apartment. If she missed the diary she didn't let on. She looked unaccountably no worse for the wear. In fact, she was fresher than ever. Her skin a little rosier, her hair a wild mane of sandy beachy curls, a wide smile on her lips. Did she get laid last night?

"Are you going to go to Palermo to deal with your passport?" she asked, taking a sip from my coffee cup before handing it to me.

"Yeah. I'm gonna leave after I eat something."

"I wish I could come with you, but I have another couple checking in any minute. It is busy for us. Five guests. That's the most I will ever have in a hotel of ten rooms. You see why the hotel does not work for me. I want to burn it all to the ground."

"You could do that. Burn it down." I had no doubt that she could and she would.

"Then I'd be poor and homeless. Don't think I haven't thought about it. There is a bus that you can take. They leave from Sciacca but you can take the taxi from right outside the city wall to Sciacca and make the late-afternoon bus and be in Palermo tonight."

"Thanks." I sipped the cappuccino. It was perfect.

"While you're gone, I'll find out more about when the town council will meet to discuss your property."

I had so much to confront her about: the diary, her cousin owning the land next our family plot, her weird dossier on me.

But before I could say anything the German husband beckoned Giusy to their table with a guttural grunt and she swished away to attend to them.

My fingers fluttered up to the Band-Aid on my head. Giusy hadn't mentioned it. Could someone already have told her how I hurt myself? Her cousin? I began to walk over to her to ask all the things but then I saw a new couple walk through the front door and into the lobby and I knew Giusy had no more time to spend on me.

Xanax helped to quell the tightness in my chest and I felt lighter as I packed a bag for my journey. Momentum will do that to you. The potential for money and security will do that to you. I threw in a pair of jeans, a couple of tank tops, a bikini, because why not. Maybe I would go to the damn beach and try to enjoy myself for a couple of days. I considered bringing the diary along for safekeeping but decided it would be safest if it stayed tucked under my mattress.

I jumped as the church bells in the town square ushered in a new hour and suddenly I was eager to get out of this village where everyone kept reminding me to watch my back.

On my way to find Caltabellessa's one taxi driver I wondered if I could make my life slightly easier and borrow Fina's car again. I turned to head back to the hotel to find Giusy when I saw a familiar face walking toward me.

His smile widened with recognition.

Luca.

SIXTEEN

SERAFINA

1924

I was the last to hear about Paola's death.

I had been away from the village caring for a young mother who was infected with a sickness of the lungs. Cettina was kind enough to watch my children while I was away. The sick woman's family was very rich and their home was close to the sea.

I slept for five nights in the servants' quarters to avoid too much exposure to the germs while I spent the days preparing tonics and applying menthol salves to the woman's body.

When I returned to Caltabellessa Paola's name was on everyone's tongues, the gossip thick and chewy as lard.

Word had come from *la Mérica* that her husband, Carmelo, had taken another wife in New York City. The guileless coward told her nothing of this. Carmelo's letters home, always accompanied by a portion of his wages, had been as officious and polite as ever.

But then three days ago Paola, our beloved baker, my savior that day on the farm, was abruptly informed by his mother that her husband had replaced her. Carmelo had written to his mamma and asked her to deliver the news. I could imagine the anger raging in

Paola's veins. This situation was, according to her mother-in-law, Paola's fault. Her husband alleged that the last time he visited Sicily, an event that occurred more than three years prior, Paola had been increasingly cold to him. That she refused to drink from his glass at meals or to share food from his plate. This was evidence of a detachment that could only be attributed to Paola finding affection elsewhere and her husband more or less accused her of adultery, though he didn't explicitly name a paramour. What was the most devastating to Paola, in addition to his lies, was his request that his two sons be sent to him to be raised by his new wife. He argued, again only to his mother, that Paola was unfit to continue to raise them in her "wild" state. His letter was incredibly civilized and rational. For him, it could be. He could accomplish all that he wanted through his mamma, never returning home to clean up his mess. Paola would be left with nothing, with less than nothing— no husband, no children, and no job. His mother was instructed to sell off the bakery.

Two nights later, believing that her honor was forever tarnished by meaningless gossip and accusations from an ocean away, Paola walked to the top of the cliffs above the village and stepped off the highest peak. Her body was half eaten by wild animals by the time she was discovered the next morning.

I wished Paola had waited even one more day, that she had confided in the rest of us women. I had to believe that despite the rumors we would have found a way to help her.

It was Cettina who told me the news when I returned from the seaside to reclaim my children. She delivered it in an impassive tone that was completely unlike her.

"She betrayed her husband," Cettina said simply at the end of the story.

"Did she?" I pushed her. "I have never heard of Paola being with another man. And what man would she be with? There are no men here."

"There are men in Sciacca who come up here. Men pass through all the time. She was always down there fetching her supplies. Remember what she said about looking at the handsome fishermen at the port after Stefano Parlate's funeral?"

"She was joking. It is not possible. She has not asked me for anything to protect against pregnancy," I said, feeling like even that was a betrayal to reveal. But you can't betray the dead. And besides, it was true. Other women had asked me for protection, and I never breathed a word of it to anyone. I would keep their secrets because it was not my place to judge how a woman wanted to safeguard her body. Maybe they *were* committing adultery, maybe it was a fear of rape, a fear that was very real when there were less men of a certain age around to protect us from itinerant travelers. I had also helped several of the left-behind wives eliminate pregnancies while their husbands were away. Even then, I never asked questions. "Paola was not the kind of woman to stray. She works hard and raises her children, takes care of her crippled mamma. She bore her load with the patience of a donkey."

"Even the donkey is an animal prone to the basest of instincts. Why would she have killed herself if she were not guilty?" Cettina countered.

"How can a woman ever prove her innocence?" I asked. I hated arguing with Cettina about anything, but especially about something so close to my own sins. I often worried she could reach into my head and pull out the terrible things I had done, the things I couldn't stop doing.

I had met with Marco at least once a month since that night he had stitched my head. Always outside of town. It was often during the daytime, when we both had excuses to be away. From that very first night, I had known it would happen again. It felt inevitable, which didn't make it any less wicked or any less desirable.

We said it would be the last time every time, always knowing we were lying. The first time we were truly entwined took me completely by surprise. Marco was a kind and generous lover in a way I didn't know was possible. Being with him never felt like an obligation. He was as enchanted by me as I was with him.

How did I feel sitting with Cettina, my best friend in the entire world, a woman I loved more than my own sister, my own mother? My mind twisted itself into knots to justify my actions. Marco told me again and again that he and Cettina had not been together in that way.

Cettina had told me herself that she had no interest in sex, that all that mattered to her was raising the children, that it brought her every joy she would ever need. I believed her and for years I understood. I had felt very little in the way of desire for a long time, believing it to be something that had simply passed me by. But Marco's touch changed all that. Where once there was nothing, there grew an all-consuming ache for the next time we could be alone, for the next time his lips would find their way to every unexplored place on my body.

I could justify all of it when I was with him and yet I hated myself when I saw Cettina, which is why I often avoided being alone with her, which made me despise myself even more. There was also the problem with her brother Carmine. He had been missing since the day the Black Hand died on the farm. There were rumors that Carmine was in trouble with the money men, the ones who worked with the man who died in my arms. Cettina had mentioned her brother only once since the incident. It was the day she examined my still-bruised torso and told me she would never forgive him and then spat on the ground next to my feet to seal her promise. But we did not discuss the details of what had happened to me. I still believed I was the only other one who knew about the man's death that day. I thought Carmine had left town not to protect me from what he saw as a crime but rather to protect himself from blame.

My body had healed, but I never left the village alone. I always had a companion on the roads to and from town and often that companion was Marco. We took too many chances, I knew that.

There was the time he rented a boat from the harbor in Trapani and sailed us to a deserted beach on the rocky shore of an island an hour off the coast. "We should stay here forever," he murmured. His lips skimmed my bare shoulder where the skin was raw from the sun and the sand. He laid me down on my back and kissed my breasts, my stomach, each movement deliberate and slow.

Afterward we grilled fish over an open flame before sailing back to the harbor. When we were blown off course and pushed farther and farther out to sea, I did not care if I disappeared or drowned right then and there. I was so happy and content and madly in love.

I never told anyone because the only person I wanted to tell would be the one destroyed by it. So when Cettina asked me why I had been looking so happy I told her it was because I loved the work I was doing. I loved being able to treat an illness, heal a burn, set a broken bone back into place. This was not a lie. I loved my work the way Cettina loved raising her children, and frankly my children too since they spent more time at her house than at mine. My happiness brought her great joy and she listened for hours and hours when I told her of the new advances in medicine I'd been reading about in the journals Marco had gotten for me from people he knew in Palermo and in America. I dreamed of crossing the ocean myself, not to join Gio but to train with a doctor who could teach me more advanced surgeries and cures. It was a ridiculous dream. I told Cettina all about one of my joys and left out the other.

Paola's funeral was small and took place on land outside the village. The church would not bury her in the cemetery. Her mother-in-law refused to bring her boys to witness their mother's final shame. I was the last one to leave the gravesite, the one to close her eyes and kiss her cheeks, to apologize to her for the many ways the world had failed her.

———

When the flu made its way up the mountain, I tried something new to keep us all safe. I asked Leda, the tailor, to help me stitch together old bedsheets and other linens and turn them into tents. I dragged mattresses out of houses and set up an outside clinic on the edge of town where germs could be more easily disseminated by the winds blowing in from the ocean. The fresh air was good for the lungs, and it was easier for me to treat our patients, both young and old, in a single place. The tents protected all of us from the sun and I saw many more people recover than the other villages did. This was when Marco got his idea:

"If you had more space, you could build a real clinic."

"If I had an airplane I could fly to Rome." I gently mocked him the way I always did when he mentioned his big and impossible ideas.

"There is land below the village, the abandoned abbey next to Cettina's family's farm. My family has owned that land for as long as I can remember and we have never used it. There is a building and a well for water and it could be yours to treat the sick outside of town, away from the healthy people. I can give it to you."

"The land where I was . . ." I didn't finish the sentence out loud. The land close to where I was attacked by Carmine.

"Carmine is gone and the land has always belonged to me."

"What would people say about that? About you just giving the land to me," I asked.

"They would say the mayor gave the town doctor a place to treat our people."

"You know I am not a doctor. And that is not what they would say."

"It is what they should say."

"There is a difference between what they would say and what they should. We have been so careful." I said this even though I knew it wasn't true. I kissed him right then as if to underscore my point. We were alone in his car, parked far out on the coast overlooking the sea. It had been longer than usual since our last meeting, and I did not want to be talking. I wanted his hands on my body, his tongue on my skin. We had so little time. But he was insistent.

He knit his brow in consternation. "We can do this. I can do this."

"Gio would never accept the land."

"It would be in your name."

"No one here would accept a woman owning the land."

"I am the one in charge here and I accept it."

I reached over and began to massage the tight muscles on the back of his neck. I ran my other hand across the inside of his thigh hoping to entice him away from this wild plan, but he was undeterred.

"I can make it happen soon."

"It would make people talk about us."

He slammed his hand on the steering wheel so hard I retreated into my own seat. "They talk about everyone. They talked about Paola and look what happened to her. It was a tragedy. We cannot let their talk rule our lives. You can save more people if you have space to do it. It is for the good of the village and for you. I love you. I want you to have this."

It was the first time he uttered those words and I never expected to hear them. I had never heard them from a man's lips, not my father's, not my husband's. I had only heard them from Cettina, who told everyone and everything how much she cherished them.

"I love you too," I whispered. I meant it. I loved him with a ferocity that sometimes burned greater than my love for my own children. I didn't have a choice about loving my children, but my love for Marco was something I chose every day despite the dire consequences. "I love you too." Louder this time. I wanted to shout it.

He turned to me and instead of kissing me he placed his hands on either side of my face, his massive palms covering my cheeks. "I cannot give you everything. I cannot give you all of myself, but I can give you this. Please let me."

What choice did I have? I let him.

SEVENTEEN

SARA

Luca somehow managed to get better-looking overnight. It was almost unfair how attractive he was, an assault on us average-looking people the world over.

"*Ciao*," I managed, my heart stumbling at the sight of him in his white linen shirt tucked into loose khakis, the collar unbuttoned the perfect amount.

"What are you doing up here?" I asked.

"I brought Fina home this morning. She fell asleep at my place. She's a lightweight."

"How old is she? She looked so young to be a cop." And to be Giusy's girlfriend, I thought but didn't say.

"Twenty-one," Luca said. "You can join when you are eighteen here. But she is a baby, yes. I often feel protective of her. I was going to the hotel to get her car keys. Do you have them?"

"I gave them to Giusy," I said.

He paused and glanced away. "I also wanted to say how very sorry I am for what I did to you there in the ocean. I was playing, teasing. I thought you would think it was funny. You seemed so tough. I thought you might just think it was fun. I did not mean to scare you like that."

A smile crept up on my lips. I wanted to ask him what made him think I was so tough, but I knew the answer. I knew what I looked like, how I carried myself. *Philadelphia* magazine had actually called me *the leader of the city's tough new breed of cool girls in the culinary world.* It was because of my tattoos. It was easy to mistake a woman with visible tattoos as both interesting and unapproachable. Cool, even.

For a long time I *was* tough. I did hard things. I pushed myself. Before becoming a mother I took chances. I believed in myself. When had I allowed self-doubt to creep in? The constant uncertainty of keeping a small creature alive was the start. And then losing my restaurant destroyed my confidence and self-esteem. The last time I felt tough and strong was when I stood up to my investors and told them we had to keep paying our employees' health insurance. They essentially told me to find a way to keep our profits in line with our stellar reviews, or else. How could we open another location, how could we franchise, if we didn't make more money? The answer was that we couldn't. Or I couldn't. I accepted defeat. I closed the restaurant. I was tough and then I wasn't. My strong body became a costume, a shell.

Luca was still mumbling in a fairly adorable way.

"I was surprised," I told him. "No worries."

"No worries," he mimicked me in a bad American accent, cocking his head.

"It's like *tutto bene.* All good. So if you brought Fina back, when did Giusy return?"

"Not long after you, actually. She hitched a ride up." This was surprising, and concerning. Could she have been in the house when I was snooping? Watching me?

"What are you doing now?" Luca asked.

"Trying to figure out how to get a ride to Sciacca so I can catch a bus to Palermo."

"I can drive you."

"Oh no. I don't want to be a burden. I was going to see if I could get Fina's keys back maybe and take her car."

"I know that she has plans to be out of town tonight for a meeting so she will need it. Just let me take you," he insisted.

I needed a ride. The town's single taxi was nowhere in sight. Luca was, without a doubt, the sexiest man I had ever seen in real life. Why was I saying no? "That would be great. The Palermo bus leaves Sciacca at four thirty."

Luca stuffed his hands deep into his pockets. "I can take you all the way to Palermo. We aren't open yet. The restaurant. It is still a couple of weeks before the season. I have things I can take care of in the city. I don't mind a drive and I owe you an apology."

"You already apologized."

"A man can always apologize more, can't he?"

"They can. And frankly most of the time they should. But they never do."

"So I'll take you. Are you ready?" he asked.

"As ready as I'll ever be."

"We go."

As we headed to Luca's car, the old man who had sketched my portrait when I arrived strolled out of a grand-looking marble door next to the bakery.

"*Buongiorno, signore*," Luca addressed him.

"*Buongiorno*, Luca," he replied, tipping the brim of his straw hat. I figured he wouldn't remember me, but he turned his warm smile my way and studied my face the same way he did while he was sketching me. "The American Marsala." He made me sound like a special on the menu at the Olive Garden.

A plump woman covered head to toe in white flour emerged from the *pasticceria* and thrust two pastries in Luca's hands without a word before kissing both his cheeks and disappearing back into her shop. The old man said something I didn't catch and pointed to me.

"He drew your portrait?" Luca was surprised.

"He did," I replied. "It was amazing! The best picture I've ever seen of myself." I thanked the man again. He nodded and made a motion with his hands as if to say it was nothing and then he made another gesture like he was brushing the two of us away. Luca kissed him goodbye, and we continued to the car.

"You must save that portrait," Luca said as we walked through the town wall's ancient arch. He pointed me in the direction of a gleaming green Alfa Romeo.

"Oh, I will. I don't think anyone has ever sketched me before."

"It could be worth a lot of money. He doesn't do portraits any-more."

I raised an eyebrow and let out a small laugh. "Is he a famous street artist?"

The car churned up a cloud of dust as we headed out of town. "A famous sculptor. One of the most famous in all of Italy, actually."

"What's he doing here, then?" I regretted the words the second they left my mouth. I sounded like a terrible snob.

"This is where he was born, and he says this is where he wants to die. He bought that house by the bakery, the nicest home in town. Giusy didn't tell you his story when he sketched you?"

I shook my head but remembered the commotion among the crowd in the piazza after he handed me the drawing.

"I will tell you. We have a couple of hours at least."

When we got settled in the car, Luca apologized that he had to take a phone call from one of his suppliers. I shrugged to indicate I got it. Those kinds of calls were once the chorus to all my days. I gazed out at the savage landscape, trying to avoid staring at Luca's profile while he drove despite the constant fluttering in my stomach every time his hand nearly brushed my thigh when he shifted gears. Like him, the car was too gorgeous. His restaurant must have been doing quite well.

He eventually hung up the phone, ignored a sign for the freeway to Palermo, and headed for the sea.

"If you take that road you will go to the town of Marsala. Your last name. Maybe some of your people were from there."

"I have no idea."

"Do you know where the name Marsala comes from?"

I raised an eyebrow. "As far as I know it's just the name of a chicken dish. A way to cover the cheapest, fattiest cut of chicken in flour and wine so it tastes delicious."

Luca proceeded to lecture me. "Marsala comes from the Arabic, Marsa Ali. During the Arab conquest of Sicily the Muslim rulers landed close to here and renamed many villages, including Marsala. Also fun trivia for an American, the name for the village of Corleone was taken from the great Arab military man Kurliyun. A fact that somehow never made it into that famous movie of yours. Are you in a rush?" he asked.

I shook my head. I didn't want to be. I'd been in a rush for the past decade. Right now, driving in a car alongside a boy with no concerns about time had a wonderful teenage quality to it that I didn't experience enough as an actual teenager.

"Tell me the story of the man who drew my picture."

He pulled in a deep and dramatic breath and I appreciated the pageantry. "He was a shepherd boy, very poor. Born after the First World War."

"He didn't look that old."

"He's probably close to one hundred. Our men live forever here. There's something in the olive oil."

"And your women?"

"They die exhausted."

It was meant to be a joke, but it also rang quite true. Luca continued. "From the time Nicolo could walk he cared for the sheep, going up and down the mountain, from dawn until dusk, speaking to no one, communing only with nature is how he tells it. The sheep did not belong to his family. They were owned by much wealthier people. The husband and wife who inherited that land came from Palermo and they were never able to have children of their own. It is said that the rich woman took a liking to Nicolo when he was very small and invited him into their magnificent home to see their paintings and sculptures. In his downtime Nicolo began to whittle pieces of wood that he found on the ground using the dull blade of a carving knife. At first he made sheep and deer and then moved on to human bodies and faces. The things he could do caught the attention of the whole town by the time he was a teenager, but no one knew what to do with him. Here is the thing about Nicolo. He didn't speak, not a single word. The rich woman's husband died, but Nicolo continued to stay with her. His benefactor bought him new tools, the kind he needed to chisel rock and sculpt clay and soon he was creating massive sculptures in her gardens and courtyards. You can see them today. Many of them are in the town and in Sciacca."

"So what happened next?" I asked, riveted.

"The rich woman paid for him to go to the Academy of Fine Arts in Palermo and then he disappeared from here. He went to the mainland and studied with the modern masters and quickly outpaced them. He began showing his sculptures in Florence, Turin, Rome. He traveled abroad. He became very famous and very wealthy."

"When did he come back?"

"When I was a boy. He once told me that he had gotten to see the entire world and that there were many places that were beautiful and broken, many people who were beautiful and broken. But that his home was the only place where he could be both of those things."

"Wait," I interrupt. "When did he start speaking?"

"When he left. He could always speak, apparently. He chose not to. He said he didn't think anyone wanted to hear what he had to say, that he didn't think anyone was listening to him until he became an important man."

"That's sad."

"Now I think he has more power than the mayor, because he has more money than anyone in town even though he never shows it off."

We eased onto another road along the top of perilous white cliffs, plunging into the sea. I wanted to tell Luca a story in return, perhaps about Serafina and the diary I found, but then he motioned down to the sea.

"Would you like to go? Lay in the sand for a while? Take a swim? I will not pull you under. I won't even go into the water. I swear."

I nodded and he slowed to take a sharp turn to the left, onto a road that wound down closer to the water. We went another mile or so.

"Ooooohhh," I suddenly exclaimed. "I want to go there." I pointed in the opposite direction from the sea, at a massive building that I recognized as a Sicilian big-box grocery store called Conad.

"Are you hungry? We can get food from a bar on the beach."

"No, no. I just want to go in and look around if that's OK." How could I have explained it to him? My deep love of grocery stores, especially grocery stores in new places. How they were these fluorescent tinted windows into the everyday lives of the people who lived in a place. I adored strolling through the produce aisles, guessing what was fresh and local and what had to be transported by boat from a continent away. The prepared foods in the deli section told me what busy people bought for a quick meal. A well-manned butcher station showed an appetite for meat in a place. You never saw a smaller butcher station than in a grocery store in Northern California where everyone professed to be more vegan than everyone else. I'd only been out of the country once before this trip, on my honeymoon to Mexico with Jack, but I spent several hours in grocery stores in Cancún and Tulum, reveling at the local delicacies.

"We shall go in," he agreed. "We could make a picnic for the beach." He pronounced it *peek*-neek."

"I'd love that. Meats, cheese?"

"Bread? Wine?"

"All of the above."

Inside the whoosh of the automatic doors, I inhaled the familiar grocery store dry air-conditioning.

"Do you want to find us the snacks?" I asked. "I'm going to look around."

He nodded, hooked a basket around the crook of his elbow, and was gone. A man who could navigate a grocery store on his own without a shopping list would never know how truly sexy he was.

First, I clocked the different flavors of potato chips: flowered mustard, cherry tomatoes, carbonara, pesto! I snatched up a bag of mint and peperoncino, exited the aisle, and returned for the pesto chips, because you truly did live only once.

I was delighted to see cartons of Mugello milk in the dairy section. It was a legend among small dairy farmers in the States. I had it once when a friend smuggled it back from a trip to Florence. Mugello is made exclusively from cows who live in the rolling green pastures around Tuscany and their claim is that happy cows make happy milk, which I completely believe because I also think happy cows produce fattier and tastier steaks. Mugello was the richest and creamiest liquid I'd ever put into my mouth and I wished I could open one and drink it straight from the bottle right in the store, but I controlled myself.

My sense of control disappeared when I reached the aisle with the fig preserves and pistachio cream. I should have grabbed my own basket. By the time I ran into Luca rounding the corner I was cradling an armful of food like it was a lumpy baby and he let out a laugh reminiscent of a delighted five-year-old riding a merry-go-round for the very first time. He'd upgraded from basket to cart, which was now filled with cheeses, cured meats, two loaves of *pane nero di Castelvetrano*, and small containers of delicious things like olives and anchovies.

"Are we stocking up for the week?"

"I cannot help myself," he replied, taking the chips and jars from my arms. "And, it seems, neither can you."

His refusal to let me pay made it all feel like a very comfortable third date even though we'd never been on a first or a second and he was just doing me a favor with this ride. We chattered about various local delicacies on the way to the car and as we drove across the strip of concrete to the sea. The beach was positioned on a spit of land between two massive granite cliffs that rose above the horizon like the jaws of a wild animal. We carried our food in the cloth bags Luca kept in the trunk and made our way along the narrow trail to the water.

"This is one of the most popular beaches in all of Sicily. You can't find a patch later in the summer. It is still early in the season and there are no tourists from up north yet so we will be fine," he told me.

The path led us to an expanse of powdery white sand nestled between the rocks. Jagged cliffs formed a perfect oval of calm sea with languid turquoise waves lapping quietly on the shore. Orange lounge chairs dotted the beach along with bright-red-striped umbrellas. Maybe a dozen families spread out on the chairs and blankets. A group of teenagers had set up camp close to the water, lazily smoking long, skinny cigarettes and lounging in the desultory way of teenagers the world over. A baby howled in demonic despair as its mother left it alone to try to tackle a toddler sibling making a beeline for the waves. The moment we took off our shoes we were approached by a trio of toned young men wearing bright yellow Speedos. They offered us chairs, umbrellas, and a drinks menu. The sand was carpeted in the tiniest perfect pink shells that made a pleasant crack beneath my toes.

"My god, this is the exact opposite of the Jersey Shore," I mumbled as Luca slipped the Speedo-clad beach boys some cash and followed them to a spot that wasn't too close but also not too far away from the water. I excused myself to slip into my bikini. In the bathroom, the mirror reminded me that my boobs still sagged from breastfeeding and my belly would never retain muscle tone again. But the rest of my body was strong from the butchering I used to do and I liked most of what I saw in the reflection.

While I was gone, Luca had prepared a feast on a towel splayed out on one of the chairs. Thin slices of dark bread smothered in the fig preserves were topped with salty anchovies. I brought one to my lips and let the fruit juice and briny oil drip generously down my chin. I could feel Luca's eyes on me, how he liked that I was eating and enjoying the things he'd prepared for me.

He asked me to tell him about myself. His direct questions about my restaurant indicated that he'd already googled me.

I began when I graduated from culinary school and started working in restaurants around Philly. I told him a little about how they exhausted me. How there was so much bullshit and waste and a lack of respect. I left out the fact that the entire culinary school ecosystem and the restaurant world had been a pyramid of misogynies I was always teetering on the top of, trying not to tumble off. I explained how I wanted to be back closer to the source of the food, getting my hands dirty.

"I got a job at the butcher counter at the ShopRite in South Philly and I loved it even though my mom and dad were so pissed that I used my fancy degree to work at the grocery store around the corner. After that I got to apprentice with some incredible butchers on smaller farms here and there. I made less than zero dollars most of the time, but I was happy. And then I got this idea for a whole-animal butcher shop and restaurant in Philadelphia, a place that would only source happy animals, that would make sure to use the entire animal, that would help educate people about where their meat came from. At first, I sold meat out of a trailer at farmers' markets. I also had a grill and I'd make sandwiches and ribs. Once in a while I even did some fancy steaks. That's what people loved. Getting a filet mignon in some church parking lot. I finally got the attention of some investors and then I got to open my own place."

I wanted to end the story there because I wished the story ended there, with everything working out exactly the way that I had planned. Thankfully Luca allowed me to.

"And then you ended up a celebrity on the cover of magazines." He opened the *Spuma* and poured fizzy liquid into two plastic cups. We lifted them in cheers, and I humbly dismissed his comment.

"I'm so far from a celebrity. I was in the right place during the right time for the right story. But tell me more about you."

"Like you, I hated working in other people's restaurants."

"Where did you work?" I expected him to tell me Palermo, or maybe Rome, Florence, possibly as far away as Milan.

"Brooklyn," he said, clocking, and obviously enjoying, my surprise. "I went to New York when I was twenty. We have family there. Everyone here has family there and I moved in with some cousins in Bensonhurst and they told me they could get me a job in a kitchen in Little Italy and I thanked them and then went to find work in a Vietnamese restaurant in Queens. I've been eating and cooking Italian food all my life. I can make a ragù in my sleep. I wanted to eat and cook things I'd never had before. Thankfully the Vietnamese restaurant hired me to wash dishes and then I was a delivery boy and a line cook and they taught me some things along the way. My cousins thought I was a traitor and a weirdo and kicked me out, but the owner let me sleep on a cot in the basement until I was able to rent a room. Then I went to work at a Korean place and an Argentinean steak house and a Ukrainian deli."

240

"You worked your way around the world," I said, impressed and a little envious.

"I did. Via the N train."

"Why'd you come back?"

"I missed home. Italian Americans are different from the people here. So different. I know that we come from the same place and that we are blood, but their idea of being Italian is so strange. It is all based on that movie *The Godfather*, you know."

I nodded as if I had only a passing familiarity with the film, as if my dad didn't make us watch it with him once a year.

"And all my uncles and my cousins in America thought they were tough guys even though they were not in organized crime as far as I could tell. They still talked and walked and bluffed like they were. They were plumbers. All of them. And my uncle made people call him by a ridiculous name, Frankie Meow Meow. He was a grown man who wanted to be called Frankie Meow Meow! And they would introduce me as the '*cugino* from Sicilia' like I was their connection to the Mafia. They have no idea what the Mafia is here or what it means or what they do. At first I tried to tell them about my actual life in Sicily, but that's not what they wanted to hear. It was exhausting. But that wasn't the only reason I came home." He sighed. "I missed my mamma. I missed the sea. I missed how we cook here and how we eat. Everyone ate so fast in New York. They inhaled their food. Except at brunch, when they'd stay for hours and then barely leave a tip. Oh Gesù, the brunch. Everywhere I worked was tormented by it, what will we serve for brunch? Let's make twenty-seven new dishes with eggs. There are never enough eggs. Americans are obsessed with brunch and cooked eggs. I will never understand you."

"I hate eggs. I hate brunch," I declared. "I refused to do a brunch service the first two years we were open because I wanted to spend weekend days with my husband and then my new baby. But my investors eventually told me I was being foolish and irresponsible and I stopped getting to make my own decisions." This was the part I didn't want to talk about. I quickly shifted the subject back to Luca. "When did you come back?"

"Five years ago. I had managed to save a little money working in America and some friends from growing up told me they would invest in a restaurant by the sea if I wanted to cook, and here we are."

I thought about how nice it would be to have friends put up money for your restaurant, instead of a bunch of rich dudes who demanded instant returns. I wanted to hear more, but it was hot and I also wanted to jump in the water and then maybe take a nap. I stood and stretched my arms above my head before pivoting on my heel and running into the sea, stopping right where the waves licked the sand before turning to him.

"Don't chase me this time, OK?"

He obeyed, to my slight disappointment. By the time I got back, he was sound asleep. I ordered myself a negroni from one of the passing beach boys and sipped slowly. This was a perfect day. Like the story I'd told Luca earlier, I wished I could make it end right here, because nothing ever stays perfect.

Luca snored, a reassuring flaw. He also drooled a little in his sleep and his elegant Roman nose was slightly crooked when viewed from above. His body was compact, but he had an exquisite build, like God was showing off his geometry skills. The pleasant zip of the first negroni compelled me to order a second while I took him in.

I hadn't slept with anyone since Jack asked for a separation. And before Jack there were only a couple of guys. Prior to meeting my husband, I mostly loved men who would never love me back. I started to think about the other Serafina, about how she married young, about how she met Marco later in her life after getting married and having her children, how she might have found passion when she was least expecting it.

Luca suddenly startled awake and swiped the drool from the side of his mouth. He'd caught me staring hungrily at his body.

"I want to kiss your face." He said it so simply, like it was already an inside joke between the two of us.

I wanted it too. I wanted to taste this man who had been feeding me delicious things. I wanted to put my hands on *his* body. Maybe it was the heat, or the gin, or the sight of his perfectly bronzed skin shining in the sun. I leaned down and placed my lips on his, nudging his mouth open with my tongue. He didn't hesitate for even a second even though we were on a public beach surrounded by surly teenagers and young mothers. He sat up and gripped the back of my neck with a force that surprised me, pulling my body closer to his so that more than our mouths were touching. His broad chest pushed against my breasts. My nipples went hard beneath my bathing suit, and I groaned so loudly that the noise surprised me. I pulled back.

"I will take you somewhere," he whispered. When he stood I followed. We walked past the bathrooms to the sheer cliff walls surrounding the beach. He waded into the water then disappeared below the first wave that crashed over his head. We powered through the breakers until the water went smooth and we were clear of the rocks. Then Luca made a sharp right turn and swam around the steep cliffs. I kept swimming, each movement stoking my desire. The water was cool in all the places where my body was burning. I finally saw a small opening in the rock wall, the tiniest of sea caves.

He looked back at me and gestured toward it with his chin. The passageway was tiny; I had to duck below the water and trust my instincts to keep me moving forward. I was awed as my head broke through the surface, and I wiped the salt water from my eyes. Inside the cave was a cathedral of stone. A hole in the rock somewhere above cast a ray of golden light into the water, turning it a deep emerald. Luca stood on a small patch of sand to my left. The water was quiet, the current and waves stopped by the rock walls, though probably still churning beneath the surface. If I were a religious person at all, this was exactly what I'd want the gates of heaven to look like.

I was barely out of the water before Luca put both of his hands on my hip bones and leaned in to kiss me again, softer and slower this time; his lips fluttered only briefly on mine before they moved back behind my ear and trailed down the side of my neck. His lips went everywhere as his hands reached for the clasp on the back of my bikini.

"Is this OK?"

"Yes," I gasped.

His mouth covered my nipple by the time the fabric hit the sand, his tongue tracing quick and then lazy circles that made me dig my nails into his shoulder blades. He squeezed one breast with his hand while his tongue took care of the other. I didn't want this part to end, but I couldn't wait for the next one to begin. I hooked my thumbs into the top of his bathing suit and pushed down slightly.

"Is this OK?"

"*Sì.*"

I shoved his swimming trunks to his ankles, wanting to take some control, wanting to be a participant instead of a silent bystander.

"Hi," I whispered.

"Hello."

He lay down on the sand. I straddled his hips and slowly lowered myself onto his body, leaning forward to place my mouth on top of his as he entered me. I could feel every inch of him pushing into every inch of me and I couldn't think of anything but falling deeper onto him. He clamped his teeth onto my earlobe.

"I'm close. I cannot help it."

I began to grind my hips faster and harder. I was close too, though I wanted to wait until the last possible second. He moaned and everything inside of me exploded in a hot, blinding pleasure I hadn't allowed myself to feel in way too long. I always thought sex on a beach seemed like a bit much, a romance-novel fantasy that in reality was all sand in unfortunate places. But this experience revised all my former objections.

I collapsed on top of his chest, both of us sweaty and sandy and spent.

He was still inside me when he glanced at his complicated waterproof diving watch. "I wish we could stay here, but I'm afraid the tides are about to come in and this entire cave will be full in a half an hour. Do you think you can swim back?"

"My legs are a little wobbly, but I should be OK."

Going out was harder than coming in. My body was limp from the rush of the endorphins and the current pushing into the cavern had picked up. But I managed to follow Luca into the sunshine and when we got back to the beach it was as we'd left it. No one was at all the wiser about our tryst behind the cliffs. Luca insisted on feeding me again before we got back on the road. He poured two plastic cups full of wine as we finished the bread, the olives, and the cheese. Few things in life are as fundamentally satisfying as good, quick sex followed by a meal of mostly salty cheese. We kept smiling dopily at one another like a couple of teenagers who'd just evaded curfew. The smell of sex still clung to our bodies despite the swim.

We ended up being the last ones on the beach and I could tell the cabana boys were eager for us to leave. Walking down the narrow path to the parking lot Luca's hand found mine. When was the last time I held hands with a man? With anyone besides my daughter? I liked his rough palms, his calluses and scar tissue from kitchen cuts and burns. His hands felt like my own, which had never been pretty or feminine, but had always gotten my job done and served me well.

The parking lot was empty and a part of me wanted him to push his car seats back as far as they could go, so I could climb on top of him again before we headed to the city. I wondered if he was thinking the same thing, because he stopped short about ten feet from the car.

That was when I noticed that both the driver's- and passenger's-side windows had been smashed in. Shattered glass glittered pink and orange on the ground, sparkling in the sunset. A hammer was thrown on the driver's seat, clearly the instrument of destruction, a simple construction tool with a bright red handle and the price tag still attached to the metal head.

"Do you think it was those kids? From the beach?" They had left about forty-five minutes before us, laughing, sun drunk, and silly.

Luca shook his head as he pushed me behind him and then approached the car with the trepidation of someone who thought it might explode right then and there. His entire body had gone rigid, on high alert, as his eyes scanned the concrete lot and the shrubs beyond it.

"It wasn't the kids. Stay here." He walked closer and grimaced when he stroked the side of the car.

"Should we call the police?"

"They won't be much help."

"What about Fina? Let's call her." A part of me felt the same rush and tingling of pleasure I'd felt when we were having sex in that cave, a chemical reaction to the danger and excitement of it all.

"I will. Just wait a second, OK?" Luca ran his hand through his hair and then leaned into the car to grab something from the driver's seat.

"It could have been an accident. A prank that got out of control." I babbled to fill the silence. Luca pulled a piece of paper from the car, cutting his hand on a piece of broken glass in the process. Blood rushed down his forearm. I could tell he wanted to read the note before I could see it, but I wasn't going to let him do that. It was only ten words hastily scrawled in English. A warning for both of us.

Does your wife know about you and the American whore?

EIGHTEEN

SERAFINA

I knew nothing about running a clinic, but time moved too quickly to think about how to do it properly. A new flu took the place of the old one and friends and neighbors fell ill faster than I could help them. The polio virus made its way to us, and then malaria. At first, I felt entirely helpless. I begged Rosalia to come to the clinic to help me, but she no longer had the energy to leave the mountaintop.

I tried new treatments and old treatments. Many things failed, but inch by inch I managed to do some good and we ultimately became successful. What did it matter if the walls of the old abbey were crumbling down around us, and the beds were mere mattresses on the floor? It offered a much-needed space for our villagers to heal and to quarantine away from their families.

There were the usual whispers about Marco giving me the land, but mostly there was relief that we had a place to take the sick and indigent, a place that had been so sorely needed for years. I was joined by two nurses, girls from Palermo Rosalia knew of through an old friend who worked in a hospital there, girls who needed to leave the city. They kept their secrets and I kept mine. I believed the two of them were in love with one another, but they were discreet. I caught only the smallest of intimacies, a hand placed tenderly on a shoulder or hip, a stare that lingered. I never asked them questions and in return they taught me things I could not possibly learn from books.

When I first began caring for patients, I rarely talked of my work in my letters to Gio. I did not think it would interest him, but I also did not truly want his opinion. If I never properly told him, then he could not tell me to stop. Or so went my hopeful logic. He knew about it of course, mostly from his mamma and his sisters, who didn't approve of what I did at first. And then I removed a large goiter from Gio's mamma's neck. For an entire year before that she could not speak and could communicate only through hand gestures and grunts. After she regained her voice, I was in her good graces for the first time since I had stolen her son.

I do not know what she told my husband about my work, but suddenly he started to take an interest in what I did. His letters were never very long. Writing remained hard for him and sometimes his script was barely legible. But one question, the one he repeated often, was easy to make out: "How much is the land worth?" I knew he meant the land with the clinic, not the land with our small house in the village. I did not have an answer because I honestly had no idea, and even though Marco put my name on the deed, the idea of selling it seemed preposterous. But Gio's notes grew more persistent.

"If we sold that land we could buy a home here. You and the boys could come now."

When he first left for New York, all those years ago, Gio said he would work until he made enough money to buy us a real home in Caltabellessa. The plan was for him to return to that home with his pockets full of American coins. But the further Sicily's fortunes fell, the less practical it became to stay, and the dream morphed into all of us eventually meeting him in the States at some uncertain date in the future. He wanted the boys with him. He wanted to put our children in American schools despite the fact that none of them spoke or wrote any English. The last time Gio visited, five years ago, he showed off his English any chance he got, along with his shiny store-bought suits and shoes. He was a new man, more confident than I had ever known him to be, and it could have been alluring if I had any desire left for him. But no matter how hard I tried, I could not conjure longing for my husband.

This was before I had taken up with Marco and I had fulfilled my wifely duties when I needed to during that visit from Gio. He seemed pleased by me. "Maybe we'll finally have a daughter," he said. "I would love to have a little girl." I simply smiled at him as if it were possible, when I knew that I had already taken precautions to prevent it.

I responded to his letters and the queries about the land with stories about the good that my clinic was able to do, about how it had improved outcomes for women in childbirth and made it possible to ease some of the pain of the dying elders. He eventually stopped asking about it but said we would discuss it in person when he returned, though he made no solid plans to cross the ocean. I fell asleep every night worrying that my husband would return the next morning and destroy the life I had come to love.

But years passed and Gio did not return again. Sometimes I fantasized that he had taken another wife like Paola's husband had. I began to conjure entire alternate lives for myself if Gio were to abandon me. He would take my boys for certain, and I would no longer be able to live in the village, but I began to envision a future for myself in another town, or in Palermo. I did not make much money from my work. Poor peasants traded eggs and hens, fish and tomatoes for my services but when I treated the rich I charged them what I was worth and I hid this money away, for what I did not know.

Some days I imagined I would welcome the excuse to abandon my wifely duties, to become someone new no matter the consequences for a woman alone in the world. That world was finally starting to change. I heard stories about female activists on the front lines of the independence movements in Palermo. I'd even read a paper by a woman doctor at a university there.

Of course, there would be no Marco living in Palermo, but in my fantasies of living on my own he somehow made a regular appearance. Sometimes I imagined having the tiniest of apartments where he could visit, and we could spend entire nights together and mornings entwined in a bed all our own.

I was having one of these exact fantasies when Cettina walked into the clinic. Her face was as white as a ghost, her entire body shaking.

"Marco needs you." I tried to hide my concern as I rushed to her and asked what she meant.

"He is ill. He has not been able to get out of bed this week." She managed the words through short, clipped breaths. Her hands fluttered in the air as they always did when she was nervous. "He cannot eat. He is hot with fever; the bedsheets are soaking wet. I told him I would get you and he asked me not to. He said it was nothing, but I know it is not nothing. I need you to come right away."

Cettina's shape, as familiar to me as my own, blurred around the edges as I tried to will the tears from my eyes. I wrapped my arms

251

around her, squeezing her so hard she let out a small cry. I had to steady my nerves before we went to see him. "Let me get you something to drink, my love. You are flushed and clearly exhausted. I will come back up the mountain with you, but I am sure what he has is nothing too terrible." I did my best to try to hide my concern. I had to appear every inch the rational caregiver and not a lover ready to rush to a bedside. I called out to a nurse to bring clean water and a cold towel for Cettina's neck and led her to a bench among the lemon trees outside. I held her tight and rocked her back and forth the way I had done with my babies, pressed my lips into her soft hair. When she was able, I made her drink an entire glass while she gazed out at the land to the south, in the direction of her family's farm. I promised we would go to Marco as soon as the glass was empty. Her breathing slowed slightly, and she tried to focus on something else to regain her strength.

"My brother Carmine is back," she said. "He returned last Sunday. He came to my mamma's house for dinner."

"Did he say where he has been?" I asked, placing my hands beneath my thighs so Cettina could not see them tremble as I remembered his boot shattering my ribs.

"Mostly Palermo. Also, Naples. He is different now. Even harder, meaner, if that is possible. He asked about you."

"About me?"

"About this, the clinic. All the people here. He says it is bad for him to have so many people poking around down here on this side of the mountain. He does not like anyone being able to watch him. I wish you had this clinic anywhere but here. Marco was stupid to give you this land."

It was the first time I had ever heard her question any of her husband's decisions and I could tell she immediately regretted it, given the circumstances. "We must go back up the hill. I need you to see him. You will know how to help him."

Their large beautiful house smelled of illness. It was a smell I had come to know well and one that did not bother me much, but in this case it was coupled with Marco's scent and I finally let myself worry. I tried to channel my emotions into concern for Cettina and squeezed her hands between mine. "I am sure he's fine. Why don't you put some food in your stomach and let me go in to examine him?"

I made my way to their bedroom, their personal space, a room I never saw. It consisted of two beds, close enough to one another that a person could reach across and squeeze the other's hand good night, a friendly distance.

My lover looked even worse than Cettina had described. His skin, typically ruddy and tanned, had gone yellow. His hair lay slick at his brow with sweat, and he shook beneath the thick quilt on the bed. I knocked on the doorframe as I entered but he did not stir or register my arrival. My heart banged against my rib cage, so loud in my ears I feared Cettina could hear it down the stairs.

I had seen patients like this. It began with the new kind of the flu and then infected something else, maybe the liver or the kidneys, allowing bile and poison to build up in the blood until the patient was poisoned from within. Cettina had every reason to be worried. This man who we each loved in entirely separate ways was dying. As I walked to his bedside, I struggled to maintain a facade of control, digging my nails into my palms until they bled so that the physical pain would outweigh my emotions. When I was close enough to touch him, I stroked his scalding forehead.

"I did not want you to come." He croaked the words so quietly I had to kneel beside him to hear. My hand found his beneath the sheets.

"Why wouldn't you want me to come?"

"I did not want you to see me like this. But I also did not think I could let you leave again if I saw you. I believe I am dying, Fina, and I don't want anyone but you in this room with me when I leave this world. I do not want to spend another minute pretending I don't love you."

Years of good judgment drained out of me. I removed my filthy hospital shoes and climbed into the bed next to him, pulled him to me as tightly as possible. I buried my face in his wet curls. "You are not dying, my love. I can heal you."

"Fina . . ." he began.

"Don't. Save your energy. There is nothing you can tell me that I don't already hold in my heart. We will not say goodbye, not like this. I won't let it happen, my love. I won't."

For a second, in his bed, my arms around his body, I had the thing I had been craving, the makings of a normal morning, the two of us in a small bed, lingering as long as we wished. I gripped him harder, the texture of his clothes and skin beneath my fingers the only thing keeping the moment from slipping away.

It wasn't until I heard Cettina's ragged breath in the doorway that the fantasy died inside me.

I could sense her staring at the two of us, watching us silently. How much of her carefully constructed world slipped away just then? I took too long to turn around, but I eventually had to face her. We locked eyes, saying everything and nothing in a single glance.

NINETEEN

SARA

Luca wanted me to meet his wife. He insisted on it after he cleaned enough of the glass from his car for the two of us to climb in and continue the journey to Palermo. The windshield had been spared, as was the rest of the vehicle. Whoever did it could have done more damage than just breaking the side windows if they'd wanted to. Not that their point wasn't perfectly made.

There were plenty of ways I could have reacted when I read the note they left behind: *Does your wife know about you and the American whore?* I could have been the cool girl and laughed in disbelief. I could have gone manic and screamed at Luca or I could have stayed silent. I chose the latter because it was becoming quite clear that I had no idea what I had gotten myself into and I just wanted to get to Palermo, get my passport, and figure out the fastest way to sell the land. Maybe Luca took my silence for complicity because after ten minutes back on the road he simply said, "You should meet my wife."

My mouth went so dry I couldn't swallow much less speak. I

kept shifting in my seat, trying to get sand out of my bathing suit bottoms.

"I'm not really into that kind of thing," I replied, glancing at him in the rearview mirror. Sex with near strangers on beaches, sure. Threesomes with an Italian couple, not really on the menu for me.

"That's not what I meant." He was looking at me now, taking his eyes off the road every so often to meet my gaze in the mirror. This was an easier conversation to have with someone's reflection. He was nervous, maybe about whoever shattered the windows and whether they were still following us, maybe about the note and my reaction to it. I had to stop myself from caring about any of it. Luca's wife was his problem.

"I think she can help you. She can be helpful for your situation. I didn't mean anything strange or sexual. I would not propose that. I—I do not think of you like that." Luca was stuttering now. "Agata is my wife. She has been my wife for a very long time, since we were eighteen, but we are not like that. We, how do you say in America . . . we are separate from one another?"

"Separated?"

"That is it. We haven't lived together in a very long time, since we were practically kids. She is a professor in Palermo at the university. A brilliant woman. One of the most wonderful humans I know." I felt a twinge of jealousy that I had no right to feel. "We got married because it was good for her. She had no family, no one to protect her, and I was her best friend. I love her. But we do not . . . we do not do what you and I just did."

I was cool. I was tough. I was relieved. "What does she teach?"

"History of the women. Feminism, you call it. Focusing on Sicilian women mostly. She is one of the first professors to do extensive work on women's stories dating all the way back to the Sicanian times through the Greco-Roman period and everything until now. She is married to her work and a very good researcher. I think she can help you with some of the things that you want to know about your great relative and whether you have rights to the land that she left you."

"How could she know about Serafina?"

"Because she knows more about the women of this island and the women of Caltabellessa and the laws that govern women than anyone. We can meet her in Palermo if that is good for you. I am sorry you found out about her the way that you did."

I nodded.

"We can stay at my apartment, or I can pay for you to stay in a hotel. We don't need to do anything."

"I appreciate that."

"It is weird now, isn't it? Between us?"

I sighed as we pulled onto the freeway and wished more than anything that my answer could be different.

"It's weird now."

———

We illegally parked on the sidewalk next to a grand baroque cathedral. When Luca grabbed my hand to lead me up the stone steps, I didn't pull away.

"Are we going to confession?" I asked.

He spun me around to give me a hard stare, a stare so earnest I almost kissed him to apologize for my sarcasm. "You need to know that I do not regret anything, Sara."

The church door was locked, but somehow Luca had a key.

"Seriously, why are we here?" I asked.

"Agata is doing research to restore the frescoes in this church.

They have given her an office downstairs. It is closed while it is under construction but I have a key so I can check on her."

"Maybe tomorrow would be better to see her," I suggested through a yawn.

"She is eager to s-see us now. I texted her on our drive," he stuttered. "It's not always the case with her. She has good days and bad days." Inside the entryway he turned left instead of going straight into the church, heading down a corridor of stairs to the basement crypt.

A small woman emerged from the musty darkness at the base of the stairs. Her face tattoo stopped me in my tracks. An inky black snake slithering up her left cheek. Agata's blonde hair was in a sloppy topknot and her eyes were a startling icy blue. She wore a red silk robe and green velvet slippers with pointy toes that made a shushing sound as she slid around the room. Her head only came to Luca's breastbone as she embraced him around the waist.

"*Ciao, ciao, caro mio.*"

He bowed his head and kissed the top of her hair.

"You are good?" He was speaking in English for my benefit, and she quickly switched too.

"For today," she replied.

I looked around, trying to figure out where to sit. Books covered most of the floor space, stacked as high as possible without teetering over. Next to them were manila folders bulging with papers. The top of one pile was littered with amber bottles of pills. On the floor Berber-style cushions called to mind a harem or a wealthy hipster's apartment. There was a bed in one corner and a kitchenette in the other.

"You are *the* American?"

"That's what everyone here keeps calling me."

Her tinkling laughter in response relaxed me.

"What do you teach?" I asked her.

"My course right now is Greek and Roman history, but my primary research is on female activists throughout Sicilian history."

"Agata recently got promoted to main lecturer, which is like tenure in America," Luca bragged like a proud father.

"Which means they cannot fire me no matter how bizarre my research becomes."

My interest was piqued. "How bizarre is it?"

"It gets more interesting every day. Would you like a drink?"

I spied a hot plate and a basic moka pot in the kitchenette. "I'd love an espresso."

"Me too." She busied herself with the coffee while Luca pawed through some of her papers. He pulled a black-and-white etching from one and examined it. "Are you still searching for more on Maria Testadilana?"

I walked over to look at the drawing. In it a ragged group of men were laying siege to a city or town. Many of them were dressed like peasants in ripped trousers and shirts. A few wore long robes and traditional Muslim headdresses. A well-dressed male figure, royalty maybe, was impaled on a stake atop a pile of burning crates. The buildings behind the scene were engulfed in flames. One individual stood out from the others. Initially I mistook them for another Arab man in a long flowing robe, but this person's head was bare and their hair—long, thick, curly locks—flowed freely. It was a woman brandishing a machete in one hand and a severed head in the other that she hoisted into the sky like a well-earned trophy. I pointed to her. "Maria?"

Agata approached with tiny saucers of caffeine.

"Oh, Maria," she said with no small amount of affection. "I will always chase tales of Maria, but I think I have found everything there is."

"Who is she?" I asked.

"She was many people and also no one. She was a poor shepherdess and a seller of prickly pears and an enthusiastic murderess who could slice a man's head off in a single stroke. Some scholars are convinced she never existed at all, that she was constructed by storytellers to give the women at least some agency in a revolution that ignored them and their families in favor of a male cock-measuring competition for land and power, but I know that she was real and that there were more like her. Back in the revolution against the Bourbons more women fought for Sicily than most will ever acknowledge. Alas it has never been the women writing the history of this island, so many of their names will be forever lost. But not Maria's. I will not allow it."

Agata was in full professor mode, and despite my exhaustion and the strangeness of the day, I found her knowledge, however horrific, comforting to listen to.

"Maria led a group of forty-eight men who lit Palermo on fire and murdered the Bourbon nobles and their families. In one assault she killed thirty royal guards. But the insurgents who followed her feared her power. When it was over, they planted a letter in her home, framing her for kidnapping and looting. She went to prison and disappeared. No body, no pardon. Her name was mostly lost to history for a very long time."

"When was this?"

"Eighteen forty-eight. Not so long ago, right before Sicily's so-called independence from the crown and the unification. One of the last battles in the hundreds of battles and takeovers of this island where one wealthy man from a wealthy family replaces another wealthy man from a wealthy family and then rapes this island of everything good. First the Greeks, then the Romans, the Byzantines, the Abbasids, the Normans, the Berbers, the Habsburgs, the Castiles, the pope. They were all mostly the same. This island is a potential paradise squandered by greed. It is hard to be a historian without becoming a nihilist because you see the worst of history repeat itself over and over again. It may be why I lose my mind on a regular basis."

I really liked this little woman, but it was hard to keep up. She hadn't stopped moving the entire time she talked, flittering about the room like an excited hummingbird.

Luca's phone dinged with a text. Both Agata and I whipped our heads around and gazed at him with a proprietary look. Luca frowned and typed furiously. Another ding. A sigh.

"I have to go."

I quickly downed the rest of my coffee and prepared to leave as Luca shifted uncomfortably from foot to foot. "Sara, I can take you to a hotel."

"Luca, you do not need to run to them the second they call for you. Stay," Agata almost shouted.

He responded in dialect, speaking quickly and sharply, and I couldn't make out any of it. Agata cursed and then gave up.

"Leave Sara here. It is very late. She can stay in the apartment across the street." She pulled out a key. "Dottoressa Grado is traveling and I have a key to her place so I can water her plants. It is yours."

Relief crossed Luca's face. Despite the espresso I was exhausted and a nearby bed with no one else's husband in it sounded perfect.

"You go," I said to Luca.

He didn't hesitate. "I'll be back to take you to the consulate in the morning," he promised. He looked to Agata with an explanation. "Someone stole her passport. She needs to go to the American consulate to replace it."

"You go," she echoed me, practically pushing Luca to the door. "But be careful. You don't owe them anything." She whispered that last bit just loud enough that I could hear. Luca waved another feeble goodbye in my direction, clearly embarrassed at how quickly he had to rush off to whatever strange meeting had been called for him in the middle of the night. I wondered if it had anything to do with the broken window, with the note. Before I could ask, he was gone.

Agata shook her head. "Oh, Luca. He is such a puppy. So cute, so loyal, so stupid." She picked up one of the amber bottles of pills, shook a few into her hand, and swallowed them dry.

"These help me stay awake when I am working," she explained even though I didn't ask. "Don't worry about Luca. He probably had to go check on his children."

I gave her the reaction she was looking for and she burst into a cackle of laughter that rumbled her little body.

"I am fucking with you. Too soon for that joke? Do not worry, American. He has no children and I am a wife in name only because it is easier for me than not being a wife, and Luca is the kind of man who keeps his promises and loves very hard. He is quite smitten with you. He called me right after he met you at his restaurant."

A warmth crept up my neck.

"So, no children?"

"Not that I know of." She shifted some papers around on the floor and uncovered a giant golden goblet filled with a rainbow of jelly beans. "He is going to meet the men who give him money for his restaurant. A true group of *sfigati*, losers, if you ask me. I told him not to take their money, but their offer was too good for him to turn down and Luca has quite the ego about his grand plans to turn the west coast of Sicily into a culinary mecca."

So maybe Luca's financial backing hadn't come as easily as I had assumed on the beach. Maybe taking money always came with its own baggage, no matter who gave it to you. A part of me wished I had gone with him, but that ship had sailed. I was about to ask her for the key to the apartment across the street when Agata made a sudden proclamation.

"I can fix your passport problem." She fired off a series of texts into the universe and a moment later declared, "I have a friend at the consulate, and she will meet us at nine A.M. It will make things easier for you. There are always lines and who knows how long you might have to wait."

It seemed like the perfect segue into obtaining that key. "Then I had better get to sleep."

"Really?" Her disbelief made me wonder if she had any idea that it was getting very late. "I would love to show you something if you will let me."

"What is it?"

"I can explain as we walk."

"Outside?"

"It is not far."

"Could we see it tomorrow? After the consulate?" I asked helplessly.

"No, no. It is something I can only show you at night. It will not take very long. But it is easier to show you than to explain. And we can talk about other things as we walk."

I considered asking her for one of her little pills, but uppers never agreed with me. The one time I did cocaine after a James Beard ceremony I took off all my clothes and sang "The Star-Spangled Banner" while dangling from a lamppost on Broad Street.

Sometime in the past six months my natural curiosity, the same one nurtured by Aunt Rose's crazy scavenger hunts all those years ago, had simply withered and died. My old colleagues, the closest friends I'd ever had besides my sister, still invited me to things. Want to check out this new bar? There's a wings and wine festival down at the pier. Come see the Brancusi exhibit or hear Snacktime at the Bok Bar. My excuses piled up until the invitations stopped coming. But now that old tug to experience something new was back and I hadn't realized how much I had missed it.

"Maybe another coffee to go," I said.

"We can get one on the street. *Amuninni.*" She covered her head with a purple scarf, discarded her green slippers for what looked like black cowboy boots, and slipped through the door.

After leaping up the stairs, Agata paused for a moment in the doorway to the main chapel.

"Do you want to see?" she asked me, and pulled me through the grand gilded doors before I could answer.

Frescoes of saints and angels covered every available surface. Massive marble columns flanked the pews, leading to a series of smaller chapels and altars. A ladder teetered precariously above a statue of the Virgin and her baby. Before I knew what was happening, Agata began to climb.

"Come, come. It is the best view of the Quattro Canti."

"Nope," I said.

"Please. I've got you. Do not be afraid." Her words, *I've got you*, were more of a comfort than I expected. My hands shook as I made my way up a rickety two stories onto a small window seat.

"Sometimes I sneak up here and watch the tourists take their Instagram photos in the church. They pose with their duck faces in front of the mother of Christ and I wonder if she would have been very amused." Agata giggled. "Other times I nap here. Look out the window. You are above the chaos."

Despite the late hour the city wasn't even close to being asleep. When I leaned out the window I spied an opera singer serenading a bride and groom as they danced cheek to cheek in the midst of the crowds. Vespas carrying too many passengers zipped past horses wearing jaunty straw hats as they clattered their carriages over the stone streets. Diners and drinkers spilled out of restaurants, cafés, bars, and *gelaterie*. An older man with a machete scraped his blade across a block of ice to deliver fresh granita to passersby. I inhaled the crisp night air and tried to feel gratitude for being here.

"We are a nocturnal city," Agata whispered, and she eased her way back down the ladder. "Let me show you."

Outside the church she paused at a colorful cart and bought me an Aperol spritz for three euro before beckoning me forward. We turned left, then right, then left again into a passageway, dodging late-night revelers—teenagers, tourists, and local families—as we hustled through narrow streets with names like via delle Sedie Volanti, Street of the Flying Chairs, and via Terra delle Mosche, Street of the Land of the Flies. I lost Agata in the crowds and then found her in a market selling street food. I was starving again.

Agata paused at a stall with a long line, jabbing her way to the front with her sharp little elbows. She returned to me with a carton of deep-fried potato croquettes and round little balls of marinated eggplant, each skewered with a toothpick.

"Open wide," she exclaimed, and then popped a potato in my mouth, as eager to feed me as her estranged husband had been.

"We call these *cazzilli*. Little penises, because of their stubby little shape," she said with a laugh. "And the eggplants, these round slices are *felle*, or butt cheeks. Everything is sexual here."

I laughed too, energized by the salty, lemony food, hoping this was what she wanted to show me but knowing there would be more.

"You came here because your family left you land, yes?" Agata asked.

"Luca told you."

"He did. He texted me things about you. Marsala is your last name?"

"Yes."

"Serafina Forte was your relative?"

"She was," I said, scooping the remaining morsels into my mouth.

"What do you want to do with that land?"

I hadn't been expecting an interrogation, but Luca did say that Agata might be able to help, and I was already grasping at straws. The possibility of returning home with any extra money in my bank account felt slimmer and slimmer. "Honestly I am just hoping to sell it for a fair price and go back to Philly. I have a lot of debt and shit to work out. The money would help. It's not like I could manage a plot of land across the ocean. Giusy from the hotel has been helping me. Once I get my passport, I can open a local bank account, and then see what happens from there."

"But you know there are people who do not want you to have any claim to that land at all?"

This little woman knew much more than she should about my circumstances. Suddenly I wanted to turn back. I felt exposed.

"That is what Giusy told me too."

"Oh, Giu, Giu. I know her well. Do not trust everything Giusy says. Do not trust anyone here. But for serious Giusy will always be looking out for Giusy. We have a word in western Sicilian dialect, *furbezza*, it means 'a devious intelligence.' I think about it whenever I think about Giusy." She brushed debris from one of the stone walls around the corner from the street food market. "Here we are." I noticed a rusted keyhole beneath the vines and dirt covering the wall. Agata pulled a small brass key on a long golden chain from beneath her shirt.

A steep stairway on the other side of the door led the way down beneath the street.

"Are we supposed to be in here?" Agata was already leaping down the stairs.

"Of course not."

"Why do you have a key?"

"I have many keys to many things."

I kept thinking about how she said it was no wonder she was constantly losing her mind.

Agata used her phone to light the way. The stench of rot wafted into my nose as the door slammed behind us.

"Are we going into the sewer?"

"Yes. But just for a moment. Plug your nose. You're a butcher. You're used to terrible smells." She really did know everything about me.

We walked along a narrow pathway of stones with putrid water flowing on either side. Agata skipped, the phone bouncing in her hand, creating ominous shadows on the dark walls.

"In here." She quickly darted down another tiny tunnel. I had to stoop but her head wasn't even close to touching the ceiling.

"Where are we?"

"The catacombs. The Capuchin Catacombs to be exact."

I gripped the wall to steady myself and found a handhold in the rock. Agata whipped her phone around to illuminate my fingers gripping the eyeholes of a whitewashed skull. I screamed. The sound echoed off the walls and then disappeared down the long dark hallway. The heads of the dead were everywhere, lining the walls, covering the ground like cobblestones.

"Most of these tunnels have been closed to the public for a long time, ever since the child mummies were discovered."

"The child mummies?"

"You never heard about them? They are in all the guidebooks. Hundreds of child mummies. Many of them so well-preserved they look as though they are merely sleeping."

The image was horrific and twisted my insides. "Why were they mummified?"

"No one knows. Some say their mothers couldn't bear to put them in the ground, but I don't know if I believe that. The mothers back then were used to the death of their children. The average Sicilian woman would give birth to ten children by the time she was thirty and half of them did not make it. Women loved their children, but they couldn't be precious about them. I think most of the children here in the crypts belonged to wealthy foreigners who had easier lives than the Sicilian peasant women, so they had the privilege of mourning. But we will not see the child mummies tonight."

"Why are we down here?"

Impatience laced her tone. "I told you. I have something to show you."

She ducked so low I had no choice but to get on my knees and then on my belly and suddenly I was crawling on the ground to make it through an opening no bigger than a toilet seat. I heard a squeaking, felt the claws of a rodent dig into my back, and I let out a small cry.

"I want to go back."

"You've come this far." Agata reached behind her to grip my massive hand in her little one. "Come on. You've got this." Her words reminded me of Aunt Rose's old encouragement and I kept going.

Through the hole was a long and narrow room, so deep I couldn't see to the end of it. The light tapered into the shadows. The walls were no longer covered in skulls but drawings. Agata paused in front of one and pulled a small penlight out of the folds of her pants to supplement the light from her phone.

An intricate scene on the stones depicted a group of nuns wielding what appeared to be garden tools, scythes, and pitchforks as weapons. A scrum of terrified children hid behind their flowing black skirts as an angry mob of men tried to break down a wall between them.

"The sisters of Saint Accursia protected the children born of a mother's affairs from the cuckolded men who sought to kill them. The women of Sicily have always kept track of our history in spaces like these, caves or tunnels beneath the ground, spaces where it was safe to share our stories."

I ran my fingers along the wall.

"Less than five percent of women were literate even a hundred years ago, so it's nearly always pictures and oral history. The women gathered here to tell their stories. Here and places like this." She sat alongside one of the walls and for the first time I noticed there were raised stones on the floor, seats.

"These meeting rooms are the heart of my current research, which, of course, will never be done," Agata explained. "There will always be more to learn and more to say about these places where women have been gathering in secret for thousands of years. I worry about publishing it at all. Am I betraying them if I do? Am I betraying their memory if I don't? Look at this one. This is Saint Agata, my namesake."

I inspected a drawing of a young woman, a child really, cowering at the foot of a grown man.

"This is from the third century AD. As a young woman Agata resisted the advances of a Roman prefect sent by the emperor Decius to govern Sicily. He raped her and tortured her, slicing off both of her breasts. She was imprisoned. Not him. Her. Then she was sent to die at the stake, but right as they were about to light the match an earthquake rattled the ground and knocked the executioner off his feet. She died in prison and now she is the patron saint of women who have been raped. Just the fact that we need to have a saint for such a thing in this country." Agata shook her head.

"Why are you named after her?" Before the words left my mouth, I knew it was a story I didn't want to hear. But Agata delivered it with little emotion.

"My mother was raped by a very rich man when she was thirteen. She ran away from her home. Rape wasn't a felony here until 1996, and besides, he was rich and she was poor. He wouldn't have been convicted even today. She made it to a nearby village, where a stranger brought her into her home and kept her safe for a few months. That woman had a cousin in Caltabellessa and my mother went there to give birth. She took her own life soon after I was born. I was an orphan in the village, bounced from house to house. In one of them I met Luca and we quickly became the best of friends. Giusy took care of us, like a big sister. We were a little gang. Luca married me as soon as he could to save me from the same fate as my mother. A woman with no real family is never safe. He worked and worked to pay for me to come here to go to school." Her voice stayed even as I reached out to express acknowledgment for all that she'd been through, but she brushed my hand away and bounced over to another section of the wall, another drawing. "But this next one is my favorite, the most important, the basis of most of my study." She traced her finger along the outline of a voluptuous winged woman. "Astarte."

Where had I heard that name before? Had I heard that name before?

"It sounds familiar."

"You wouldn't have heard of her. Astarte was an African goddess, probably predating the Greeks. She was Canaanite or Phoenician in the beginning. Goddess of love, sex, war, and hunting. The worship of her traveled along the trade routes. She was a goddess of self-defense and also of female conquest. Massive temples were built to honor her here in the island's western towns like Erice and Trapani and Sciacca. When the Greeks came to the island some scholars say that the worship of her disappeared, but her followers would never have let that happen. The women kept her alive. They knew assimilation was the only way to survive and continued to worship the ideals of Astarte, her bravery, independence, passion, through temples to the Greek goddesses Artemis and Aphrodite, and then the Roman Diana and Venus. Eventually, when the Christians came, the women transferred Astarte's spirit and her strength into the Virgin Mary. This is how Astarte lives on. It is one of the reasons that the island's women were so quick to accept the idea of the Virgin Mary. We transfer the love of our previous goddesses into acceptable figures for whatever time we are living in. Astarte remains alive in all of us Sicilian women." Agata pushed up the sleeve of her shirt to reveal a tattoo of the goddess on her forearm, her breasts bare and powerful in their nakedness, the horns sprouting out of her forehead so sharp they looked as though they could impale an enemy in a single blow, the massive wings curling toward Agata's elbow. I remembered where I saw this image: Fina's tattoo. The same woman, same horns. And the name. It was the toast that Giusy and Fina gave before we settled down to the meal at Luca's restaurant. I could hear the clink of their glasses as if they were with us. "Astarte."

"Is this some kind of cult?"

"It is more a way of life, a spirit, a story we pass down, a way of reminding ourselves that the only way for a woman to survive in this world is to help other women. The stories get passed down through some of the families, but they were lost for many generations until I began much of my research. Old manuscripts talking about the Astarte legends were some of the first things I studied when I began to search for the stories of forgotten women. There is a place like this one near Caltabellessa, in the cave by the Norman castle. All of us used to play there when I was a girl. That's where I discovered some of the first drawings."

Agata took something out of her pocket and popped it into her mouth. It could have been another pill or a jelly bean.

"That cave is where I discovered the first image I ever saw of Astarte. And right down the road from it, in a tiny abandoned stone house, is where I discovered your relative's diary."

"Wait. You're the one who found Serafina's diary?"

"I did. You have seen it?"

"I found it in Giusy's apartment." Somehow I didn't have it left in me to lie. "Why did you give it to Giusy?"

Agata sighed. "Oh, Giusy! Our relationship is so complicated. She works so hard. Tries so hard. But she has a darkness to her. When I was first discovering things about Astarte, the goddess, Giusy became completely obsessed with everything new that I learned. It made sense. Giusy's husband used to beat the hell out of her. One time he kicked her ankle so hard it shattered. The doctors put it back together and she walked with a cane for many years. Sometimes she still does even though she is healed. Maybe it is a reminder to herself or to other people in town that she is a survivor. The idea of Astarte made her feel like she had some power in a world where she had none. But she took it too far. We let her take it too far."

"What do you mean?"

"That is when Giusy's husband disappeared."

"I thought her husband left her."

"Oh, no. He is gone." She said this with the certainty of someone who witnessed the act of removing him from this earth with their own eyes.

"Did she kill him?" I asked carefully.

"All I can tell you is there is no way he could have survived. We did what we had to do to protect her. He would have killed her if we hadn't," Agata said sadly but without remorse.

I remembered Giusy saying that she made sure her husband wouldn't return. I wanted to know more, but I was exhausted and needed to keep the focus on Serafina. "So why did you give Giusy the diary?"

"She told me she had talked to a relative of Serafina Forte who might come to the island and maybe they would find it useful. That is you, by the way."

"Actually, it was my aunt Rose she talked to. But whatever."

"I was fascinated by the diary. I grew up hearing about Serafina as a cautionary story. What happens when a woman is left alone to her own devices, how quickly she loses her honor. Finding her diary was like a gift to me, a reminder of the importance of the work that I do, the importance of women writing their own histories and legacies. That is why I wanted to show you this place."

"But why would you give the diary away?"

"I gave the diary to Giusy in a moment of weakness. She knows how to say the right things to make me afraid of her. But I kept many of the pages."

The ripped-out pages, the words that might help me prove that Serafina had been given the land fair and square, the ones that might reveal who murdered her.

Agata continued. "In Caltabellessa they say your great-grandmother was a witch and a whore, but she was really a doctor, a healer, and a woman mostly abandoned by her husband as he sought his fortunes in America. She saved the lives of countless people in that village. She probably saved hundreds from being completely wiped out by a terrible flu with the precautions she put in place for cleanliness and germs. She was a hero and they murdered her. I was the one who found the police report too."

"Then you know who murdered Serafina?"

"I do not. After I found the diary, I talked to some of the older women in the town. Some say Serafina's lover did it to save himself. Some believe it was the family of her lover's wife or maybe even the wife herself, even though I can't imagine that. But I think they're all wrong. I think the simplest answer is always the best. I believe it was Serafina's cuckolded husband. I believe he returned home because he heard the rumors, and he murdered her so that he wouldn't have to bring her and his shame to America."

I shivered in the damp cold.

Agata made her way to the back of the room. Her arm went deep into a hole I hadn't noticed before and she brought out a large box that she unlocked with yet another key.

"I keep things in here. Things I want to be safe. I think the university searches my rooms sometimes. Or maybe I am just paranoid. I like to keep my important papers among the stories of these women." She handed them to me with a flourish. "The missing pages of your relative's diary. The ones that I kept."

I immediately tried to make out the words in the dim light.

Agata lowered herself to the floor and stretched her thin body along the stone. She closed her eyes, ready for sleep.

"Let's go back." I rolled up the pages so I could shove them in my back pocket and grasped her forearm to try to lift her to her feet.

"Maybe we rest here?" She gazed up at me. From this perspective she looked like a small child and I had an immediate urge to tuck her into bed.

I managed to drag her to her feet and then to the door. An image of the Virgin Mary was carved into it. I said a silent prayer to her that I would make it out of this grave and back home to my daughter. I finally prodded Agata into the tunnels. She mumbled which way to turn, and I had no idea if any of it was right or if we'd be trapped in an endless maze beneath the city forever, but finally I found the stairs leading to the door.

When we reached Agata's office back at the church she tumbled face-first on her couch. "I may not wake up for a while. Sometimes I sleep for two days," she mumbled into her sheets. "Get me a pen and paper. I will write the name and phone number of my friend who will help you at the consulate." I grabbed them and she scribbled down some numbers and a name.

Agata was nearly out, but she managed one more thing.

"You should not stay in Sicily. It's never safe for a woman here, but when people want something from you, they will do whatever it takes to get it. They'll make it look like an accident."

I realized too late that she never gave me a key to the apartment across the street. It didn't matter; there was no way I could sleep without reading the missing diary pages. I didn't need to delve into the text very long before I found what I needed. There were long paragraphs of Serafina recounting the exact exchange she had with Marco when he gave her the land, including one where he said he would put her name on the deed. She also wrote down the name of the bank he made the transaction with.

There was another section where she wrote about asking him whether the land was hers to sell. According to her recollection his answer was a clear and absolute yes. She could do what she wanted with the land, but he asked her one thing in return. He begged her not to leave Sicily for America.

I thought about that request. Serafina didn't leave. She was killed before she could get on a boat and join her husband. Was Marco desperate enough to keep her that he would make sure she stayed at any cost? Dead or alive?

There was also no longer a question in my mind about whether the two of them were lovers. Plenty of those passages remained. I would keep them to myself. I would protect her.

Who knew if the diary pages would mean anything to the officials, but at least I had the information in my possession. I was no longer at Giusy's mercy for every little scrap. After I went to the consulate I would find out if the bank Serafina mentioned still existed and if so whether they had any records of the deed being filed.

I kept reading. A quiver of sadness crept through me at one of the last mentions of C., Serafina's best friend and confidante. She finally wrote the woman's entire name. Cettina. It was familiar. I remember how musical it sounded when I read it from the church registry.

Serafina was having an affair with her best friend's husband. The realization was heart-wrenching. She didn't just betray her husband. She betrayed the woman who was closer to her than a sister. And if she could do that, then what other parts of the gossip and rumors that clung to her name and legacy were true?

The final page was the most chilling:

> *I never allow myself to be alone anymore. I have no doubt that Carmine will murder me the first chance that he gets. I sense danger everywhere. In my nightmares Gio returned and struck me, even Marco pushed my head beneath scalding bathwater. These men who once loved me wanted nothing more than my destruction.*

The words nestled in my gut. Her fear became a part of me as I reread a passage where Serafina said she was planning a trip to Palermo, how nervous she was to finally visit this beautiful, strange, and otherworldly place. I thought about how travel was such a privilege for her and how much easier it was for me.

There were a couple of stray blankets and a throw pillow where I could lay down on the floor and sleep for an hour. I plugged my phone into a charger I found on one of the tables and noticed a text from my sister from more than twelve hours ago.

Are you OK? I'm worried about you.

There was too much to write in a text and I didn't want to wake Agata by calling. I thought about how to explain it all to Carla as I forced myself into a brief dreamless sleep.

I left well before Luca returned and sent him a text saying I was fine on my own. I reached the consulate before it opened, finding a pleasant bench near a church down the street.

The sun was already warm on my skin, but a shiver ran through me as I got the feeling I was being watched. I looked behind me and saw a man holding his phone aloft like he was trying to get service, but I could tell he was taking my picture. His hair was long and greasy. He had a hint of a beard and sat next to a dusty brown backpack that took up more of the bench than he did. When we made eye contact, he stood and walked quickly away, disappearing into a narrow alley behind the church.

"Hey," I shouted, and ran to the street, but he had disappeared.

Was he the one who left the note in Luca's car? I considered running into the alley to try to find him, but the consulate was about to open.

As Agata had promised, her friend met me at nine on the dot in front of the shabby office building that housed the consulate. "Hey. I'm Harper," she said. She was American, her Southern accent thick and friendly. She had a long red braid that nearly grazed her tailbone and the wide-set eyes of a Disney princess. She wore a conservative navy skirt suit with an American flag pin on the lapel. I tried to imagine her hanging out with funky little Agata and I liked their juxtaposition.

"Your passport was stolen?" Harper asked as we walked into the building.

"Yeah. From my hotel room."

"And you have a police report?"

"I do."

"Do you have a copy of the passport?"

"I have a photocopy that Giusy made when I checked in."

"This will be easy, then. I can get you a temporary document that you can use as identification when you go back to America."

"Would it work as an ID if I wanted to open a bank account here?"

She stopped and looked at me with confusion. "Oh, we can't help you with that."

"I don't need your help with it. I just wanted to know if it is valid identification if I wanted to open a bank account."

"It should be. Why are you opening an account? Not that it's any of my business or anything, but most tourists don't come over here and do banking. And if you want to stay here and live here that is a totally different visa process. You're just on vacation, right?"

"I inherited some land and I need a bank account if I want to sell it. That's what they told me."

She raised an eyebrow. "They?"

"The *notaio* in the town my ancestors are from and the woman who owns the hotel I'm staying in. She's helping me. It's a long story. I know it all sounds crazy."

Harper replied with no punctuation. "You don't know crazy until you spend a year at the Sicilian consulate . . . Trust me . . . I applied to work in Rome, but they were short-staffed here with all the migrants coming in and they gave me extra pay and actually now I sorta love it and its weirdness . . . Bank stuff and land stuff is way above my pay grade though. I could maybe make an appointment for you to meet with someone here, probably not today but in like a week or so . . . anyway, you should be careful . . . I gotta tell you we've been seeing an uptick in scams about land and inheritance. Ever since those genealogy sites got big and people started searching for their relatives in different countries. Everyone here thinks people in America are super rich and when Americans reach out to their third and fourth cousins they often find out about an old villa or a family olive oil business that is looking for an all-cash investment and then they come to us and say, 'Get my money back,' and we say, 'We can't help you. You got scammed.' That's not really what we say, but you get what I mean. I can get you a passport today though, mostly because Agata asked and she has been my only real friend here in Palermo. She rescued me from some terrible men on my first night here after I had too many spritzes. I owe her a lot."

We arrived at a small office with nothing in it but a laptop and a metal desk with two rickety chairs on either side. The pale gray walls peeled beneath two framed photographs of the president of the United States and the current secretary of state, who I was hard-pressed to name. I had discovered in the past couple of years that the more dire your own personal crisis, the less impressive the bureaucratic office that fixes it will be. The space in the federal courthouse where I filed my bankruptcy paperwork and dissolved all my professional dreams was a six-by-six-foot cubicle with a yellowed photograph of Prince William and Kate on their wedding day.

Harper played Scrabble on her phone while I filled out a stack of forms. Then she took my police report and a photocopy of my passport and entered me into the system.

"I have to run a quick check to make sure you are who you say you are," she said in a lilty singsong.

My pulse sped up at the thought of a background check. I imagined Harper's silent judgment. *Why should we let you back into America with your bankruptcy and credit score in the toilet, you loser?*

But her expression didn't change as she scrolled through whatever dossier came up on her screen. She typed some more and then got up from the desk. "I'll have you out of here in five."

"Thanks," I said. "I really appreciate how fast you're getting this done for me."

"No problem at all. Anything for Agata."

My phone rang as I walked out of the consulate. "Where have you been?" Giusy's voice was wired and frantic. "I've been trying to get ahold of you for more than a day.

"They scheduled an emergency municipal meeting about the land. It is tomorrow night," she said.

"So fast? How is that possible?"

"Things move slowly here until they do not move slowly. Then they happen right away. The land developer is in town. He is visiting from the Emirates and only here for twenty-four hours. He is apparently pissed off that this is more complicated than he expected. He wants his deal closed. He wants his resort built before Italy puts in their bid to host the World Cup. And apparently he has heard about some new American TV show or movie that is going to be filming on the island and he thinks it will make more people come here."

"But the water test. The well. Weren't they doing more tests or something?"

"It is done. Your land has the reserves. Or the land that should be yours. We will not know if it is yours until after the meeting. Are you going to make it back here?"

"I'll be there." My brain churned when I hung up the phone. It was funny how checking a single thing off your to-do list—in this case, getting my new passport—could make you feel like you could accomplish anything. I hadn't been so energized in a long time. I grabbed my phone and scrolled until I found the right number. He answered immediately and within a half an hour he met me in front of the consulate.

"*Ciao, ciao, bella.*" Pippo kissed my cheeks. "Are you finally ready to go see the ruins, maybe the fish market?"

"Actually, I need to hire you to help me with some business here in Palermo and then take me back to Caltabellessa tomorrow. I need to visit a bank to inquire about some old documents and then open my own bank account and find a real estate attorney I can trust here in Palermo."

"This will be much less interesting than the ruins or the cathedral, but I can help you." He took a step back and surveyed me. "You look good. You have a shiny face. No, that is the wrong translation. You have a glow, maybe that is what I am supposed to say. You look healthier. Like a horse."

I laughed, which felt fantastic. "I think I'm just filthy and I need a shower. But you are right. I feel good." I walked to Pippo's car. "Let's go. I have a lot to do and if we get it all done maybe we will make it to the fish market."

TWENTY

SERAFINA

I woke to the slam of the front door. It was barely light out, just past dawn. My first thought was that it was one of my boys sneaking into the house. They had reached an age where they came and went as they pleased.

Against my better judgment I hadn't locked the front door before I went to sleep because Cosi had begged and begged to stay late at a friend's house and promised he would be home shortly after I went to bed. I should have known better. It had become too obvious that someone in the village wanted to do me harm.

On more than one occasion over the past few months I had found broken glass shattered on my doorstep first thing in the morning. At first I thought it was an accident, but after the second time I knew someone had put it there purposely, hoping I would step out in my bare feet. Our insolent family cat went missing last month. Since he was a kitten, he never neglected to return for at least one meal a day even when the boys were smaller and used to tie bits of twine and bells to his tail, doing everything they could to make our home a circle of hell for him.

The other night as I was getting ready for bed, I found the poor animal splayed out on my windowsill, sliced from throat to belly, blood and entrails dripping into my second-floor bedroom. Someone had bothered to climb up to my bedroom using a ladder while I slept. No doubt they watched me as I lay unconscious and vulnerable in my bed. Fear gnawed at my heart every night.

The obvious perpetrator was Carmine, Cettina's brother, who glared at me every time we crossed paths in town but otherwise had not acknowledged what had passed between us on his farm years earlier. I worried that he had told the people he worked with about how that man, the one called the Black Hand, had died, how he believed I had murdered him. I worried the Black Hand's bosses wanted revenge.

But Carmine was not the only one in town with a grudge against me. I had healed as many people as I could, but many didn't survive and grief is never rational. The blame for an untimely end in our clinic almost always fell on me. The brother who bled out after a bad fall from a ladder, the daughter who passed in childbirth. The child who would be forever crippled by a virus. My heart ached for the losses, none of which were fair or expected, but my sympathy meant very little to those left behind.

Something crashed onto the kitchen tile. I heard a low grunt and a groan. It was a man for certain. Whoever was downstairs was unfamiliar with the layout of our home. I rose and gripped the machete I'd taken to keeping beneath my pillow these past months.

The door to the boys' room was slightly open and I could see three pairs of feet sticking out from their quilts as I passed. I'd recognize my sons' feet anywhere. You could give me a lineup of the feet of a dozen boys and I would know Cosi's crooked big toe, Santo's flat arches, Vincenzo's extra-wide chubby baby feet that he still hadn't outgrown, more rectangular than feet had any right to be, pudgy bricks anchoring his round body to the ground.

I shut their door, a small protection against whatever would happen next, and tiptoed barefoot down our stairs. The narrow passageway was dizzying at such a careful pace. Whoever was in my house was still in the kitchen, still puttering about and mumbling to themselves in a low and frustrated tone. I would not scream when I entered the room. I did not want to wake the boys and force them to run down to defend me. I would take care of this myself. Bile filled my mouth as I turned the corner and imagined the inevitable confrontation, hoping my nearly silent footsteps would at least give me the element of surprise.

The intruder wore a dark gray overcoat too heavy for the season. I took in the tall, thin body leaning against the stove. There was a patch of scalp visible beneath thinning hair that used to be coarse and strong beneath my fingers. How was it even possible for me to recognize this stranger? This man I'd spent less than a year with during our entire marriage? I knew that it was not him that I recognized. It was my sons. The slope of Cosi's shoulders, the egg-shaped head of Santo. Hair the exact shade of Vin's. I knew all these body parts like I knew my own skin.

"Gio?" I backed away from the kitchen doorframe for a second and stashed the knife in a drawer in the other room.

Relief should have flooded through me; no one was here to harm me. But instead I felt a different kind of dread. Gio had not written, at least not to me, and this felt ominous.

"Fina." He sounded the same, his voice quiet, low, shy. When he turned, he did not look me in the eye, another bad sign, a sign he had heard things about me from across the ocean, things that displeased him.

I rushed over to the stove, not to hug him, that didn't feel right, but to place the kettle on the burner.

"It has been a long journey," he said.

"I did not know you were coming."

"I wrote. I told you. A month ago. I sent you the name of the ship I would be arriving on."

"I never received a letter. But it does not matter. You are here now." I kissed both of his cheeks, finally feeling a small liberation from worry that this visit wasn't unplanned after all, that he had tried to inform me. But the relief was short-lived. He had to be lying. I had never missed one of his letters, never missed one of his payments, not even through the war. Somehow the words and the money always made their way to me. It was the most reliable and most noble thing about this man. And now there were other ways to send news, telegrams, phone calls, though we still did not have a private line. And wouldn't Gio have written his mother too? I had seen his mamma five days ago. Surely she would have been out of her mind with preparations for her boy's return.

"You look good, husband. But why are you here so early in the morning?"

"The ship came in yesterday and I only just got a ride from the port."

"You must be exhausted. Why don't you go to the bedroom and lie down?"

"I would like to eat first."

"Of course." I pulled things from cupboards, olives, dried tomatoes, and sliced a day-old loaf of bread from the table. It was still soft enough that it gave easily under the knife. I smothered the bread in oil and placed it in the oven to toast. The kettle was ready. I would need a strong black coffee as much as Gio surely did.

"The boys will be pleased to see you," I said with a smile as I started to serve him. I made sure to touch his shoulder. I put all the food on one large plate we could share, remembering Paola's husband's complaints that she would not share food with him, that she denied him the simple intimacies of a proper wife.

I sliced up a tomato and drizzled everything with lemon juice before sitting next to him to eat.

"Sorry we have nothing sweet. I usually walk to the bakery in the morning before the children wake." I did not add that the offerings in the bakery were no longer worth buying with Paola gone. My husband shook his head to say it did not matter. He ate with both of his hands, ravenous and greedy.

"Food always tastes better here," he said when he had licked every crumb from the plate. "Why is that?"

"I do not know. I have never been anywhere else," I said honestly. "Would you like to sleep or wait for the children to wake up?"

Thankfully he yawned as his eyes began to droop. "I would like to sleep before I see them. I have much to tell you all this evening when we are together."

I led Gio up the stairs and into our bedroom, wondering if he would want me to lie with him, if I needed to perform my duty as his wife before he could drift off to sleep, but he answered my question by merely removing his shoes, lying on top of my rumpled sheets, and falling right into a deep sleep. I could hear all three boys in their room, and I waited until they were in the kitchen before making my own way downstairs, trying to steady my nerves before facing them.

I had known that my world would fall apart sooner or later. I'd felt my reckoning coming since that morning Cettina and I locked eyes over Marco's broken body. That morning I had eased myself out of his bed and beckoned her forward to tell her that her worst fear was true. Her husband was dying. She momentarily put aside what she'd seen, gripped my hand, and asked me what we should do. Not her, not I, but we. Hadn't we always been a we, ever since our earliest days? I was more yoked to Cettina than I was to my husband, maybe even my children.

"We cannot let him die," she insisted.

There was only one thing I could think of and even that felt like a false hope. "We need to get him to Palermo. There is more that can be done for him there than I can do here. There are real hospitals. There is new medicine. It may give him a chance."

Armed with an opportunity to save her husband, a chance she never had with the first man she married, Cettina sprung into action. "I will figure it out. Stay with him. Keep him comfortable. Do whatever you need to do to make sure he knows he is cared for."

Whatever you need to do. That phrase lingered long after she left the house. I stripped his body of his sweat-stained clothes, bathed him with a sponge, and gave him enough morphine to take away his pain. I found clothes and prepared him for his journey, all the while kissing his face, his hands, his bare chest, telling him that I loved him, that I would always love him.

Cettina quickly found Gaetana, who had inherited her dead husband's car but who did not know how to drive it. Gaetana called on Leda, who could drive but had no car. The two women arrived within the hour, ready to be put into service.

"No one can know how sick he is," Cettina insisted to all of us. "If the wrong people found out that our mayor was this ill, you know it would not be good." We knew. We swore. Cettina stayed back with the children after helping us lay Marco down in the back seat, his head in my lap. I was careful how I touched him in front of the other women. He never once opened his eyes.

I knew only one doctor in Palermo, knew of him was more accurate. I had read his articles about experiments with mercury, copper, and sulfur to fight off infections of the organs. Once we arrived in the city we managed to ask around and find the hospital where he worked and the nurses there directed me to an office in his private home. Driving through Palermo's confusing grid of streets took many hours and many misunderstandings. Leda nearly drove the car into a livery station after making a wrong turn, but eventually we found the house. How did I look to this doctor when I arrived on his doorstep, a bedraggled peasant with stains on her dress? I gave him no time to react. I sputtered out the situation—that I came from a small village, that the mayor of the town was desperately ill, that the doctor in our town thought he had an infection of the liver that had progressed quite far. The man's eyes flickered with interest when I described Marco's symptoms. He was eager to try new things and even though I cringed at the idea of Marco being an experiment, I also knew I could not let him simply waste away back at home. The doctor accepted Marco as a patient and kept him at the house for treatment. That was many months ago and I had not been back to Palermo since, though Leda had visited with Cettina and reported that Marco was making slow and steady progress. Cetti had not spoken a word to me since then. She didn't meet my eyes in the market or at mass, where she was often accompanied by her brother Carmine. I was terrified to approach her, but I forced myself to behave as I normally would in the hopes that we could come to terms. When I went to her home her children answered the door and said she was not available. She no longer looked after my boys for me while I worked, and sometimes I brought Vin to the clinic with me.

So yes, I had been waiting for some kind of reckoning, the air around me feeling thick with the possibility for weeks. I just never imagined it would come in the form of my husband.

The boys were already eating at our round kitchen table once I made it downstairs, picking at the scraps Gio and I had left behind.

"Your father has returned," I told them as simply as possible. I always wondered what the word *father* meant to them. I imagined he was like the character in a story they had heard over and over again. But did Gio's absence make them resent him or revere him? We never spoke of him. I read them his letters. I told them he was working hard to make sure all of us could have a better life, and they never asked questions. I kept the one photograph I had of him above the mantel. Vin had barely any memories of Gio. Cosi had the most, but they were so fleeting. Of course once I told them he had arrived they wanted to see him. I told them he was asleep, that they should go to school and do their afternoon chores, that we would all meet for a meal later.

Before they left, Cosi pulled me aside. "Does this mean we will be going to *la Mérica*, Mamma?"

"I do not know what it means, Cosimo." He frowned a little. For as long as I had dreamed of escaping this village, I could hardly imagine uprooting my family now. Even though times were hard for our village, my children always had enough and what they did not have they did not know about. Cosi's nervous stutter echoed my apprehension. He kissed me on the cheek and whispered, "I love you, Mamma. We will be good no matter what happens or where we go. Good as bread." He dutifully walked his two younger brothers to school. My stomach was in shreds when they were out of my eyesight.

I spent the next few hours rushing around town, gathering supplies and ingredients for a feast worthy of my husband's homecoming. I had no doubt I would be hosting my mother-in-law and Gio's sisters. I knew without being told that I would be relegated to my kitchen for the next week, and I tried not to let resentment overtake me.

When I returned home, arms heavy with food and wine, Gio was awake and riffling around the bedroom, opening drawers. My drawers. I stood in the doorway and cleared my throat in a manner I hoped was not accusatory. "Can I help you find something?"

He looked properly chagrined that I had caught him going through my things.

"I was looking for a comb," he told me, and used his hand to sheepishly flatten pieces of hair that had curled away from his scalp in his sleep. Maybe he hadn't been trying to invade my privacy at all. I found my hairbrush for him and indicated he should sit on the bed. I climbed around the mattress behind him and began to brush what was left of his once lovely hair. He let out a deep, contented sigh as the bristles passed over his skull and I thought he would reach for me, but instead he simply let me continue until his hair was neat and orderly.

"I should start the meal. Will your mamma be coming?" I had not yet told anyone in town about my husband's arrival.

"She does not know that I am here. I wrote only to you."

"I never got the letter."

"I do not know why."

It was strange that he hadn't informed his mother. He usually told her everything. He wrote to her more often than he wrote to me, or at least I assumed that was the case given how much more she knew about the daily happenings in his life than I did.

"I will walk to her house tomorrow," he said. "And surprise her. Today it can be just us, you and me and the boys?"

"Of course."

"When will they be home?"

I had been out doing the shopping for the entire morning and lost track of time. "An hour, maybe more."

"Could we go for a walk before they return?"

"Aren't you afraid of running into your mamma?"

"We can walk up the mountain, away from town. I want to be able to glimpse the sea."

I tied a veil around my hair to protect it from the harsh, sandy scirocco winds that had been blowing in from the coast for weeks. When we fell into step next to one another it felt like a stroll with an old friend. But there was also an undercurrent to our silence, the discussion we would have when we stopped walking. Gio seemed as nervous to begin as I was. Every time I thought we would pause at a pleasant overlook, he kept going, until we were at the very top of the mountain, the place where the trail peeled off to Rosalia's home, mostly empty since her passing a few months earlier. I stored many of my medical supplies in her old house to keep them away from my children. I often imagined living alone in the stone hovel, the peace and the loneliness. She left me the house and everything in it, not that she owned this land or that the old medical journals and surgery tools were worth anything to anyone but me. I had been the one to hold her hand as she passed out of this world and into the next and I would always remember how peaceful, almost joyous she appeared as she was going. It was ultimately a disease of the heart that took her, something we could never fix. She'd been coughing up blood for months, but I gave her all the morphine at my disposal, not even worrying if I had anything left. When she was able, she wanted to talk and I wanted to listen. She told me she never regretted not having children until she met me. She never wanted them and she was lucky enough to avoid the unchosen fate of many of the women in our village. But when we met, she understood what it meant to pass knowledge and learning down to someone. That was what gave her peace in the end.

"You will do more than I ever could," she insisted with one of her final breaths.

I thought about her words as I waited for my husband to tell me my fate. He sat and rolled a cigarette from a pouch of tobacco hidden in his jacket pocket. After smoking half of it he finally said what he had come home to say.

"It is time for you to join me. For you and the boys to join me in America."

I said nothing. That was a mistake. I should have expressed joy. In my silence he rolled another cigarette as I gazed over the rippling fields and the sea wondering what he knew of my life. Did he want to take me away from here because he'd heard rumors about me and Marco? Was it because of my work, the shame of having a wife who earned money doing a man's job? These were questions I could never ask. I could not even manage to say, *Why now?* because it would be understood as disobedience. So I nodded like a mute idiot, hating myself for my silence. He continued.

"The situation here is not improving. I probably hear more of the news than you do." In his voice I heard great condescension. "The unification of Italy continues to do nothing but destroy Sicily and Sicilians. It has been much worse since the Great War. The northern Italians are our new conquerors. And worse, now all of Europe steals from us and gives nothing in return. There is much anger here and many believe there will be another war and Sicily will suffer. They won't even let us speak our language!"

I knew what he spoke of. Marco and I talked often about the rise of the militant journalist Benito Mussolini and his new political movement, which was trying to marry the desire for socialism in the peasant class with the kind of nationalism befitting a unified country. Mussolini's supporters called themselves the Blackshirts and formed sects called the *squadristi*. They attacked anyone they believed to be anti-Italian, which included those who saw ourselves as Sicilians first and Italians only when necessary. I had treated several men who were attacked by the *squadristi* in Sciacca for daring to fly only a Sicilian flag and speak only in dialect. Mussolini wanted to force us all to only speak proper Italian. He was smart. By stealing our language, he could steal our voices. The *squadristi* used torture, sometimes even on children, to gain information about who was loyal. And, as always, us regular citizens were caught between the politicians and the *mafiusi*. We all knew the violence would only get worse.

But I feigned ignorance about all of it and nodded for my husband to ramble on.

"I have opportunities for us. I have been working hard and made many connections. I no longer owe any debts to the men who helped me get on my feet when I arrived in New York. I have enough saved to bring you and the boys and my mamma. If we sell our house in town, we will have enough money to purchase a small amount of land and build a house in a city outside of New York. Lots of us have been moving there."

"We would not be living in the city of New York?" I asked. Not that it mattered. Not that New York was any different from any other city in America to me.

"The work is hard in the city, and we are still poor by their standards. Any apartment we could afford would be small. You would need to work too. But if we move to Scranton in Pennsylvania that would not be the case. And if there is more money, I can invest in a small business I can pass down to the boys. That's why you need to sell that land that was given to you by the mayor. That extra money could support our family for generations."

This was why he'd come home. I had stopped responding to his queries about selling the land with the clinic on it. I didn't even know if I had the power to do it. Marco had given me a flimsy deed that declared the land be used for a hospital. I never went to a bank or met with an official.

Gio grabbed both of my hands and stared into my eyes. He was begging me for something for the first time in our lives and I remembered the young man I once held through the night as he cried about the horrors he'd experienced in the sulfur mines. I wondered what he had seen and done in the new country that I hadn't bore witness to.

"You will never need to work again if we sell that land. You can stay home and care for the boys the way I know you have always wanted to but couldn't because I was gone. We will have more children in the United States. I know you needed extra money and that is why you worked. It is my fault."

I tried to quiet Rosalia's voice in the back of my head. *You will do more than I ever could.* That would not be the case when I joined my husband in the strange city of Scranton. I would be put back into my place in the home. He would keep asking for more babies. My intellect and my talent would wither. I would slowly die.

I kissed him on the mouth then, the correct response from a wife who is given the gift of being cared for by her husband, of not having to work, of getting to leave for a new life in America, the land of every immigrant's dreams. "It is complicated. With the land. It was given to me to be a clinic. I will need to talk to Marco and he is not here. He is very sick. But I will see what I can do. We should get back to the house and back to the boys." Gio spun me around when I turned away from him, more violently than I expected.

"I am not asking you, Serafina."

"I know that, Gio." I wrenched my arm away from his grip. He did not have it in him to grab at me again and I quickened my step back to the house, taking the longer route through town, knowing Gio did not want to call attention to himself yet.

He did not mention the land again when we ate with the boys. Instead, Gio regaled them with stories of America, of tall buildings that touched the clouds, of immigrant men who became millionaires through hard work and perseverance. The younger two were entranced by the stories. Cosimo remained skeptical and gripped my hand beneath the table.

That night I lay with Gio as I knew he expected me to. It took only moments and passed in a pleasant silence except for the rhythmic creak of the bedposts. My husband, for his part, was satiated. I woke before the sun in the morning, leaving him in my bed. It was fortuitous that I was the first one to reach our door. An envelope had been slipped beneath it in the night and I immediately recognized the handwriting I never thought I would see again. Two sentences from Marco:

Come to Palermo. I need to see you.

———

Despite the crowds and the poverty, the intensity of everyone and everything, I loved being a stranger in a strange place.

Palermo crackled with vigor, the sounds and smells assaulting all of my senses at once.

It was a miracle I made it to the city at all. When I first read Marco's note I dismissed a visit as impossible. I burned it after I read it and once the words had turned to ash, I tried to forget them.

There was simply no way I could go to Palermo to meet Marco. Gio would insist on coming and I could not imagine surviving any scenario with my husband and lover in the same room.

For the past couple of weeks Gio had strutted around Caltabellessa like he was a rich man in his fancy felt hat and suit, a returning conqueror. He sat for hours with the old men in the piazza puffed up with tales of his success in New York City. Gio was home for two weeks when he fell ill. Just a cough and a fever, nothing more, but it knocked at least a little of the hubris out of him. He complained that the illness came from the unsanitary conditions in our village, told me it was yet another reason we had to leave. He used it as another excuse to press me again to learn more about selling the land.

I took advantage of the opportunity. I said there were things about the deed that I could only learn from Marco and that I would have to go to Palermo. I said this only because I knew my husband was too sick and exhausted to argue or to try to accompany me. I knew he would let me go if it meant we were that much closer to getting the money.

I found a ride in a truck with the fishmonger from Sciacca who delivered fish to our village once a week and to Palermo once a month. For a few lire he said I could join. Gio had his mamma taking care of him, doting on him, making her own plans to prepare a move to America, and telling anyone who did not ask that her son was now a rich man who would be taking care of her for the rest of her days in a house with plumbing across the ocean.

The fishmonger and I stayed silent the entire drive. I was grateful that we had paid him enough money for me to sit in the front of the truck. There were three others from Sciacca riding in the back, tightly packed in with the bulgy-eyed cuttlefish.

The monger dropped me close to my requested address and said he would return to the same spot for me at the same time the next day. Marco knew I was coming. I had sent a letter and told him not to respond.

I spent an hour wandering through the streets of Palermo to prepare myself for our meeting. Finally I returned to the heart of the city, the Quattro Canti, to the doctor's grand baroque home behind the church of San Giuseppe dei Teatini.

When Marco greeted me at the doctor's front door, I nearly collapsed right there on the stoop. He gripped both of my arms before I could stumble, and pulled me into the most elegant courtyard and garden I had ever seen. Fan palms lined white-pebbled paths surrounding a massive marble fountain fit for a palace, not the home of a doctor. I was astonished at all of it, at Marco standing on his own two feet when he had previously been at death's door, at the luxury of the property, at how intensely my body was reacting to being close to him again. I did not even realize tears were streaming down my cheeks until Marco brushed them away and led me to a bench. He was still far from well. He walked with a cane, favoring the left side of his body over his right. His color was off, his skin the sallow yellow of sun-dried turmeric. The most shocking change was his head. His curls were gone, his head shaved all the way to the scalp. But he was upright and mobile. He was able to steady me as I tried to get my bearings. Somewhere within the depths of the garden a door slammed and I startled.

"Dottor Lombardo is leaving to teach a class at the university,"

Marco informed me. "We are alone except for the maids and the cook. But we do not have to stay here. We can go out into the city. I have been preparing for your visit for weeks, saving up all my energy. There was a part of me that could not bear for you to see me like this." He ran his hand over the shiny skin on top of his head. "But I put my pride aside."

I pulled him to me, brought his head to my breast, and kissed his smooth scalp over and over.

"How is this possible?" I whispered. "I thought you would be close to death."

"Me too," he said, sighing in pleasure at the touch of my lips. "But the doctor would not give up. After I arrived, he gave me a shot of something that helped me regain consciousness. I told him to do whatever he had to do. Some days I thought he was a monster. Some days I thought he was a saint. I think you need to be a bold mixture of both of those things if you want to heal the way that he heals. But I *am* healing. Look at me. I am standing on my own two feet, walking, eating. He assures me that eventually I can return home."

Home. Our town. The place I would be leaving as soon as Gio and I could get our affairs in order.

"Marco, I have something to tell you."

"I have things to tell you too, my love. But first can we find something to eat? I was so excited by your arrival that I was not able to eat anything this morning and now the cook has taken her rest. I haven't ventured too far from here, but there is a trattoria close by with an excellent lunch. You and I have never eaten at a restaurant together out in the open. I would very much like to take you."

"Let's go," I managed.

He grasped my hand, and we strolled through the streets of the city like husband and wife. We arrived at a restaurant called the Casa del Brodo dal Dottore with a sunny-yellow exterior and an impressive stained-glass door depicting the doctor saints Cosma and Damiano, both of them penniless healers of the third century. I raised an eyebrow at the scenes on the door, hoping Marco would explain. "Lombardo's brother owns this restaurant. It has been in their family since the 1890s and it is famous for its broth, which the doctor believes has medicinal properties. I do not know if that is true, but it is tasty."

The inside was small, only eight tables. A waiter brought out a carafe of red wine and Marco poured two glasses, toasting us.

"To our future."

My heart sank at his toast, knowing what I needed to tell him, that we had no future together, that I would be leaving soon. But I wanted to delay this as long as possible.

"Tell me everything the doctor has done to you," I said in response.

"I do not even know most of it." He took a sip, considering what to reveal. "He has removed a lot of my blood and replaced it with the blood of others. I do not know where it all came from, whether it came from a body that was alive or dead. He thought it was best that I did not know all the details. It could be animal blood for all I know. Wouldn't that be something? To have the blood of an ox?" It was clear Marco had an intense respect for this man, and so did I after seeing how well my love was doing.

The waiter brought out two steaming bowls filled with thick broth. "*Tortellini in brodo*," he announced.

The tiny hat-shaped morsels of dough fell apart in my mouth, revealing baked cheeses and pork mixed with unexpected spices, cinnamon, maybe cardamom. The broth was hearty and satisfying;

it tasted of the sea and the land all at once, briny and sharp. I finished within minutes.

"My compliments to the chef. This is glorious."

"You are glorious." Marco took one of my hands in his and I traced the thick blue veins visible through his skin with my free fingers. "I want to take you all over this city."

"You are still a sick man," I asserted. "And we are already being too bold, eating out in a restaurant like this. You never know who will see us, even this far from home."

"Please let me take you around to the places I have discovered while taking my daily walks. The doctor insists on them. He says that staying in bed for days on end is the primary reason so many patients remain ill. The blood must be moved through the body."

When I finally agreed he left some money on the table, and we headed back out onto the street. I pulled his hat lower onto his brow and hid my hair with a scarf, for all that did to disguise the two of us as we walked hand in hand through the melee of via Vittorio Emanuele. Young boys squeezed in close to us, wanting to sell us painted postcards of the city. We dodged wheelbarrows filled with oranges, lemons, poppies, and sumac. Larger painted carts were pulled by donkeys in elaborate feathered headdresses covered in bells that jingled as they trotted by us.

I was ashamed of my simple dress and black mantilla. Women in Palermo had shed their traditional costumes and wore bright tailored outfits. Some of the stores along the viale della Libertà even bore the signs written in French boasting CHAPEAUX DE PARIS. Marco led with authority, as though he had been walking the uneven stone streets of Palermo his entire life. We tripped up the steps of the grand Teatro Massimo. I stopped to marvel at the massive lion statues flanking the theater and reached up to pet one. "Lombardo told me they brought real lions and elephants onstage for their operas," Marco explained once we'd descended back to the street. He plucked a pear from a rickety bench displaying fruit and vegetables in every color of the rainbow, some shapes I'd never seen before. We ate it together at a fountain surrounded by seats that were filled with pilgrims and families, priests and nuns. Music came from a bandstand constructed to look like a small Greek temple.

Everywhere I looked, beautiful buildings loomed over us, as high as the cliffs above Caltabellessa, many of them covered in chiseled statues of goddesses who gazed down upon us with concern. Inside the grand cathedrals the golden icons blinded me with their splendor, though outside of each of them the stairs were littered with beggars.

Marco and I passed beneath a stone arch to a calmer, cleaner lane. No more pushcarts or animals, only a couple pedestrians. "This is one of the oldest streets in Palermo, or so they say," he told me. Intricate blue and yellow tile work surrounded the windows and doors. Wrought-iron balconies, barely large enough for one, teetered over our heads. Sheets hung from their railings, threatening to flap right in our faces. Many of the crooked wooden doors were flung open and I gazed through them into courtyards much like Lombardo's, the entryways to much grander spaces, their modesty cloaking the wealth.

We strolled in silence for a couple more blocks. Marco dropped my hand and held tight to my arm. I could not tell whether it was in exhaustion or anticipation.

Eventually he paused in front of an imposing stone wall covered in vines and fragrant white plumerias. He pushed aside some of the greenery, revealing a small door in the stone that swung open at the slightest touch.

"How did you find this?" I asked.

"Magic."

"I do not enjoy teasing."

"The doctor told me where to look. He knows everything about these streets. Like I said, he truly is a remarkable man."

What I was looking at right beyond the entryway might have been a church, but it was far less ornate than any of the other churches I had passed in Palermo with their elaborate carvings and stained-glass windows, their spires and cupolas reaching as close to heaven as possible.

"Look up," Marco instructed.

There was no roof.

"It was never finished?" There was a bygone grandeur in the unfinished ceiling and the simple bare walls.

"It was meant to be a monastery in the sixteenth century, but the Ottoman raids on the island halted the work and the stone that was meant for the ceiling was diverted to build new walls to protect the city."

"It is peaceful in here."

"It is. I have spent many afternoons in silence, sitting right over there." He pointed to a low stone bench in the shade of a fig tree. Palms and yucca sprung from the healthy green grass covering the ground inside while violet wisteria climbed the walls.

"Then that is how we should spend this afternoon," I said, and led him to the bench, hoping I could compel him to finally rest. "In silence."

"Hopefully not in silence." Once we were sitting, he wrapped an arm around my shoulders. "Or maybe some silence." He leaned over to truly kiss me for the first time since I'd arrived. I clung to him like a newborn would cling to its mother, desperate and hungry. I grasped his arms, his neck, his waist, all of it smaller and frailer than it had been months earlier. I don't know how long we stayed entwined like that, but we were both breathless when we finally broke apart.

"I love you, Serafina," he said as he traced my cheekbones with his index finger.

I pulled away. "Marco," I began. I did not have all my words ready for him. I had expected to find a dying man. I had expected to say my goodbyes, to tell him that I would soon be following my own husband to our new country. I hadn't expected to have any reason to stay. But he kissed me again before I could continue and eventually he pulled me to my feet and into the shadows of what was meant to be a private chamber of the old forgotten church. The floor was nothing but dirt and soft leaves, and it still felt like the most luxurious mattress in all the world.

For the rest of Palermo it was merely another autumn day. For the two of us it was everything. We made love and then fell asleep in one another's arms. When we finally wandered out of the ruins I was starving, and Marco bought me an entire rich meal prepared right in the street. He paid a half lire for two *pani c'a mèusa,* light and fluffy pieces of bread filled with succulent meat and peppery *caciocavallo* cheese grilled atop a fire perched in the gutter. We ate it with our hands, juices dribbling down our chins.

We eventually found our way back to Marco's small quarters. Inside there was only a bed and a porcelain tub that on closer inspection I saw was filled with steaming hot water.

"The nurses fill it every night before I go to bed. It is part of Lombardo's treatment, a bath as hot as I can stand at least once a day to sweat out the disease. Would you join me in it?" He was already gently removing my dress, kissing my bare neck and shoulders.

My skin turned pink once I was in the scalding water, but Marco wrapped his arms around me from behind. "Give it a few seconds. Let your body relax."

Like magic, the heat stopped searing my skin and I allowed myself to sink into Marco's embrace, closing my eyes and trying to savor the moment.

"When I thought I was dying, you were my only regret," Marco said, twisting my damp hair between his fingers. "The fact that I didn't wake up with you every morning and fall asleep in your arms. It was the only thing I knew I was doing wrong in my life."

"What you want is crazy," I murmured.

"Does it have to be?"

"You are too good a man to abandon our village, much less abandon your family."

"But what if we found a way to make this work too? What if we could travel here to Palermo more often? You could study with the doctor. I could receive my treatments. There are ways we can be together. And it will not be long before our children are grown and there might be other options for us."

I knew then that I had to explain that his dreams weren't simply crazy, they were impossible.

"Gio has returned." I said it to the wall opposite the tub, unable to turn and meet Marco's gaze. "He has been back for nearly a month now. He says that it is time I join him with the boys."

Marco's grip on me tightened. I usually welcomed his touch, but this was too rough.

"My love," I began.

"I cannot let you leave."

I had never heard this kind of sharpness in his voice. "You do not have a choice. I do not have a choice." I twisted out of his grasp and turned to face him, straddling my legs on top of his, drawing his face to mine.

"I almost lost you the day that I brought you here. But now we have both been given a second chance to be good, to fulfill the vows we made to our spouses in front of God. I would love nothing more than to wake up in your arms every morning of my life." My voice cracked as I imagined what that would feel like. "But we have always known that was impossible."

His eyes blazed with a fury so intense I worried he might strike me for merely stating the truth. I stroked his cheeks, gently kissed his lips, and tried to use my softness to defuse him. But as quickly as his anger was ignited, it began to dissipate. He sank low into the tub, the fight drained out of him, the reality of our circumstances setting in. It was as good a time as any to tell him the rest.

"Gio wants me to sell the land with the hospital on it, so that he can start a business in the new country," I whispered.

"So that is why you came. Because your husband asked you to?" he scoffed. "Because you need money."

"No. No, my love. I do not care about the money. I will tell him it is impossible."

"But it is not. That land is yours to do with as you wish. Sell it if he needs money. I do not care. Sell it tomorrow. Go to the Banco di Sicilia on via Roma. I filed a copy of the paperwork there. They have what you need. But, Serafina, you must promise me one thing."

"I cannot promise you anything." I had no agency in this situation. None at all.

"Sell the land, but do not leave. Give him what he wants. Give him money. But do not leave me."

He was still a sick man and I worried that he would only get sicker if I took the dream of our future away from him. So I lied.

"I will not leave you." I wanted to mean those words with every ounce of my soul. My whole body ached. Bile rose in my throat as if I had swallowed quinine, but I managed a meek "I love you, my darling. I love you."

Marco and I were both shivering by then. I found two towels set on a chair at the end of the bath, helped Marco to his feet, and dried us off.

We didn't make love again that night. I let myself linger in his embrace for only a few moments after opening my eyes before I rose and got myself dressed before he was awake. I paused for a moment, leaning out the window, clutching onto the marble sill and breathing deeply to fortify myself before gently kissing his lips one last time and walking quietly out the door.

———

It took the entire day to return home. My house was dark, and my front door would not open. My key did not turn in the lock. My first thought was that I was doing something wrong. That the door not opening was a trick of my exhausted mind, but then I realized that something, or someone, was behind the frame preventing the door from opening. I heard a movement, the scratch of a chair moving across the stone floor, a clatter of metal falling to the ground, perhaps a key stuck into the other side of the lock. I tried once more.

When the door finally creaked open I froze, afraid to enter my own home.

Gio stood a few paces from the door, his legs wobbly. I winced at the smells coming off my husband: sweat, liquor, sickness, and unwashed skin. His feet and chest were bare.

"Where are the boys?" I asked. How I hoped they were home and safe in their bed, close by in case I needed their help.

"My mother's house."

I tried to walk around him to reach the stairs to the second floor, but he blocked my path.

"What did you learn about the land, Serafina? About selling it."

I lied. I had decided that if I couldn't keep my promise to Marco and stay in Sicily, I also could not sell his land. I could not take his money. I was not a prostitute. I quickly told Gio the story I had invented on the drive home. I told him that I learned that it didn't legally belong to me, that it belonged to whichever doctor ran the hospital, that it was essentially public property. I told him I had misunderstood the transfer of the land because I was stupid about such things.

Gio raised a hand in the air as if to strike me. When I cowered backward he thought better of it and wilted onto the floor. He glowered up at me.

"What in the devil have you been doing while I've been gone? My mamma has suspicions about you. She mentioned them when I said you went to Palermo to meet with the mayor. She says the two of you are too friendly. She said I put too much faith in you."

I stared him directly in the eye. "Everyone in this town suspects everyone else of something. You know that."

"My mamma said I should beat you to remind you of your honor."

I reached my hand to his cheek and discovered it was wet with tears. I hated him in that moment, but I consoled him anyway.

"My darling, the rumors are just gossip. There is no truth to them. I will keep inquiring about the land. But we will sell this house. There will be plenty of money from that. Soon we will be in America, all of us together."

I had been foolish to go to Palermo on my own and I'd eventually learn I'd been foolish about other things. It would be months before I realized the extent of my folly, before I knew without a doubt that the child growing in my stomach was Marco's and not my husband's.

TWENTY-ONE

SARA

The meeting at the Caltabellessa city hall was already underway by the time I made it back and the chamber was packed. This was clearly the most exciting thing happening in town. It was a pageant, a spectacle, and I was the main event.

A scrum of elderly women, dressed head to toe in long black dresses, huddled by the entrance. One of them reached for my hand as the heavy door slammed behind me, her touch warm, the skin of her palm paper-thin and soft.

"Diu ti binirici." God bless you.

The cavernous meeting room had to be three stories high with rows and rows of benches that resembled church pews. A massive Sicilian flag hung above a mahogany podium flanked by two long tables where six older men sat in high-backed wooden chairs, three on each side. I assumed they were various municipal officials. A smaller Italian tricolor flag fluttered begrudgingly next to the Sicilian banner.

Giusy's halo of massive black curls was obvious in the front row. She turned back to look at me along with the rest of the room, all of them clearly waiting for "the American" to arrive. Giusy was a vision in a perfectly fitting white suit with a low-cut black blouse beneath, her boobs pushed up to within inches of her chin. A gold chain, its links the size of quarters, hugged her neck like a dog collar. She strutted down the aisle in impossibly high red heels while carrying a matching bright red cane in her right hand, which she tapped onto the stone floor in a staccato symphony as she approached me. The sound of the cane reminded me of Agata's story about what happened to Giusy's husband, Giusy's *furbezza*, her devious intelligence. Giusy would do whatever it took to survive, and I knew I should never forget that.

I still allowed her to take my elbow and escort me to her row like a reluctant bride. She was the only friend I had in this town.

I sat between Giusy and Raguzzo, the *notaio*. He offered me a smile, his braces gleaming in the fluorescent lighting. In the aisle behind us, I spotted the men who assaulted me the other day, Armani Belt and his slob of a friend.

When I sat down he whispered: "*Porca puttana.*" I didn't turn.

"He called you a pig slut," Giusy translated for me.

"Yes, I know," I hissed back, adding, "Why didn't you tell me your cousin owned that land?"

Her eyes widened in mock innocence. "I thought I told you."

"You didn't."

"You must have forgotten."

"I didn't."

Giusy turned to her cousin with a wide smile and a flick of her fingers beneath her chin. "*Vaffanculo a chi t'è morto.*" Then she said to me, "I told him to go screw his dead relatives."

"Aren't they your relatives too?"

"I meant he could screw the relatives on the other side of the family. You look good. Did you get a tan?"

"I got some sun. You look spectacular."

"I know. So that man, right there." Giusy pointed to the front of the room. "The little one shaped like an avocado. He is the mayor." Giusy gave a wave to the mayor by wiggling the same four fingers that she had previously used to tell the other men to fuck off. The mayor walked to the podium, where a young woman, a secretary who appeared to be barely out of high school, brought a wooden box for him to stand on so that he could reach the microphone.

He cleared his throat and greeted the crowd before bowing his head.

"He's so dramatic. He's praying," Giusy said.

Once he was finished blessing us, the mayor spoke in a mixture of Italian and dialect that would have been difficult for me to follow if Giusy didn't provide a steady stream of narration.

"The land just below the village containing the remains of the old abbey and village hospital is under consideration for purchase by Sheikh Khalid Al-Falih." She pointed to the group of Middle Eastern men across the aisle from us. Four of them wore gray suits, white shirts, and ties. They sat confidently with their hands in their laps. They flanked a fifth man in a long flowing robe with a red-and-white-checked scarf over his head—the sheikh, I assumed.

"The mayor is saying that the sheikh is looking to purchase the land in addition to the adjoining parcel in order to build a new seven-star resort with a golf course and a spa that will bring tourism to the region and save us all."

"That's what he said?"

"Essentially. Most of the land belongs to the Puglisi family, that donkey fucker sitting behind us."

"Your cousin. What's his actual name?"

"Antonino. But we call him Nino. Now the mayor says the other parcel of land in question may belong to you. He says the town council will decide if you are the rightful owner and if you are allowed to sell it to the sheikh."

Nino and his compatriot stood up and walked to the podium. His friend kept his mirrored aviator sunglasses on and clutched a bulge in his belt that I knew was his gun, as if he might have to prevent an attack at any moment. I would have laughed if everyone else in the room were not so deadly serious and silent.

"Nino is saying the land has always been in his family, since the very early days of this village," Giusy said once her cousin began speaking. "He says they defended it against invaders from far and wide. The Normans, the Germans."

"And you thought the mayor was dramatic."

"Sicilian men are so emotional. Haven't you seen the Italian soccer team when they're playing in the World Cup? Always falling to the ground and crying. Women do not have time for that kind of emotion. We have too much to do. Now my cousin is saying that he welcomes the partnership with our Arab brothers, the kind of friendly alliance that will usher in the rebirth of Sicilian commerce and tourism. Who wrote this for him? He says we cannot allow an American capitalist to come in and steal land rightfully belonging to a Sicilian. He says your deed is fake, that you created it on a computer with Photoshop and that you are nothing but a scammer and a fraud."

In the wake of this character assassination all eyes in the room fell squarely on me, most of them narrowed into slits.

"Don't worry," Giusy whispered. "We will get our chance to speak."

I was the lead in a play that I hadn't tried out for, had never even seen the script for, but it was sure as hell time for me to write myself in. Nino continued for a few moments more, basically accusing me

313

of being a colonizer with questionable morals and motives. Giusy eventually stopped translating.

The door in the back of the hall creaked open and once again everyone pivoted, eager for another character to take the stage. I recognized him, but it took me a moment to remember where from. Then it clicked. The man from yesterday morning, the grungy guy on the bench who took my photo, was walking into the hall and sneaking a seat in the back row.

"My secret weapon," Giusy said.

"You know him?"

"I invited him."

"Who is he?"

"A reporter."

"Did you have me followed in Palermo?"

She pretended not to hear the question. "You being here, this dispute over the land, an American woman versus members of the Cosa Nostra. That's interesting for a reporter. No?"

"The Cosa Nostra?"

"My cousin. His friend. I told you all about him when we went to dinner. They are associates for the Abruzzi Family. Always have been. That farm hasn't made money in years, but they let the Abruzzi store their drugs on the land and then they transport them in the sheep's asses when the carcasses are shipped to the mainland. But the Sicilian government has cracked down. So my cousin wants to get rid of the land. He has big dreams of moving to Ibiza and becoming a DJ and a rapper, but to do that he needs money. He has two girl-friends and they both have kids, so he will need to pay them off if he wants to leave. He was counting on selling his land and your land to get enough to be able to tell them both to piss off and to finance his dreams of becoming Tiësto. But now you are here and he is angry."

Giusy teetered up the aisle to take her turn at the podium. Raguzzo scooched closer to translate for me, but his commentary wasn't nearly as thorough or as colorful as Giusy's. She held up a copy of the deed for the land and pointed to me.

"She is saying that since more than a million men left Sicily around the turn of the century that all of us have family members in America. Some of us have been supported by them over the years. She says Serafina Forte wanted you to have this land."

When Giusy mentioned the name Serafina Forte, groans erupted from some in the room. Yet when I turned, I saw the group of old women in black dresses perk up and I took a closer look at them.

Calculating the women's ages was impossible. They could have been sixty or a hundred and ten. They couldn't possibly remember Serafina, if they were even alive before she was murdered. But their mothers would have known her. There was even a small chance that some of the older ones had been brought into this world by her hands.

Giusy ignored the discontent in the room and continued. She said there was nothing wrong with an Italian American returning to their homeland to claim their legacy and that I was the rightful owner of the land.

Raguzzo nodded along. "Giusy is good. She is earning her twenty percent."

"I thought it was ten percent."

"I am sure it is a sliding scale. What is money anyway? I will go next and say that I believe your deed is legally binding, that you are the rightful owner of the land, and then there will be time for discussion."

When Giusy stepped down, Raguzzo replaced her at the microphone. He gave his official two cents and opened the floor to the audience.

A local man in pants tighter than pantyhose asked a rapid-fire succession of rhetorical questions about whether the land ever could have legally belonged to my great-grandmother, whether it was given in good faith or she tricked the owner into passing it on to her with her magic.

"He is an idiot. He works for my cousin," Giusy explained. "He wants to remind everyone in the village that she was a witch who used her feminine powers to tempt men."

The man stepped down from the podium and was followed by another who said the exact same thing. Then Nicolo, the sculptor, stood and slowly made his way to the front. A hush settled over the entire room.

"What's *he* doing?" I asked Giusy as I rooted around in my backpack for the documents I obtained in Palermo, trying to figure out how I could inject myself into the proceedings.

"I do not know." She looked as surprised as everyone else in the hall.

Nicolo spoke in clear and careful Italian with perfect diction. I wondered if it was for my benefit but then I looked at the sheikh, who no longer had his translator whispering in his ear, and I realized he must also speak Italian and that Nicolo wanted him to understand.

Nicolo's voice was smooth as fresh cream and he mesmerized the crowd with his showmanship, clearly honed from years of courting art investors in America. In simple prose he said he knew Serafina Marsala only briefly at the start of his life, when he was taken to her clinic and she treated him for malaria. For months she nursed him back to health. He described her careful bedside manner and the way she looked after everyone in the clinic. She was a godly woman, he insisted, a good woman, a woman who did much for the village, who saved hundreds of lives during the terrible flus that ravaged the island in the 1920s. I glanced at the old women in the back of the room and saw them nodding along. Tears formed in my own eyes, but I squeezed them shut to keep the waterworks at bay. Bursting into ugly sobs would do nothing to help my case.

"Serafina Forte Marsala deserves our respect and so does her kin, one of whom is here in this courtroom." He nodded to me and finished with an admonishment. "We have demonized a woman who did nothing but keep our village alive. Why? Because we enjoy petty gossip? Let this girl who has traveled so far claim her rightful inheritance."

I almost expected a standing ovation once he was finished but it wasn't that kind of crowd. Still, the nods of respect Nicolo received as he hobbled through the center aisle of the room and right out the door were enough to show his message was acknowledged. He leaned in to squeeze my shoulder on his way out. I wished I could follow him, but instead I took advantage of the empty podium and approached it. I'd practiced my speech, writing it all out in Italian in Pippo's car.

"I am Sara Marsala. I know I'm a stranger to your town. I've only just arrived but I want you to know how much this village meant to my family. I was sent here by my great-aunt Rosie, who was born here nearly a hundred years ago. This place meant so much to her and she wanted me to bring her remains here. It was her final wish."

One of her final wishes, I added to myself.

"I am named after her mother, Serafina, the woman Nicolo spoke of. My family in America has always regarded her so highly. I knew nothing but wonderful things about her when I was growing up. But I was surprised when my aunt Rosie left me a deed with her name on it. Probably as surprised as all of you are to see me here."

That, at least, got a few chuckles from the crowd.

"I visited a lawyer in Palermo yesterday to confirm what Signor Raguzzo has told you. He validated the deed and ran a check of records from the original bank. I have all the documents for you to review."

I placed the sheaf of papers in front of the town council before returning to the mic.

"I know that I have come here under strange circumstances but I'm grateful that those circumstances finally brought me to this beautiful place."

Kill them with kindness was another of Aunt Rose's favorite sayings, though she often added the caveat, *and then cut wind as you walk away.* I could feel her in the room, could almost smell her musky drugstore White Diamonds perfume.

I had no idea how to end my speech. I almost bowed, but that would have been weird, so I just muttered, "*Grazie.*"

The mayor replaced me at the podium, announced that the town council would review all the relevant documents, and declared the matter closed for public discussion with the bang of a gavel. He said there'd be a break and then other topics on the agenda would be discussed. I walked to the edge of the room as most of the crowd dispersed, uninterested in the rest of the meeting. Giusy turned around to meet the mangy journalist's eyes. He stood and made his way to the sheikh's crew, who had yet to exit. He pulled an old-school reporter's notepad out of his pocket, which gained him a tad more of my respect.

Giusy grabbed me by the elbow and pulled me to the door.

"You didn't tell me you were going to a lawyer," she spat out.

"You didn't tell me your cousin owned the land. Clearly we don't tell each other everything."

Neither of us blinked until I spoke again. "I wanted to come prepared. I wanted to find out for myself that the land was mine."

"Well, you did that. Good for you." Giusy kept looking over her shoulder at the reporter. "He's doing exactly what we need."

"Should we be over there talking to the potential buyers, introduce ourselves properly?"

"You are so American! Absolutely not." She pushed me out of the building, lit a cigarette, and drew in a deep drag before continuing. "These are businessmen. They want this land. But they don't want a ton of press and they definitely don't want their names linked to any of the Sicilian crime families, which is what Luigi should be asking them about as we speak. The Arabs don't care if you own it or if my prick of a cousin owns it. They want this sale to be easy. Luigi will tell them he's writing an article about a young American woman coming to Sicily to claim her family's legacy and how the Cosa Nostra has been trying to stop her. The sheikh, or his people, will get spooked, they'll tell the mayor to rule in our favor, in your favor, and the money is yours."

I wanted to breathe a sigh of relief but none of it could be so simple.

"Why would Luigi kill a good story?"

"Because there are millions of stories in the world and if we win I will give him some money and some sex and I also know a few terrible secrets about him that I could tell his mamma. Luigi belongs to us."

The last sentence made my heart skip a beat. Giusy collected secrets the same way she collected the trinkets she stole from hotel rooms. She liked to keep people indebted to her.

"Should we go celebrate?" Giusy stubbed out her cigarette and lit a second. This time she offered me one, but I refused.

"There's nothing to celebrate yet. I gotta call home," I said. "Can we talk more in the morning?"

"Sure. You OK to walk back by yourself? I'm going to have a drink with Luigi. You will have money, Sara. All your problems will be solved." Suddenly her arms were around me in a too-tight hug. "Your aunt Rosie would be proud."

I hugged back and gave her the smile she needed. "I can make it to the hotel on my own. But I'm starving. Is the kitchen open?"

"It's unlocked. Make yourself something," she said over her shoulder. "My home is your home."

———

The hotel was quiet. I couldn't find the light switch in the kitchen but the full moon outside the window lit the path to the old fridge. I pulled out a beautiful cut of sirloin steak that I assumed Giusy was saving for a braciole and cooked it in near darkness, letting my old instincts kick in. I heated some butter and oil in a cast-iron skillet and sliced the meat into thin strips so it seared quickly, shaking some sea salt and pepper over it as it crackled. I savored the waves of invisible heat rising from a sizzling pan, stroking my cheeks, and I ate the steak straight from the flame the second it went from red to pink. Since I'd arrived on the island people had been feeding me. Pippo, Giusy, Luca, Agata. I desperately wanted to feed myself. The steak disappeared in less than a minute. I was exhausted, but also a little high on the possibility of selling the land and getting the money, of reopening my restaurant in a new location, of having enough to hire a good lawyer. I'd be one step closer to being with Sophie whenever I wanted. I pulled out my phone. The Wi-Fi was working down in the kitchen. I dialed Jack.

"You finally figured out the time zones," he said instead of hello.

"Put Sophie on."

"She's about to go swimming with my parents."

"Then she hasn't left yet."

"I don't want to get her all upset. When she hears your voice she spends the rest of the day asking for you," he said.

"Of course she does. I'm her mom and she shouldn't have to ask to be with me." Yes, I had agreed to let Jack stay at the house with our daughter all those months ago. But he had made the choice to try to keep me out of my daughter's life. This was the first time I'd directly confronted him about our new custody situation and the conviction in my voice felt intoxicating. For the past few months I'd been too afraid, too convinced that he was right, that he was the more competent parent. But that was just Jack's version of the story.

"Get my daughter, Jack."

He put the phone down. I could hear Zelda's nasally voice saying something about how they needed to get down to the lake. Jack snapped back at her and then Sophie's singsong filled my ears.

"Mamma, I miss you so much. When do I see you?"

"So soon, honey. When I get back I'll get up to the lake as quick as I can."

"How long until you give me hugs and kisses?"

"Three or four days, baby."

"Then you can see my new unicorn floaty and I can show you how it helps me swim? I named him Travis."

"I'll see it soon, baby."

"OK! GOOD! Loveyoubye." My heart melted into my stomach as the line went dead.

I was in bed by the time I realized that I hadn't called my sister back. My exhaustion was too overwhelming to go downstairs where

I would have service. I stared up at the mural on the ceiling, the orgy of fantastical beasts sneering down at me, and slipped into the deepest sleep of my life.

———

Someone was staring at me. I knew it before I even opened my eyes. I could feel their gaze on my skin, and yet, for a few moments, I stayed curled on my side with my eyelids shut, willing this to be a strange dream that would disappear the moment I acknowledged its existence. Then I felt the tip of a blade dig into my lower back, right above my tailbone, into the space between my sacrum and my spine.

"Get up."

Of course I recognized the voice. Did I really believe this would all end so easily? His belt buckle gleamed in the sliver of light from the bathroom. I rolled away from Nino to the other side of the bed. He yanked me across the sheets by my biceps.

"Get your hands off me," I managed, though the knife was now pointing at my lower abdomen, directly in front of my left colic artery, the one that could cause a pig to bleed out in less than a minute. "I'll scream. Giusy will hear me."

"Who do you think let us in?" His teeth gleamed as brightly as his belt.

They dragged me down the stairs and threw me in the back seat of a car parked on the narrow street in front of the hotel. A cloud passed over the moon and there were no lights on the street so I didn't recognize it right away, but once the engine revved up I saw that the windows were missing. It was Luca's Alfa Romeo. Giusy helped these men take me from her hotel and they were driving me away in Luca's car. I should have listened when I was told to trust no one.

TWENTY-TWO

SERAFINA

1925

I felt like I was going mad. Most nights when I couldn't sleep, I walked the streets to try to calm my blood. My strange wanderings only lent credibility to the rumors about me.

When I finally fell into a tortured rest there was nothing but pain. In my dreams Gio beat me, Marco drowned me in a boiling bath. These men who once loved me wanted nothing more than my destruction.

Each morning I woke with a jolt, certain that disaster was imminent.

I thought about ending my pregnancy nearly every day. But I delayed and delayed. I still worried Marco would take another turn for the worse, and for that reason, and many more, I needed to keep his child alive even if it meant terrible things for me. For us.

I did not have to tell anyone for many months. My symptoms were few and the ones I experienced were easy to hide.

Gio had set sail the day after I'd returned from Palermo. When he woke the next morning the demons of drink had left him, and I was unsure how much he even remembered of the night before. He was apologetic but still skeptical of me. He met with the *notaio* to find out how much our home in town was worth and whether there might be any willing buyers.

It was our luck that the official knew of a man who planned to return from America in just under a year who was looking for a home for the family he had started across the ocean with an Irish-woman he met in a place called Philadelphia. This raised Gio's spirits and he treated me kindly until he left for the docks in Palermo.

Months later, right before I started to show, I wrote to Gio to tell him that he and I were blessed with a child and he was delighted, even though it would mean another mouth to feed. He wrote me back saying that he hoped the baby would be a girl and that I should wait to make the voyage across the ocean until after she was born. He said that he planned to travel to the city of Scranton to settle himself before we all arrived.

Marco also wrote to me every week, despite the obvious dangers of doing so. The letters came to the clinic, where I still worked every day. In them he begged me to return to Palermo, stating in no un-certain terms that he was desperate to find a way for us to be to-gether. If one of those letters fell into the wrong hands, what would happen to us? I did not dare respond.

There were already those in town who gave my growing stomach strange glances, including Gio's own mother. When I passed Cet-tina in the street she averted her eyes from me. I wrote her long letters of apology and slipped them under her door, but I never re-ceived a response. In mass I sat in the row behind her and Liuni, now a strong and beautiful boy, no trace of his earlier illness in him. Cettina did not turn around. Eventually, I was so desperate to con-nect with her that I grasped her arm on the street and spun her body toward me. She was hardly surprised. It was as if she'd been waiting for me to do something for all these months. The look she gave me was friendly but unfamiliar. It lacked all the intimacy we had spent a lifetime sharing.

"I wish you all the blessings for this new child, Serafina," she said to me. "And I have been wanting to thank you for all that you did to save Marco's life. I expect that he will be home soon from Palermo and it is all due to you." I wanted to shake her, to slap her. Where was the girl who had kissed my forehead before I walked into Rosalia's house for the first time so many years ago? The girl who had promised to take care of me, no matter what? My questions were selfish, of course. I was the cruel one, the culprit, and I deserved much worse than her coldness.

"Thank you, Cettina," I murmured, and let go of her arm.

———

I was as large as a barn when someone set my clinic on fire. They threw a bottle filled with gasoline through the window.

There was only one woman and her tiny infant in there when the fire broke out. The baby was fresh from the womb and I had been having trouble coaxing the afterbirth from the woman's body. I feared an infection. I'd been massaging her belly for hours and finally took a rest after applying a poultice of mugwort and marigold to her navel while she slept. I was lying on the mattress next to them when it happened, but I was so very lucky that I was still awake when the window shattered and the flaming bottle hit the floor. I moved as quickly as my clumsy body would allow me to smother the flames with a blanket to slow them down enough to get the new mother and her baby out of the structure, but all of us watched helplessly as everything inside burned.

I had no doubt about who did it. Cettina's brother Carmine had

continued to make his irritation at our proximity clear. He'd recently invited a group of men, some low-level *mafiusi* deputies from
the western coast, to live in his farmhouse. From the way they
stared at me I knew Carmine had told them that I was the reason
the other man died on the farm years ago, that he had blamed me
for what happened in order to absolve himself.

I saw the flames when I closed my eyes at night. In my dreams
they devoured not just the hospital, but my home, my children, my
entire life.

In my daily life I felt attitudes toward me shift due to the rumors
I knew Carmine had started about me. He exaggerated the number
of patients who had lost their lives in my care, told anyone who
would listen that I was casting spells on the pregnant women and
the children I delivered. All the goodwill I had built up over my
many years of service was slowly eroding.

As I got closer to the day my baby would enter the world, I grew
more anxious. In addition to being terrified about the bad actors
around me, I feared that the second Gio held our child in his arms
he would know that she did not belong to him, that even if he
didn't know for sure he would question me and see the lie in my
eyes. Could I really keep up the farce for the rest of our lives? It was
true that women had lived with bigger secrets, but I worried this
one could not be contained.

One night I woke to bedsheets completely soaked through with
blood. My boys Santo and Vin were at my bedside.

"You were shouting in your sleep, Mamma. We have to get you
help. Cosi has already gone for the nurse."

I remembered Cosimo's birth, how I blacked out and came to
with Rosalia breathing into my mouth, giving me air, bringing me
back from the brink of death. There was no Rosalia to save me now.

I knew my nurses would do their best. I hoped they would save the baby. I couldn't help but think how much easier everything would be if I were gone.

When I reached my hand between my legs, I was certain my fingers would graze the top of an infant's head, but I felt only more blood. Vin screamed; the sound echoed off the walls of the house. I surrendered to the dark.

————

When I woke I heard the nurses chattering about me outside of the door, worried that I might not make it. I felt no pain and realized from the cloudiness in my head that I must have been given many doses of opium. I could just make out a blurry shape across the room, a woman holding a child.

Cettina.

No. That was impossible. I was in a dream.

A ray of sunshine caught my best friend clutching my child next to the window, but nothing about it was warm. The light was cold and white, and I shivered despite the heavy wool blanket covering me up to my breasts.

Noticing I was awake, she walked to me, tracing her fingertips along the child's tiny skull, following the curve of her clamshell ears.

"You should name her Rosalia, after our beloved witch," Cettina murmured.

"Why are you here?" I wasn't certain that I even said the words out loud until she answered.

"They told me you were dead. For a moment it was true. You were gone, but then the nurses brought you back to life."

"Were you pleased to hear that I was dead?"

"I love you, Serafina. I have always loved you. But our love has grown complicated. You know that. I came here to say goodbye and I was grateful when I did not have to do that, when the women saved you."

She sat down beside me, and I finally glimpsed my little girl in her arms. Small, but not too small. A month early. Of course early was better than late according to the math I had done in my head. When Gio was in Caltabellessa I had lain with him twice and then my blood came. He had fallen ill and we didn't lay together again. Then I left for Palermo to see Marco. I thought I was visiting a dying man so I took no precautions against pregnancy. When I returned, I did not have relations with my husband again. I thanked the Virgin Mary for making my daughter come to me early. I thanked my new daughter. I couldn't help but think she was trying to protect me. But then the girl opened her eyes, and I knew that nothing could protect the two of us.

Babies' eyes can be many colors when they are born. In our village they are often dark, but sometimes they are blue or gray before turning to a muddy brown like my own, like all three of my boys', like my husband's. This child had clear green irises, as light as a blade of new grass in the morning sun. This child had Marco's eyes, a fact that we would never be able to disguise, a fact that cursed us both.

When we were younger women, it often felt like Cettina and I could slip into one another's thoughts and try on the other's pain during our most difficult moments. Over the years that power had left us. I had no idea what Cettina was thinking when she placed the child into my arms and kissed me on the forehead. She whispered into my ear, the moment marked by a single ragged breath.

"I do love you like my own blood, but you cannot remain in this world."

TWENTY-THREE

SARA

I gasped for every breath. They shoved me face down in the back seat of the car, my hands tied behind my back. Nino's tall hench-man sat on my ass, the tip of the knife still digging into the small of my back. Every time I thrashed around, he shifted his weight and I could feel his erection through his thin sweatpants.

Eventually he yanked me up into a sitting position. We sped through streets not built for cars. Hard left and right, right again. A slam of the brakes, turn, turn, turn. Daedalus's maze.

I'd assumed the men would take me out of Caltabellessa, down the mountain, but we kept climbing higher and higher. The road turned to dust. Scraggly branches scratched at the sides of the car.

We passed the old Norman castle, the cave of the dragon. If I could loosen the ropes on my wrists I could elbow the asshole in the face, roll out the door, and make a run for the cave's opening. I'd be cornered, but at least I'd have a chance.

Nino parked Luca's car in a small clearing of rocks and waist-high shrubs. He walked around to the back, opened the door, and dragged me out by my ankles, making sure my face slammed into the ground when he let go. He kicked me once, twice in the ribs. I heard a crack. From there he lifted me into a standing position.

"We should teach her a real lesson before we kill her." The tall one exited the car and stood bowlegged in the headlights, one hand stroking his crotch.

"We will just get rid of her," Nino said in English. He wanted me to know what was going to happen next. He wanted me to be afraid. "It needs to look like an accident." We were close to the edge of the cliff, and I didn't need to be able to see to the bottom to know the drop was more than three hundred feet straight down into a chasm of jagged rocks. "Or not an accident. But maybe like this crazy bitch killed herself. Get the car to town. I'll walk down when I'm finished here."

Within moments the tall one was in Luca's car, heading back to the village. Their plan was so simple, really. If they got rid of me then there would be no obstacle to selling their land and my land along with it. They would get all the money they'd expected to get before I barged into their world. Nino would be able to pay off all his baby mammas and buy an apartment in Ibiza or wherever. But what I didn't understand was why Giusy was helping them after everything I thought she'd done to help me. There could only be one answer. Money. They must have agreed to pay her more than she'd ever make from me selling the land. Of course, she had no real loyalty to me. I remembered what Agata told me back in Palermo. Giusy was only out for herself.

The tip of the knife poked into my back as Nino prodded me closer to the edge of the cliff. It would be impossible to overpower him, but I could twist and turn and force him to cut me and show signs of a struggle on my body so that whatever happened next wouldn't look like an accident. But the threat of the pain of the blade slicing further into my spine was worse than the instant death of smashing into the rocks so I remained limp as he kept nudging me on.

My feet teetered at the edge. I heard a movement behind us, the unmistakable sound of footsteps. When I turned Giusy stood in the sliver of moonlight. She pointed a handgun directly at us.

Nino released a sharp hot laugh into my ear. "You are a cold-ass bitch, cousin," he said to Giusy. "I knew I couldn't trust you, not even with everything I promised you."

Giusy's emerald eyes blazed in the moonlight. She shifted her weight from foot to foot like a boxer.

Nino mocked her. "Put the gun down, Giu-giu. You are so dramatic, you silly slut." I made the most of his momentary distraction, shifting my wrists right and left, the skin chafing against the twine binding them.

Nino kept going. "What is your plan? You'll kill all three of us and get the land and the money for yourself? You know you won't get away with it like you did when you offed your husband. They'll throw your saggy tits right into jail. Then who wins? The Arabs? The mayor? Don't be a stupid bitch. Put the gun down and help me throw the American over the edge."

I could hardly make out his words with my pulse roaring in my ears. Giusy took one step forward, and then another.

She was a half dozen feet away from us when she raised the pistol over her head and shot into the sky. The crack of the gun distracted Nino enough that he completely loosened his grip on me, sending me tumbling to the ground. Suddenly I heard the clatter of metal on stone. An object had been thrown at my feet, a carving knife, one with a sharp curved blade on one edge and a nasty point on the end, the kind farmers have been using for slaughter for centuries. You hook it into an animal's skin, pierce through a major vein, and then drag it up their torso to gut them. Before Nino could regain his footing, I squatted down and twisted my hands behind me, managing to grab the handle from the dirt. Giusy knew that a gun would be useless for me, but a knife in my hand was an extension of my own body. I twisted the blade around and around until the twine at my wrists began to fray.

Nino was back on me in an instant, cackling at Giusy again.

"Giussssssssssy. I knew you wouldn't have the balls to shoot me. You're a coward." Her eyes filled with hate and disdain, with years of memories of being called an idiot, a bitch, a whore. Nino's own knife was back in my spine. A rustling in the darkness. He turned toward it, letting me pivot on my bare heel, sharp rocks grinding into my skin. An image flashed through my mind. My daughter at my funeral, eyes glassy and confused. Her memories of me already fading. Adrenaline surged through my body as I broke completely free and plunged the knife as deep as I could into the softest part of Nino's belly before gripping the handle with both of my hands and pulling upward, flaying his entire abdomen open. He fell to the ground in a pool of blood, his expression a mixture of surprise, terror, and respect.

I dropped to my knees in the dirt next to Nino's body, doubled over, and gasped for air. A metallic taste filled my mouth. I must have bitten my tongue when I plunged the knife into his belly. I clawed my way back from the edge on all fours, desperate to get away from the corpse. Time stopped. My body felt cold and hollow.

When I finally looked up, I expected to see Giusy beside me, but she was gone.

Many minutes later, a cop car emerged from the darkness. It parked and Fina got out, along with the police chief I'd met on my first night in town. They surveyed the scene, the knife in my hand, the blood, Nino's lifeless corpse. Fina's expression held not even an ounce of surprise.

"I'll have to take you in," she said to me.

I'd already offered up my wrists for the cuffs.

"*L'ha ucciso?*" the detective asked me with an uncompromising glare.

I felt lost in a fog as I blinked up at the kind-eyed older woman from the consulate they'd assigned to help translate for me even though I didn't need her. I understood exactly what he'd asked: Did you kill him?

My whole body shuddered. I ached. At least one, maybe more, of my ribs was definitely broken, and the pain in my abdomen throbbed. Salty tears rolled down my cheeks.

My brain was dense with pain, shock, and guilt. I tried to speak but my breath was so rapid and shallow the words wouldn't come out.

And so I nodded.

"Do I need a l-lawyer?" I eventually stuttered.

"One has already arrived," the woman from the consulate proclaimed. What the hell was she talking about? Was this another one of Giusy's connections? I wanted nothing to do with that. So far I hadn't told anyone who questioned me that Giusy was up on that mountain. I didn't even tell Fina, but if anyone knew Fina did. All of this was a setup. It was a setup from the moment I walked into Giusy's hotel, or maybe even before then. I knew in my bones that Giusy had a plan from the moment she first spoke to Aunt Rosie. I shook my head as hard as I could despite the pain radiating in white-hot circles around my skull.

"No. I don't know what you're talking about. I didn't call any-one. That's not my lawyer."

"I will show her in."

"Don't," I said even more forcefully than I expected. But the detective and the diplomat were already gone.

I leaned my head against the cold metal table and tried to will consciousness away. I could smell myself, still in my filthy clothes, still covered in blood, some of it mine, some of it his.

It was a long time before the door creaked back open, maybe an hour.

"Sara."

My sister's voice.

"Sara!" Louder this time. It couldn't be real. I must have fallen asleep with my head on the table. I was dreaming. But Carla was very real as she pushed past the detective so forcefully he stumbled into the wall.

"Sara, what the fuck have you gotten yourself into?" She was practically on top of me, smothering me, kissing my head, my face. I buried my own face in her hair and let the tears flow freely.

"How did you get here? How did you find me?"

"I was already on my way after you didn't answer my texts, you lunatic. I blew all our frequent-flier miles on a same-day flight to Rome and went on standby to Palermo. I've been in the air for a day. And then I came to town to find you. I went to the hotel you were supposed to be staying at and no one was there and then I came to the police station. They told me you were at the police station, and I thought, 'What the hell did she do now?' and instead of saying I was your sister I told them I was your lawyer and here I am." She shoved me away to arm's length to examine me. "Honey, you're covered in blood."

"They haven't let me go to the bathroom to clean up."

I glanced over at the door. It was closed and we were alone, but I knew they were listening to us.

I crumpled onto the floor and leaned against the concrete wall, pulling Carla down next to me. I needed to be as close to her as possible and I couldn't do it in a chair. I lowered my voice to the slightest whisper.

"What am I charged with?" I shivered, dread twisting through my insides.

"Nothing," Carla said, almost surprised by my question. "They didn't tell you that? Assholes. They can't charge you for protecting yourself. The female officer said she saw everything. That man was attacking you. She said you got ahold of the knife in his belt and stabbed him. You saved yourself. I think they're mostly scared you're going to make a big deal of this with the embassy. That guy has a record a mile long. He should have been in prison nine times over. They haven't stopped apologizing to me since I got here."

So many pieces were missing from that version of events. Yet I knew they didn't matter. Relief flooded through me even though the dark truth remained. I had killed a man and no matter how terrible he was, no matter how much he deserved it, I would never be able to forget it or entirely forgive myself.

My sister was still recounting this alternate version of reality. "The officer says the owner of the hotel heard a fight in your room and when she went to check on you, you were gone. She called the police. They had a report of screaming on top of the mountain from someone else and they went to check it out. The police officer got there just as you were struggling and saw you defend yourself."

Mostly lies, or at least a creative distortion of the truth. But what did it matter? Even if I did have proof that it had happened any differently, what could I tell them that wouldn't incriminate me, that wouldn't send me to prison for life, keep me away from my daughter forever? I would learn to live with the guilt of taking a life if it meant not abandoning Sophie.

"Sara, babe. I'm so sorry I let you come here alone."

I put my head in my sister's lap. She stroked it the way she had when we were kids.

"Do Mom and Dad know what happened?" I murmured.

"Yeah. They're waiting for you outside that door."

"What?" I struggled to sit up.

"I'm kidding. They don't know anything, and they don't have to. I'll get you home."

"OK." I wanted to fall asleep with my sister rubbing my head and I wanted to wake up at home in my own bed in Philadelphia. I wanted to forget the look in Nino's eyes as the blood drained out of his body. There was only one thing I had to do before I could leave.

"We need to spread Rosie's ashes."

"We can do it tomorrow morning before we go. I found an Airbnb on the edge of town. Let's get you a shower and a few hours of sleep. I can go get your things from the hotel."

"I can get them. When can we leave here?"

"You need to sign some things and we're free to go. I asked that everything be written out in English. No one is going to Amanda Knox you. The consulate is making sure of that. They've written up an account of what happened, about how you were attacked and a document that says you won't be pressing any charges. Unless you want to press charges?"

I ran the tip of my finger along the yellowed rubber on Carla's ancient black Chuck Taylors, the twins of mine. This was what she'd written on them, a line from the Meredith Brooks girl empowerment anthem we listened to on repeat back in the nineties, *I'm a sinner, I'm a saint. I do not feel ashamed.*

I shook my head no and let Carla strip me of my bloody T-shirt like a toddler. She took off her own Temple Law hoodie and pulled it over me. The sweatshirt was soft and smelled like home. My sister left and returned shortly with a doctor who bandaged my ribs, wrapped me up like a burrito, and gave me some kind of pain medication much stronger than Tylenol. I'd still need to go to the hospital at home to get checked out, but I could move more easily.

It took several more hours to get all the paperwork in order. I read over the documents and the statement they wanted me to make. It was all as Carla had described. I signed and just like that we could leave.

I killed a man, and we were able to walk out of the police station without even a slap on the wrist. None of it seemed real.

I couldn't shake my suspicions. I knew I'd been placed on top of that cliff to do exactly what I did, to eliminate him from this situation, to help Giusy somehow get the rights to his land, to all of the money. I had no doubt that she would be the next in line to inherit.

Giusy had used me to commit the perfect crime.

The sun was barely over the horizon and the streets were empty except for the stray cats. I remembered Giusy's warning to always be kind to the stray cats because they keep the souls of the dead. One of them nuzzled the back of my calf and when I flinched it swatted a sharp claw against my ankle, drawing blood. The souls of the dead. I thought of Nino.

Carla insisted I go straight to sleep but I wanted to get my things from the hotel myself. At the piazza I directed her to a bench where she could wait for me. Unlike the day I arrived, the front door to the Hotel Palazzo Luna was open, almost welcoming, but the lobby was empty. Every step upstairs brought a pain to my ribs, but I ignored it and continued to my room.

Giusy was stretched out on my bed, still as a corpse. For a moment I believed she might actually be dead and my heart quickened, but then I saw her chest rise and fall in an easy cadence and I knew she was simply waiting for me.

I let the heavy door slam to announce my presence, but she didn't startle. She merely opened her eyes, propped herself up on her elbows, and gave me a nervy smile.

"You're going to get your money," she said.

I could have said I didn't care about the money, that it was ridiculous to risk my life for some cash, that it was blood money now, but those were lies. I needed it.

"Good. I opened a bank account in Palermo. I'll have my lawyer contact you and Raguzzo. You can wire it."

She snorted and rolled her eyes. She looked incredible, sleek as hell in a black silk bomber jacket and matching shiny black pants that stopped just below the knee. The perfect blend of tacky and chic. But I knew what to look for—the concealer caked over the purple circles beneath her eyes, the scratches at her ankles from walking through brush and thorns to surprise us at the top of the mountain and then to sneak away.

"You're so formal now. You'll have your lawyer contact me. Pah! I'll make sure you get the money. They'll start working on my side of the land transfer by tomorrow." She lifted her jewel-encrusted vape pen to her lips and took a puff.

"You're the owner of Nino's land now." I didn't phrase it as a question.

"With Nino dead, I'm the beneficiary. He's not legally married.

His two older brothers are dead. I'm the next oldest cousin. It goes to me."

"You knew they would never convict an American woman after she was attacked by a man, a criminal, here. You set this whole thing up from the beginning. You brought me here to kill him."

"*We* killed him," Giusy said.

"But no one knows that."

"I know it and you know it. Remember what Luca said down at the restaurant. When he told you about how the fishermen here kill the tuna. They work together. They cooperate to herd them into the chamber of death. No one man can kill a tuna on his own, but together they succeed. Much like us."

Giusy needed to say all this out loud. She needed to be seen. None of it would matter if she couldn't share it with someone, if someone else didn't see all the pieces she set in motion.

"We will get his money and money can equal power," she whispered.

"We? You and I?"

"My daughter. Fina and I."

The front of my throat tightened. I felt stunned. What the hell was she saying? It didn't make any sense. "Fina is your daughter?"

"Of course she is my daughter," Giusy replied as if it were as plain as the nose on her face. But her smirk let me know that she enjoyed my surprise, that this was information she hadn't wanted me to have until now. I finally realized that her secrets and her decisions to share them were about her sense of control. That and the fact that knowledge was currency.

"With Nino gone his business will also fall to us," Giusy kept explaining. There was a wicked thrill in her tone.

"His business?"

She leaned in closer. "It is my turn to take a hand now. It is time for things to change. The Cosa Nostra is weak in some parts of the island because the men have been lazy. Nino was an idiot, but so many are. You know the saying. The mother of fools is always pregnant. And in Sicily . . . she is always having twins. But I am not lazy. And I know the new ways of the world. I know computers and crypto and the dark web. Fina has found herself a place with the police. We can help them and now Nino's bosses know it for certain. They know I have what it takes. I have proven myself."

"You told me the Cosa Nostra was ridiculous. You told me they were losing their power." I snorted.

"They will never lose it. Things are different now. The good bosses. They are like CEOs, businessmen . . . the power will never go away. It only changes. It is hard to explain. I once heard it described as a festering cold sore that subsides and seems invisible and then erupts more powerful than ever. It will erupt again soon."

"I thought you hated them."

I'd struck a nerve without meaning to. "I am doing what is necessary for me and for my daughter," she seethed.

"Fina has a good job."

"The police make shit money. And they get no respect. I will make her real money. I will give her and her daughters and her daughters' daughters a future."

My brain sifted through all the new information. I didn't have the wherewithal or the words to wrap my head around how much bigger this was than me. Maybe I shouldn't even bother, but I had to try. "You had me kill Nino to prove you are worthy of taking over his work with the Mafia, and now you're telling me all this. Jesus Christ, Giusy. Isn't there like a code of silence or something?"

"You watch too many movies. And do not take the Lord's name in vain like that. I tell you things because I trust you. Are you judging me? You have no idea what it is like to live here, how I have been treated my entire life. I did what I had to do and it worked. I will get the money for the land that is rightfully mine. You'll get yours. That dirtbag is dead, that man who has probably hurt and raped dozens of women without remorse."

My stomach roiled with anger and fear. "He could have killed me."

She finally ruffled with irritation as her lips curled into a sneer. "That wasn't going to happen."

"You can't control everything."

"I knew what I was doing. You were never truly in danger."

I almost believed her.

"Was Luca a part of your plan too? Him taking me to Palermo. Him taking me . . . to the beach." Disgust and shame flooded through me as I imagined Giusy ordering him to sleep with me.

"No. No. Luca threw us for a loop. It is why we tried to warn you off him on the beach. In the parking lot. But that did not work. We didn't plan on Agata either, but whatever. It was fine. It was all fine."

"But his car?"

"It was not his car. It belonged to Nino. Nino was his big investor and Luca liked to impress people by borrowing the fancy car. My cousin was not very happy that I smashed the windows of his prized Alfa Romeo but that does not matter now."

A small relief. I wanted to believe that Luca was a mostly good person, that he had no previous knowledge of what Nino planned to do to me on top of that mountain. I agreed with most of Agata's assessment of him—exquisitely sweet, a puppy, adorable, loyal. That was how I wanted to remember him.

"Did you have my passport stolen too?"

She nodded. "I wanted you to need me."

My clothes were still strewn all over the floor. I got down on my knees and stuffed them into my duffel.

"Why aren't you more grateful?" Giusy asked.

"Grateful to you? I'm grateful to be alive," I spat back.

"You're alive because of me."

"I almost died because of you."

Giusy stood so quickly I wondered if she was about to cross the room to punch me in the face. Instead, she made her way to my armoire to extract the box of Rosie's ashes. "Rosie wanted this for you."

"Give that to me." I closed the distance between us in a couple of seconds. "You don't know anything about her."

"I've been talking to her and writing to her for more than a year." Giusy was animated now, revving up to her preferred tempo. "We FaceTimed and chatted for hours. I may have talked to her more than you did since you were so busy when she needed someone the most."

A low blow and she knew it. I wanted to lunge at her, to make her take those words back, mostly because I knew there was truth in them. "Stop it. I was always there for her." The lies we tell others. The lies we tell ourselves. "So you talked and FaceTimed. She was just a part of your plan. You found an old woman an ocean away and preyed on her?"

Giusy shook her head. "She found me. I did this for her. I did this for my cousin Rose."

I took the bait.

"What are you talking about, Giusy?"

"Your aunt Rosie first found me through one of those DNA sites that locates your relatives for you. She found me because I was also her relative."

As I thought back to what I knew about my family tree, Giusy filled in the holes.

"Rosie wasn't your great-grandfather's daughter. She was the child of an affair with Marco Domenico, the mayor of this town, the husband of Serafina's best friend. She was able to pass her off as your great-grandfather's and get her to America, but everyone here knew the truth. That's why Agata gave me her diary. I am related to Marco. This hotel, it was once his home."

"And Aunt Rosie knew this?"

"I told her almost everything I knew about how we were related, about the affair. I told her everything except about the murder of Serafina. She was unwell and I did not think she could handle that. I promised her that I would do more research and that I could tell her things in person, and then eventually, when she knew she would not make it, I promised I would tell you and help you however I could. But for so long she hoped she would get better and that she could bring you here with her, that we could all drink negronis together, is what she said. She told me you and I were very much alike. That's when she sent me the magazine article about you, and I was so proud to be related to you, cousin. I thought, this is a woman like me, a woman who wants more from her life. And then those Arabs came around looking to buy the land. I told Rose about that too, about how my male cousins would take it. She told me I shouldn't let that happen, that I needed to stand up for myself, stick my tits out and show them who was boss."

Stick your tits out was a classic Aunt Rose instruction, one she'd been giving me since before I even hit puberty. Giusy was telling the truth.

"So I did this for her and for us. I would like you to believe me, but if you don't I still did what I promised her I would do. I helped you and I gave you an adventure. And you will go home with enough money to fix your life."

"Do you want me to thank you?"

"I want you to respect me," came Giusy's sharp reply.

"I have absolutely no lack of respect for you." I said this honestly. I didn't forgive her, but she would always have my respect.

She lowered her voice and her gaze. "None of this was an accident or fate. I did this. Let me enjoy it. I have been underestimated my entire life."

I knew something about being underestimated and I also knew I wasn't going to let it happen again.

"How much are you making off the sale of your cousin's land, Giusy?"

She seemed surprised by the question, but she clearly wanted to brag about her good fortune.

"It looks like a million."

I took a deep breath and channeled my late aunt. I stuck my tits out.

"Then I want my cut. What is it? Ten percent. Or was I supposed to give you twenty percent if you helped me sell *my* land. I'd say I helped you out quite a bit by getting rid of Nino. I'll settle for fifteen percent of your million, in addition to what I sell my land for, because face it, Giusy, you couldn't have done it without me and there are plenty of people I can talk to in the embassy about exactly what happened last night."

Giusy wasn't the only one who deserved respect.

She stretched out a long curl and let it spring back into place. "I will give you what you deserve." Then she reached beneath the bed. I flinched. Was she going for a gun because I asked for the money? My entire body tightened and I lunged toward the door. She cackled at my fear. "That is probably fair for you to get some of my money." She stretched out her hand to give me the thing she'd reached for. Serafina's diary.

"I knew that you took it from my house. I have cameras, you know. But it should be yours. You can keep it."

"Give it to Agata for her research. I know Agata took some of the pages out, but some are still missing. Did you take them?"

She bristled with indignation at my question. "Not very many."

"What was on them?"

"Just stories I liked to read. The ones about Serafina's relationships with the women in town. The things they did to help one another, all the little things they did to fight against the, how do you like to say it in America? The patriarchy? Those women were a force. They ran this town. That is what Agata studies, the women who work and live just beneath the surface of history. The women whose stories are never told. The women like Serafina. The women like us. I like reading them because it reminds me of the time when women ruled. I am sad that the period was so short; that the women were forced to join their husbands in America, or the husbands returned and took away their new power. But I believe times are changing. And I believe women will rule again."

I had no doubt that Giusy would rule over her own small fiefdom here. I only had one last question.

"The pages you took said nothing about who murdered Serafina?" I asked. "She didn't suspect that anyone wanted to hurt her in the end?"

Giusy shook her head. "She suspected that everyone wanted to hurt her in the end. But she did not write all the way to her death. The journal stops. I have thought much about it. It could not have been her husband, Giovanni, even though many people believe that it was. He took the baby in and he raised her. He would not murder his wife and then do that. He would have given the baby away if that were the case. Others think it was her lover. My own great-grandfather Marco. But he loved her. Could it have been a crime of passion? Perhaps. But I do not think so. From her writings, from what I know, he was not that kind of man. He was not capable of that sort of thing. I have my own theory. I am no Inspector Montalbano but I think it was Marco's wife, angry at Serafina for disgracing her. They were best friends, close as sisters, and Serafina played her for a fool. I do not think we will ever know. But we do not need to know exactly *how* her life ended. That is not what your aunt wanted for you. Rose wanted you to learn how she lived, how she persevered against all of the odds, and I have given you that. Serafina was a badass woman like us who wanted more than the world was willing to give to her. She found a way to live on her own terms."

"Until they killed her for it."

"Yes. Until that."

I didn't shove her away when Giusy leaned over to hug me. My heart hitched a little at her affection. "Do not feel sorry for yourself, Sara. Women are like the cats. We have nine lives. It's that most of us do not realize it. You will go back to America and you will thrive. It is what Serafina would have wanted. She died so that you could have that. Never forget her."

"I won't," I mumbled.

She embraced me even tighter as she whispered in my ear, "I will see you one day in America."

———

I woke up to the million-dollar view, the craggy cliffs, the rolling hillside, an expanse of azure sea. My sister had booked the Airbnb sight unseen, didn't even bother looking at the pictures, but it turned out both of the bedrooms overlooked the edge of the village, giving visitors the Sicilian postcard that was even better in person.

A voicemail from Luca had come in overnight.

"I heard what happened to you. Sara, you have to believe that I did not know anything about it, but I should have done better. I should have stayed with you that night in Palermo. I am so very sorry. I was called to meet with Nino thinking it was about the restaurant but all he wanted was to take his car back. If I had known he would be driving to . . ." There was a long pause. The thought ended there. "Please call me. I would like to see you before you are gone. Or after. I was thinking that maybe I would make a visit to America, to New York City, visit family, friends, maybe pick up some work in a kitchen later in the year. Who knows what will happen with my restaurant now. Maybe I could see you in your home city?"

Maybe, I thought, but didn't call back. I was thankful for our time together. He saw me as a woman again, as someone worthy of desire. I hadn't felt that way since becoming Sophie's mother and that was something to be grateful for.

I held on to Carla as we walked through town to her rental car. My sister supported my weight as we scuttled down a narrow stairway and into the main piazza. Carla broke away from me for a moment and dug into her bag, leaned down, and placed something on someone's stoop.

"What are you doing?" I asked.

"Rosie's mugs. I brought a couple with me."

"That's perfect," I whispered, reaching into her bag to help her.

Carla yawned. "I need a coffee before the drive. I don't suppose there's a Starbucks here?"

I pointed toward the *pasticceria*.

"Espresso. In there. Grab me one and something to eat too." I stood on the edge of the fountain and admired the sculpture at its center, Nicolo's sculpture. Unlike most sculptures of women the world over this one didn't look downtrodden or overly pious or pissed off. In fact a hint of a smile tickled her lips, her eyes alight with a joy rarely afforded women in art. I took a familiar comfort in her face.

Too familiar.

I couldn't believe I hadn't seen it before. I pulled the only picture I had of Serafina out of my backpack to confirm my suspicions before walking to the grand marble door next to the bakery.

Nicolo opened after a few knocks. He didn't look surprised to see me. I pointed to the statue in the fountain. "May I ask you something?"

He followed my gaze. "You look like her."

"The statue? You carved her based on a real person?"

He clearly thought I already knew the answer to that question, as if it were obvious.

"It is Serafina," he said quietly.

"She looks happy. No. That's wrong. Maybe 'happy' is the wrong word. She looks content, satisfied. Satisfied and strong."

"She was all of those things. Her strength is what I admired most about her and there was a lot to admire."

"You created this from your memory of her from when you were a child? You were so young when she treated you for malaria. And so ill. How was it possible?" This woman was much older than Serafina was when she died. In stone Nicolo gave her the years that were taken away, or so I assumed.

A mischievous grin illuminated the old man's face.

"This is Serafina as she was in America."

Maybe I was slow from the pain pills the doctor had given me. Maybe his words made no sense. "You imagined what her life would have been like if she had made it to America?"

"This is her as I saw her in America."

"Excuse me?" I glanced at the *pasticceria*, wondering how long my sister would be gone.

"Serafina was not murdered," he said. "She left this village alive." His revelation knocked me off-balance and I had to sit on the edge of the fountain.

He carried on, seeming to know we were short on time.

"For all of my life, I never expected anyone to buy my artwork. But there are always rich men and women who think your art should be bigger, be appreciated by more people, and they kept introducing me to the people who did that kind of appreciating and in the 1950s a rich patron sponsored me for a show in the United States. We visited five cities in five weeks."

"Imagine my surprise when I walked into a gallery in Atlanta and I saw her. I thought my mind was playing tricks on me, or maybe she was just a woman who bore a striking similarity to the one who saved my life all those years ago. She crossed the distance between us and wrapped me in her arms. She told me how proud she was that I had made such a splash in America, that she had always known I was destined for great things."

"Serafina?"

"Serafina. She had been living in a small town about an hour's drive from Atlanta, and she read a big feature article about me and my work, and she came there. I can't imagine it wasn't without risk. She'd kept her secret for so long, how did she know I would continue to keep it for her?"

"That's not possible. She was murdered here. It's all in the terrible police report."

"I do not know everything. I only know what she chose to share with me, but she did tell me quite a bit of it and for years I have wondered why she decided to tell me," Nicolo continued, his voice low and warm. "But as I have gotten older it does make some sense. We want someone to hold on to our stories when we are no longer on this earth. I sketched her face on a napkin as she told me what she had done. I kept that napkin with me for the rest of the American tour. I used it to make this statue. It was my model." He looked up at the sculpture's face with a reverence usually reserved for saints or celebrities.

"And no one in town recognized her?"

He shrugged. "We see what we want to see. The town wanted to believe she was dead. And the ones who did know it was her had no reason to tell."

"But how?" I didn't even know what questions to ask.

"Like I said, she did not give me all the details. Women are good at keeping their deepest secrets. She did say she knew she could not go to America with her husband, nor could she stay in the village. She seemed to know we were kindred spirits in that way, that we were two souls who longed to escape. I know she had help with staging her murder, but she never revealed who gave her that help. I can guess though."

I shouldn't have been surprised by the emotion the story brought up in me, but it hit me with a suddenness. I reached for Nicolo's hand and squeezed it hard. "Keep going."

"She had money to escape, though she didn't say where it came from. She took a steamship through Rome rather than Naples or Genoa, the routes many from our area traveled when they went to America. She was processed in Baltimore and found it simple to give whatever name she chose."

"What name?"

"I do not know. She never told me. She said she left Baltimore and boarded a train south to Richmond, Virginia. She had been put in touch with a woman there who could be trusted, a cousin of someone from the village. That woman was a housekeeper for a wealthy old man who needed a private nurse. Serafina cared for him until he died. With a recommendation from the man's family, Serafina was able to get other nursing commissions and soon it didn't matter that she had no medical training in America. Her face was filled with a vibrant light as she told me how she began to deliver babies in your country, first for rich women in their homes and then for the poor in city hospitals. She eventually received an actual nursing degree. Her pride at that accomplishment filled the entire room."

His own face was bathed in awe at the memory, and I realized that I might have been the first person he had ever shared this with.

"Did she remarry?"

"She never mentioned a single man. But she did talk about her children. The women from the village kept her informed about how they had grown and what they were doing. Serafina was especially interested in her daughter. She regretted leaving the little girl. She gave me a sealed envelope with the child's name on it and asked if I would send it to her once Rosalia was grown into an adult and once her father had passed. I could open it right before I sent it, she told me. It was the deed to the land that is now yours. I sent it to your aunt Rosalia thirty years ago as Serafina asked me. I sent it with a note explaining how her mother had cared for me when I was young and how she gave this to me before her death, which was true, even if I didn't say when exactly she died or that she did not pass in Caltabellessa."

Aunt Rosie had known about this family land for three decades, almost as long as I had been alive, but she never did anything about it until the end of her life. Maybe she didn't believe it was real. Maybe she didn't want to know the whole truth, or maybe, like many women of her time, she was afraid to venture out of the perfectly constructed world she had created for herself, to discover something that could change everything. I would never know. What I did know was that she gave the land to me, that she passed on her birthright and her mother's legacy to me, that she chose me even when I was at the lowest point of my life.

Carla appeared then with two steaming paper cups of espresso. She smiled at the old man still holding tightly to my hand.

"*Ciao*," she said brightly. "*Mi chiamo Carla.*" I pictured her practicing her Italian on her Duolingo app on the plane on the way over.

"Carla, this is Nicolo. He is a wonderful sculptor. He created this statue in the middle of the fountain." I gestured above us.

"*Bellissima!*" Carla exclaimed. She didn't see the resemblance. Why would she? Who ever looks closely at the faces or expressions of the women immortalized in stone all around the world? I'd tell her everything eventually, but it wasn't the time. Nicolo kissed Carla on both of her cheeks, then turned to me.

"You will have a fascinating life ahead of you, Sara Marsala. Just like her." He nodded up to Serafina's figure smiling down on us. "She created her own destiny when everything was stacked against her."

I gazed up at Serafina's statue. She'd endured a lifetime of setbacks and still managed to reinvent herself and find a new path in life. I'd had my share of pain, but nothing compared to hers. Maybe permanency was not the only metric of success. My marriage didn't work out, but I got a wonderful daughter out of it. My restaurant was a great success, just not forever because forever is hard. Maybe I couldn't do it all and be everything to everyone and that had to be OK. Like Giusy said, money could equal power and I would have plenty of it. I didn't want power exactly, not like Giusy. I just wanted options. I wanted a chance to get back to the basics that I loved—a small butcher shop, a grill, setting my own hours so I could spend time with my daughter, no investors telling me to expand, to franchise. No fucking brunch. I was getting a do-over and I wouldn't take it for granted.

"Nicolo, would you do something for me?" I rooted around in my backpack until I found what I was looking for.

"You are giving it back to me?" he asked as he gazed down at the portrait he had sketched of me.

"I was wondering if you could give it to Luca for me."

"Of course," he said. "I am sure he would appreciate it very much." That sly smile returned before he leaned in to kiss me on both of my cheeks. As he hobbled back to his house, Carla put an arm around me and leaned her head on my shoulder.

"So Sicilian! I love a chatty old man first thing in the morning. Did he say anything interesting?"

"I'll tell you on the plane. It's a very long story."

I reached into my duffel bag and pulled out one of the ziplock bags that I had divided Aunt Rose's ashes into. I grasped a handful. I'd thought I would be squeamish about touching them, but there was nothing but love in my heart as the dust filled my hand. I gently scattered it into the fountain at Serafina's feet.

"Sara! You can't put them into a public fountain. What if it goes into the town's water supply or something? Gross!"

"I doubt it does," I said to my sister. Then with more authority, "Someone told me it flows out to the sea." I had no idea if this was true, but it didn't matter. A little dust wouldn't hurt anyone and there was something wonderfully macabre and right about everyone in this town consuming a little bit of Rosie. I grabbed another handful and then another.

"Nicolo," I called out before he reached his door. "Would you watch our bags for a little while? Could I leave them in your place?"

He nodded. I tossed our things through his massive door and grasped my sister's hand as tightly as I could. When I led her through the streets to the dusty path up the mountain I was suddenly overcome with the urge to take Carla around the town, to show her its broken beauty, the narrow alleys, the imposing castle, the remnants of Greek and Roman and Saracen ruins. I wanted to make its charm and strangeness come alive for her. The idea of it made me smile so wide my cheeks actually hurt. Carla grinned back at me.

"I missed seeing you like this," she said.

"I missed feeling like this. I have some things to show you."

But first I wanted to fling the rest of Rosie's ashes from the very top, right outside the cave where everyone believed Serafina perished, the same place where I almost lost my life, the place where Serafina found a way to start hers all over again.

Once we made it to the peak Carla stared out at the sweeping vista in awe. "Maybe we shouldn't leave."

"Oh, no. We can't stay here," I said. "But who knows, maybe we'll come back someday."

I took advantage of my sister admiring the view and stepped backward to the curved rock that formed the dragon's ear. I leaned in and whispered.

"I've fucking got this."

EPILOGUE

It was Cettina who reported my murder to the police, but the idea of staging my death belonged to both of us. We invented the plan late one night in the weeks after my Rosalia was born.

After I nearly died giving birth to my daughter my old friend did not leave my side. Cetti laid beside me in bed as I healed. She fed my child from a bottle when my milk did not come in and she nursed us both to good health. That was when we made the plans.

I could not go with the children to join Gio and I could not remain in Caltabellessa. We believed my husband would accept little Rosalia as his daughter if he had no way to question it. If I went with the children to America, he would always wonder, he would ask questions. His mother would pry, and I could not hide my secret forever. Without me there, with an orphaned daughter and a deceased wife, Gio would accept the story he was told and raise all my children. Rosalia would be his, the little girl he had always wanted.

We thought about how to do it, how I could disappear. We thought about Paola, how no one spoke about her any longer, how her life and death had simply been forgotten, erased. Pretending to end my life wasn't an option though. I did not want to bring yet another sin to my family.

Someone had to hurt me.

Cetti volunteered to be the one who went to the police with the story about my body.

"They will either believe me that someone else murdered you or they will think that I killed you myself for being with my husband, and no one will blame me. They will dismiss it as a *delitto d'onore*, nothing more than an honor crime. Either way they will not question me," she said practically and rationally.

"Cetti." I reached for her.

"I love you. I have always loved you. My first word was your name. And I love my husband. I am happy that the two of you found so much in one another. I do not blame either of you. I have the life I want. I'm a mother to all those precious children. You never longed to be a mother and now you are so much more. Everyone got what they needed."

A memory came into my mind, so clear and sharp it was like it happened that very morning and not decades earlier. The two of us ripping locks of hair from our heads, braiding them together and throwing them from Cetti's roof into the wind to pledge ourselves to one another.

We shouted a prayer into the sandy gales:

Bread and bones we are cummari to the grave,
Bread and rice we are cummari until paradise.
Closely united so that you cannot escape,
Fly, hair, go to the sea.

We were five years old.

"I love you," I whispered to the adult Cettina in front of me.

"I know," she said back. "I have always done my best to protect you. Remember the first time we visited old Rosalia?"

I remembered. Holding her hand as we stumbled, me nearly turning back, Cettina's lips on my forehead as she told me to keep going. I nodded.

"Let me help you one last time."

And she did.

I had no illusions that Cettina was being completely selfless. I believed her when she said she still loved me, when she said she wanted to protect me and care for me. But I also knew her life would be easier with me gone from the village, from Marco's entire world.

Gio wanted me and the children to join him in the summertime, when the ocean crossing was easiest. He wrote and asked if I needed him to come to fetch all of us, but I assured him we would be fine on our own. I also told him that I would take care of selling our house in town, that I would make sure the money was transferred across the ocean before we left. That gave me four months with my baby girl, and I spent every waking moment with her and the boys. I even strapped Rosalia to me when I trained the nurses to take over my work. Eventually I bought the passage for all of us for the June 30 crossing from Palermo to the city of Philadelphia.

I sent one final letter in May. I told Gio that the sale of our house was delayed. That I needed to stay behind. This was true, but it was delayed because I had waited to meet with the *notaio*. I said I would send his mamma and the children ahead of me and follow them on the next ship.

Leaving my children was the impossible part. The boys were

nearly grown and I kept telling myself that if we had stayed in Sicily or if I had gone with them, they would have left me to work in a matter of years anyway. With the boys I knew that I had already done my best. I had raised them, shaped them, been both their mother and their father. I was proud of the young men they had become, and I knew they could live on their own. I knew they would always remember me.

Baby Rosalia would never know me. I would never be able to tell her she was wise, brave, and kind, that she could do anything her brothers could do if she put her mind to it, no matter the constraints the world put on a woman. And yet, as much as I loved her from the moment I woke and saw her tiny body in Cettina's arms I knew without a doubt that she would be better off if I were gone.

I traveled with all of them to the boat docks in Palermo. "Do not cry, Mamma," Cosimo had murmured to me as he gently rewrapped the blanket around his baby sister. I had made sure that the ship that would carry my children would be able to provide for Rosalia's nourishment by hoarding condensed milk for their journey. We also knew of another young mother, the cousin of a friend, who would be traveling at the same time. She promised to nurse my child as her own if need be, and I knew my mother-in-law would make sure Rosalia thrived. "We will take good care of her," Cosi insisted. "And we will see you in two months. As soon as you get the house sold."

"Yes, my little lion, so soon," I had lied to my boy. "So soon."

I clutched each of them furiously to me, trying to hold on to some small piece of them and imprint some small piece of me before I let them go.

Our house in town was sold within the week after they left. Once the money from the sale came, I wired it across the sea, but I kept the deed for the other land below the mountain, the one with the clinic on it, for myself. I saved it, knowing one day I would leave it to my daughter.

I thought often about Gio's words about what my life would be like when he brought me to the new country. I would never have to work again. I did not see that as the same prize he did because I also remembered the old witch's words to me: *You will do more than I ever could.*

That premonition echoed in my head every time I wavered about my plan to disappear.

"Never tell Marco what we did." I made Cetti promise. "Let him think I'm dead. Please," I begged her, and she agreed. He was another part of my life that I had to let go if I wanted to continue to live, and if I thought he was looking for me I'd never stop imagining the two of us together.

All of the town's women mobilized to help us. Gaetana volunteered to be Cettina's other eyewitness. Together they told the authorities they found my body on the top of the mountain and that they buried me themselves to spare my children the horror of what had been done to me. I didn't know what they told the officers about how exactly my corpse was ravaged, but I was certain it would have been convincing. We knew the many ways a woman's body could be harmed.

They filed an official police report and Leda drove me out of the village in the middle of the night. We went straight to Palermo, where I boarded a boat that took me to Rome and then to Baltimore in America.

Cettina wrote to Gio about my death. She begged him to tell the children I passed away from the flu. He promised her he would. He was already constructing their own mythology in America.

I knew that Gio never remarried, which surprised me at first. But he had become used to living without a wife for so many years, perhaps he no longer needed one. Besides, he had his mamma. I knew that he and my boys all worked in the coal mines of the Pocono Mountains, painful labor, which broke my heart, but I also knew they invested the money in a good and safe business within a few years and built themselves a nice house. I knew Cosimo became a town alderman but never married. He sent love poems to Cettina's stepdaughter Silvia until the day he died. Vin was a wild child and then an unruly man. He fixed motorcycles in their auto body shop and then took off riding one across America. He spent the rest of his life on a commune in California with the hippies. I was delighted that Santo fell in love with a Sicilian girl named Lorenza who worked in a fancy department store in New York City. I heard he met her when he traveled to the city to see the big tree lit up in Rockefeller Center. He had three boys with her. When I learned of the car accident that took their lives, I didn't leave my own home for two weeks. Rosalia, thank the Virgin, took in their children. My daughter, Marco's daughter, had always been at the top of her classes. She won a scholarship to a teacher's college and many years later she even received a master's degree in education. All that news reached Caltabellessa and then made its way to me. Cetti wrote me letters for the rest of her life, at least one a month, and eventually we spoke on the phone, which cost us both a small fortune.

She also kept me updated on all the town news. I had always worried our greatest sin was our pride in our work and that bad things would happen to all of us women for our impudence. I was not entirely wrong. Saverina's brother-in-law returned and took over her duties as butcher, telling her that her work was undignified for a respectable woman, that what she had done for a decade was suddenly vulgar, and when her husband died from the flu in Missouri she was left penniless. The widow Gaetana's house was raided by highwaymen who knew she lived there alone. They took everything, including her car, and left her broken, lifeless body on the steps of the church. Ninetta became pregnant while her husband was away. Her brother-in-law had her charged with adultery and thrown in jail. His barren wife raised her child. When she was released, she packed up her things and left the town without a penny to her name. Many of our women friends were summoned to America to be with their husbands and resume their domestic labors. I often thought about seeking them out, but I knew it would only open old wounds.

The only time Cettina and I did not speak was for a month when Marco died only ten years after I left. Cetti took on the traditional ritual of mourning and did not leave the house or speak to another soul for many weeks. Marco had remained the town mayor until his final days. Cettina told me that in his last hours he tried to tell her everything about the two of us. His final words were to tell her he loved us both.

"I betrayed you," she told me when we finally spoke of it. "I told him everything we did. How we lied. How you were alive. I told him at the very, very end, and it was worth the betrayal. He died with a smile on his lips."

Over the years Cetti and I talked many times about her making a trip across the ocean to see me, but cancer took her before she could make the journey.

By the end of my life I truly believe I did accomplish the things old Rosalia thought I could accomplish. Each time I learned something new I felt she was with me. She was there when I assisted in an open-heart surgery as a licensed nurse. She was there each time I set a bone or placed a newborn baby in one of those new incubators that kept them warm and healthy. She was there when I got my degree and walked across the stage clutching it to my chest at the age of fifty-five, joy and pride coursing through my veins.

I never saw my husband or my boys again, but I made sure that I saw my daughter's face before I died. The month after I was diagnosed with an illness I knew would take me within the year, I traveled up to Philadelphia on a train. I always felt like the richest woman in the world when I traveled on a train, and throughout my years in America I had ridden them as far away as Florida and San Francisco. America certainly was as magical as all those advertisements in the newspapers had promised. Every city sparkled with a different kind of possibility.

Rosalia's home address in the Poconos was easy enough to find in the white pages. After arriving in Philadelphia, I rented a car to drive the two hours into the mountains.

I pulled up to Rosalia's house in the middle of town, the house that would have been mine if I had come to America with my husband. I did not have a plan for what I would do. I worried I would be overcome the moment I saw her, that I would rush out of the car and run to her, tell her I was her mamma, and scare the hell out of the poor woman, then well into middle age. She might call the police, tell them a crazy old lady had escaped from the senior home and someone needed to come take her away.

No, I could control myself. I had controlled so many things for so long.

She walked out of her door soon after I pulled the car behind a hedge in front of her neighbor's home. She was fifty-four that year, yet she carried herself like a much younger woman, head held high, bright red lipstick curled into a smile as she sauntered out to her own car, a black Mustang convertible. When she got in, she put the top down and turned the radio up so loud I could hear it down the street. I didn't know the song, but it was something catchy and I watched in awe as she shimmied and danced in the front seat of her car, performing for no one, moving her body only for herself.

Tears pricked my eyes. A tremble of sorrow traveled through me. I felt the weight of her small body in my arms from the last time I held her. Despite the heady rush of nostalgia and longing, I was content just watching her. I never could have imagined this woman, not in my wildest dreams. She was so much more than I ever expected.

I hid, lied, and disappeared to create this marvel, this brilliant, educated, independent woman singing alone in her car in front of a house that she owned, a woman beholden to no man. I saved myself, but I also gave my daughter the chance to be her own person.

I watched her for maybe a minute more before she pulled out of her driveway, checked her lipstick in her rearview mirror, and blew herself a kiss.

AUTHOR'S NOTE

I come from a family that loves to tell stories, that loves to embellish stories, a family with little regard for the details of actual events as long as they can captivate an audience over the dinner table. There is one story that has been told time and time again, the story of my great-great-grandmother Lorenza Marsala's murder.

According to family lore Lorenza was murdered in Sicily more than a hundred years ago. Her story was mostly retold at family reunions, funerals, and weddings. Lorenza's husband came to America to make money, to carve out a better life for his family as many Sicilian men did back then. Lorenza was left behind in the village of Caltabellotta with her children. Her husband eventually brought all of his brothers over, then his sons. His wife was left to sell the family farm, but she never made it to the United States.

Some relatives said she was murdered for being a witch, a *strega*, who used her dark magic to manipulate men. Others said she was a healer, a doctor. Some claimed it was the Mafia, particularly a man they referred to as the Black Hand.

These small wisps of my great-great-grandmother's narrative

knotted into my brain for years. I kept asking myself what it would be like to be a wife and mother left alone while your husband took off to work in a faraway country. What would you have to do to be considered a witch? What lines would you have crossed, or rather, which of the left-behind men did you upset?

On one trip to Sicily six years ago I heard similar stories from some of the older women, stories that had been passed down to them. They told me that when the men left Sicily, women became empowered for the very first time. They learned to read and to write and to do the accounting. They often took on men's jobs. This was necessary but also often dangerous. And that was when I began to write Serafina's story. From the beginning I knew I wanted to use the faint threads of my great-great-grandmother's story as a starting place for a novel. The aforementioned details were the kernel I used to imagine *The Sicilian Inheritance*.

I picked up this manuscript and put it away many, many times over the past five years. Every time I got pregnant again and when I gave birth to two daughters I thought about the stories we pass down about women, about how we talk about their ambition, their passions and desires for more from a world that is often unwilling to give it.

I've been to Sicily several times over the years and a lot of the details in this book about this rugged, beautiful, and intensely broken place come from my own experience. But I also consulted books and academic texts to find historical details and color about the two time periods I wrote about.

The writings of Sicilian author Maria Messina were incredibly inspirational. Messina is one of the only published authors to highlight the real daily lives of Sicilian women. I also devoured *Little Novels of Sicily* by Giovanni Verga.

My local library was able to track down a rare copy of the anthropological text *Milocca: A Sicilian Village* by Charlotte Gower Chapman. I consulted it often to learn more about interpersonal relationships and divisions of labor in small Sicilian villages.

I gathered many sayings and words of dialect from these older sources. One of these is the word *mafiusi*, an early word used to describe the Mafia. I use that instead of *mafiosi* in the chapters from Serafina's perspective.

I read and reread John Keahey's *Seeking Sicily*, Jamie Mackay's *The Invention of Sicily*, and *Women of Sicily: Saints, Queens & Rebels* by Jacqueline Alio. I am indebted to them for their immense knowledge of the island and its history.

I also consulted several academic texts, including "Women in the Classroom: Mass Migration, Literacy and the Nationalization of Sicilian Women at the Turn of the Century," by Linda Reeder, in the *Journal of Social History* and "Conflict Across the Atlantic: Women, Family and Mass Male Migration in Sicily, 1880–1920," also by Linda Reeder, in the *International Review of Social History*.

For information on the modern-day Mafia, particularly the women involved in it, I consulted the books and articles of Barbie Latza Nadeau, particularly her book *The Godmother: Murder, Vengeance, and the Bloody Struggle of Mafia Women*.

The town of Caltabellessa is entirely fictional. I chose not to set the story in Lorenza's birthplace of Caltabellotta so that I could blend together various aspects of many different rural mountain towns in Sicily.

Serafina's and Sara's stories are purely fiction, but at the end of the day what I hope the most is that their stories would make my great-great-grandmother proud.

ACKNOWLEDGMENTS

There were so many times when I thought this book would never make it to bookshelves. I began writing it six years ago, when I first found out I was going to become a mother. Something about that massive sea change in my identity made this story call to me. I stopped and started again many times over the years and there are many people who encouraged me to keep going. First, my husband, Nick. He pushed me to just "write the whole damn book"; to write it just for me before I decided what to do with it or how to introduce it to the world. It was the best advice I could have gotten because it allowed me the time and space to let the ideas marinate, to allow the story to unfold the way it was meant to.

Zack Knoll was my earliest reader and editor. His advice in shaping my first narrative was invaluable and this book would not exist without him. My incredible agents, Pilar Queen and Byrd Leavell, told me I had something special on my hands after their first read. Their constant enthusiasm for this project inspired me to persist on this journey over and over again. They have become so much more than agents. They are now trusted friends and advisers and I could not do this without them.

My fabulous editor, Maya Ziv, read the submission for this book on her own Italian honeymoon and we were immediately simpatico. I was lucky enough to hash out plot details and twists and turns over many a Sicilian meal with her. The entire Dutton team has been a dream and I am so grateful for all the work of my publicity and marketing team of Nicole Jarvis and Lauren Morrow. Helping readers discover books is harder than ever and they have been tireless in their efforts to get this book into as many hands as possible.

My coauthor from *We Are Not Like Them* and *You Were Always Mine,* Christine Pride, is usually one of my early readers and editors, ever since we met when she was my actual editor on *Charlotte Walsh Likes to Win.* She is the best at reining me in when I get off track. Many other early readers—Brenda Copeland, Andrea Peskind Katz, Glynnis MacNicol, Hannah Orenstein, Regan Fletcher Stephens, Sun Park, Sarah Pierce, Lesley Grossberg, and Casey Scieszka—offered valuable feedback, insightful commentary, and the very necessary cheerleading I needed to keep me afloat.

Thanks to the village of support that helps care for my children while I write, without whom I couldn't do anything.

And a final thank-you to the three delightful and maddening little souls who made me a mother, who changed the way I see the world, and who constantly remind me of the magic in the everyday.

ABOUT THE AUTHOR

Jo Piazza is a bestselling author, award-winning journalist, and critically acclaimed podcast creator. Her books have been published in ten languages and twelve countries. Jo's podcasts have garnered more than twenty-five million downloads and regularly top podcast charts; and her journalism has appeared in *The Wall Street Journal*, *The New York Times*, *New York* magazine, *Marie Claire*, *Time*, and numerous other outlets. She lives in Philadelphia with her husband and three feral children.